THE MAKING OF AN
ENGLISHMAN

THE MAKING
OF AN ENGLISHMAN

By

W. L. GEORGE

NEW YORK

DODD, MEAD AND COMPANY

1914

TO

THE SMALL FRENCH BOY

WHO IN 1894 FIRST CALLED ME

JOHN BULL

AND TO

THE YOUNG ENGLISHMAN

WHO IN 1902 FIRST ADDRESSED ME AS

FROGGY

I DEDICATE THIS BOOK

7088

CONTENTS

PART I

CONTENTS

PART IV

PART I

CHAPTER I

RULE BRITANNIA

I

THE dark young man who had just come out of Holywell Street, a little uncertain, as if he had lost his way, crossed the Strand with hesitation. He drew back as some hansoms came careering towards him, made as if to return to the pavement, then ran across to St. Clement Dane's. He paused awhile on the island, looked at the faintly red sky over the Cecil. There was dubiousness in his movements, the dubiousness of the stranger in a large town, who is anxious to find his way and, because of his pride, reluctant to ask it; there was interest too, the stranger's revealing interest in houses with unfamiliar faces, in the traffic which in foreign lands so perversely clings to the wrong side of the street. At last he seemed to muster resolution as he turned eastwards.

Some minutes had elapsed since the booming of the quarter from the bells of the nearest church, and as the young man stopped again to look at the Griffin, he seemed to listen to the endless confirmation of the surrounding chimes. They came muffled and faint after their long journey from St. Paul's and Westminster, shrill from St. Dunstan's and the Chapel Royal; the chimes seemed crisp and aloof, detached in aristocratic fashion from the rumble of the omnibuses and the sharper clip-trop-trop of the cab horses. The dark young man walked slowly, his eyes and ears very aware of all this unfamiliarity and its intimations of unpenetrated mysteries. There were church bells and horses in his own country, but these had an undefinable personality of their own, not to be gauged by a difference in the casting of the metal or in the hands

3

that controlled the beasts. And there were other sounds too, in this not over busy Fleet Street of the night, sounds which bore witness to the transitory importance of something that hung over the town.

There were no crowds. Indeed, the omnibuses rolled westwards, empty inside, and but half-loaded on the top. But every street corner had its newsboy, aggressive and raucous, shouting incomprehensible extracts from the *Echo* and the *Star* under the dim gas-lamp. And the newsboys, bent double under their loads of rosy papers, fleeted past with an air of urgency. There was excitement in the air, a little fever, as if everybody were thinking of something that had just happened and of its reactions upon something infinitely more important which might happen soon. And because every Londoner was thus oppressed his town was oppressed; all these people, hurrying or strolling, those screaming boys, fixed, statue-like policemen, those few whose cookshops and public-houses were still open, carried, closely wedded with their cares and their merriment, a common preoccupation.

The dark young man was influenced by this atmosphere and knew its causes. He must needs have been blind and deaf not to have felt some excitement in this town, where all day he had seen men and women buy the same papers three times over in the hope of finding news which would bear out or give the lie to the dirty placard he now stared at. The placard roughly stuck on the stones at the corner of Fetter Lane bore the words:

FALL OF MAFEKING

The newsvendor had long deserted his afternoon pitch, gone back to the office to bring the false promises of fresh quires, but the placard remained as a dirty memento of disaster, to be trodden on by angry boots, dumbly stared at by passers-by as they tried to believe it was not true. All through that Friday afternoon the stranger had listened to the wild rumour of the streets, the march of Plumer, his defeat, the death of Baden-Powell, the suicide of Eloff, all those mad untruths which rise from the battlefield like disturbed crows. He was stirred, he could hear in spirit those guns that roared and rumbled so many thousands of miles away, and he could smell the smell of battle: dust, sweat and hot rifle grease. A stranger and unlinked with this England, he could not drive from his mind the familiar photographs of those long, mud-coloured lines of young men, face upon the ground in the shallow trenches.

He thought with pleasure of the brown lines, thrilled, choking a little as a man chokes when moved to an exultation in which are pity and some fear. For him the Boer enemy was the shadowy foe of the Kriegspiel, not real as the brothers of those real men among whom he walked. He had no interest in the struggle but he had to share in it, as he could not have watched a brown dog fight a white one without favouring one of the two colours. Though detached he was a partisan, and because he had eaten bread in England and heard her men speak, perhaps because England was quietly folding him in her clumsy, good-natured arms, he was for England and against the *vierkleur*. He wondered why he did not, for the sake of his own republican tricolour, desire the victory of the *vierkleur*: that question he could not solve; he merely thought of the thin brown line and stood dumb with those English in front of the dirty placard on the stones.

II

The young man reached Ludgate Hill, looked awhile at the railway bridge, at St. Paul's, dazzling white in the moonlight and split in two by the black spire of St. Martin Ludgate. He turned back, and, as again he approached the Griffin, a premature clock chimed half-past nine. The stranger stopped. On the opposite pavement he could see three men and a girl, who looked up to the upper windows of a building. That moment had an undefinable quality of hush, as if the world were an audience waiting for the curtain to rise on a play the title of which they did not know. There was nothing to arrest these people's attention, nothing to make them stop, save, perhaps, the secret influence of some event which winged towards them as they waited. The silence grew heavier, then broke. From far down one of the lanes the mouths of which frame the emptiness over the river, the stranger heard a sound. The other watchers heard it too, turned about, strained towards it, as if they could hardly believe in its reality. But the seconds passed, and they knew that this was real. They heard it, the faint voice: " Hip—hip—hip—hurrah."

The four watchers suddenly became a little knot of people. The sound rose up again, and now unmistakable as if it were the voice not of three or four men but of many scores. " Hip—hip—hip—" roared the phantom in the lane, " —hurrah." And then the silence died. As if some magician had struck into life the very stones, they seemed to spurt men and women in solid black lumps, from every porch, from every lane, from the lit-up warmth of every public-house. A hundred windows burst into brilliance and as suddenly were obscured by clusters of men and girls. The phantom in the lane roared again, rival roars rose up; then the shouts merged in one steady, throbbing sound. It was the sound of cheering, and it grew as the news spread rapid as a stain of oil from their centre in Fleet Street to the farthest suburbs, the sound of cheering without rhythm or measure, of cheering so uncontrollable that the " hurrahs " of it covered the preliminary " hips," the sound of rival songs, of " Rule Britannia " and of " God save the Queen," and of all the things in London fit to make a noise—pianos, horns, trays and kettles far away, of whistles too. As the youth leaned back against the wall, wedged in among a shouting, incom-

prehensible crowd, he could discern in the roar the sharp
quality of those whistles.

At the upper windows of a newspaper office appeared
two men who carried a white linen band. It was unrolled, and the roar grew yet more massive as the crowd
read three words, roughly scrawled:

MAFEKING RELIEVED

Official

London had quickened. The desert of Fleet Street
seemed to have sucked in all who were within the periphery
of its voice, as swiftly and as invincibly as an electro-
magnet collects iron filings when the current passes. As
minutes piled on minutes, tense and fleet as seconds, London emptied itself into the streets from drawing-room,
theatre and kitchen; the ever-new miracle of the Press
repeated itself, as if the editors had foreseen the event,
for already the tricolour poster of the *Evening News* war
edition was in the hands of boys, who could be seen fighting
their way out of the lanes among the greedy crowd. While
some snatched at and stole the precious sheets, others thrust
silver into the boys' hands. The crowd swayed, unable
to move, crushed itself against the other crowds that had
formed as magically at the Mansion House and Charing
Cross. Here and there, wedged among the people, was
a four-wheeler or an omnibus, whose horses were too listless
to take fright. Time passed, but unperceived; London had
forgotten it, wanted only to sing, to cheer, to embrace. But
a purpose must have formed, a restlessness have come,
for the crowds suddenly felt the desire to move. It was
not the desire of panic, the desire that dictates fright,
but an orderly, if exultant desire to do solemn, triumphant
things, to line up and as soldiers to march to nowhere,
just to march and to feel the earth tremble under the
trample of rhythmic steps. The Fleet Street crowd, bound

together by the alternation of the national songs and of
" The Absent-Minded Beggar," began to move towards the
West, and I . . .

III

Yes, I! I, who sit at a square knee-hole desk as I
write these lines, one of those English desks the Americans
have invented, it was an incredible other I who marched
with those Englishmen to that Trafalgar Square . . . to
Trafalgar Square where stands the monument of the
admiral who crushed my countrymen. It was not then
incredible, but it is now incredible that I can have been
what I was, that there was a roll in the " r's " of Trafalgar.
For I have lost the " r's," and the feeling of Trafalgar,
lost the feeling of Waterloo, lost them so completely that
like a born Londoner I have forgotten the blood and smoke
that soil those rich names and that they awake in my mind
no idea save " open space " and " railway station."

On the table is a top-hat. It is an ordinary top-hat,
and that is extraordinary: it is absolutely impersonal,
unoriginal, affords no key to the one who wears it; its
brim is neither very curly nor very flat, its crown neither
very high nor very low; it is the sort of top-hat everybody
wears, the sort of top-hat which has a steady thousand
brothers between Piccadilly Circus and Hyde Park Corner.
I would not know it in a crowd, and I am glad, because—
well, that would never do!

It is positively an English top-hat!

And because it is an English top-hat, and because everything in this room into which has crept a faintness of
London fog is English, so English that it is old English,
because I see English papers, English chintz, and English
books, and English china, and an English typewriter (made
in America) on a Sheraton table (made in Germany),
I am glad that all this is English, so English that even
America and Germany are succeeding in being English,
just as I, the Frenchman, am English.

I am glad, and when I think of the young man who marched to Trafalgar Square, with a swollen, bounding heart under the waistcoat he had bought in the Boulevard Montmartre, I am amazed. It is I, yes, I am sure of it when I look at his photograph. Or it was I. It was a young man of twenty, dark, with black eyes and rather arched eyebrows, hair that ought to have been shorter, a well-cut mouth enough, shaded by a long but rather thin black moustache. Other documentary evidence, my military book, tells me that he had an " ordinary " forehead, an " average " chin, that he had no " stigmata." And my present figure leads me to believe that he stood about five feet nine in his boots, never having been measured otherwise, that he was fairly broad and that his hands and feet were rather small.

A passable portrait this, but no work of art. It lacks life, inspiration, and I suspect that no effort of mine will ever endow it with either, for I don't know him any more. He stands in a world I have left behind; he is my ghost and he wears the surprising clothes that ghosts wear; (where do they get them?). I understand him perfectly and I don't sympathise with him, for I can't feel as he felt. I see him; he walks, smiles, speaks; he makes jokes and he makes love; he has political ideas, and standards of honour, and habits, and nasty envies, and bubbling generosities. He is quite the most wonderful toy in the world, but he is not I.

England has poured him into another man.

I have called him " the stranger," and I have done right, for he is a stranger even to me. I know well enough why those Englishmen impressed him, but it is extraordinary that they no longer impress me. I gather that if he could rise again it is I, the Englishman, would impress him, and that I would cast over him the critical, albeit tolerant look of the Englishman. The roast beef of old England has done its work well!

IV

As we marched towards the West I bought a whistle for a shilling. And from Wellington Street onwards I blew it to exhaustion, blew it with a fine sense of martial demonstration, tossing the squeal of it into the slaty night in honour of the great race which had produced Gladstone, Cromwell and Shakespeare. I remember those who walked to the right and left of me; there was a working-man of some sort, who maintained upon me the stare of a squinting eye and exhaled one of those subtle, penetrating trade smells which blend so curiously with the aroma of beer; the other was an elegant old gentleman with the clipped white moustache and the brick-coloured cheeks of the re-tired soldier. Neatly pinned across his shoulders was a tricolour newspaper placard. And the backs and heads in front! how high were the heads held, and how square the shoulders! One back seemed to own no head, for it was humped, and so bowed that I could not see beyond it. But a hand belonging to that body held up on a stick a bowler decorated with strawberry leaves. The English hunch-back, carrying his ducal headgear, had his share in the glory of the night.

We marched onwards, and I could not hear a word spoken, though mouths opened towards ears, for the roar of us, and our whistling and blowing of horns, and the tramping of our feet engulfed anything that we might personally feel. There was no I, and as we reached Trafalgar Square, where I linked arms with the odorous working-man and the elegant old gentleman, there was no They. There was nothing save an enormous exultant We, a We too big for classes and nationalities, a hurrying, intoxicated We, bursting with relief and self-complacency.

Round and round Trafalgar Square, where the tide of us had swept the corners clear and swallowed up those people who projected from the pavement, almost in step as we sang—

"And when they ask us how it's done,
We proudly point to every one
Of England's soldiers of the Queen. . . ."

Round and round Trafalgar Square, past the National Gallery, the black windows of which confessed that the custodians were shamefully in bed, past the two hotels, their windows blocked with people assembled to cheer us and to wave Union Jacks, past the full mouth of Whitehall, down the hill of which I could see whole fleets of omnibuses, stalled, helpless and loaded with overflowing clusters of men and women.

Round and round Trafalgar Square, with throats full of ridges choked by dust, and with sweat upon our very eyelashes. Upon the parapet of the Square sat half-a-dozen girls together, who wore all of them dusty black coats; as I passed I could see they were singing, for their mouths all worked together, and they swayed together from right to left and back. For us they waved their dirty handkerchiefs, and then they were dragged from the parapet and patriotically kissed.

Round and round Trafalgar Square. The working-man, who still maintained upon me the stare of his squinting eye, dumbly pointed to a four-wheeler, stranded in Pall Mall East, among the seethe of our overflow. On the roof stood a man in evening clothes with a woman in a low dress. Hands in hands and face to face, they danced a furious dance, leaping up and down like puppets on a wire; the man's white tie had flown loose, and as the woman danced her earrings left behind them little striæ of light. Some of her fair hair had escaped, the man had lost his hat; they danced in abandoned joy.

And round and round Trafalgar Square. And round and round again.

We met some mounted police and split upon them like waves on a breakwater. We streamed north, up Charing Cross Road, and, as we came, those who faced us turned and led us; I was still linked with the old gentleman, who grinned inanely now and hung wearily upon my arm, and with the working-man. In front I could still see the hunchback: his stick had bored a hole in his bowler; he carried the hat with the strawberry leaves upon the crook and had decorated it further by sticking into the hole his Kruger-headed pipe.

As we passed I could hear the singing better, thanks to the echo of the walls. And, drunkenly excited, I too sang to them that Britons never, never would be slaves. From the windows of the Alhambra peered clusters of girls' heads, for all the ballet was there—golden curls, and black curls, and red curls, and gorgeous loose manes; I had a vision of the Alhambra as an extraordinary animal with two flashing eyes of incandescent burners and a hundred white arms outstretched. From the roof of one of the theatres they were firing a toy cannon as fast as they could load it.

At Shaftesbury Avenue we were stopped by a cube of policemen, and, before we could break down their puny resistance, we heard the fifes and drums. We heard them faintly from the north, and suddenly they burst in upon us, leading the Endell Street Boys' Brigade. Fife and drum in front, the boys marched past as if truly British Grenadiers; they resolved themselves into bright, smiling faces, glittering buttons and neat dummy rifles.

> " Whene'er we are commanded
>   To storm the palisades,
> Our leaders march with fusees,
>   And we with hand-grenades;
> We throw them from the glacis,
>   About the foemen's ears
> Sing tow, row, row, row, row, row, row,
>   To the British Grenadiers."

The boys vanished, were seized and hoisted on shoulders; as we poured on towards the north I could hear the determined band struggling to play on as the crowd bore it aloft.

And so through the Carnival of Friday night and of the next day. Carnival! I carry for ever in my memory the vision of the Union Jacks on long bamboo poles, of the paper hats, the B.P. buttons and the patriotic handkerchiefs. Did I not act my part in all of it? Defend an English girl in Piccadilly from the patriotic ticklers? and see near Marble Arch a great and patriotic fight outside a public house? And I raised my hat to Kirk, the butcher, who waved his sheets from his bedroom window because he had nothing else to wave.

. . . .

For two days they fought and made love and drank, and rode decorated bicycles, and mobbed Volunteers in so friendly a spirit that these took to riding in cabs.

I have confused memories of two nights when I could hardly sleep, for they were rioting in Oxford Street and letting off fireworks; for they were rioting in the soul of me, the Frenchman, as I lay in bed all a-throb with the triumph of these English, trying to sleep and too tired to do so, too excited to do aught but thrill at the animal splendour of them, unable to repress my habituated lips as they hummed:

> " And when they ask us how it's done,
> We proudly point to every one
> Of England's soldiers of the Queen. . . ."

CHAPTER II

HAIL! FRANCE, AND FAREWELL

I

THERE has always been an England for me, and though I am or was a Frenchman, I have always been as conscious of England as of France. For, all through my childhood, I heard the words *Angleterre* and *Anglais* occur often in my father's conversation; no doubt I heard him alternately revile and belaud those English, who mattered so very much to the Bordeaux shipbroker he was. If every port in the world is somewhat English, then Bordeaux is almost a colony of the new Carthaginians, those Carthaginians who are Romans too; there is an atmosphere of England about the names of many who sell stores and sails and coal, and caulk the bottoms of the ships, which affects the old, while the young are subject to football and Charles Dickens. We are complex, we *Bordelais,* for we are dark, vivid, noisy; we twist our moustaches before we have any to twist, and strut every one like a Cyrano de Bergerac in mufti: yet, and perhaps because our city would decay if an earthquake were to lift it from the waters, we have the greedy spirit of commercial England, her vigour and her obstinacy. We like the rough games of the North; we drink spirits as readily as wine; we cash the sovereign at sight and make a profit on the deal.

It is this peculiar atmosphere created an England in my mind, an England represented in early days by a Consul who, said my father, was a *cochon.* That Consul! I never saw him, never knew his name, but I felt him to be the grey eminence behind that cardinal of ours,

14

the harbour-master; he did not mean anything precise, for he did not mean soldiers, and it is difficult to realise who is who if he does not mean soldiers when you are a very little boy. He was just an influence, something solemn and potential with which you could do anything you chose if you owned it, something like a tableful of money. I have never seen a tableful of money, and I suppose I never shall, for I have little use for money, being so much fonder of those things which money buys; why then the British Consul was always associated in my mind with a table covered with coins from edge to edge is a little mysterious, unless there be in the very far back of my brain some phrases now forgotten which have marked its lobes, phrases in which " Consul," and " francs," played equal parts. It is certain that this secret power must have meant money, and that England must have shared its glory. As I grew up, England very much meant money, and now I, an Englishman of sorts, still find it very difficult to prevent the golden sovereign from eclipsing the pale sun of the isle.

In those early days I became aware of England as of something that was partly real: not so real, of course, as the housemaid, Eulalie, or as the dog, a black, golli-woggy dog, or as the Chinese box with the eight corners in which chocolate seemed mysteriously to grow by night. No, England was real to me in the sense that God and the wood of the Sleeping Beauty are real to a small boy; it was an undefined country, but it was emphatically somewhere. I once asked my father where England was. I must have been about six years old. I stood by his side in a black velvet suit with a lace collar of which I was very proud, for it was one of the first *Little Lor' Fontlroi* ever seen in Bordeaux; besides rumour said that the Parisians, those people of Olympus, had not the like. I watched the big ships steam down the Gironde towards the sea, and while my father talked, as he continually did, I thought that the big ships were

like the fat, painted ducks which Eulalie set afloat to
please me in the flooded kitchen sink. *"L'Angleterre!"*
shouted my father. I remember nothing else. I see
him, not as he was then but as he was in late years,
and set that older figure upon the wharf. It is a tall,
corpulent man, still darker than I am, who wears a silk
hat upon massive black curls; he has choleric dark
eyes, his nose is aggressive; his mouth and chin are
hidden in a thick mat of hair that runs up to his brown
ears. Through the lobe of each ear a fine gold circlet
has been drawn. I shut my eyes and I see my father,
arm outstretched towards the North, pointing with his
stubby brown finger across the Gironde to the opposite
shore. He talks, he talks, he shouts, he glares at me
kindly; by periphrase and crackling Gascon adjective he
tries to enlighten me, and I listen to him unmoved, well
accustomed to the roaring of the metallic Southern throats.
I feel beyond that stubby finger the unknown country:
it is distant, for the half mile of Gironde water is my
ocean. But I feel the mysterious country, and because
it is beyond the water it is a romantic land. The rest of
the episode is foggy, but memories of a white garden-wall
enable me to reconstruct it. I feel that I looked at the
wall anxiously, for it was very high, not less than six
feet, and wondered whether, if I stood on the top, I should
see the country to which went the ships. I have also an
impression of opera glasses, delicate things studded with
red and green stars, which usually reposed in the sacred
drawer with my mother's black silk dress, her Indian multicoloured shawl and the little dancing shoes with the high
heels, shoes so small that, when I once stole in and put
them on, I found they were not much too large for me.

I think *Little Lor' Fontlroi* stood on the wall, and with
the jewelled opera glasses vainly swept the northern
horizon. The last impression of the adventure is one of
physical pain, of maternal brutality no doubt, for my
mother's hand is narrow and long; its fingers are delicate

as the limbs of a deerhound, but they must have been very hard.

II

Some years elapsed before I knew that I was a Frenchman, a subject of the Republic, for there was a distinguishing quality about this English dream, a dream made up of fantastic anticipations; it was a quality of romantic realism: I saw England not as she was, but as she might be. I have said that England was to my mind the toy that my model railway was to my hands, for the unconsidered fragments of conversation which fall into the greedy ears of a little boy impress him indirectly. They do not evoke definite pictures, but they lay trains of thought; the word "unconstitutional," used by my father when I was eleven, never meant anything to me, but it lodged in some part of me, irritated me into questions to Eulalie which yielded no intelligible answers, into profound reflections which perpetually oscillated between England, the moral inkiness of lies and the existence of a Divine Spirit. Likewise, in earlier days, England set me thinking and making cosmic pictures with ships, fogs, elephants and plum-pudding. This was not, after all, so bad a synthesis of England; I have always been synthetic rather than analytic; I have always wanted to construct, and if I have analysed at all it is because I wanted elements with which to create the lovely imaginative.

The imaginative! I have loved it as much as the logical. It was my French mother, the thin girl who came from Tours in the early days of the Third Republic to marry that noisy southerner, my father, gave me the logical. She came, prim, narrow, economical, dutiful and pious, with a neat little ordered mind, a mind very like a bookcase. On one shelf she kept family history, conventions and customs; another, a large one, contained devotional works, which were not exactly religious works; the other

shelves were crammed with books of reference, such as
*The Care of the Child, How to Feed Husbands, Home
Finance*. I think I understand my mother fairly well—as
well, that is, as a man can understand a woman—and I
have never felt there was, on the shelves of her brain,
one romance or one book of verse. And yet, sometimes,
when I bubble with emotion, I ask myself whether there
was not, is not (for my mother lives) just one book, a bold,
sinful, delicious book of passion, which she pulls out
guiltily at night, to read a few pages. If there be such
a book in her library, I am sure she craftily hides it behind
the others; it must be her own and beautiful secret, which
would cease to be beautiful if I set eyes on it.

I like to remember her as she was in the 'nineties:
demure, cruelly neat. She invariably wore black, much
to my father's annoyance, save on orgiastic days, when
a wedding, a christening, or a visit to the theatre demanded
grey or dark blue. I am sure that she was very unhappy
in grey, that she thought she looked like a cockatoo. She
was quiet, hard and incredibly efficient: Eulalie, a half
negroid Bordelaise, might roar in the kitchen, stamp, vow
that she would leave rather than reduce in the stew the
percentage of oil, but my mother's thin pipe pierced
through Eulalie's coppery clamour, and in the end the
percentage of oil was reduced. If, in her rage, Eulalie
smashed a dish, my mother would deduct the cost of it
from her wages and solemnly hand her, with the balance of
the money, the hardware merchant's receipt.

I owe you such shrewdness as I have, *maman,* and I
have always loved you more than my father, even though
he did jog me up and down on his enormous knee, take
me to the wharf and teach me to tell which ships were
loading for the Brazils and which were about to beat round
the Horn or the Cape to the China seas. Not even the
ten-franc piece he gave me on my twelfth birthday can
outweigh the subtle atmosphere of your love—and of mine,
for are you not *maman?* The mysterious French *maman*

who had so much love left to give her little boy because
she took to herself a stranger when she took a husband.

If, with love, my mother gave me the logical, my father,
with love, gave me the imaginative. He had brought it
ashore from the phosphorescent seas which swell below
the Line; as a seaman he began, and as a seaman he
ended, though he tried very hard to be a shipbroker.
Everybody knew it, and nobody called him Monsieur
Cadoresse: they called him *le capitaine*. He was, says a
dirty old piece of paper in my dispatch-box, born in
Bordeaux in 1838. Another dirty paper records that in
1879 he married Marie Lutand; others show that I was
born in 1880, that four years later my sister Jeanne came
into the world.

My father vanishes with the last paper, for he was
drowned in 1893. He merely passed through my life,
and I shall have little more to say of him, for his burly
ghost never disturbs me; this means that he never visits
me, for my father's ghost would not slink by in the unobtrusive English way: his ghost would come on a high
wind, shout like the spirit of Pantagruel and borrow all
the chains in purgatory for the pleasure of rattling them.
He was probably a happy enough man, for he managed to
be so busy as not to have time to think. A sea-captain
at thirty, he impulsively bought up the decaying shipbroking firm of Barbezan & Co., and ebulliently boomed
it into such prosperity that he was able, at the age of
forty-one, to abandon his loves, his gambles, his fights
and his drinking companions for the sake of his slim Marie.
I have not been told the story of those heroic days, and
therefore can do no more than guess at them, for the
London agency of Barbezan & Co. was founded with
" young Lawton " a few months before I was born. I am
conscious of the growth of the London agency, a little of
the decay of the Bordeaux firm. My father must have
been failing, or " young Lawton " must have been too
strong for his old French partner. I know that the activi-

ties of my father did not affect the firm, and he too knew it, for, in the last year of his life, when the land was being taken from him by those bold young English hands, the sea began to call him.

It called him, and then it took him. On a sunny May morning I went with my mother and little Jeanne to see the quondam shipbroker sail on a great four-master. The twenty-five years of his inaction had unfitted him for command, but the young skipper was kind; he understood that old *Capitaine Cadoresse* must be allowed to stand by his side on the bridge and to shout a few orders to the monkey-like sailors.

I shall never forget his peculiar figure, as the little busy tug contemptuously towed out the big ship that was taking rolling-stock to La Martinique. I suppose he was ridiculous, for he refused to wear the blue serge of the Englishman; he stood, legs wide apart, his frock-coat flapping about him, his silk hat on the back of his curly black hair; a streak of red silk under his waistcoat showed that he wore a sash. He sailed out with his ship, a replica of one of those fat Marseilles sea-captains who helped Napoleon in the 'sixties to vie with England in the Levantine seas. He went down with the great four-master, probably on an uncharted rock.

III

And so away with my father. He fell like a leaf in my path, and like a leaf blew away. He did not leave us poor, for my mother was bought out by "young Lawton" for a lump sum and an annuity. "Young Lawton" came from England, and that was an exciting affair. I was called into the drawing-room, which always made me feel nervous and respectful because it had a strange smell, the smell of rooms which are seldom opened.

I remember it—a sweet, faintly-scented smell, with a touch of rot in it. When I walked into the drawing-room on that June morning, the sun was streaming on the stiff

Empire sideboard and couch, on the prim garnet cushions, the arranged footstools; but a morbid fancy seized me: my mother sat on the couch, dressed in black, and " young Lawton " stood with his shoulders against the black marble mantelpiece, dressed in black too; my sister Jeanne and I paused inside the door, two small figures in new mourning. It was then the smell seized me and I was sure that it was the smell of a fresh grave. So deeply did this strike me that I hardly answered when Mr. Lawton spoke to me. It was some minutes before I realised him as a tall, slim man, who was not at all young as I understood the word; he was then thirty-eight. But soon he interested me, and I tried not to laugh (feeling that I ought not to laugh until my father had been dead at least a month) though his French was rather bad. " Well, young man," he said gravely, " and what do they teach you at school? " I did not know what to say, so replied: " Everything."

Lawton laughed, and one look at my mother's shocked face made me realise that these English had no heart. Or no manners. But I liked his amazing face, for it was regular, clean-shaven and kindly; of course his was a secretive, economical laugh, not the good roar of the South. Still—it was friendly, and I liked to think that he might laugh louder. I vaguely admired his reserve. And I liked his smooth, fair hair, like the coat of a well-groomed horse, his slim build, his calm blue eyes. Also I had never seen such brilliancy of polish on any French collar.

" Everything," he repeated after me; " well, that's better than nothing, which is what they teach us in England."

I looked at him suspiciously. Surely he would not say that if it were true. Then, being my mother's son, I cut the knot:

" Don't you know anything, then? " I asked.

He smiled. " No, not much."

His modesty surprised me. This could not be true. But what was the use of knowing things and not letting people see it? " Don't you want to know things? " I asked.

" No. It's doing things that matters, not knowing how
to do them."

I pondered this for some time; it was an interesting
idea, an idea quite outside the curriculum. But there was
a flaw:

" If knowing things doesn't matter, why do you say
it is better for me to learn everything than nothing, as
they do in England? "

My experience of thirteen years told me that at this
stage my father, or any ordinary human being, would
have struck the table with his fist, shouted at me, told
me to hold my tongue. But Mr. Lawton did not move a
finger, nor raise his voice; he looked at my mother and
said:

" This child is amazing."

Then my mother gave us the ancient French hint to go
away by telling us to go into the kitchen and see whether
she was there. I was not to see Mr. Lawton again for
many years, but I believe that I thought of him all the
time. He was just the incredible Englishman, a creature
of stone, incapable of anger or satisfaction. His extraordinary ideas did not appeal to me, for he contradicted one
sentence by another; how did England get rich if she did
not know what she thought? To do, instead of to know:
that was interesting, but do what? Mr. Lawton had drawn
an impressionist picture of England. In half-a-dozen
sentences he had shown me the viscera of his country: self-
confidence, contempt for learning, muddle-headedness and
the habit of infinite success. Fortunately, or perhaps unfortunately, some of the blanks were filled in later by
Dickens, Walter Scott, Kipling and Conan Doyle.

IV

They came later, these English writers, as I worked
my way up at the Lycée. I have little to say of my
schooldays: I learned, and then again I learned. Later

on I took degrees. To this day I am faintly surprised
when an Englishman talks of his school, as if it were the
only school, for I am quite sure that there is as little
difference between the Lycée at Bordeaux and the Lycée
at Lille as there is between the workhouse at Dover and
the workhouse at York. My school treated me as if I
were a goose doomed to produce *pâté de foie gras*. The
games which seem to make English schools illustrious and
competitive, we played them, but we played them after
school: we did not, as they do in England, steal the school
time from the games.

When I read the memoirs of other men I find it difficult
to understand how it is they remember so well the faces
and the sayings of every master and of every boy; there
is a minuteness in their evocation which makes me
suspicious, for those years at school, between the ages
of ten and fourteen, seem to me so futile, are indeed so
futile, that I can hardly see them. Or I lack the mental
telescope. I was a prize boy, and, every year, I staggered
down the red cloth of the platform stairs, with half-a-
dozen books on my arm, and several crowns of laurel
drooping over my nose. I cannot sketch those prize-giving
days: I might say that the head master had a beard, that
old Gargaille was fat, but that is all—and I might say
that I learned things, but I have forgotten them, I have
forgotten even the curriculum.

The truth is that school was an unemotional affair because my memory enabled me to learn readily and to
recite facts with parrot-like facility. I did not know the
thrill of rivalry, the agony of defeat. I remember very
much better a magnolia in the park, which flowered every
year and far into the autumn. Every morning I passed
that tree. It was loaded with blossoms so large that my
two hands could not cover one of them. They were white,
flushed with pink, and ruffled like the short feathers of
a swan's rump. One day, when no keeper was about, I
drew one bloom down, very tenderly so as not to hurt it:

the sun had warmed it, and it felt soft and firm like a
woman's cheek. I buried my lips in it, and it softly
breathed into my lungs its insidious, heady scent. A dozen
times I think I kissed that heavy blossom, and I remembered, when the winter came and the tree stood stark naked,
this caress of my first love.

It was emotion called me then, emotion about to sing
its swan-song when Chaverac died. Chaverac! Perhaps
I have never loved anybody as I loved Chaverac. I so
openly worshipped him, and he so obviously accepted my
homage, that our form ceased to call us Cadoresse and
Chaverac, but invented for us the joint name of Chavoresse. I cannot even now believe that he was an ordinary
person, this boy, one year my senior, for I could not
have so loved him and hated him unless he had had some
quality. Or I am too fatuous to think so: to this day
I am sure that every woman I have looked on with favour
possessed some charm which no other woman had, and I
am almost as assured of Chaverac's matchlessness.

Chaverac was, when I first saw him, fourteen years old,
short, dark, curly-headed, like any Gascon, or rather,
he would have been curly-headed if his hair had not been
close clipped. Set in his brown skin, his red lips seemed
dark; they smiled over splendid white teeth, but it was
his eyes held me—deep, greenish eyes with brown specks.
I liked to think that his eyes were like pools of water in
the sun and that the specks were the shadows of the leaves
of overhanging branches.

We had become friends simply, fatally. In those days
I had lost the assertiveness of earlier years, I was shy,
unpopular, and therefore became shyer and more unpopular. One morning I had been bullied by three or four
big boys and stood smarting, too proud to cry, against the
brick wall of the play-yard. I wanted to cry, not so much
because I had been pinched, because my arms had been
wrenched, or because I had been jeered at, as because my
unready tongue had cloven to my palate; I was logical then,

not ebullient. Now they had gone, and a flood of gorgeous invective was rising in me. How great it would have been if it had burst at the right moment! Chaverac, who had never before spoken to me, came close, examined me and said:

" You've got a funny face."

That is how one offers comfort when one is fourteen. But Chaverac had helped me, relieved the congestion: my pent-up invective burst from me. Chaverac listened to the end and said placidly:

" Those fellows are pigs."

That was just like Chaverac. He understood then as he always did, and it is not wonderful that I could always talk to him. With me he always smiled, remained unruffled; he was willing to be worshipped and willing to be hated; he was critical, always interested and never fired. At the age of fourteen he was a Laodicean, a man of the world, and as such he drew from me naught save what suited him: calm, light and debonair, he was the elective affinity of my impulsive roughness. We were French both of us, but in those days I had all the passion and he all the acumen of our race.

I need not dilate upon the adventures of that year, for nothing of any kind befell us. Ours was the inarticulate companionship of boys; I do not think he wanted to confide to me anything of his hopes, and certainly I did not know how to do so myself. Chaverac lived within himself, liked well enough to see me kneeling at his shrine, but was content to hear me talk of Gargaille, of the merits of Dunlop or Clincher tyres, of Lawton the amazing Englishman. He did not feel the need to do more than stimulate my conversation. I still think that he enjoyed the sense of mastery it gave him to know that he was the only person to whom I talked freely.

My intercourse with Chaverac was therefore made up of vast outpourings of facts, of small ambitions, and

proximate desires. If it was magic to meet him on the
way to school, to take tea (that is bread, fruit and sweet
syrup) in Madame Chaverac's cold flat near the Quinconces,
to tell him in the play-yard how I had got full marks for
composition, it must have been because I was desperately
searching for love. Having no idol, I had to make one.
But I could make no heroism, and Chaverac would no
doubt be to-day almost forgotten of me if his death had
not worked in me a mental revolution.

We were both keen cyclists, and I think I must withdraw, unsay that I could ever have forgotten this companion of my leisure. For who save Chaverac could scorch
so hard as to catch up with a passing motor-car? And
who save Chaverac could sit in the sun and mend a puncture
without complaining? And who save Chaverac would have
romantically refused to carry a lamp, but decorated his
handle-bars with Chinese lanterns? It interested him to
be romantic, I believe. Yet I might have forgotten if he
had not died, for his death became horribly intermingled
with my happiness.

One Sunday morning we had cycled some ten miles
south, along the Garonne. It was hot, and we had stopped
on the crest of a hill, while Chaverac wiped his forehead.

" Hot," he said.

" Yes, hot," I replied.

It was good to think that we should both be hot. We
looked down upon the river as it glistened between the
meadows like a stream of hot metal and, as we looked,
I wondered what Chaverac thought. He did not seem
much concerned with the sweep of the river or the purple
vineyards, which rippled down terrace after terrace from
our feet to the water's edge. He was not for nature,
Chaverac, he was for me and for what nature meant to
me; he was content to make me his æsthetic vicar. So,
while he still placidly wiped his round, dark head, I looked
my fill of the ruly river, its little burden of barges, pleasure
boats; I looked at the excursion steamer, which seemed

no larger than a launch, and was crowded with a thousand black, ant-like things.

Beyond the vineyards and the Garonne were the meadows, the tall poplars, the atrocious villas which the builder was beginning to shoot forth into the country. Beyond curtains of trees, in the north-west, was the denseness, the shadow that concealed Bordeaux. A smokestack was sharply outlined in the clear air, and thus graceful. I enjoyed a sense of peace and of attainment, for we had painfully climbed this hill, pushing our bicycles; below us lay the broad white road that circled round it: I could see two bends in it, far below. We stood side by side, saying nothing but content, for we were alone, as two can be on a peak, and by knowing each other knowing all.

It was because his eyes covered and warmed me with their definite look of understanding that I knew Chaverac to be my good companion, the being who for me alone had emerged from chaos. Up the other side of the hill a cyclist was coming towards us. I could see him grow as he rose, his cap ridiculously fore-shortened and his attenuated feet almost invisible. I watched him a little resentfully, for he was intruding, coming uncalled into a world which I could share with none other than Chaverac; he grew and I saw him, an absurd figure with a cap that was too small, squat calves which no benevolent trousers hid. He had, and I saw it as he raised his face towards me, the general air of roughness of men who suddenly swerve across the path of bewildered old ladies, race motor-cars, do all the things we did, but in uglier fashion. The man stopped by our side, mopping his forehead, then looked at us as if wondering whether two boys could help him.

" I say," he asked Chaverac at last, " what's the best road to La Sauve?"

" Straight on until you come to the bridge," said Chaverac, pointing to the hot white road.

" Ah! There's no short-cut, I suppose?"

I looked at the man and suddenly felt a queer, insane hatred of him. I hated his flaccid, white face, his rosacia-touched cheeks and the straggling black bar of his moustache. I hated him because he was inadequate and unconscious of his inadequacy. And his cap, his small cap, his squat, stockinged calves.

"No, there's no short cut," said Chaverac. He was polite; he always was polite, unruffled, even when talking to men of this kind, creatures that should be mocked and flouted. I felt I must speak, spit some insult at him.

"Unless," I said, with a savage ring in my voice (and it surprised me), "unless you go down there." I pointed down the almost sheer side of the hill, through the purple vineyards, to the metallic river. The man looked at me, amazed and angry, like a bull which glares at the sun on leaving the toril; it pleased me to see the angry glow in his eyes, to feel that a flick of my tongue had done this, pierced the silly sufficiency which clothed his flaccid, white face. But I was frightened too, as one is frightened when one has mischievously pushed a lever and the machine begins to work.

"What?" said the man. "What do you say? What do you mean? Do you take me for an *imbécile? hein?*"

I said nothing, but looked at him in a conflict of emotions. I hated him and his ugliness, the mean, stupid satisfaction which could not laugh at itself because too uncertain and weak, but I despised myself because my joke was feeble. True, I had hurt him, and that was good, but how weak had been my sling and how despicable my game. Also I feared him as red rose in his white cheeks.

"*Hein?*" he said again, and lashed himself into fury. "I ask you a civil question and you—you answer me as if I were an *imbécile*. I am not an *imbécile*," he repeated so angrily that I felt intimately that he knew himself to be one; "it is you the *imbécile*." He took a step towards me. "*Imbécile!*" he muttered again. And, as his right hand moved I involuntarily stepped back. I was driven back, I was afraid of him even though I despised him.

"*Ah?*" he sneered, showing yellow, irregular teeth. But I had stepped back and, very subtly, his self-esteem had suddenly regilded him. He did not strike, but shrugged his shoulders and turned to go down the hill. Only once did he turn towards the spot where I remained, frozen and horribly humble. "*Imbécile!*" he cried and with unimaginative emphasis: "*Sacré imbécile!*" Soon the white road swallowed him. Then he reappeared in the first bend, passed through it and was again swallowed up, reappeared in the last bend. I saw him turn his head towards me, his absurd little head, under the cap that was too small. It was too far to see his lips, but for me they moved, and the invisible medium that linked our warring spirits conveyed to me his monotonous, inaudible insult: "*Imbécile! Sacré imbécile!*"

Chaverac had not said anything. He had watched the scene with phlegm. Indeed, there was almost amusement in his brown-flecked green eyes; he smiled jovially rather than ironically.

"Chaverac," I faltered. But I stopped, I could say no more. I was overwhelmed, raging; I knew that my underlip trembled and that again there was welling up in me that frightful torrent of abuse which swells in the breast of the impotent. Oh! if only the man could come back—I felt hot at the idea of the words I would use. I saw myself, too, smashing my fist into that putty-coloured face, tearing at that straggling black moustache. I was blood-lusty and Chaverac knew it, watched me with his queer air of critical pleasure in the sensations of others, watched me as if he were a vivisectionist observing the effects of a drug.

Then I leapt to my bicycle and threw all my weight into the pedals, so that they might carry me more swiftly from the horrid spot.

V

There was a shadow between Chaverac and me. It was nothing at first, a trifling obstacle, an awkwardness such as parts master and dog when the man has trodden on the dog's foot and it returns, whining and wagging its tail, protesting while it is caressed that the pain was nothing. Chaverac had ultimately caught me up on that fatal day and had tactfully left the subject alone; he had diverted the conversation to some inoffensive topic, such as tyres, and Bowden brakes, borne with my sullen silence, made jokes, pushed the memory into some far corner of his brain. At first I felt grateful, loved him for it. But he could not wash out the past; he knew and I knew that I ought to have struck the man, at least insulted him. I ought to have inflicted on him injury for injury, and my honour would have been clear, or I could have hurt him more than he had hurt me and have been a hero. Because I had wantonly and stupidly wounded him I ought to have wounded him again. I had not done so, and this because I had been afraid, afraid of gibes and blows, afraid because he was a man and I a boy. There was no hiding it, I had behaved like a coward. I knew it. Chaverac, too, knew that I was a coward. Each knew that the other knew, and it was intolerable to share the secret.

We made desperate efforts, Chaverac and I, to shoulder our burden. We struggled so desperately for our old intimacy that we saturated it with gall. We looked suspiciously into each other's eyes, suspected traps. If I wanted, as I did in those days, to talk of Vaillant and Caserio and the other Anarchists, I held back, and the sweat of fear rushed to my brow, for Anarchism meant killing and courage, and I was a coward. I had had my chance and lost it. And Chaverac, too, suffered, even though his teeth still flashed in forced smiles; he dared no longer ask me to cycle with him, for he knew what a joint expedition must recall to me. We chose our subjects; then we spoke less, for now we had to think before we spoke for fear that we should open a wound. At last we hardly spoke at all, but walked homewards side by side, defensively silent. I no longer put my hand on his arm, for I uneasily felt that he might be sullied by my coward's touch.

We had terrible dialogues.

" Good-morning."

" Good-morning."

" Hot, isn't it? "

" Yes."

That was all we had to say, we who had chattered, remembered, planned. Everything was going, for everything was poisoned and was withering. It was terrible to meet, to see in each other's eyes a pity that was turning into fear. We had to meet, for we could not even part: the memory held us, it was our secret, the gnawing thing set like a canker in our affection. To part, to avoid these looks, would have been the heavenly relief that follows on the amputation of a ruined limb, but we could not part, because we did not dare; we could not break the link, for to break it would have been to confess, either that the one remembered or that the other understood. We could know, but we could not confess.

How the horror would have ended if time had not stepped in as a surgeon rather than a healer, I do not know; in insults, recrimination perhaps, in some exhibition of rancour, when he would have told me that I was a coward and that he despised me, when perhaps I would have struck him as I ought to have struck my enemy, unless —and this was another horror—unless again I proved myself a coward. I hated him because I had loved him. I could have borne disgrace before another, I could not bear it before him. But time helped us and the world helped us. They altered the hour at which a private tutor expected me; they developed in the history master an interest

in Chaverac which kept him back for a few minutes after
the lesson, while I escaped alone; they even strengthened
friendships we had both flouted in the days when we were
one.   I know that, as I hurried away while Chaverac
spoke to the history master, the voice of the past screamed
to me that I should wait, but I hurried away with Adam's
averted face, for I had fallen.

Strengthened by accident, our parting grew more definite.
We missed each other, mistook places of meeting, discovered urgent engagements on Thursday afternoons and Sunday mornings.   Our fellows observed the difference,
taunted us, asked whether " Chavoresse " was dead.   Ah!
that was the true suffering, this public exhibition of our
distress.   The steadfast cruelty of the boy scented out at
once that something was amiss, pestered us with quips
and questions, hunted us from the playground because we
feared its jeers.   We were outcasts because we were butts,
and yet we could not come together again.   We were two
Ishmaelites madly fleeing from one another in the desert.
Even our families tortured us, tortured us with questions,
surmises as to absurd quarrels, made barbarous attempts
to bring together two boys who could only sit face to face,
tongue-tied, full of hostility.

Time passed, and with it some of the pain, for the boys
grew tired of their game and our parents forgot our
tragedy.   There was nothing left save an awful emptiness
where there was not yet room for hatred, nothing but
strangling constraint.   All had gone—pleasure, peace and
interests.   I skulked where I had walked merrily.   Later
only did the past goad me yet further, when Chaverac
had become so intimately associated with it that he bore
some of the blame, when I began to hate him, to grow hot
with rage when I saw him, to shiver with passion when
I thought of what he had seen.   My mother had forgotten.
She knew only that I was moody and fierce-tempered.   The
doctor ordered me a sedative.   I lay under my cope of
lead.

One Thursday evening when I had been out alone, my mother took me into the drawing-room. The smell of the grave was in it still; formal and black-clad, she was a worthy messenger.

" I have something to tell you," she said.

" Ah!" I said listlessly, though her tone was grave.

" You must be prepared—it is dreadful——"

" What is it?" I asked in a choked voice. I knew— I knew—Chaverac——

" He was cycling—he slipped—he slipped under a dray."

" Is he dead?" I can still hear my flat voice.

" Yes—oh!—oh!—what is the matter? What is the matter with you?"

I see my mother's face now as I write, the fear and surprise in her eyes; I see her outstretched hands with spread fingers. She was pale, almost grey, but I know that warm blood had rushed to my cheeks, that relief had burst from me in a great sigh. I was free—free—alone in possession of my shameful secret. How lights must have danced in my eyes!

VI

I do not shrink from this confession. That which is, is. My story shows how singularly the materialistic child of twelve had evolved into the morbid, introspective boy of fourteen. But that boy had yet to grow into a youth and into a man, to undergo other shocks, change again as swiftly as the wind, gain and lose convictions, adopt attitudes and be moulded by those attitudes until they became part of his character.

The death of Chaverac meant more to me than relief from an obsession. It snapped the links that bound me to my fellow man, it made love, emotion, detestable. His death restored to the throne logic and materialism. I had given my soul and, circumstance aiding, my gift had been flung back to me, soiled and unknowable.

I had done with the soul. When I was sixteen I had done with faith. I was thrown back upon my brain, and sudden interest in my work rose up; unfettered by emotion I turned to the intellect. I decided to be rich, powerful, hard. I decided these things in the abstract, and then looked for a peg on which to hang them: that peg turned out to be England.

VII

I have said that I never forgot Lawton; indeed, the brilliance of his linen collar hung for years before my dazzled eyes. That white collar meant England, very much as the magnolia meant France. It meant more, for it was one thing to try and be intellectual and hard, and another to be like Lawton; I had the young generosity of the South, and if it could not out in friendship it must out in admiration for something, in an ideal. The years between fifteen and eighteen were crowded by study, by the dull memorising of facts; I gained nothing from my education save information and, if my companions had not helped me, I should have been an intolerable prig. But they helped me, in the indirect way in which youths help one another, by support mixed with chaff, for they were not all unsympathetic to my ever more vivid English dream.

I remember three of them especially, at the financial school. We were then all four seventeen, keen, combative, different in some way known to none save ourselves from the hundred others who mean nothing to me now. Those others have mostly vanished; some have left behind them names without faces, Dubourg, Arbeillan, Valaze; and some have faces without names, dark, southern faces mostly; and yet others are nothing save a brown suit or a white hat. But the chosen three will never quite die for me; there was Luzan, a well of intelligent and bubbling gaiety, who thought argument was a sort of mental catch-as-catch-can. Luzan writes to me once a year or so to this day, and tells me that my views are idiotic; whenever I change them they are still idiotic. There was Lavalette, the best dressed young man in Bordeaux: he is now the best dressed man in Paris, but he is not a mere fop; he has a discriminating if desultory appreciation of the arts and (this endears him) an undiscriminating but sedulous love for England. As for Gobot—I have lost sight of fat, jolly Gobot, with the round, pink face, the piggy, intelligent eyes, and the booming voice. Ours was a heterogeneous company, for Luzan was the mocker, the Puck, the miniature Anatole France—Lavalette was the old French grace blended with the new French *chic*—Gobot embodied all the solidities, stupidities and shrewdnesses of the bourgeois. And I? I was the hot, restless spirit who felt quite sure that he was cold and judicial.

Of course, we never played games, we had a better thing to do, and that was to talk. I do not suppose we overlooked anything in those two years, neither faith, nor woman, nor politics, nor the histories of our families, their weddings and their scandals. We were perfectly frank and perfectly unashamed; we were not cribbed nor shy— indeed, we affected more liberty of view than we possessed. We were atrociously bad form, and it was splendid. One conversation, especially, I remember, at the end of my second year, when we finally settled *la question anglaise,* as we called it in pompous imitation of the diplomatic jargon.

"Those English," said Gobot, "are nothing but land-grabbers. That Fashoda affair—why, if we'd had a decent fleet we'd have sailed up the Thames and bombarded London instead of letting Marchand die in a swamp."

"Which swamp," said Luzan maliciously, "takes the form of promotion, the *Légion d'Honneur* and a triumphant reception in Paris."

"Marchand morally died in the swamp," said Gobot, stodgily, "killed by the Englishmen. He'll never be a general, the Government wouldn't dare. Our Government

never has the insolence of the English; the English have
that one quality and it's useful to them."

"Oh!" I protested, "the English aren't so bad——"

"Who stole Egypt?" cried Gobot.

"And who let the Germans crush Napoleon III?" asked
Luzan. He smiled wickedly, and I knew he was playing
with the sincere Gobot.

"You're right, Luzan, and who killed the other Napoleon? shut him up in an island? and who set Europe
on him and never fought at all?"

"*Pardon, Gobot,*" said Lavalette, smoothly, "there was
Waterloo."

"Waterloo!" roared Gobot. His fat, pink face became
dark red, and his piggy eyes began to flash. "Speak of
it! why, it was the Prussians won Waterloo, the English
sent hardly anybody with their *Wellignetonne*. England
never fights, she sends money to hire armies, just as she
hires men for her own, and then she swindles everybody
when the war's over. Who stole India? the English.
And who stole Canada? the English. And who talked
of helping the Balkan Christians and let the Turk have
them? the English. Land of Liberty, you say, Cadoresse? Did the English help Poland? No! we helped
Poland while the English were filling their pocket with
North America. And wasn't it the English fought China
to keep up the opium trade? the poison trade? And
wasn't it the English who taught the Indians to drink
themselves to death? Hypocrites, liars, Bible-mongers,"
roared Gobot. "They don't send out missionaries, they
send out commercial travellers. And all the women drink."

We were silent as Gobot suddenly laid before us the
result of the elaborate history we are taught; as his voice
rose I felt a foreigner in my own country, for I had no
share in this smouldering fury of the French, who have
always found in their way a rich island nation, a nation
grabbing islands merely to prevent other nations from
travelling freely, a people always ready to lend money to

their enemies, to side, in the holy name of splendid isolation, with anybody whom they could exploit. As Gobot went on, raucous, and therefore weakly absurd, I suddenly saw him as small, thought of him as one of Kipling's monkeys whom the other animals would not notice.

"All the same," said Lavalette, patting his perfectly oiled head, "they are the only people who know what a gentleman is."

We discussed the gentleman, as expounded by me; he was a queer creature, as I took him from my reading, mainly a person who hunted the fox, and told lies to save the honour of women. We discussed Protestantism and whether it was better than the Catholicism we all of us practised, but did not believe in. Gobot was still raging historically, for Luzan had him well in hand and was drawing him back and back, from treaty to treaty and defeat to defeat; they had got to Blenheim, and by and by would get to Agincourt, to Crécy. Meanwhile, as we all four walked slowly round and round the little park, Lavalette and I were better employed on English literature, which we could both read in the text.

"Those two," said Lavalette, tolerantly, "they don't understand; what's the use of talking to people who read Walter Scott in French?"

I looked approvingly at Lavalette. I do not think anybody else had ever so wholly satisfied my æsthetic tastes. He was then nearly six feet tall, very slim, and, because narrow-chested, graceful as a reed. His long neck carried a well-poised and very long head; his mouth was small and rather full-lipped; it made me think of a tulip. But better than his glossy black hair, his delicate hands, which he exquisitely manicured, I remember the sorrowful gaze of his grey eyes. Immense eyes with the opalescent whites! how kindly you appraised and discounted my crudities!

"They do not know," said Lavalette, "and that's why they talk. Why, the way they hate the English shows they don't understand them; also it shows that they are inferior to them, for one never hates an equal, one respects him."

"That's true," I said; "boxers shake hands before they fight."

"They do. That's the English way. You find it in all the books, in Kipling, in Conan Doyle; you find phrases like 'playing the game' and 'not hitting a man when he's down.'"

"You don't find it in Dickens," I said.

A long pause ensued while we thought this out.

"No," said Lavalette at last, "you don't. And I've read him through, almost. That's curious."

"What's curious?" asked Gobot from behind.

We told him. He did not know Dickens well, having read only *David Copperfield* in French, but pointed out that perhaps Dickens did not play games.

"Perhaps that's why," Luzan suggested; "games make a difference."

Then we all four spoke together, Gobot because he always talked and Luzan because he always contradicted; but Lavalette and I had got hold of something and were very excited.

"That's the answer," I said at last; "the Englishman is a peculiar animal because his temperament has been altered by games. He thinks life is like football."

"With rules and rights—" said Lavalette.

"A Protestant in the playing field—" said Luzan, with a sniff.

"A Protestant everywhere," I said, as if illumined. "He's always ruled by something, by a code, a habit. That's why he had a Parliament first, that's why he does not fight duels—"

"He wants to save his skin," growled Gobot.

"Are duels dangerous?" Luzan asked, thus diverting Gobot from the attack.

Lavalette and I walked on, full of a new realisation; this idea of the rule of games being made the rule of life was fascinating; one felt one had suddenly come upon the meaning of this cold, restrained English life. Of course, it was restrained, for the people respected the rules.

I think we discussed England for the rest of the afternoon; Lavalette persisted in being literary, in comparing Walter Scott with Dumas. " No fire," he said, " except in *Ivanhoe,* but elegance. Now Dumas brawls in taverns. His cardinals are braggarts and his kings are merely vulgar. Of course, Walter Scott is a bore, but such a gentlemanly bore."

I think we understood Walter Scott pretty well, the severity of his courts and the high-falutin sexlessness of his historical romances; and Conan Doyle, too, we understood. His Englishman was Sherlock Holmes, the cold, hard, shrewd and brave man, and Watson—how English was this splendid, stupid Watson who could listen and do what he was told. Dickens we suspected as an oddity and a sentimentalist, but he made London seem romantic and very comfortable. As for Kipling, Lavalette and I almost gave him up, or rather we gave up his passionate, poetic side, tried to draw from him a picture of another Englishman, the calm Anglo-Indian, so haughty, so efficient, and so brave.

We created an Englishman from anything that came handy. It was, on the whole, a fairly good lay-figure.

VIII

And so, through these early years, when the world was dawning, I saw life as a map divided up into diverse countries; one was the land of art, another the home of business, a third was marked " love." The first interested me in rather stereotyped fashion: my affection for the arts rested upon my rebellion against our graveyard drawing-room; the second drew me a little more, for it was mixed up with England: commerce and liberalism in ideas made up for me the soul of the island. As for love—well, I am

French, so I did not suppose there was more to know about it than I did know when I was eighteen. Love had not stolen upon me softly like spring into an English hedge; it had come flaunting, brazen and mercenary in the train of the senior rowdies of the school. If I suspected now and then, when I thought of Agnes and David Copperfield, that it had some fugitive charms not to be found in Bordeaux, I thrust back the idea. Intellect was the real thing, woman was the pastime. I knew all about her and all about love. I knew nothing about either, and I might never have known if I had not come to these islands where love burns with a clear, white flame, a flame which does not scorch as does that of the French brazier, but beautifully and intimately warms.

IX

Then Mafeking. But I have told Mafeking.

" Land-grabbing again," said Gobot when I came back; " *cochons.*" I smiled in an exasperating and superior manner. I knew.

X

Unroll again, film of my life, and show me my dead self in movement. You show me a young man in a white smock, sweeping the barrack-yard: the army. Then the young man in a small room at Montauban, in red trousers; his belt and bayonet lie on the bed; his lips move as he whispers English irregular verbs: " throw, threw, thrown . . . blow, blew, blown—": idealism. The young man again, in full regimentals, with half-a-dozen more of his kind; they are at the *brasserie,* have had a little too much to drink; the young man holds upon his knee the tolerant singing girl who goes round with the plate: seeing life.

.   .   .   .   .   .

We sat in the drawing-room, my mother on the right of the black marble mantelpiece, Jeanne on the left, I by the table. I noticed that our three chairs marked the three angles of an equilateral triangle. The magic of the prim room seemed to compel geometry in attitudes. It possessed the one fender on which I had never put my boots, and I had never smoked in it. I tried, that morning, for the regiment had given me assurance, but there was no zest in the performance, or the damp air of the room had affected the saltpetre. I looked at my mother, slim, pretty and black-clad; at my beetle-browed sister, realised our group as a family council, a dry, loveless thing, fitly held by the stiff Empire couch and the garnet-coloured footstools. The room smelled of death, and suddenly I knew how glad I was to say good-bye to this hardness and formality, to go to England, free, living England.

"And so you are going to-morrow, Lucien," said my mother. "I hope it is for the best."

"*Oui, maman,*" I said, thinking of the morrow.

"Your father always wanted you to go into the branch. I had hoped you might stay here and go into the house; still——"

My mother paused; she had never been able to realise the change, to accept that "the house" was in London, that the Bordeaux firm was the branch. For her, the Bordeaux firm was still august, dominant, as in the days of my father and his frock-coats.

"Still I suppose Monsieur Lawton knows best. You'll write to me, Lucien."

"*Oui, maman.*"

I knew I ought to have said more, but life and adventure waited.

"You will get on, of course. Your father always hoped to leave you the house. Monsieur Lawton knows that it was understood; so you must work hard, Lucien. You are very fortunate, for we are not dependent on you: Jeanne will have a little money, and we shall marry her soon."

I glanced at Jeanne, who sat playing with her fingers.

She was rather a pretty girl, small and thin like my mother, demure, but she had under heavy black brows my father's splendid eyes. She did not move when my mother calmly announced her intention to "place her" with some man.

"There's no hurry about that," my mother resumed. "Jeanne's only eighteen. Have you packed? No? Well, you must do it to-day. And mind you take brandy for the crossing. Your thick socks will come home to-night."

I was going to thank her formally when she suddenly did something she had never done before: she sighed, and allowed one large tear to roll down her cheek.

"*Maman!*" I cried. And before I could hesitate I had broken the coldness, I had thrown my arms round her and we were both crying, while Jeanne sobbed as she knelt by my mother's side and held my hand. I was twenty-two, "an old soldier," and I wept. But, even as I wept and promised my mother to write every week and return every summer, I could hear the roar of the English beyond.

XI

The cliffs of Folkestone stood up, white and green, exactly like the French cliffs, yet unlike.

The wet, green country, the oast-houses and the hop-fields were left behind. Townlet after townlet, deceiving me, promising London, then dwindling into fields again. Then denser townlets, smokestacks, building plots. The sea mist had thickened, was becoming yellow.

I saw the houses in their gardens, then the bronze Thames in the moist, yellow air, the Houses of Parliament standing out like black bluffs against the pale sky.

CHAPTER III

INTRODUCTIONS

I

"This is it, Mr. Cadoresse," said Mrs. Hooper.

She had preceded me and now stood in the middle of the room, while I remained on the threshold. I had a moment's hesitation for this was the first time I had seen an English bedroom; the hotel at which I stayed during Mafeking week and the semi-public rooms of the Lawtons' house had not prepared me for the homely feeling of this sleeping place. For a reason I shall always feel and never quite understand there is a difference between a bedroom in an English house and one in a French flat; if the Englishman's house is his castle his bedroom is his keep. But Mrs. Hooper was talking again in gentle tones:

"I hope you'll be quite comfortable, Mr. Cadoresse. Anything you want—there's the bell near the bed. I suppose you'll be wanting to get ready for dinner, so I'll leave you if you've got everything."

"Thank you," I said. "I don't want anything. A fire, perhaps."

It was October and I felt chilly. When I left Bordeaux the magnolias were loaded with blooms. Here the air was misty and raw.

"If you like, Mr. Cadoresse, though we don't generally light fires before November."

"Oh! it doesn't matter, it doesn't matter," I said. I felt reproved. I had broken some law. I wanted to apologise, to explain abundantly, but I found that Mrs. Hooper had gone, quietly, without adding another word; she impressed me by her negativeness. She wore no notable clothes: a dark blouse and skirt, so far as I remember; she dressed her grey hair neither very tight nor very fancifully; she did not gesticulate, nor welcome me warmly, nor appear churlish; she did not call me " Sir " in pro- pitiating manner, nor was she familiar; she was neither servant nor hostess. I have met many Englishwomen like her: the number of things Mrs. Hooper was not and did not was amazing. But I did not think about her very long: my room interested me. My room had an air of permanence, for I would then have been embarrassed to find other quarters in a private house. A stranger, I was like a shipwrecked sailor for whom the desert island be- comes home. Against the wall furthest from the window was a black and brass bed; before the window stood a small table, covered with an old red cloth and bearing a swivel-mirror; a marble-topped washstand with a yellow- tiled splasher, a mahogany chest of drawers at the foot of the bed, and three mahogany chairs made up, with a brown-painted hanging cupboard, the furniture of the room. All these pieces of furniture struck me as too small, too compact; they left the room bare, save for thin red cur- tains at the window; the room felt too light, too airy. I missed the heavy canopy which shut me in when I slept in my French home, the blue eiderdown, the darkness, the comfortable thickness of the stuffs.

And yet Mrs. Hooper had not attained the sanitary horror of modern English houses; I was spared the linoleum that chills the feet and the distempered walls that chill the heart. At least she had laid down an old red-and-brown carpet, which was probably not very well swept; on the yellowish rosebud-decorated wall she had hung three engravings: " The Peacemaker," " In the Garden of Eden," and " The Jubilee Procession," while a red, blue and gold text tried to induce me to remember that the Lord was my Shepherd and that I should not want.

On the whole, however, I did not dislike the room and

I was introspective enough to realise that I would get used to it, that the dog can, after a while, sleep well in the cat's basket. It was nearly seven. I began to unpack my clothes, to lay them out on the bed, hurriedly, for my evening clothes, my smoking as I still called them, seemed scattered among the others, while my shirts, French laundered, had mostly had a bad time on the journey. When, at last, I was ready, I realised that I somehow fell short of the Lawton ideal. I was a neat, dark, slim youth, not ill-looking, but my ready-made black tie did not content me; my shoes were well enough, but I had that day seen a fashion-plate in a newspaper which proved that on these occasions Englishmen wore pumps; and, in some undefinable way, my linen did not reach the Lawton standard. It never did quite reach it until four years had elapsed, when a sympathetic man told me that I should send it to a *French* laundry. Incredible!

At last I stood in front of the mirror, in the midst of the quantity of clothing two small trunks can discharge, critically considering the candidate for the English quality. I found I had not greatly changed since that historic night when I marched down Shaftesbury Avenue with a thrilled heart, while (and I reminiscently hummed the refrain) the Englishmen sang:

> " And when they ask us how it's done,
> We proudly point to every one
> Of England's soldiers of the Queen."

" *Pas mal,*" I said aloud to the figure. I liked the arch of my eyebrows and the increasing thickness of my moustache. Good dark eyes, too, but I suddenly determined to get my hair cut the very next day. Still, the hair would have to pass for that evening, so I opened the door and, as half-past seven struck, followed a pungent smell of cooking to the ground floor.

I passed between the red-papered walls to the hall, which was decorated with a pair of buffalo horns, a gaunt

hatstand and a print of the Heenan *v.* Sayers fight. Then
I hesitated in front of the doors, for nothing told me
which was the dining-room. To open the wrong door
would be annoying, because it would make me look a fool.
I should not have been in the least bashful if, on opening
the wrong door, I had found Mrs. Hooper in a bath but
I could not have borne being made ridiculous.

Suddenly I heard muffled peals of laughter; a door
opened, the laughter became shrill, and a young girl,
running out, nearly rushed into my arms. I do not think
I shall forget that first picture. She came, light, bounding,
and she is fixed in my mind upon one foot, a Diana
Belvedere; she was laughing still, and I could see the
quiver of the light on her brown curls, the white glitter
of her teeth, and the sparkle of her dark eyes. But, as
I looked, her expression and her attitude changed. The
eyes were cast down, long lashes lay on full, faintly
blushing cheeks; the mouth smiled no more, and I saw
nothing now but the very pretty and very prim English
miss. We stood face to face for two seconds, while I
searched my brain for a suitable English sentence and
some qualification of the rule that in England you must
be introduced, and as I searched I thought I had never
seen anything so delightful. But the English miss eased
the strain, threw me a glance which took me in from
forehead to shoe, smiled and, with much dignity, passed
me by.

As she went she murmured: " Good evening, *Monsieur* "
(alas! she pronounced it approximately " Mersser ") and,
with persistent dignity, climbed the first three or four steps
of the stairs. Then dignity seemed to desert her, and
she ran upstairs, on sole and heel, loud and gawky as a
boy. This did not kill the charm but intensified it by
making its elements incongruous. I had no time to think
more of her, for the room she had come out of was evidently a bedroom; at least I could see a bed in it, so I
boldly turned the handle of the other door.

Three people looked at me with extreme calm. I thought of the calm of fish. One of them was Mrs. Hooper, as I had seen her half-an-hour before; the other was a girl, younger than the other, not at all pretty, but still worthy of a glance, for she had flaxen hair, china-blue eyes and a milk-white skin; the third, an elderly man, I judged to be Mr. Hooper. He was a small, thin person, as undecided in colouring as his wife; his mild eyes made me think at once of the younger girl, obviously his daughter; he stood leaning against the mantelpiece where burned no fire (of course, not in October), in a black frock-coat the silk lapels of which were not very fresh. Mr. Hooper was rather bald, looked about fifty; he seemed so mild, so genial, so unruffled, that I wondered whether an immense aggressiveness lay under his mask.

I had not time to analyse further, for I was struggling with an internal rage. I, Lucien Cadoresse, was wearing the wrong clothes, was being ridiculous. I thought of running from the room, of putting on my tweed suit again, but then I should have been more ridiculous. It was a ghastly situation and I nerved myself to bear the chorus of protest. But there was no chorus; Mrs. Hooper said:

"Allow me to introduce you to my husband, Mr. Cadoresse, and to my daughter Louise."

Mr. Hooper said: "Glad to have the pleasure——"; Louise, or Lulu as she was called in ordinary circumstances, mumbled and blushed. Then the girl I had met in the hall came in, now quite demure, was introduced to me as "My daughter Maud." Fully mustered, the family was doubtless going to protest against my clothes. But Mr. Hooper said:

"Very cold for the time of year," and rubbed his hands.

"Much colder than in Bordeaux," I replied, expecting this to lead up to an allusion to my bare shirt front.

But Mr. Hooper began to question me on "the meteorological conditions in the South of France," as he called them. I satisfied him as well as I could, which cannot have been completely, for Mr. Hooper had one of those thirsts for miscellaneous information found mainly in the City of London and in the North Country, which nothing can ever assuage. Of indifferent health, too poor to indulge in games, bound to daily labour which he was not vigorous enough to realise as uncongenial, Mr. Hooper had developed a desultory acquaintance with every branch of knowledge, from Sanskrit to wood-carving; he knew some French, a little more than no German; he could quote six Latin tags and one Greek one, but he couldn't spell that one; he was fond of history, that is history *à l'anglaise,* as it is expounded in *A Favourite of Henry XXIX,* and the like; he knew where was Taganrog, for he had had to look it up, but could not at once locate Moscow on the map; he liked to know how many dollars went to the pound and was quite content not to know how many gulden went to the pound. Mr. Hooper's mind was an unlimited patchwork quilt of ideas and facts; occasionally the ideas clashed and the facts did not dovetail, but those little imperfections did not interfere with the progress of the quilt. He never looked for a piece with which to fill a hole when the facts did not accord: a new piece always went end-on to the others and the mental quilt grew larger and larger; it would have smothered him in time if he had not continually lost bits of it, which made it manageable.

Mr. Hooper loved a fact. In later days I repeated to him the joke in *The Man from Blankley's,* to the effect that the area of the Great Pyramid is exactly equal to that of Trafalgar Square. He did not laugh, but with great relish added the fact to the quilt.

While, that evening, Mr. Hooper entertained me with a schedule of compared temperatures which showed that isotherms had escaped his attention, I examined the room and its inhabitants. The dining-room was emphatically an English room; it had red paper, well covered with inferior oil-paintings of still life and steel engravings of British regiments holding the pass or the ford, as might be. Opposite the window was a large mahogany sideboard, awk-wardly carved, on which stood a cheap tantalus, some siphons and the bread platter; there was also a bottle of ready-made dressing. The mantelpiece carried an elaborate oak overmantel, on which were accumulated brass ash-trays, little china pigs, and some Goss, two bronze candlesticks which did not match, some prospectuses and letters. Into the looking-glass were pushed two or three cards, one of them an invitation to a Conservative meeting at a titled lady's house. This I know, for it stayed there many weeks. Yet the room did not displease me; it was cold, the chairs were ugly, the carpet felt thin and the table appointments seemed common, the plate dirty under the glaring gas, but it was comfortable, it was untidy. I had left formality in France, and I knew it when those people spoke to me so quietly, without trying to entertain me, when they re-frained from commenting on my evening clothes.

Mr. Hooper said: " The dinner is late, my dear."

Mrs. Hooper said: " The girl will bring it up in a minute, Alfred."

I looked at Lulu, who at once blushed, then at Maud. Maud's eyes met mine with a boldness that suggested either absolute innocence or deliberate challenge; I found out later that it contained a little of each: that mixed quality is an English monopoly. I looked her full in the eyes, which I could now see were dark-brown, analysed her in detail; she stood the test very well, and it was singular to find her almost a woman and so much of a boy, for her figure was slim and straight, and yet I foresaw that within two or three years it would show all the gracious curves of maturity. Under my cool inspection, which took in the thin brown stuff of her blouse and the low dressing of her hair, she remained composed, but at last she smiled at me from the corners of her mouth, and looked down at her feet. My heart was beating a little when the gong was struck in the hall and the little maid entered, carrying the soup.

"I regret we cannot offer you hordoovers," said Mr. Hooper archly, "but radishes are not in season. We might have had some sardines, though; Ethel, where are those sardines you opened for breakfast on Tuesday?"

"You know you had the last of those this morning, Alfred," said Mrs. Hooper. "Besides, sardines don't keep when the tin's open."

"Melon," said Mr. Hooper.

"How can you, Alfred! Melon in October! Mr. Cadoresse will have to live as the English live," said Mrs. Hooper, "and of course we can't expect him to like our cooking."

"Oh, I'm sure it is excellent," I said, as I tasted the soup. It seemed excellent, for I had never before tasted clear soup devoid of grease; this particular soup was just oily water, but it was strange, and therefore good. "I want everything that is English."

"You shall have it," said Mr. Hooper. "I flatter myself we are a true British household, though of course we are not prejudiced people. Oh, no, we are quite cosmopolitan, Mr. Cadoresse. I remember once, when I was in France——"

I listened while Mr. Hooper gave me in detail the list of the dishes he had partaken of at the "Hôtel de France," at Neuchatel in 1896. Meanwhile the two girls were carrying on an animated conversation in low tones.

"Yes," said Lulu, "there she was, Mother, with the pink hat on she wore on Sunday."

"Orange, you mean," said Maud.

"When I say pink I mean pink," Lulu replied.

"And when you mean orange you say pink," said Maud, sprightly if a little acid.

"Pink," said Lulu. Her china-blue eyes were bovine in their obstinacy.

"S'pose you think I can't tell pink from orange," said Maud.

"And you wouldn't believe it, the whole thing only cost

two francs," said Mr. Hooper. " Now in Soho it's even cheaper, but I don't care for those places. I always feel the kitchens are not quite nice."

He spoke the last words between inverted commas; Mrs. Hooper laughed dutifully and I joined in, feeling it was the thing to do.

When the roast leg of mutton was brought in, on a dish that was too large and flooded with warm brown water, Mr. Hooper carved, remarking:

" Mutton thick, beef thin."

The girls were still wrangling.

" Fathead," Lulu muttered.

Maud looked at me with a faint smile that clearly said: " See how I suffer," and replied: " Think I'm colour-blind? "

I thought I should take the opportunity and said:

" The brilliance of your eyes, Mademoiselle, demonstrates that there is no justification for the accusation."

There was a pause, during which Lulu blushed at the compliment addressed to her sister, but Maud did not blush: she made a bread pill and gave me a little smile. Mrs. Hooper said:

" Now, Mr. Cadoresse, no French compliments. You will turn my young ladies' heads."

" My head's all right, Ma," said Maud.

" May be it is, and may be it isn't," said Mrs. Hooper, fondly gazing at the curly brown head, which I judged to be unruly. I was helped to baked potatoes, caked with grease, to nameless green food, which had apparently been moulded and then cut into slabs. The water jug was handed me without question, and I missed the usual wine.

" How did you leave your dear mother, Mr. Cadoresse? " asked Mrs. Hooper. " Mr. Lawton said she was very sorry to part with you."

" Oh, very," I said.

" She's not thinking of coming over to England? "

" No, I don't think so," I replied.

"Well, I'm not surprised. It seems so easy travelling, sitting in a railway carriage and doing nothing, but it does tire one so. Why, I remember when I went to Paris with your pa, girls, I was that tired I had to lie in bed for two days, and you'll never believe it, but your pa had gone along to the bathroom the first morning when I heard a knock at the door. I thought it was him and said, 'Come in,' and in came the waiter with my breakfast. I don't think that's usual, is it, Mr. Cadoresse?"

"Oh, quite," I replied. "He would come to the bath-room if you rang."

There was a short silence which showed me that I had gone too far, and the position was not eased by Maud, who suddenly burst into a fit of giggles, which recurred at frequent intervals.

"Stop it, Maud," said Mrs. Hooper; "silly."

"Can't, Ma," the girl gasped.

"Well, if you can't," said Mrs. Hooper resignedly, "we'd better change the subject. Yes, I was that tired, Mr. Cadoresse, I couldn't even go and see that church; you know—the church they call the little cakes after——"

"The Madeleine?" I said at random, for I do not know Paris well.

"Yes, Madeline. But I went to the shops."

"Ah!" said Lulu softly. "I'd love to go to Paris and see the shops."

"They are lovely shops, aren't they, Mr. Cadoresse?" said Maud, who was recovering. "Oh! I'd love to go to Paris."

"You must wait for your honeymoon," said Mr. Hooper, facetiously.

"Don't see why," said Mrs. Hooper. "They're no better than Whiteley's, I'll be bound."

While stewed apples and custard were being served, a friendly debate on the merits of French and English shops took place between the father and mother, but Maud and

I exchanged frequent friendly glances and covert smiles. Lulu had lapsed into sulky silence, and steadily ate.

II

It was a singular atmosphere, made up of the contest between ambient dulness and the sparkle of Maud. It is perhaps too much to say "dulness," for my first impression was one of sobriety, sedateness; the conversation was absolutely stupid, but then it was exactly the conversation that would have been held at a French bourgeois table where—and I have never so far convinced the English that I speak the truth—the arts and scandals are passed over. All the foreignness of it lay in the Hoopers' abstention from inquiries which would have struck me as normal enough: not only had they not mentioned my unsuitable clothes, but they had not asked what my father was, whether he was alive, how much he earned a year; they had not asked me whether my sister was marriageable and whether she had a *dot;* they had not even tried to find out what I thought of them and their city.

Those English people, did they care?

I realised that these were *petits bourgeois,* that Mr. Hooper could hardly be worth more than six or seven thousand francs a year, and yet their manners were excellent. As they ate, they dropped no food. Yet classes did not mix in England: therefore they must have copied. I considered Mrs. Hooper faded, dowdy, stupid, yet perfectly dignified; and Mr. Hooper limited and dull, yet bound by some code not to trouble his guest with questions. They were copying, those two; they must be copying, or I was drawing incorrect conclusions from my abundant English reading. In those days I had not discovered gentility and the tests by means of which the genteel man is distinguished from the gentleman. I felt almost humble in presence of these self-effacing people, and I rather resented their lack of interest in me.

But those English people, did they care?

Lulu I dismissed as a stupid girl of sixteen, and I was right. She was a very English type, and an ordinary one, for most English girls are stupid, and that is why they are so seductive. They are not hard, purposeful, as are our women; they do not know anything, and therefore they are grateful when anything is told them. They are the perfect slaves we love; they are seductive because they are innocent.

Lulu, however, was not seductive that night; she might have been in my eyes, for she was so unaccustomedly pink and white and flaxen-haired, but there was Maud. Lulu was born to be overshadowed by Maud, and, I suppose, knew it. While I analysed the Hoopers I looked at Maud; often our eyes met, and I fancy she did not try to escape my gaze; indeed, on finding that I looked at her small hands as she made bread pills, I am sure that she became yet more industrious at the game. Little hands, I have not forgotten you; you were broad in the middle, but you tapered to a point, and small white fingers too, you tapered, you blushed at the knuckles and joints, and you glowed into coral at the tips. Small, delicate hands, with the girlish roughness that made me think of *crêpe de chine*, you were warm and animate; folding upon my hands, you were tender as the wings of a fledgling bird.

III

We passed upstairs. More of England was revealed to me, for the entire first floor was made into a drawing-room; the folding doors had been removed and, as the gas brackets gave but little light, the room seemed very large. It was the glory of the house, it was as glorious as our own drawing-room, and it claimed brotherhood with it; nothing was missing except the smell of the graveyard, and I realised that whatever may differ from country to country some things are not national, but human. The drawing-room was white and gold, the paint was rather dirty and the gold tarnished, but still it was white and gold. There was a large settee, covered with tapestry; two armchairs and a number of small ones, either gilt or cheap mahogany, were dotted about. On a shelved black bracket stood an elaborate tea-set, which was never used for tea; there was, on the mantelpiece, an imitation Sèvres clock, out of order, between two tall blue jars filled with pampas grass. On the walls were framed photographs of pictures by Burne-Jones, also portraits of the Queen. In the " ell " stood the cottage piano, the back draped in a piece of Japanese printed cotton. I was chilled by the rigidity of it; while Mrs. Hooper sat down by the mantelpiece and began to embroider a tablecloth, the two girls nudged and whispered on the settee. I was very uncomfortable, for I had had no coffee; it was the first time in my life I had had no coffee after dinner. Perhaps because of that I moved restlessly about the room, went to a table in a corner on which were heaped albums and books. I opened some of them at random, looked at photographs of ugly old people whom I did not know; albums and books were dusty, as if seldom opened, but they interested me, and I noted titles, unknown authors. I found *Ships that Pass in the Night,* and *Under Two Flags,* some sixpenny editions of Merriman.

Mr. Hooper came in, said good-night. This, he regretted to say, was the Debating Club night. He was expected to move the vote of thanks after the debate. Quite an important paper: " Machiavelli."

I promised to come on another occasion. Mrs. Hooper embroidered steadily, I dared not smoke, I heard the girls whisper mysteriously:

" Of course, I wasn't taking any," Maud confided.

Mumble from Lulu.

" No fear! " vigorously from Maud.

" Maud, my dear," said Mrs. Hooper, " won't you show Mr. Cadoresse your picture postcards? "

Maud did not seem unwilling. She took from the small

cabinet under the shelved bracket a large cloth-bound album, laid it on the book-table after pushing away the dusty literature, and sat down. I came and stood beside her while she began with pretty demureness to make me look at every card.

"That's from Gib," she said, "and here's another from Malta. I put 'em all together cos they came from my cousin Tom. He's in the navy."

I detected some pride in her speech and became absurdly jealous of Tom.

"We always thought he'd go for a soldier," she added, "but he didn't. There's another he sent from Bombay with a nigger on it. Old Funny-hat I call him."

There was an interval during which "old Funny-hat" and "going for a soldier" were explained. My English was good, but it wasn't exactly English, and it did not include this kind of phrase. Indeed, my early intercourse with Maud was one long (and usually inadequate) English lesson.

"Here are some from France. Oh, I get a lot of those from pa's friends—Paris, Dieppe, Troovil——"

I was not listening to her. Leaning over as she turned the pages, I looked at the delicate white neck on which clustered the brown curls, at the small hand which pointed at the cards. She must have known, for she chattered on, giving me no opportunity to speak, and from time to time she looked up at me, with a faint smile on her lips and a soft but arch look in her humid brown eyes.

Because she was a stranger she was adorable. Then I thought of coffee.

"I get 'em from everywhere. You could have sent me one from Border if I'd known you before you came——"

"You silly kid," said Lulu, looking up from the pink evening paper; "you couldn't know him before he came, could you?"

"One has to mind one's P's and Q's with Miss Clever,

Mr. Cadoresse," said Maud to me. Angry, she was adorable, for she flushed.

"Don't bother Mr. Cadoresse, dear," said Mrs. Hooper, who still embroidered; "perhaps he's seen enough."

"Oh," I protested, "it's very interesting. Show me some of Spain, Miss Hooper. I've been there."

Maud looked up at me; there were in her eyes appeal, triumph and gratitude. "Here's one of Saint Sebasting," she said. And as she pointed with the right hand she laid her left hand on the table, as if by inadvertence, so near mine that I could feel the warmth of it. The minutest distance separated them. Yet it was a distance, and when hands do not touch it matters very little whether there is between them a yard or the tenth of an inch. I leaned over her to look at the card.

"Bullfights," I said with an effort. And, as I moved, our hands touched. They touched very softly, but definitely. The whole side of her hand was against mine, and this was very wonderful. We did not move. For some seconds we were silent while each could feel the beating of the other's blood.

"I shouldn't care to see a bullfight," said Maud smoothly. "Horrid, messy things. And it's so cruel to the horses. We wouldn't have 'em in England. Our Dumb Friends, S.P.C.A., all that sort of thing, you know."

She chattered on while I stood by her side, quite unable to speak, my throat dry and my cruel desire for coffee quite forgotten. She chattered as if she were perfectly cool, while my hand felt numb and rigid. And still she did not take away her own.

These English girls, do they know when men touch their hands?

Suddenly she shook her brown curls, moved her hand; the spell was broken. She laughed, and I gave a heavy sigh.

"You're not saying anything. Penny?"

"Penny?"

Explanations. Then Mrs. Hooper suggested that Maud should sing. She went to the piano. She played a rollicking, rhythmic tune, a tune of the " Waiting at the Church " type; not one word did I understand, but I knew that I wanted to beat time while I watched the white throat swell and the brown curls dance staccato.

" Very pretty," said Mrs. Hooper, after Maud had sung in an unexpected fit of sentimentalism, " Good Bye "; " very pretty. Lulu, you might run upstairs and find me my other reel of red cotton."

Maud began to improvise a melody of her own—a gay, splashy thing, very much like the first tune she had played.

" How long that girl is," Mrs. Hooper murmured.

Maud broke down in her impromptu, began again in another key. Mrs. Hooper went to the door.

" Can't you find it, Lulu? " she called up the staircase. Then, after a pause: " It's in the top drawer—oh, never mind, I know where it is——"

Mrs. Hooper had gone. I was alone with Maud, alone with a young girl. It was impossible. How could one be alone with a young girl—but then I remembered English liberty. Of course. Maud looked at me round the corner of the piano. In the bad light I could see her smile.

" Baby can't see. Baby blind," she said in another voice and a different language. " Baby go quite blind if Frenchman don't light other candle."

I leaped rather than walked to the piano, but my hand shook so that the match missed the wick.

" Shaky hand. Late nights, naughty, naughty," said Maud.

I looked down at her, and she smiled at me. I bent towards her, and still she smiled without moving. My hand went out, groped on the keys of the piano, found her fingers, and grasped them.

" Ouch," she murmured; " you're hurting."

But her smile had not vanished, and a very faint, pleasant scent came from her hair. Without a word I slipped my arm round her shoulders and kissed her, trembling a little, clumsily, half on the lips and half on the cheek.

She remained passive for a second, then drew back.

" Now then, saucy," she said, but she was still smiling.

When Mrs. Hooper returned with Lulu and the red cotton, the two candles were lit and Maud was banging at a noisy tune.

IV

I found sleep difficult. I had stood a long time at the window, looking into the desolate little garden. The fog had gone, and under the rays of the moon I could see against the wall the dim shadow of a faded rose, while two bushes of Michaelmas daisies reared up, straggling and gaunt, in the stone-spattered flower bed. Many things occupied me; I had not forgotten that I had had no coffee, and now that my excitement was past the desire seized me again. Indeed, I am not sure that my memory of the epic kiss was not tainted with the gnawing need. When I think of coffee I feel like an opium-eater. If ever I am sent to gaol I shall go mad.

I did not at once think of the kiss, for I am a sybarite; I like to recreate my impressions one by one and as they formed, and I like to give them climaxes followed by flat periods; I like them to pass through my mind like a well-ordered play. And I want my climaxes to be larger and larger and more significant, so that I may ring down the curtain upon my dream-play, while I bow with actor and author and clap my hands in the royal box. So I resolutely thought about the old Hoopers. I had not, I felt, analysed them very well, and how could I? I had none of the English measures with which to appraise them, I could estimate them only according to French values. But the prestige of England clung to them; I was enormously impressed by their calm, by their disregard of my views and their regard for my comfort. I was paying twenty-seven and six for board and lodging, and it seemed as if I were paying my money for hospitality.

Mr. Hooper was more evident than his wife; I was surprised by the generality of his interests, by his spareness and his youth. In a rigid, unimaginative way he was still studying politics, he took trouble to know something of my people, he was seeking. True, when he captured an idea he slew it and embalmed it. Butterfly hunter! But still, he was inquiring, he wanted to know, and there was romance even in the despair of his dry quest. His wife troubled me more; I saw her as gentle, refined, courteous; I gathered that she had no power of action, but much power of resistance. Nothing would break Mrs. Hooper: if an earthquake had precipitated Westminster Abbey into the Thames I felt she would have remarked: "What extraordinary weather we're having—I wonder where I put that bodkin." Obviously she could control Lulu, who had left no impression on me at all, except that she was sulky, but could make nothing of Maud; I could see that she loved Maud, thought her an infant prodigy, that Maud's singing was more than an elegant accomplishment, that it was a family rite. While I watched Maud's full white throat swell, I had also noticed Mrs. Hooper's head nod in time, and seen her smile at me when the songs ended. "There! what do you say to that?" was in every smile.

But evidently Mrs. Hooper did not greatly care whether she controlled Maud or not. The girl could do no wrong, and—perhaps this English aloofness extended to the family circle. Perhaps they let each other alone, just as they let the stranger alone. The whole evening seemed to be a lesson in non-intervention. Mr. Hooper had gone without explaining in great detail where he was going to, when he would be back; Lulu had read a novelette without being asked what it was and whether it was interesting; and when Maud could not cease giggling because I had made an undesirable joke, Mrs. Hooper had said, "If you can't stop, we'd better change the subject." It was so amazing that I hesitated to conclude that the English do not care what happens.

One thing, though, I felt assured of: Mrs. Hooper would certainly care if anything happened to Maud. This liberty of theirs must be limited by some custom or rule, and I felt sure that she would not condone the intrigue into which I was entering. Of course, this was an intrigue. . . .

"You haven't done badly," I remarked to the elegant figure in the looking-glass; "you've started a love affair, you've only got to go on."

I felt certain that I had nothing to do but go on. Of course, Maud was deceitful and hot-blooded; I shouldn't have much trouble with a girl like that, for she was ready to fall into any man's arms, and if she wasn't—I laughed contentedly: I knew all about women and their ways. One feeling I did not have, and that was one of hesitation in presence of adventure; Frenchmen are not made like that.

CHAPTER IV

MISS MAUD HOOPER

I

IF there were in London no Oxford Street it would have to be invented, for without it straying groups of foreigners would prove a perpetual nuisance to Streatham and Hornsey. I was introduced to Oxford Street by the inside of a hat, which advertised the fact that it had been bought there; in later years the street became definite, thanks to a chromo taken from a Christmas number. That grateful chromo showed "Oxford Circus on Christmas Eve," a wonderful vision of carriages, splendid horses driven by liveried coachmen, enormous policemen, and gay young women with rosy cheeks, mostly dressed in furs, followed by dandies who did not disdain to carry parcels. There was a fox-terrier, too, for fox-terriers were fashionable in those days, and "bits of blood" in the shafts of hansoms; burly Pickwickian coachmen obviously made jokes (of course, bus-drivers did). There radiated from this early product of the three-colour process a jollity, an irresponsible love of food, drink, light. Indeed, I was a little disappointed because London did not turn out to be as like a Christmas card as I expected: but I was not very disappointed, for it had another magic.

It had the magic of Oxford Street. It was not that Oxford Street was so very broad, for it would be lost in the Champs-Élysées, or so very beautiful: it was for me more than a fine street—it was an English person. The Americans had not yet got hold of it, smirched it with façades of new brick and stucco, or Portland stone; its houses were not very high, and they were houses, not warehouses. I liked the shops and their poor show of plate-glass, the crude display of their wares; it was interesting to compare our idea of showing off boots, which is to put three patent-leather pairs in a nest of green velvet, with the hundreds of boots, the festoons of boots, the bewildering array of shoes for the road and shoes for the bed, of slippers and top-boots, of dandified pumps, and rough, spiked hoofcases for the golfer and the football-player; I could stand and gloat over this kind of show; it was enormous, Falstaffian; it suggested large appetites, needs and the fulfilment of needs. Oxford Street was more English than Bond Street because it was not modish; it did not receive the clothes of the French and Viennese, the enamel of the Russians, the promiscuous patents of America; beyond a little Italian glass and some Indian goods, the latter pardonable, after all, because colonial, its wares were English. They were rather dear, neither beautiful nor ugly; they were abundant, and most of them would last for ever. For ever! that feeling still clings to Oxford Street, to those undefiled portions which threaten to crash down into the road, and it is incredible that they will ever so crash. They have always been there, those shops which intrude into the houses, and I guess their intimacies, their corridors, the clumsy steps which join house with house until an emporium arises. Above the drapers are the ghosts of dead kitchens, of the parlours and the best bedrooms; and there are doorsteps on which once stood grave merchants, reading the *Morning Post,* to know what they should think of Mr. Pitt.

I still have, as I walk that street, the sense of the illimitable which is bound up in the streets that run from east to west. On one side I can feel the rich places, their parks, Stoke Poges and its churchyard, Wiltshire, rolling plains, Bristol and the open sea; on the other I wind away with Oxford Street, through business and slum, to the docks, the Thames that is like the tongue of the sea, and then again the sea, with, upon its breast, the big ships filled to the bulwarks with East Indian spices, and furs, and bales of wool. Over all and, as it flaps, making in the wind sharp sounds like the slam of a loose door, is the Union Jack.

Eternal England, that no revolutions ruffle, who return to régimes discarded because you never discard that spirit of order and power which lies under the régimes, you are like Oxford Street. You are indirect, you do not drive through international life as did the bolder Rome; while Rome built those roads which despise rivers and mountain, you built Oxford Street and its vassals from the Bank to Shepherd's Bush, tortuous, broken by angles, here wide and there narrow, inconvenient but persistent; you give way to the obstacle—then surround it; you fight no battles with the soil, and yet you conquer it, indomitably driving your road, quite careless of beauty and content if the road can serve, unwilling to take a path other than that of least resistance. You erect no monument, you are too busy being a monument. Conscious of ancestors, you do not strive to have ancestors, and because you are too big to be conscious you are ancestral.

II

Almost every day I walked along Oxford Street, from my home with the Hoopers in St. Mary's Terrace, along the Edgware Road, until I reached Fenchurch Street, the bewildering City which housed Barbezan & Co. So much did it bewilder me that I confided my impressions to the not very sympathetic Maud. But she was not entirely unsympathetic: indeed, she was, for an English girl, strangely curious of my affairs; I would not have talked of them with her if she had readily responded to more amorous moods, but I was ready enough to share with her the impressions I accumulated so rapidly that they hurt: not to talk is always dreadful for a southerner, and I think I would rather talk about anything than not talk at all.

For Maud was proving a puzzle to me. When I went to my room and acted the dream-play, which ended in the adventurous kiss, I thought I saw quite clearly the sequelæ of the deed. I thought of other kisses, less rapid, more reciprocal; I imagined responses, had no difficulty in conjuring up a softer and yet mysteriously aggressive Maud, who would tell me that she loved me, that I had but to ask to be given.

I had no doubts at all: a girl who so openly attacked me the first evening could not be difficult to win. I was not in love with her; if she occupied my mind at all, she was merely one of my comforts. She was the woman sent by the kindly Providence of Lovers to fill, for the time being, a certain part of my life. She was charming, provoking and—convenient. It was thus with a degree of confidence that I threw one arm round her shoulders when, the next evening, I met her on the first floor landing, outside the bathroom where she had washed her hands. Just before I did it she was smiling; she looked deliciously demure, for her eyes were half-closed, and her attitude, as she rubbed against each other her still moist palms, was almost quakerish. But as I touched her, her expression changed. She put out both hands against my shoulders, pushed me away:

"Now, then, Mr. Frenchman, none of your monkey tricks."

I laughed, tried to break her resistance. Coquetry, of course. But there was something else in the coquetry— obstinacy, I supposed, for we fought silently on the landing for some moments. I was the stronger, drew her to me, but she bent her head down, pushed the curls into my face. I kissed the warm brown hair, and, as I did so, she half freed herself, and I saw this was not coquetry, for she was flushed and the pretty mouth had set in a straight line.

"Let me go," she whispered; "leave go, can't you. I won't have it. D'you think I want you messing me about? No fear!"

She wrenched herself free, and I looked at her in amazement.

" Crumpling my blouse," she grumbled, as she patted it. " What d'you take me for? Rag-doll? or what? "

" But, Maud——" I faltered.

" Not so much of your Mauds, Mr. Frenchman. Have a shave and try Miss Hooper."

I was puzzled by the seemingly irrelevant advice to " have a shave," and, while I thought, took her hand. She did not withdraw it, looked at me with a faint smile.

" Sorry you spoke, aren't you? Well, you needn't look sulky about it."

" I am not sulky," I said.

" Yes, you are. Cross old bear. Baby quite frightened."

I understood that I was forgiven, but I knew better than to accept forgiveness: the only way to gain absolute forgiveness from a woman is at once to offend again. So, without another word, I pulled Maud towards me; there was a slight show of resistance, soon vanquished. But, before I could kiss her, her lips rested a second on my cheek, firm and cool, and she escaped:

" No more, Mr. Frenchman," she said, with some dignity; " I'm not out for choc'lates, just had grapes."

She ran down the stairs, laughing, and I went to my room. I had something to think about: Why had she repulsed me? Then kissed me? then repulsed me again? Coquetry I had met before, but not this kind of coquetry; I knew the methods practised by my own countrywomen, by which man is encouraged, discouraged, then heartened, and the French rack is no kinder than the English: but in those cases there had been no prefacing caress. With the first kiss came the downfall of the defence, the acquiescent rout and capture of the defender. It was not so here: apparently an English girl, or at least English Maud, could with impunity hold the hand of the man who attracted her, even clasp him in her arms; she could rely on her own powers of resistance.

Strictly speaking, I did not " learn about women from 'er "; I learned about her from other and later women. I understood her much better after parting from her and was surprised to find her different from her old self when I met her again. Maud was a very ordinary English type, a type to be found in none save Anglo-Saxon countries; she was unawakened in the passionate sense, and I do not think that the kiss of Prince Charming himself could have roused her from her sleep. She could attain a passionate stage, to maintain the metaphor, akin to somnambulism, but she was never awake. She was made up of two strands, one positive and the other negative. The first was the strand of interest, money, adornment, cheap excitement, eager vanity, and there are many splendid mates, English, Latin and Slav, who have such a strand in their composition: la Dame aux Camélias was so made, and Cleopatra somewhat. But it was Maud's negative strain made her different from any Latin, Teutonic or Slav woman I have ever met. Her capacity for resisting caresses, for showing that she did not want them, her ability to live without love, without emotion, her self-contained and neutral attitude, I have met these traits again and again and believe in their reality only because of their recurrence.

Paradoxically enough, Maud, or I will say the Maud-type, is aggressive. It prepares for seduction by clothing itself as little as it may, by using the powder, the rouge, and the scent of the man-huntress; it ogles, it rustles, it drops its voice to tender murmurs, it invites, it clamours for capture—no, not capture, pursuit. For the array for seduction is not the prelude of desired defeat: the intention is to restrict to a sham fight the reality of the engagement. The Maud-type is the exact counterpart of the fowler, the man whom victory bores when it is in sight—victory, that is, in the accepted sense. The victory of the Maud-type consists in instigating attack, defeating it and instigating it again; if the victim shows signs of flagging he must be cajoled, and minor privileges may be granted. If it be clear that he is almost disgusted, that he will not attack the main position, an outpost is suddenly evacuated; he occupies it, surprised, advances and is at once repulsed, as if he had been ambushed. But the Maud-type never intends him to win: the struggle is real, and if the victim suddenly perceives that he is being tricked and retires in anger he is immediately forgotten when other quarry presents itself. My intercourse with Maud was made up of these continual strategic advances and retreats. So determined was she to hold me, for purposes she hardly defined to herself, that I was often surprised by the extent of the concessions she would make to achieve her object. She had moods in which minor surrenders and acquiescences were so many that my triumph seemed assured—but were they moods or policies? I do not pretend that such girls are entirely devoid of emotional feelings, but these are buried very deep; there is gold in some abysses of the sea, and it is therefore untrue to say that there is no gold there: but nobody has ever been able to dive deep enough to secure it. There were days when Maud would of herself take my arm in a quiet street, others when she spontaneously offered caresses; she seemed to yield, but she never yielded. I do not think she wanted to, and I am not sure that she could. She had a fierce dislike of love in its robe of red and flame; she understood it solely in the flirtatious pink and tinsel of musical comedy. She was afraid of it, because she felt it to be brutal, big, and earnest. She did not want anything to be earnest, she wanted things gay, comic. But she would make concessions to me so that I might continue to flatter her by pursuing her, so that I should pay. The Maud-type knows one thing very well—that man must pay, and pay for nothing save exasperation. It does not consider, as does its analogue in America, that man is bound by chivalry and disinterested courtesy to supply candies, novels, ice-cream and seats at the theatre; but it does consider that man must supply the English equivalents of those things on a limited pleasure contract. It wants them so desperately that it sometimes gives more than it intended, and in later life it often takes for granted that it must give everything for greater delights, such as the use of a motor-car, fine clothes, and Brighton holidays, but throughout it does not want to give. It wants to take. If it can take everything for nothing, good; if everything for something, unfortunate; if it must take something for everything, it does so resignedly. Between Maud and me there was an ever open contract which we never signed; she never taught me to bargain, for I am of those who give heartily and take greedily, asking no questions: she was all implicit bargain.

III

In the name of English liberty Maud was sent with me on the eve of my entry into Barbezan & Co., so that I might find in romantic Oxford Street the shops I needed.

" Funny sort of shirt you've got on," said Maud; " stew 'em in tea in Border, don't they? "

I assured her we did not stew shirts in tea.

" Well, I only asked. And, of course, you've got to get your cuffs sewn on. No, you can't get a ready-made tie here. Can't tie it? Don't be silly, I'll show you, Frenchy; anybody can see you aren't sailors over there."

" My father was a sea-captain," I said, rather curtly, for this annoyed me.

" Well, he might have taught you to make knots. My cousin Tom—he's in the navy, you know—he taught me. Of course, your hat's too small."

" Perhaps that is because my hair is too thick," I suggested, with an attempt at sarcasm.

" Yes, 'tis, get a haircut," said Maud, who did not perceive the irony; " but even then it's sizes too small. Boots, too; you don't want a point to them, if you aren't going to pick your teeth with them, and you're just bursting out of your gloves."

"So are you," I said, for the criticism was galling.

"Now you're being nasty. Well, do what you like. I don't mind if you look like a picture postcard. You're one of the toffs, one of the kid-gloved Dandy Fifth, I don't think."

She turned her back on me, began to gaze intently into a window full of bead necklaces. I was still angry, but her irritation killed mine, and I could see under the cluster of her brown curls a gleam of white neck which moved me to repentance. I took her by the elbow and made her turn towards me. She smiled a little.

"Now you're sorry, aren't you? Leave go of my arm and say so."

I apologised, and being humbled was forgiven. But I was also subjugated, the outfit was taken out of my hands.

"He wants a couple of blue ties," she explained to the shopman.

"Excuse me," I said, "as I am dark——"

"That's all right. You put him up those two in poplin. . . . Oh, no, don't trouble, he's a Frenchman, *he* doesn't know. And now you just run along to the linen department, tea-caddy."

Tea-caddy! I, Cadoresse, for her "caddy" and then "tea-caddy."

"You know what I told you: just as tight round the neck as you can stick it, and cuffs sewn on, and five and six's the price, with a bob off for six. You can get half-a-dozen coloured ones while you're about it, and mind you don't get mauve, 'cos it washes out third time."

"I don't like coloured shirts," I said.

"Well, you've got to like 'em. I'm not going about with a blooming mute."

This was Maud in her element, enjoying the new and amusing sensation of dressing a young man. The occu-

pation did not show her up at her worst, for she had
somehow learned how a man should dress; at least she
had the instinct which, left to itself, makes for flashiness,
but, when educated, ends in correctness. She had, for
men, the sharp ideas of fashion which she derived from
the rapt contemplation of popular actors; they influenced
her enormously. She could not have said whether trousers
should be pegtop, whether collars should be double or
wing, but she responded to influence so well that she
spontaneously rejected the thing that was not the thing
of the day: when it became the thing of the day she as
spontaneously suggested that I should adopt it. The triumph of clothes was attained when she could say of a
passing man: " This is It."

I was difficult to fit at the hatter's.

" No wonder. I often think, you're barmy on the
crumpet," Maud commented, who had then known me for
a week. " S'pose they were clearing a job line the day you
got your head. Still, you aren't worse than pa, with
the bald bit at the back under the brim."

I found her good company, this cheerful, energetic girl;
she was less managing than adventurous; amused by the
" spree," she threw all her energy into an occupation which
she would have voted a nuisance if it had been habitual.
She was so pleased because she was doing something new
that she did not reprove me when I squeezed her hand
behind the liftman's back. She even pouted at me the
imitation of a kiss. While charming, she remained com-
petent, or rather voracious; she was bent on extracting
rebates for quantities; she asked for shop-soiled goods, as
if she were a thrifty French housewife. But thrift
was not the motive; she displayed the street-arab acute-
ness of those who systematically make a show on small
means.

At last I was equipped. I had been in four shops, and
an undoubtedly English wardrobe was travelling towards
my room. I suggested lunch.

" What'll ma say? " said Maud, doubtfully. Then: " who cares? We'll say we waited while they wondered what it was 'd blown in. An' if she doesn't like it she can lump it."

" Lump it? "

" Do the other thing."

I accepted the unintelligible explanation, and we looked for a place to lunch at. It was past one o'clock. The pale, silvery light of November made the grey pavement faintly opalescent where patches of nocturnal moisture lingered; the sun was not shining, but I could feel that it was shining behind the colourless haze, and though I wondered for a moment whether, in Bordeaux, it was streaming on the red and purple leaves of the beeches, I did not feel homesick. For was this not pulsating, vigorous England; jolly, warm England? A green Atlas came towards us, its team gaily trotting; the omnibus rolled as it went, like a big, fat forester, or some enormous bloated scarab. Busy, sturdy England, and pretty, white-necked English girl, I . . .

" Penny," said Maud as usual.

" I was thinking of *restaurants*," I lied, having learned her language.

" Oh, we don't want a ristorang; too nobby; you come along."

Maud led me to one of those shops where people have tea at one o'clock and fried eggs at four. Four or five companies maintain many hundreds of them, and I remember that it struck me as splendid that there should be hundreds of these shops; it was a large idea, it conveyed a notion of national appetite; and the uniformity of the arrangement, the levelling of Bond Street and Chiswick, held a suggestion of democracy. The more uniform things are, the more they are part of a civilisation.

" You better have a Kate and Sidney," said Maud; " it's English, quite English, you know. Hi! Miss."

The black-clad, slim Miss responded sulkily to the shrill

cry, smiled when I looked at her. English girls still smile when I look at them, even when I hardly notice them; my eye has habits.

"You needn't keep a glowing orb on her," said Maud, as the girl left, charged to bring us a "steak and kidney pudding, with boiled, and half a veal an' ham pie, and two coffees." "I didn't bring you here to make goo-goo eyes . . . codfish."

"Oh! but she was so pretty, Maud," I said, innocently. "All the English girls are pretty. She had hair like the sunshine—not like yours, of course; that is like the nuts in September."

"Been kissing the Blarney Stone, Frenchy. But you don't come it over me like that, even if I haven't got hair like the moonshine or whatever you call it. Pretty! It's a lot you know about it; why, she's just a job lot of broom-sticks. And you should give up that habit, looking at girls with that 'take me away and bury me near mother' look of yours."

"Look at that one with the green eyes and red hair," I said, mischievously.

"Carrots!"

"And those two, the dark ones. They can't be English——"

"S'pose I'm not English," Maud snapped. She was angry, provoked by my open admiration for the others. She leaned her elbows on the table, propped her face upon her hands; two dimples appeared in the rosy cheeks. I bent across the table.

"You're the Rose of England," I said; "not the Rose of England I thought I would find, you know, the White Rose. You're the beautiful, warm red rose, and your eyes are like brown crystals, your hair is like mahogany, and it shines like it, and your mouth is like red velvet round two rows of pearls."

"My!" said Maud, smiling; "you can tell the tale, Caddy. Where did you learn English?"

" I've always been learning English, I knew we should meet."

" Tell me another."

" I really did."

" Don't say ' I really did,' you dummy, say ' honest.' I tell you what, Caddy, you talk too well, you give yourself away."

It was true; it was the grammatical excellence of my speech exposed my foreignness: it has cost me years of patient labour to learn to speak as badly as the English.

I began to eat my first steak and kidney pudding: I do not think I have ever tasted anything so delicious as that first pudding; I remember the tender consistency of the suet, the solid quality of the gravy, and the thrill when the palate that expected steak suddenly discovered kidney. And I suppose that, after the oil of my fathers, I liked the sensation of potatoes flavoured with nothing but warm water. While Maud daintily pecked at the veal and ham pie, nibbling like a bird, she talked incessantly, just then of her people.

" Oh, pa," she said in response to a question; " the dad's all right. He's a dignified old cock, but you mustn't mind him, even if he will go on about his talky-talkies. You just tell him a little bit out of *Answers* once a week and he'll be happy like the larks in May."

" What does he do? "

" He's in the City, like you; the same sort of job; that's how he got hold of you from a fellow in Barbezan. We've been wanting a lodger. Oh, but don't let mother catch you saying that: you're a paying guest, you know; ma's so genteel——"

Maud began to laugh, and I laughed too when she explained the distinction. I liked this brusque, laughing girl, for I saw she had no snobbery; at least she never showed signs of it except when she met the " skivvy " in the hall on best hat days. Then Maud was " quite the lady."

" They're all right," she summed up, " but they're a
bit full of themselves. Lor', you wouldn't believe the
row there was when I said I'd go to the 'Cademy last
spring. It wasn't genteel. I'm going to be an actress,
you know."

" Is there a conservatory here? " I asked, translating
at random.

" I don't know what you mean by a conservatory. I
go to Madame Tinman's—Mother Tinman they call her
in the profesh! *You've* heard of her. What! not heard
of Mother Tinman? What did they teach you in Border?
Anyhow, I go there four times a week. Singing and
dancing's my line; singing's what I like:

> " Oh, mother dear, sing me to sleep
> And beg the angels my soul keep . . ."

she hummed. " What d'you say to stewed fruit next? "

While we ate the stewed fruit she expatiated on her
work at Mother Tinman's, and I wondered at her small
appetite, for she had left half her pie; few French girls
would have done that. She seemed enthusiastic, and I
dimly realised that to this peculiar education of hers was
due the difference which existed between her and her
parents, and stodgy Lulu. Taken at sixteen from the rigid
gentility of Mrs. Hooper's home, from the limitations of
a budget of some two hundred and fifty a year, she had
been plunged into the artificial atmosphere of the outer
stage. At Mother Tinman's, I found out by degrees,
singing lessons were given by professionals who were
resting, and while voice production of a kind was taught
to the voiceless as well as to the gifted, the pupils were
well fitted to earn money.

" You should hear old Bella Billion," said Maud:
" ' Never you mind if you can't go up to D,' she says,
' you just keep your eye on the man in the stage box.
One wink for him and a nice goo-goo for the gallery boy.
Twirl your sunshade, twirl away, tooraloo, and never

you mind the words so long as you've the limelight on your pearlies; the chorus's the thing, my gal; you sing it to the gallery boy until he shouts it back at you. And let him know you've got a knee and frillies that weren't washed in printer's ink. Up and down, me dear, an' round an' round, goo-goo, tooraloo, that's how you do the trick, my gal.' Lor', it's enough to give you a fit on the mat."

I don't think that for many months I understood Maud and the jolly looseness of her talk, but there is no forgetting that extraordinary language of hers; its vocabulary is not very large. Bella Billion and her like, the talk of cars and of trips to Maidenhead, of salaries of a hundred a week and the indiscretions of peers, all this had created in Maud's pretty head an amazing confusion. Gentility, propriety, all the English starch had already been taken out of her by coarse English irresponsibility. But, and this was amazing, personal aloofness remained. I laid my hand upon hers, pressed the pointed fingers.

"Give over," she said as she snatched her hand away.

Why did we go so freely? I wondered. Matchmaking? no doubt, since marriage leads to love, they say, more surely than love to marriage. And English liberty too. English liberty, how difficult it was to understand you were not licence.

CHAPTER V

BARBEZAN & CO.

I

THE old firm received me well enough. The office was large and rich; it occupied a whole floor in a new Fenchurch Street skyscraper, and conveyed an impression of well-oiled machinery. Letters were numbered and sorted by the office boy into baskets, one of which was known as *the* basket because it stood on Mr. Lawton's desk; after Mr. Lawton had dealt with them they were distributed by Mr. Hugh, mechanically acknowledged in polite, stiff letters which began by " Sir " and ended in " yours obediently." I never heard of one unacknowledged letter. They passed into obscurer baskets, were collected by a junior clerk, who checked their numbers, traced any that Mr. Lawton had held up in defiance of his own rules. At last they went to the card-index, an innovation which rather clashed with our formality, to the files. We never lost a letter, forgot one entry. We were never short of brown paper and string.

The extraordinary part of it was that this caused no fuss. How things got done in that noiseless, swift way, between ten and five, I can explain only by saying that we never talked about work. We talked of other things, and accordingly these grew confused, but work was done in silence and seemed to demand no conferences. I believe silence is England's secret, and I bore many a snub before I acquired the habit. I had not been in Barbezan a week before I began to learn that I, the foreign correspondent, must do my own jobs.

" What is the address? " I asked Mr. Hugh Lawton,

who had handed me a slip bearing, with the notes for a letter, the name ' Marillot.' " And the whole name? "

" You must look it up."

" Yes—but do those ships dock at Pauillac? "

" I cannot tell you."

I was minded to ask whether the tons referred to were " short " or " long," but refrained, for Mr. Hugh had already turned away and, in his cold, precise voice, was telling Purkis he would need supplementary bills of lading for the *Florabel* shipment. I realised, as I watched the smooth back of his head, that I had been thrown into the water, that nobody wanted to know whether I could swim, that I would have to find all this out. I might drown— but then, if I struggled I would not drown; such is the English way of teaching people to swim.

Magic English business, when I think of you to-day, I have my boyish impression of England as wealth; your wheels revolve silent and steady, grinding out gold, without waste of material or time; you pass from father to son, you endure for ever, and you are a concern so sacred that you must be shielded from the prying eyes of woman. There are three kinds of Englishmen who entrust no secrets to their wives: Cabinet Ministers, Freemasons and business men, and as the latter are more numerous than the other two classes they set the tone for their race. The English business man is most interesting when confronted with a new appliance or a new idea; he sniffs it like a dog who is offered a piece, let us say, of wild boar, or some other outlandish food; he feels it is good, but novel; it must be looked at, smelled, pawed, tossed in the air to see whether it falls properly dead and harmless. At last it may be nibbled, then greedily eaten. Then the two, dog and Englishman, sit up, and declare each in his own way that he has hungered for this for years, that he has made special efforts to procure it and that he is not in the least afraid of novelty.

That was how Purkis received the calculator. Purkis,

when I first knew him, was elderly: I met him in Moorgate
Street last week and he is as elderly as ever, but not a day
older though ten years have elapsed. On the calculator
occasion he appeared to me as a short man, with a square
face and sparse brown hair in which ran some silver streaks.
Small and very delicate hands contrasted with his bulky
body, especially in his familiar attitude, when he leaned
his shoulders against the mantelpiece and crossed his hands
upon his rather aggressive paunch. Purkis looked so
broad, then, that I had to think of a frog.

That was the attitude he adopted when a new idea
arrived in Fenchurch Street. Purkis would examine it
with suspicious grey eyes, clench his little hands upon his
large stomach and say:

"What are we coming to next?" or "I don't know
anything about it."

The first formula meant that Purkis was willing to
tolerate the intruder; the second that he didn't want to
know anything about it. Remove the bauble. Purkis had
said "I don't know anything about it" to the German
canvasser who now stood in front of him, amiably blinking
behind his gold-rimmed glasses and quite unaware that
Purkis had pronounced sentence, that all he had to do was
to take the calculator out and hang it.

"Ver' goot thing," he remarked, genially. "It will do
all calculations."

The German turned from the impassive Purkis to me,
in whom he divined interest: "You say figures. I
multiply."

I made up a terrific sum, a multiplication of five or six
figures by five or six more, behind which trailed treacherous
decimals, the sort of multiplication I hope never to have to
effect. The German threw me a gratified glance: "Ver'
simple, ver' simple," he muttered, as he deftly seized lever
after lever, pulled each one down to the indicator figure
while my fantastic multiplicand appeared in the upper
frame. He smiled at the machine from under his yellow

moustache, seized the lever; half a dozen rasping sounds, click, more rasps, another click, rasp, rasp, rasp. The German drew back, pointed triumphantly at the machine; he evidently looked upon the product as a work of art.

" So! " he said, triumphantly.

" How do you know it's right? " asked the calm voice of Mr. Hugh, who had come in.

The German drew himself up, as if tempted to hand the questioner a card and a cartel, then decided to clear the machine's reputation.

" I prove it now," he said. He looked at Purkis defiantly, solemnly handed me a slip on which he had written the multiplicand. A quick shift of the levers, the product became a dividend, the multiplier a divisor; the lever was rotated towards the operator and, preceded by a tornado of clicks, the quotient suddenly showed the figures of the written multiplicand. It was exactly like a conjuring trick.

" Ver' simple," he declared, as a cherubic smile illumined his rosy face.

" That's rather ingenious," said Mr. Hugh, and began to finger the levers. " It might be handy for those long statements of gross weights. What do you think, Purkis? "

" I don't know anything about it, Sir."

" Oh, I egsplain—" the German protested.

" No, I understand. How much does it cost? "

" Twenty-six pounds——"

" All right. Send in the bill."

While the German wreaked his vengeance on Purkis by explaining to him everything that might be done with a calculator, I was able to meditate on the swollen rashness of these business methods. Twenty-six pounds! The English must be very rich, but—I found this out later, they do not like small expenses; if the German had wanted twenty-six shillings he would have had no order; there would have been nothing impressive in his new idea.

" I don't know anything about it," said Purkis ungrate-
fully, as the German left the office. He did not; I am
sure that he does not yet know anything about it, and he
never will; he will do the gross weights statements himself
with a pencil, but he will not touch the calculator; no
junior has ever used it in his presence without being told
to take the damned thing into the waiting-room. The
calculator may grow old and decayed; it may even get out
of order and thus become thoroughly respectable, but
Purkis will never recognise it: in his own phrase, " that
would never do."

Certainly Hugh Lawton was of a different type. He
had recently come down from Oxford (in those days I
said " up ") with a pass degree and, though he has never
told me so, I now know from a chance reference to " notions " that he had been through Winchester. Hugh Lawton was then twenty-three or four, and so very much of
a young Roman that some uninformed girls called him
" The Greek God." Six feet tall, broad-shouldered, slim-
hipped, with a high, white forehead, calm, blue eyes, a
nose on the bridge of which there was but little thickness
of skin, he attracted attention even in this England, whose
sons are the sons of Apollo; he had a long, thin-lipped
mouth, a resolute chin; his large white hands were always
in good condition, though never manicured. Upon his
loose limbs clothes hung so easily that I was reminded
again of a Roman statue whose toga and limbs are hewn
of one piece. Indeed, it was pathetic to see him stand
next to Purkis: there was such sharp contrast between
their trouser knees.

I do not want to dwell upon Hugh Lawton's clothes,
though they were a bitterness to me in those early days;
he had his father's recipe for white collars, and his ties,
always faint in shade, must have been specially made for
him, as I never managed to match them. But his clothes
were significant because they expressed him, very much,
I suppose, as mine revealed my own individuality. It is

not enough to say that Hugh never appeared with a red
tie or a purple shirt: it was impossible for him to do so;
it could not have occurred to him to buy such things. The
things he did buy were so neutral that they were, in a
sense, a negation rather than an assertion of attire; like
most Englishmen of his class he was dressed, while I was
got up. He could do nothing so positive as get himself up.
I have never yet seen signs of his doing anything positive.

The strength of Hugh Lawton lay in his abstentions.
He did not speak much, he did not gossip, he did not
plead or urge; twice only in his intercourse with me did
he lay down views, and they turned out to be those of
his class. But if he did not obtrude himself he did not
draw back; he stood, as his nation has stood in every part
of the world until the world, tired of wondering whether
it would go away, let it stay. In the more familiar atmosphere of his father's house he laid down views from
time to time, and this does not go counter to what I have
said of his silence and the two breaks that took place in
it: the dinner-table and drawing-room remarks were hardly
views, they were statements, and *ex parte* statements only
in so far as they were repetitions of equally motiveless
statements taken from his newspaper. Though a Liberal
he was no Liberal partisan: he was a Liberal because his
father supported the Liberals, a Liberal by right of birth.

How Hugh Lawton came to tolerate Liberalism I do
not yet know, unless he tolerated it because he accepted
conditions as they were. His indifference was foreign to
the restless spirit of rank-and-file Liberalism; I never felt
that he approved of the Liberal creed, but I am quite sure
that he did not disapprove of it; certainly he had not
attained acceptance of his party's theories by dint of
scepticism. Certainly! I do not know that I dare say
"certainly," for Hugh Lawton must have had a secret
life; he must have had, because I never found that he had
a public one; I never knew him to express his admiration
for a movement not comprised within the party creed; he

had many friends but I do not know whether he cared for them; I have never been quite sure that he fell in love, though he paid moderate and impartial attentions to many friends of his sisters. He cannot have been so neutral; some mental modesty must have concealed—what? And when I speculate on this problem I am carried away by my prejudices; I think of another Hugh Lawton, out for adventure in the shining armour of idealism, and of yet another, with flushed face and glowing eyes, intent upon the pursuit of some base passion. What did he do? Secretly drink? Smoke opium or gamble near Tottenham Court Road? Pursue some strange loves? I don't know. I shall never know; it is impossible that there was nothing behind that rigid face—no desire, no hope, no lust. But how is one to find out?

His tastes were not evidence, for they were not definite. He saw, I believe, most plays as they came out, one night the latest " Girl," the other some gloomy importation from Sweden; if a play was produced at, say, the Haymarket, he went; if it was produced at the Court he did not. It did not matter what the play was, it mattered what the theatre was, who the players were. I think he read a few books, not many, but the contrasts were amazing; he shrank neither from the *Life of Gladstone* nor from paper-backed novels which were finally stolen and enjoyed by the housemaid. He liked games: that is, he played them, but he displayed no enthusiasm. He neither ate much nor drank much, nor smoked much, but he did not openly disapprove of teetotallers and non-smokers. Infrequently he swore, but without conviction. I believe he did not swear because he was irritated, but because most men swore.

The mystery of Hugh Lawton is the mystery of England, and it is insoluble; no steps are taken to guard it, but I suspect it is guarded by the immense inarticulateness of the English. They do not feel the need to explain themselves; if others explain them they do not protest. Perhaps they do not understand, and perhaps they do not care. But in those days I felt this English mystery as a reserve of power; I knew that Hugh Lawton would never give himself away, never lay himself open to attack; he was the tortoise, typical of his race, able to bear all blows on its shell and resolved on one thing only: that it would never, never, never put out its head.

I admired, and I still admire Hugh Lawton. I admire him impersonally as a statue, an opera or a principle, a thing the appeal of which is inherent in itself and not dependent on clamorous expression. Though I do not completely understand him, I feel him to be fixed. He is permanent, he is like the Oxford turf, mown, watered, and rolled for three hundred years; a western civilisation has made of him a finished product, and it may be that his existence is a presage of defeat; breeding cannot go higher, but it can go lower. Too much he towers over the underman, and too unconscious is he to be the overman; he is the finest product of the average of his race, the apogee of the commonplace, and with him England stands in apotheosis.

II

Hugh Lawton stood as a banner, dignifying Barbezan & Co.; his commercial training was less than mine, but he had commonsense: that is to say he was so afraid of committing himself that he was never likely to do the wrong thing: whether he was likely to do the right one was open to question. He was, at that time, head of the tranship-ment office, where I suspect Barker did the work, with little Merton, the junior, while I took over the correspondence in French and German under the kindly rule of old Purkis. (They called him old Purkis when he entered the office at the age of twenty-five.) Old Purkis, who loved only one thing in the world, his garden at Penge (he really did live at Penge though he called it Sydenham), had made a close friend of Farr, his second, because he too loved, in order, his garden at Hornsey, then his son Norman, then his wife, who was the most wonderful woman in the world. Farr was about thirty; he had a round, white face with two black currants stuck in for eyes, and the snubbest nose in the world. I think I disliked him at first sight because black hairs grew perpendicularly from his wide nostrils. Then Farr saw me make a fool of myself, and that I found hard to forgive, as hard as it had been to forgive Chaverac, the witness of my cowardice.

After I had been a month in the office Farr saw me, one afternoon, putting on my hat. I forget where I was going to. He called me back. "Oh, Cadoresse," he said with hesitation, "as you're going out, do you mind paying this cheque in? It's five to four and the sergeant's out, while Lord knows where Tyler is. You don't mind, do you?"

I hesitated, for it did not seem to me right that the foreign correspondent should do commissionaire's work. One must preserve one's dignity. Still, I took the cheque without a word and went out with an air of erectness intended to convey that I was condescending. When I reached the bank I looked at the cheque, a large one, for over two thousand pounds and, though I knew that a cheque already endorsed and crossed with the name of the bank was of no use to me, it pleased me to be handling even the dummy of so large a sum. I pushed the cheque and paying-in book under the cashier's little railing; he glanced at the cheque, turned it over, made a tick on the foil as he tore out the slip, and pushed the book back with a mumbled "all right."

I waited. A liveried commissionaire gently pushed me to show that he had his business to do. At last the cashier looked up.

"Yes?" he said.

"I am waiting for a receipt."

"Receipt?" He had blue eyes, and they bulged under his raised white eyebrows.

" Yes, a receipt for this cheque." I showed the paying-in book.

" We don't give receipts."

" But——" I faltered.

" 'Urry up," the commissionaire remarked.

" Banks don't give receipts," said the old man sulkily. " Here." He held out his hand for the book the commissionaire was putting through the bars. The push became harder. I found myself being edged along the counter. I remember protesting again, being pushed still further away, for two clerks had hurried in as four was about to strike.

I left the bank more dismayed than angry, for I had not seen the commissionaire leave, with or without a receipt; besides, nothing showed that he had paid in cheques; while I did my own short business I remember the oppression of the affair; I wondered whether this were serious, what Barbezan & Co. would say; at any rate I could swear I had paid the cheque in. I rehearsed my speech, to be delivered in the witness-box; it was a fine, manly speech; I squared my shoulders as I delivered it. When I returned to the office my heart was beating, and I laid the book in front of Farr, pale but determined.

" They did not give me a receipt," I faltered.

" A receipt? What do you want a receipt for? "

" Is it not right we should have a receipt? "

" What do you want a receipt for? "

The stupid repetition angered me. I hated the white face and the rigid black hair.

" We fill up a form in France and we always have a receipt," I said, obstinately.

" Well, we aren't in France."

" It's a curious way to do business," I persevered.

" Oh, don't be a silly fool."

In the moment of silence that followed I felt my cheeks grow very hot. He had insulted me! And in that moment the whole of the scene on the hill, so many years ago,

unrolled on the film that obscured my eyes.   Never again!
At least this time I would be no coward.   While, with
extreme dignity, I took out my card case, I had a vision
of this low fellow neatly spitted on my sword.   The
point, I felt certain, would stick out between his shoulder
blades.

"Lord!" he gasped as he took up my card; "what's
this?"

"You have insulted me.   You will receive my seconds
to-morrow."

Farr's currant-like eyes became larger than I had ever
seen them before; his open mouth showed irregular pointed
teeth.   Suddenly he threw himself back in his chair, and
roar after roar of laughter came from him, while I looked
at him severely, my right hand on my hip.   Barker, who
was at that time consulting a reference book on the corner
table, looked up.

"What's the joke?" he asked.

Young Tyler came up to us, as if by accident, and framed
in the door I saw Merton.

"He—Cadoresse——" Farr gasped, pointing a stubby,
white finger at me.   Then he collapsed again, waving my
card.

A group formed about us.

"Take his collar off," said Barker.

"Give the gentleman air," Merton suggested.

"No, no," Farr wheezed; then he recovered.   "Cadoresse has challenged me.   I'm in for a bloomin' duel."

Then they all laughed, and I could hardly understand
them, for they talked all together, and Purkis, who came
in to ask what the noise was about, exploded into feeble
titters.

"At your disposal, Mr. Shivaleer," said Farr, bowing,
with his hands on his chest; "but I choose the weapons.
What do you say to safety pins?"

"A gentleman fights with the weapons of gentlemen,"
I said, but I was no longer secure in my dignity.

I was overwhelmed with pleasantries; Barker suggested squirts; Merton asked whether we would all go to B'long for the week-end and would I show them the sights after honour had been satisfied. Even Tyler, my despised junior, ventured to ask whether breastplates were barred.

I turned away, I twirled my little black moustache as I went to my desk. I ought to have known better than mix myself up in a brawl with my inferiors.

" I don't know anything about it," Purkis summed up as he left the room.

Of course not. His sort didn't.

III

I suppose I was a silly young man. Perhaps I was morbidly sensitive rather than silly; I resented anything that displeased me in England, less because it displeased me than because I could not bear to think there was anything displeasing in England. The duel represented one of the gaps in my knowledge of the English; I had not read enough modern literature to understand that Walter Scott was properly dead. I found myself famous in the office; the word " shivaleer " clove to me, or I was called " the Knight," and " Cyrano," for Coquelin had recently come to London. I was subjected to chaff, the chaff I have found so difficult to grow accustomed to; I had to get used to being asked how many frogs I had had for breakfast, to be hailed with " Hullo, socialism," if I wore my favourite red tie, to be told not to go for my landlady with a fork if the peas were hard.

Chaff! Amazing island in English reserve! right to jovial and reciprocal insult! Englishmen could not tolerate that which they do if they were not phlegmatic, lymphatic. I have not yet found out why an Englishman who will not venture to ask you how much you earn a year will address you as " goldbug " if you buy a sixpenny paper. We Frenchmen don't chaff: we dare not; if we did, we should be fighting all day. I do not like chaff now—it makes me a little uncomfortable, I am never quite sure that I know the ring of it; but I have accepted it as I have accepted that the duel is dead. It is enough for me that the English should chaff and that their differences should be settled by fist or writ: they can do no wrong. So determined was I already in this attitude that I apologised to the detested Farr, but my reputation did not decrease; it spread over the rest of the office and entertained it for weeks. It even reached Hugh Lawton, who suddenly added to the end of a letter he dictated to me:

" I heard about your duel, Cadoresse. It's not done, it really isn't done."

Well, if it wasn't done I wouldn't do it. I might not, in Rome, do as the Romans did, but in London I would certainly do as the English did. Was I not going to be an Englishman? a real, beef-eating, beer-drinking, sporting Englishman? A fury of Anglicisation came over me. I watched Barker furtively as he worked, for he was very well dressed, and as I was still far too proud to ask for the address of his tailor, I covertly examined his coat when he went out to wash. The result was not quite a success, for I chose an aggressive Donegal tweed, and, as I felt my clothes were too tight, had it made several sizes too large. It fitted me as a sack does a potato. I was nicknamed the teddy-bear. Then I had my hair cut very short.

" 'Ello, Dartmoor," said Maud, playfully, when I came home. I realised that I talked too much: I became wooden. I even thought of shaving off my little black moustache, but Maud would not hear of it. I was going to be English, one of these splendid calm people, whose temper was so easy that insult could rebound from them; I was going to be silent, self-reliant, purposeful, in brief Olympian. And I was going to speak English like an Englishman.

In those days I overdid it, for I was not content with continually noting idioms, looking up new words and grammatical rules: I wanted to obliterate from English the intruding Latin, I was as enthusiastic as the German who substituted " Fernsprecher " for " telephone." You will picture me, then, at six o'clock, in a deserted office and quite unmindful of Maud; I have a French dictionary and an etymological dictionary and I translate from a newspaper:

> " Our constitution, derived from the customs of ancient England, is a monument which no Cabinet will venture to destroy—"

Latin! good enough for the English, but not for a would-be Englishman.   I remember my patriotic translation:

> " Our laws, which have come down to us from our fathers, are a tower that no henchman of the King will dare to cast down—"

The word " tower " was a great trouble to me; " henchmen of the King " was, I felt, a subterfuge made necessary by the non-delegation of the powers of the moot; yet it could pass, while tower could not.   But there seemed to be no Anglo-Saxon idea of monument, and the Elizabethans were so woefully foreign.   The Elizabethans were not good enough for me, and I had not yet discovered Miles Coverdale.

My enthusiasm was damped by another of those little incidents which make up the history of my first months with Barbezan.

I had come to London well primed with commercial phrases, my tongue glib with " yours to hand of the 8th inst.," and " as per contra," and the other barbarisms, but I began to rebel.   I did not like these sentences, which could be translated almost word for word into any one of the atrocities the world chooses to call business forms. I decided to redeem the unliterary City, and I decided to be original.

It is digressing to tell what I suffered because I was not allowed to be original or distinguished, but I digress as does a sheep in a new and succulent pasturage, where it leaps towards a tender shoot before it has munched the one it has just bitten off; they are too rich, those English fields. I suffered from obscurity because I had never known it before; as a child I had recited fables to admiring elders; as a boy I had stacked my prizes in the drawing-room and exacted tribute whenever the graveyard was opened; and then it had been youth, more academic success, modish clothes, minor prowess in athletics. I do not think I had ever hit a tennis ball over the net without looking to see whether the performance was observed. In England, as Hugh Lawton said, this was not done. And though the avarice of this country when praise is asked of it, galled me, I accepted it as a harsh but beneficent tonic: was it not the custom of this northern Rome to give no credit, to recognise naught save duty done?

But I had to swallow my tonic, and it was nasty. If the draught contained in the duel was unpleasant, others, as bad and worse, had to be swallowed too. The famous Saxon business letter was one of those. I have forgotten the bulk of it, but I believe that in my enthusiasm I began by telling our correspondent, who had asked for a rebate on Barbezan's commission, that " We begged to acknowledge his writing of the fourth of last month "; I then went on to " We must say, in answer, that we cannot grant that our share in the yield of the business is over great—" I assured him at the end, having been instructed to say that our " charges were so inadequate as barely to balance our working expenses," that " our share was so small as to be less than our need."

I was called into Mr. Lawton's private room. He sat at a large knee-hole desk—a handsome man, then close on fifty and very like Hugh. In front of him was my remarkable screed.

" *Qu'est-ce que c'est que cela,* Cadoresse? " he asked, taking it up.

" That is the letter to Burland & Co.," I said.

" Yes," he said after a pause; " that's all very well. But why ' our share in the yield of the business is not over great? ' Why not ' the commission is in accordance with current practice '? "

This did not sound like a very good phrase, even in City Latin English. But I ignored that, fell back on my main defence:

" Mine," I said, carefully choosing my words, " is written in Saxon, in Gothic alone."

" In Gothic alone," gasped Mr. Lawton. Then he began to laugh, while I stood in front of the desk, very mortified and rather angry. " But what do you want to write Gothic for? You'll be making up charter-parties in black-letter by and by."

" Gothic, or Saxon," I said, and paused reverently, " is a wonderful tongue, Mr. Lawton, it is so full of meaning, so concise——"

" Concise," said Mr. Lawton, wickedly, " is not Saxon. You are falling from grace."

But I was too excited to feel his shaft. I wanted to tell him how much I loved the word " craft " and hated " art," how inferior " remarkable " was to " wonderful "; I was making a bad case, I was carried away by analogy; in my mistaken philological zeal I branded as Low Latin honest Frankish words which had strayed into French. I buttressed my view with Shakespeare, the Bible and Fletcher (whom I had never read); I stuttered in vain efforts readily to find Saxon equivalents of " psychology " and " retrograde." I tried to make him feel my craving to be English, historically English.

He listened up to the end, without interrupting me, holding his chin in his left hand. Then he looked up at me with amusement in his eyes.

" So you're going to be the John Bright of Fenchurch

Street? I'm sorry for you, Cadoresse, you'll have a rotten time. But, really, are you only a silly ass or are you pulling my leg? What are you doing?"

I blushed and confessed that I had noted the idiom in my pocket-book, for inquiry.

"Well, you're trying, anyhow," he said, laughing again. "But you'd better not go too far. I'm afraid you're *plus anglais que les Anglais,* Cadoresse."

The letter was rewritten. But, a week later, I received an invitation to dine at Lancaster Gate, of which I shall have something to say; that was a very good ending to the affair; at least it seemed good until Muriel Lawton quietly asked me whether I was the "Girondin Ancient Briton."

IV

I had repressed my desire to talk of Maud, though Barker was occasionally arch about a certain Dora whom he favoured for lunch, while Tyler and Merton frequently exchanged within my hearing views on women where biblical substantives and Stuart adjectives curiously clashed with modern Cockney. Prudence or reserve prevented me from doing likewise, for, nothing is, after all, so interesting to talk about as women, especially conquered women. But then I had not conquered Maud. Three months had elapsed, and I did not seem to have advanced much beyond the stage I attained the first evening, though our opportunities were many, while the tolerance that surrounded us was almost incomprehensible. Lulu did not trouble us, any more than she troubled anybody else; the sulky flaxen-haired girl had not in three months exchanged with me more than a dozen sentences beyond daily salutations. Lulu seemed to live in a dream, and I realised that this was a dream of romance induced by her fierce appetite for novelettes. If I met Lulu in the hall she was either coming in or going out with *Bella's Millions* or *Daisy and the Duke;* sometimes she was coming in with a bundle of these things, which she bought in the Edgware Road at the rate of seven for sixpence; and though they evidently served her as a drug, she was not ashamed of them. Perhaps they were a habit rather than a drug, and they bred in me another habit, that of thinking of her (infrequently) in her studious attitude: china-blue eyes and mouth open, absolute inexpressiveness; she seldom laughed or wept; she read. And then she forgot. This I know, for Lulu left novelettes behind her like a trail; I found them on the dining-room sideboard, in the drawing-room, in other places the most remarkable of which was not the bath-room. So I ventured to experiment, to steal a novelette from the new set she had left on a chair and substitute an old one, which happened to be clean. I told Maud, but she remained unmoved.

"Bless you," she said, " *she'll* never know."

Certainly she showed no sign of knowing, for she read the old novelette right through. Maud was not afflicted with the same disease: her reading, in addition to the *Daily Graphic* (discarded a few months later for the *Mirror*), was made up mainly of the *Era,* which she went through from title to printer's name, and of the *Sporting and Dramatic,* in which she held a sixth share with five other members of the Tinman Academy.

"We draw for it once a week," she confided to me; "comes in handy for cutting out; got Sarer Bernard out of it this time, stuck her in the looking-glass."

I found out that Maud had plastered the wall-paper in her corner of the bedroom with pictures of a number of actors and actresses and especially of comedians. One picture postcard, too valuable to be put in the album, was signed " Yours sincerely, Dan Leno."

"He did 'em for the lot of us this summer, when old Tinman took us to his special."

This is hearsay, for I had never entered the bedroom Maud shared with Lulu, and I never entered it to the end. I once caught Maud on the threshold before dinner, but as I moved she slammed the door in my face and did not speak to me that evening. Truly Mr. and Mrs. Hooper were justified in their trust; they accepted that Maud and I were great friends, could afford to let us wrangle and talk all the evening in the dining-room. The family never assembled in the drawing-room after the first evening.

"You don't mind, Mr. Cadoresse, do you?" said Mrs. Hooper. "I think the dining-room's so much more homey."

I agreed, and for my part, never put my evening clothes on again to dine at St. Mary's Terrace. We settled very comfortably in the dining-room, where Mrs. Hooper went on working tea-cloths and table-centres, to be given away in due course on birthdays and Christmases; Lulu stolidly read of peers, honest maidens and motor-car elopements (I wonder whether they elope in aeroplanes in the modern novelette); Mr. Hooper was out three nights a week, debating, or attending Masonic meetings: on other nights he often engaged me in conversation as to "The history and customs of foreign peoples" or read his substitute for the Bible, Fyfe's *Five Thousand Facts and Fancies*. Meanwhile I worked with grammar and dictionary until Maud, jealous of my absorption in anything but herself, though she did not seem particularly to want my attentions, suddenly threw a newspaper or one of her mother's reels of cotton on my open book. Maud always threw, and an expression in her eyes told me when she was about to do so; it was her instinct: in a Swiss hotel she would have thrown bread by the pound.

"Maud, my dear, how can you?" Mrs. Hooper would say, with a look of reproach in her mild eyes. But Maud could, and her mother had given up serious interference. Sometimes we made too much noise, disturbed Mr. Hooper in his study of *Five Thousand Facts and Fancies;* on one of these occasions he raised his head and remarked:

"Since you've got to make so much noise, Maud, you'd better go up to the drawing-room and try the piano."

" Talk of bright ideas! " Maud cried; " you take the biscuit, Pa."

" I wish you wouldn't talk like that, Maud," said Mrs. Hooper, helpless but admiring. " Don't turn *all* the gas on, dear."

" I won't turn any gas on at all. You can listen, and hear me read you off the Dead March in Saul, as sung by Mr. Dutch Daly, Esquire, all done by kindness and by the light of my glowing orb. Come along and be the stalls, old coffee-pot."

" I wish you wouldn't call Mr. Cadoresse ' coffee-pot,' " moaned Mrs. Hooper.

" Well, he is a coffee-pot, aren't you? Or is it the Red Lion you slip round to every night on the Q. T.? "

" It's only coffee," I said as I opened the door for her. " Honest Injun."

" That's right, we'll make a John Bull of you by and by, I don't think."

It was not the first time I had been allowed to accompany Maud to the icy drawing-room, where she tortured the old piano into songs in which were weepings and wailings and gnashing of wires. It no longer struck me as extraordinary to be alone with her; I was contented, having had my coffee at a dreadful little Italian restaurant in the Harrow Road; I was in the after-dinner gallant mood.

" Stop it," said Maud, freeing herself from my sudden grasp as we entered the dark room. " Stop it, I say. I won't have my hair pulled."

I kissed her at random on neck and cheek, seeking her lips.

" Oh! do behave," she protested weakly; then she pushed me away. " If you don't stop it I'll go downstairs again." I released her. " There. That's better. You be good." She kissed me lightly on the cheek, murmured " sauce-box," and eluded me in the dark.

I lit the candles for her, as I had learned that she must

not be coerced; she had to be irritated by indifference or
handled as lightly as a butterfly.

"You dare," she said warningly, and began one of her
noisy tunes. She smiled, rolled her brown eyes and shook
her curls. Smiling all the time, she sang a tune I had heard
already at some hall. It was incongruous to hear this
pretty girl declare that:

> "It ain't all 'oney and it ain't all jam,
> Wheelin' round the 'ouses a three-wheeled pram . . ."

And it was delightful that this dainty creature should
sing of slums, babies, pubs, lodgers, sausages and cheese;
it was unexpected; she was the flower on a dunghill. I
laughed as she sang, and she smiled more broadly. She
winked roguishly, and I went to her side, gently stroked
the back of her firm neck; she seemed indifferent to the
caress, went on with her song:

> ". . . I 'aven't any money, I got nuffin' to eat,
> I'm walkin' round the 'ouses on me poor ole feet . . ."

I leaned down and softly kissed her neck, first on the left
and then a little further, and then again, surrounding her
plump neck with a ring of kisses. She continued to sing
without resenting or seeming to appreciate the caresses.
Did she know I was kissing her? Yes:

"Oo," she said at last, "you're tickling."

But still she went on singing, and she did not strike a
single wrong note though I went on caressing her neck,
playing with her soft brown curls. And even when I suddenly grew rough, seized her chin and kissed her mouth,
she showed no anger: as soon as I released her she burst
out with:

> "Good-bye, oh, rose of summer's sowing,
> Good-bye, oh, flower-scented wind . . ."

"Oh, do give over," she protested angrily, for I had
put my arm round her waist, lifted her off the piano stool;

I crushed her against my chest, covered her face with greedy kisses; a thin film hung over my eyes, so that, round a candle, I could see a zone of purple.

"Maud, Maud, my darling, my angel, I love you, I adore you," I murmured thickly into her hair. She did not struggle, she seemed frightened as I grew bolder. And for a moment she seemed to respond to my passion; she coiled one arm round my neck, and as our lips met I had the terrible thrill of victory.

"Do you love me?" I asked.

"Oh, go on."

"You do."

"Well, perhaps I do."

"Say it."

"Say it," I repeated fiercely, and I think that in my anger I savagely shook her.

"I do love you."

And with that I had to be content; never did she say simply and splendidly, the "I love you" for which I waited. She seemed to respond, she did not rebel against my caresses, but she had her fixed limits and, if I grew over-bold, would repulse me without showing offence or content.

"Now then, that'll do," she said at last that night; "stop it. What d'you take me for? Bit o' butter-scotch?"

She sat down at the piano, leaving me angry and perplexed, and began again:

> "Good-bye, oh, rose of summer's sowing,
> Good-bye, oh, flower-scented wind . . ."

I looked at her meekly, full of dim realisations. And yet she smiled as she sang, practised her stage tricks, lauguished first to the right and then to the left, and looked up towards a gallery crowded by her imagination with "boys" to whom she winked. I saw her as every-body's thing and wondered why she could be nobody's thing; I questioned whether she loved me, liked me or preferred my attentions to none; it was very difficult to make her out.

"Well, sulky," she said, as she finished her third song. The jocularity of the address did not seem to clash in her mind with the last words of her lyric:

> ". . . We'll meet again in heaven blue."

I did not reply, still looked at her, sunken in my ugly mood.

"Look here," she said brightly. "I'll have to give you a good old talking-to if you go on like this." She stood up, leaned an elbow on the piano and rested her head on her hand. "I didn't say I wanted to spoon. No fear. Why don't you wait till you're asked? 'Stead of sitting there with a face like yesterday. You take my tip and don't make so free."

"I didn't make free with you," I said, acidly.

"Well, if that's what you call not making free I'd rather not know what you do call making free."

I stood up, went to the wall and vacantly gazed at a picture of the Queen, while Maud sat down with a thump on the piano stool and thundered out another music-hall tune. I thought bitterly that she was playing it very badly, that anger could make her miss notes, while caresses could not. At that moment I hated her, and half resolved to go to my room. But Maud, on finishing the noisy tune, was banging an accompaniment to a monotone of her own composition:

> "I don't care, I don't care.
> Let him go to Paree-Mayfair,
> I don't care, I don't care.
> Let him go to Paree-Mayfair."

For some two minutes I bore with this nonsense, which grew louder and louder and more purposeful. I knew it as half-defiance, half-signal. It made me tingle; I felt

like a bull that becomes angrier with every thrust of the
banderillas.

" Stop it," I shouted as I strode to the piano.

The laughing eyes were fixed upon me, the red mouth
was open, and I could see the white throat swell as she
screamed her idiotic refrain. And her gibe was so subtly
aphrodisiac that I did not know how much her youth and
grace drew me. I hated her, despised her; I wanted to
seize and twist her firm neck, shake her, kick her; and a
sense of degradation mixed with my delight as I clasped
both arms round her, lifted her off the stool:

> " I don't care, I don't care,
> Let him go to Paree-Mayfair . . ."

Maud screamed as I carried her to the sofa. And then,
for some moments, there was silence while I caressed her
with a ferocity born of my baulked hunger for her. She
laughed on a high note; she did not struggle though I
knew I was painfully crushing the hand I held, though
a heavy curl fell across my face as I bent to kiss her.
She did not return the kisses I pressed upon her eyelids,
her neck, her lips; she remained quiescent in my grasp,
as if aware that she would struggle in vain, as if conscious
that the brute must dominate awhile until fluting reason
can be heard. But as I held her I was revengeful rather
than joyous, for I knew that hers was but a partial surrender, that she was paying in small favours for attentions and pleasures, that I would never break the steely
barrier of her coldness, that on my exceeding the limits
formulated by her sex-policy I would be repulsed and
dismissed. Oh, in her own language, she wouldn't give
herself away.

She sat on my knees, one arm round my neck, limp and
half-smiling; she seemed tired, as if some content had
come to her out of the wooing my prudence had restrained.
But there was no heat of excitement in the hand I held:

it was firm, cool, able no doubt to carry without tremor a glass brimful of water. She would not spill a drop. And I knew bitterly that my eyelids were moist, as if something inside me had cried out with pain and had tried very hard to weep.

She sat up and away from me at last, pushed up her flying hair. " My! " she said; " you're a bit of all right, you are." A very little, grudging admiration filtered to me through the phrase, but she eluded me as I tried to clasp her again.

" No," she said, firmly. " Never no more again, Mister. One might think you were barmy on the crumpet the way you go on, pulling a girl about like a rag doll. If that's the way they do it in Border I'm not surprised you got the hoof. No," she added, a note of anger in her voice as I seized her hand; " it's closing time, house full. Keep off the grass, I tell you," she cried as she stood up, " and talk sensibly or——"

We talked sensibly. I tried to tell Maud what I did at the office; I described old Purkis, Farr and the perpendicular hair. " Don't be dirty," was her comment on my description of Farr; Tyler and Barker gained no appreciation, but she seemed interested in Hugh Lawton.

" Sounds like a bit of a toff."

Oh, Maud, if I had met you ten years later would you not have said Hugh Lawton was a k'nut!

She pestered me with questions. How old was he? What was he like? But exactly? Yes, she did like 'em fair. Was he his father's partner? Would he be? Would I? She was interested in everything that was material; she did not know that there was anything non-material. She did not love; she spooned. She had no ambitions; she had desires. She could not feel remorse; she could know that she had put her foot in it. She did not believe in God; she could fear hell.

Hugh Lawton appeared as a shadow on her mental screen, my superior because he bought his ties in the

Burlington Arcade, while I bought mine in Cheapside, just as I was superior to the young men who bought their ties in Edgware Road. Money, rank, position, prospects—she could understand all that, but I could make her understand nothing else. I tried to explain the Saxon business letter.

" Oh, German, you mean," she said, vaguely.

I gave it up. I tried to make her see what it meant to be an Englishman, to feel, to think like one.

" Oh yes, I know," she said; " didn't you say you could get out of camp, or whatever it is, if you naturalise? "

We could talk only of facts; we could hardly talk of love. For her love was a subject with two compartments; in the first she put questionable jokes, which I now realise she did not quite understand; in the second was a singular cloying composition: hand-holding on the Front at Brighton, moongazing on the River, ultimate marriages involving nightly attendances at the halls or theatres; there was a strain of melancholy in it: the young lover was quite as pleasant dead as alive, for one laid flowers on his grave, and one was " true " to him; later on one was comforted by an older man, whom one met by " mother's grave." One married the older man, and somehow, after lying in one's own grave, one might meet the first love in heaven. There were love-letters too, but she called them " silly talk."

All this mixture of mental sensuality and sentiment rested on a paradoxic foundation of ignorant purity. Maud was cold, or rather unawakened. She had not been told: she had heard, at Tinman's, in the street, but she had not been marked by her knowledge; she had not connected the fragments of enlightenment which had come her way. Essentially English, she had few curiosities and did not devote to the theoretic side of passion the thought and research hardly a French girl neglects; the subject did not interest, did not attract her; she knew " in a sort of way," and did not want to know any more.

Indeed, she often repulsed me with a sharp " Stop it," when I tried to correlate in her mind the impressions I found there.

You were pure in your own way, little flower of the London gutter.

V

Of course, the Hoopers were trying to entrap me into marriage. I found that out later, with some surprise, for, in my own opinion, I was not a *bon parti,* and I did not realise that a young man with a salary of a hundred and twenty a year could be appreciated by the genteel Hoopers. I did not, for years, grasp that an English girl can leave her father's Kensington house, his brougham and her skating club to control a suburban brick box and a twelve pound " general." Nor did I understand that Mrs. Hooper would have been quite satisfied to see Maud installed with me in an upper part in the Harrow Road, that she accepted her husband's view: " Young people must not expect to begin where their parents left off." Besides, Maud had not the dowry usual in civilised countries, I think, and, even now I am a little uneasy when the English girl plunges for love and nothing a year.

They are too hard on the *dot,* those sentimental English, who, by the way, shrink from *dots* and insist upon marriage settlements. I like to think that a girl does not come penniless into her husband's house, that she has the option between maintaining her financial independence and, therefore, conjugal affection, or helping her husband in his career, or keeping her money to educate her children. In spite of my own record I still distrust those matches made in hot blood, without regard for class, suitability, monetary chances. And I don't like to think of all those English girls sold in marriage to the first bidder, lest there be no second. We sell to the best bidder, the English to the first. And they do sell, for what can a penniless

woman do in presence of a hated but moneyed husband?
Love! yes, there's love—but after all, why marry?

So I never thought of marriage with Maud. I wanted
to marry an English girl some time, a girl I would love, but
ideas as to suitability were fast set in my mind. I could
not have introduced Maud to my mother if my mother
had had experience of English girls. And I wanted a girl
with some money: I was not going to hunt money, but
one must have money. I looked upon my affair with Maud
as an adventure, just as she looked upon it as a flirtation;
I still hoped to bring it to a satisfactory end, and until
that time could not brag of it at the office, but of Lottie
I could brag and did.

For I was not faithful to Maud. There was no reason
why I should have been, as faithfulness is, after all, no
more than acquired insensitiveness; also faithfulness cuts
one off from experience. In this respect only did I make
exceptions to the British code I was adopting; I could
not bring myself to find other eyes dull because those of
Maud were bright. They were not dull, and they were
rewarding, for there are not two looks alike, two smiles
as witching, and the tender break in a woman's voice
when she murmurs and laughs low is never twice quite the
same. Those soft low laughs are all of a family, but different. Appetite for adventure, for an excitement that
was mainly mental, drove me into perpetual conflict with
women. I had to look into the eyes of the waitress when
I ordered my chop, and if I made her blush it was a
success: I took this blush back to the office and hung
it up like a rosy curtain across the Fenchurch Street
window. In the Underground, in the streets, on the top
of jolting horse-buses, where propinquity combines with
the excitement of release from work to saturate the air
with aphrodisiac vapours, I had eyes for all those fair
heads and curly brown heads, and clear blue eyes and bold
black eyes, tokens of some fiery southern ancestry. To
this day I cannot walk the streets without disquiet, so

treacherously soft and treacherously pure are these English girls.

For they are pure, and I was not very successful. Indeed, if I had not had the persistency of the spider I would not have continued my pursuit of them in the face of the snubs which I received. They were afraid of me, the foreigner, for the cold mantle of their purity let through disquiet when I drew near; I have been told, and have no reason to doubt it, that there is no banter in my black eyes. I have never looked upon a woman, old or young, without there being a caress in my glance, however casual; I have no talent for banter, I never flirt, I am always dangerous. They knew it, and if they did not snub me, soon they gave me short answers, were " surprised at me " or " wouldn't have thought it of me." One of them, at Earl's Court, I think, threw me a frightened glance and ran away. But even if I had never succeeded, I would still have tried, for I had in my life the young bachelor's demon, loneliness. Often Maud was out with a " pal," or " studying " at the halls; then, after a while, I looked up from my books, gazed at Mrs. Hooper, knitting or embroidering, at Mr. Hooper, deep-buried in *Science Siftings* or *Tit-Bits*. A placid air of content hung over them, while Lulu, in an armchair, read at extreme speed some tale of dairymaid and duke. The atmosphere was—stuffy, and there was about the very gas an air of finality: it would never, never turn into electric light. I would make an effort, mumble out: " . . . but worship and humbug are exceptions; though the accent be on the first syllable the final consonant is redoubled." Then I would memorise the double ps and gs, contrast the words with " refer,"—worship, worshipping—refer, referring— until the rule began to slip away and I ceased to know whether the typical word was pronounced " refer " or " reffer."

Up to my room on those nights. First a vicious casting of my body upon the bed, accompanied by an internal cry: " What shall I do? what shall I do? " Then a steady gaze at the text, " The Lord is my Shepherd, I shall not want." In the bad light I had to guess at the queer old English characters. A muttered curse on all clerics, springing from my Jacobin temper. There was nothing to do, I wanted to do nothing. I leaped off the bed, walked round the room, examining each article, yellow-tiled splasher, old red cloth, swivel mirror; the pictures next, the wretched sentimental " Peacemaker." Costume-play love! pah! Then " In the Garden of Eden," a clerk and a typist, in nineteenth-century fig-leaves. The Jubilee procession troubled me on those nights; it always seemed to think me emotional, hysterical, un-English.

But at last I had looked at everything, felt mental nausea in front of my books, looked into the garden, then sodden with winter rains. I would stand for some moments in the middle of the room, slowly walk to the window, stare into the blackness, walk back to the bed, then back to the window. Pause. Then I would begin to go round the room, slowly, hands in pockets, head down. As I passed, the dirty carpet lost all its pattern. I began to walk faster, round and round, half-conscious of impressions, black window, empty grate, dirty boots. Faster and faster still, like a convict in his cell or a beast at the Zoo. I went round and round the room, which seemed to grow smaller all the time; I was like a squirrel in its wheel with a night's turning in front of it. And, as I turned and turned, one thought speared my loneliness: what shall I do? what shall I do? And again and again it came, ebbing and flowing, like successive waves beating upon a shore.

At last I would seize my hat, rush out of the house, slamming the front door to get some noise into my life. Sometimes I would walk aimlessly on, eyes towards the ground, as fast as I could, contemptuous of traffic and butting into passers-by, until I stopped quite suddenly at Hendon or Shepherd's Bush, just tired and dulled enough to want my bed. And on other nights I would climb into the gallery of a music-hall and stare at the backs of the people in front of me, or drink whiskey on the top of stout in a public-house, just to exchange a word with a barmaid or find interest in a " drunk." Or I would engage in long, aimless pursuits of women who had caught my fancy. Once I ran after a cab laden with luggage and offered my breathless services after a two-mile sprint. One must do something, one must.

It was on one such night I met Lottie. I had walked a long way, far beyond Notting Hill, when I caught her up—a slim, fair girl. The obvious shopgirl, badly dressed, with cheap lace sticking out of her old, modish gray coat and two visible brooches. I found out a little later that she wore two more—also a pendant and a necklace of sham pearls.

" Are you going far? " I asked.

" Just about as far as turn-back," said the girl. I saw, as she looked at me, that she must be twenty-five. Fair hair, blue eyes, pale face: five more years of good looks and she would be old.

" May I go with you? " I asked.

" No, thanks," she said; " not out for chocolates, just had grapes."

But this is only the small change of London gallantry. Soon I was walking by Lottie's side, holding her arm, unrebuked.

She did not mind, she prattled of her " people " in Norfolk, of her situation at a stationer's, of Kew and Earl's Court, and didn't I think those railway bridges cost a lot of money to build? She did not mind my going with her, she did not mind when I kissed her in a silent street of villas, she did not mind kisses, fervid or tepid. Lottie did not want anything or object to anything; she had never developed; even her taste for pleasure was faint: she did not long for Sunday afternoon River trips, she merely liked them. I took her for a misty walk in Richmond Park, three days later, and she never took my hand, nor drew hers away when I grasped it. She never asked me my name, thus never knew it: I was a " fellow," and when for a few brief hours I was a lover, a " fellow " I remained. Not for a moment did any enthusiasm leap up to meet mine, and when I dropped out of her life, out of sheer weariness, I do not suppose she suffered. She could not forget; she had nothing to remember; doubtless she went from a " fellow " to a " fellow."

The ignominy of it lay heavy upon me sometimes, and often I swore that not even the walking round and round in my room would drive me to this. But it did: what can one do? what can one do? Ignominious as was this adventure, the first of many, it was, however, an adventure, and I had to brag of it. I began by throwing out hints to Barker; I would in any case have done so, but he began by talking of Dora.

" She's a little bit of all right, is Dora. And I rather think yours truly is a bit of a favourite with her."

" How can you tell? "

" Oh, I go late—perhaps that's my little plan, and there's never more than two or three at her tables at half-past two. So she comes and sits down and gasses away about this, that and the other, and we have a fine old time. Blime! if I wasn't a married man——"

" What does that matter? "

" Now then, now then. None of your continental ways here. They won't wash. Besides, Cadoresse, you don't understand English girls; they're not after you like flies round a honey-pot."

Memories of Maud collided with memories of Lottie and others, and I looked inimically at this handsome, well-brushed young man who stood before me like Don Juan lecturing Casanova. It was absurd, I reflected, that a suburban puritan should masquerade as a gay dog, and more absurd that so attractive a young man should be a puritan. For Barker looked very smart in his soft, dark grey tweed; he managed to buy good clothes in Poultry

for three guineas, while I failed in Sackville Street for
five. He had an agreeable, open face, tanned once a week
on the golf course, fine gray eyes, a small, beautifully-cut
mouth; but for a small chin and a very slight narrowness
of forehead he would have been as handsome as Hugh
Lawton. He exasperated me, therefore, for two reasons.

"Aren't they?" I said at length. "Well, they're not so
farouche as you think, Barker. There's——" I was going
to say "my landlady's daughter," but honesty twisted the
phrase: "Many of them are quite easy. Why, you can
talk to English girls in the street."

"Oh, you can," said Farr, who had come in as we
talked; "but everybody knows that sort, they don't
count."

I suddenly understood an English attitude: two kinds
of women, the accessible undesirable and the inaccessible
desirable.

"I cannot tell whether they count," I said, "but——"
I told them the story of my meeting with Lottie, of
my subsequent meetings, fully stated her in terms of conquest. I enlarged upon the adventure: Lottie's hair shim-
mered like gold, her pale eyes became as deep, blue, sunlit
pools; in my story she was fervid, passionate; she became
the Golden Girl; a lovely romantic light (shot with the
fires of passion) flowed over Notting Hill.

"Go on with you," said Barker at last; "you rotten
dog."

"And what did she say to that?" Farr asked. There
was a glow in his ugly little eyes, and the black hairs
moved as his nostrils twitched.

Ah, this man liked my story; puritan Englishman, what
is there under your black coat? I elaborated the story,
filled it with response, made it dramatic; a histrion, I liked
to play upon Farr.

"Well," he said at length, exhaling a puff of breath
from his white cheeks, "she's a——"

How can men say such things? or such words? I am
not yet used to the English vocabulary. And to apply such
words to love!

For it is love, it is always love. Even inarticulate, even
formal, even cold, it is love and always love, and because
it is love it is wonderful. I am in love with love. It
makes me happy to know there are lovers, thousands, millions of lovers, and it makes me miserable to think I
shall die, because then I shall no longer know love. It
made me shudder when he suddenly dragged from my poor
little adventure its coat of many colours. But Barker was
not coarse; he had none of Farr's hateful sensuousness, the
sensuousness which, among his like, expresses itself in
words from the fishmarket. He lectured me:

" You know, Cadoresse, it sounds very nice and romantic,
all that, but what about the girl? Have you thought of
what it means for her? "

" It means for her what it means for me."

" No, you silly old josser; you're all like that abroad.
You don't understand women; you think they're just like
you. Well, they aren't: they feel disgrace and lose their
self-respect. Why, there's no knowing what harm you may
have done the girl; you may have ruined her life for all
you know."

I suggested that as Lottie was not my first adventure
I might be deemed not to be her first, either.

" That's got nothing to do with it," said Barker, severely;
" it's your responsibility all the same. Put yourself in her
shoes, and perhaps you'll see she can't hold her head up
again; she feels dishonoured, she may break her heart over
it, refuse to marry somebody else."

" Oh, stuff," I said.

They laughed: that was not the word I ought to have
used, but I could not bear to use their word.

Barker went on with his reprimand. As an enlightened
chapel-goer he had to turn me from the path of sin, and as
he talked I understood the Englishman better, understood

the depth of his illusion about women. Barker saw woman
as a calm, passionless, charming creature, anxious, in his
own words, "to marry to have someone to take care of."
He was not mercenary, and could not believe that woman
was mercenary; he could not believe that a woman could
want anything her husband did not want; he credited
her with no initiatives, with desiring nothing save dresses
and babies. Barker thought that women did not mind,
at thirty, being spinsters in their fathers' houses, if those
homes were comfortable. If in those days there had
been militant suffragettes he would have told them to go
home and mind the baby. He loved his wife, who represented woman; he looked upon her as an ideal and as a
type: religious, domesticated, obedient, gay, loyal and
respectably romantic. He would have given her to drink
his last drop of blood but would not have spared her
a penny for a newspaper. He thought she was perfect,
that woman was perfect, that woman was so noble and
beautiful that she must be set on a pedestal and worshipped: but she was never to get off the pedestal and do
what she liked. According to Barker it was the husband
knew what his wife liked, and her tastes conformed singularly with his own.

I began that day to see why Englishwomen are so
bored.

At the end of the lecture Farr abruptly said:

"Heard that limerick, Barker, about the young lady
of Turin?"

The limerick was recited. Disgusting. Then came two
jokes out of one of the weeklies, where wit was absent and
foulness abundant. Barker laughed uproariously.

"Heard that story about——"?

A very pretty actress was dragged through the gutter.

Tyler came in, contributed his quota to the conversation, and little Merton drew near, sniggering and squirm-
ing; a nasty, hot blush climbed up his rosy cheeks. Clearly
this abominable talk bore no relation to actual fact; it

was just talk: they never connected those stories with living men and women.

These Englishmen! They keep their ideas apart, like dogs each one kennel, lest they should fight, I suppose. Or no, the process is less conscious; they have their standards and their lists of points, with which to classify the dogs. One kind of dog goes under " spaniels," another under " retrievers," and so on, and there are kennels for mongrels and kennels for curs, and kennels for pariah dogs, and there is a big, secure pen for " foreign dogs." They padlock that one and put barbed wire round it for fear they might themselves go too close and be bitten. One thing they never do, and that is connect the mongrel and the spaniel and say: " Both are dogs."

Good, pure women and " bad lots "—that is all they see. It is no use saying that convention can make the first out of dullards, or that romance can lift the second upon wings and carry them up aloft: that would interfere with the classification.

CHAPTER VI

THE HEART OF ENGLAND

I

I HAVE not done what I set out to do. I have been too critical, allowed later and more judicial impressions to fog the sharp, partisan views I took of England in those early days, and to clear the chaos created in my mind by their conflict. I cannot, now that I speak English so well that people ask me whether I am Scotch or Welsh, now that I conform to English conventions and believe in a few of them, restore the freshness of the mind I brought from France. I figure the past as one may trace out on some very old Italian fresco a faint design over which an economical iconoclast painted another picture. I could not see England for the English.

I gave them all more or less heroic qualities (except Farr, whom I endowed with undeservedly villainous traits), because I understood them only in flashes. They always came out with strong, high lights. A flash, and I saw Barker, for instance, as the moderate, sober, honest man, a little narrow but perfectly calm, irrepressibly calm —and then I saw him no more. I have said that I thought him limited, uninformed on the woman question, but I excused him to myself. I was always the advocate of the English: if they injured me and advocacy became impossible, I refused to prosecute. Thus, silly old Purkis stood as the rock of security, Tyler, Merton as energetic, intelligent young men, finely pure (as a rule) and incapable of playing anybody a dirty trick. Hugh Lawton represented for me in the flesh what the young wrestlers on

113

the Embankment represent in bronze. Oh, Olympian Hugh, where is the laurel-wreath that sat so well on your currycombed head?

It is because I saw no more than the main lines that I understood the English: it takes a foreigner to do that. If an Englishman struck me as pure-minded, he was Galahad; if strong, he was Hercules; if bad, he was Jack the Ripper. Nowadays I judge men, perhaps better, perhaps with more regard for shades of temperament, but not so surely; I do not so readily part the lions from the unicorns. I judged violently, in a prejudiced spirit, and I almost invariably approved. If I had hesitations as to the genteel Hoopers, as to the clerks of Barbezan, I think I had none about the Lawtons after the august dinner. It took place in January. Invited because my Saxon business letter had amused Mrs. Lawton and because my status was, thanks to my name, not quite that of a clerk, I found myself, at half-past seven (for the dinner hour had not yet travelled to a quarter-past eight) inwardly a little shy and outwardly very bold, seated at a large round table between Mrs. Lawton, a sprightly, good-looking matron, and a delicate fair-haired girl, Edith, her daughter. I have no very clear memory of the first lap of the conversation, for the preoccupation of clothes, after all these years, still hangs stifling over the occasion. I was again wearing the wrong clothes. I always was, and to this day I am never safe in this country where the wearing of the black is governed half by rules and half by intuitions; whether I choose tails or dinner jacket, black tie and waistcoat or white, I am never sure that I shall be in the majority. Now clothes is the one thing in the world in which a Frenchman who is trying to become an Englishman does not want to be original. When he is not trying to become an Englishman, he does want to be original, and I have vivid memories of a white lace tie I used to wear, now unfortunately lost, before I realised that Englishmen stared at it bewildered, as if they were

Hottentots confronted with a motor-car. But, that night, my trouble was not confined to my tie, which was black. One seat away was Edward Kent, a short, fair young man, who looked as if he shaved three times a day; his tailcoat was moulded into him, his tie and waistcoat sat, precise and intolerably white, on his plump body; Mr. Lawton too, wore tails, but for mysterious reasons a black waistcoat, while Hugh, to make my unease complete, had dared a dinner jacket with a white waistcoat and tie. I judged this to be modish, but remained cheerless, for one thing was quite clear: I was not white enough. When, in later days, I tried to be white enough, I was generally too white; I could never grade entertainments, gauge the difference between dinners " Class A (family and two intimates)," and dinners " Class B (four strangers)," and dinners " Class C (unlimited ostentation)." Nor could I distinguish between the livery of the master of the house, that of youth, that of the guest—between the livery for food, the livery for song, the livery for the dance. In Hugh's 'Varsity phrase, I managed to dress either as a " cad " or as a " bounder." He never said this of or to me, as that would not have been like Hugh, but such was his classification; for Hugh there were only the dressed, the underdressed, the overdressed. It took me four years of labour to enter the " dressed " class frequently. English syntax was much easier. But, that night, as I rolled anxious eyes from the chattering Mrs. Lawton to the shy Edith, when " cad " and " bounder " were unknown terms, I felt like a waiter or a mute. I hardly knew what I said, as I glared at the opposition clothes, though little seemed to be expected of me save to listen. Mrs. Lawton had nothing to say, but she said it very prettily; in my perturbation her gossip was very comforting.

" You must dislike this weather very much," she said, " after the South. I know what it's like, for I simply can't stand London after the middle of January. I simply *have* to go to the Riviera."

"Riviera?" I said blankly, quite unable to connect this word with the *Côte d'Azur*.

"Yes, the Riviera. I generally go to Cannes, or Mentone, though that's getting impossible now the Germans have found it out. Of course, there's Monte Carlo, but there's too much noise, too many people! what I want is a quiet place, just to sit in the sun——"

Mrs. Lawton developed at immense length her idea of a quiet life; I smiled as much as I could, I tried to smile with my ear, I suppose, and I do not remember what she took to be a quiet life. I have a vague feeling that its quietude was rather eventful. Meanwhile I inspected the guests, Hugh and Mr. Lawton, who were as rigid and polite outside as inside the office, and then my cheerful neighbour. Mrs. Lawton was pleasing enough. She looked about thirty-seven or eight, but at the time was actually forty-three, for she had the Englishwomen's secret of looking much less than their age, probably because they do not grow up; she was dark-haired, buxom, and her colour, though a little ruddy over the cheekbones, was agreeable. I failed to find upon her face a trace of powder or rouge, and regretted it a little, for the loveliest features in the world are set off by the subtle wickedness of these artifices; yet I liked her, her gaiety, and her triangular eyes. It was Mrs. Lawton's eyes made one look at her twice; to say they were triangular is the only way of saying that the eyelids drew close together at the outer corners of the sockets, while they parted a little wider near the nose. This gave the grey-green pupils an astonished, kitten-like air. Mrs. Lawton's eyes were too well-bred to ask questions, but they always seemed a little surprised when information was volunteered. She had given those eyes to her daughter Muriel, who now sat almost opposite to me, and showed exactly what her mother had been twenty years before. Indeed, had Muriel not been the taller, and had not her shoulders been rather thin, she could well have passed for her mother's younger sister.

Muriel did not return my scrutiny, for she leaned unashamedly towards Edward Kent, who now sat stroking his little fat chin, while his manicured hand played with his glass of hock. I could hear his thin, piping voice, the conversation which secured him invitations to dinner.

" I really am, I really am," he protested. " You think I never do anything, Miss Lawton, because I never have anything to do. Now that's where you're wrong. It is the lazy people are the busy people because they are so unused to work that what they must do takes an awful long time."

" Paradoxes," said Muriel, raising a pretty, thin shoulder.

" That is to say, truths. Truth, you see, lives in a well, and you don't know that when you see the well. It's the same with paradox: you find truth in it, but you must haul her out."

" Mr. Kent," said Muriel, " you are tiring me out."

" You should take more exercise, then——"

" Oh, spare us, Mr. Kent," said Mrs. Lawton, suddenly forgetting me and the Riviera and leaning over towards the entertainer, " and tell us what happened at Caux."

For several minutes I was left out; while I ate the thin slices of saddle of mutton and found out I liked it with red currant jelly, I saw that Louisa Kent was flirting with Hugh. She was very pretty, I thought, with her dark hair, her rosy colour; she had her brother's little fat chin, but on her it was charming instead of being faintly ridiculous. She was talking quickly, in tones too low for me to understand what she said; perhaps she did not want to be overheard, though there was nothing in the placid smile which flickered about Hugh's beautiful lips to show that he cared. It was extraordinary, but evidently Muriel and Louisa were " making up " to the men, and these did not even swell as conquerors, they basked in the sunshine that was their due.

Indeed, no man seemed to think of the women, except Mr. Lawton, whom I could hear gently talking to Edith about Brussels, which he seemed to know well.

"Oh, you must ask Mr. Cadoresse," he suddenly said, with a laugh.

I turned in time to catch a faint smile and the quick, shy look of the girl.

"Yes?" I said. "Can I be of service to Mademoiselle?"

"Oh——" She paused, blushed. "It's only father. He says that it's not Bwar der lar Camber. He wants me to roll my r's like—like——"

"Like me," I said.

Edith blushed so hotly that her neck and shoulders grew pink, and I thought her pretty. Insignificant, of course, as blue eyes and fair hair make a girl, but pretty.

"Oh—I didn't mean—I didn't say that—I really didn't."

Her eyes were downcast and I wondered whether there were tears in them. I felt I had been clumsy, that I had trodden on a little flower.

"Cambrrr," I said, reassuringly.

She looked up at me, smiled, shook her head.

"Try," I suggested. "Cambrrr."

But she would not try. She sat smiling and blushing, nervously tapped on a fork with thin, white fingers that trembled.

"My little girl mustn't be shy," murmured Mr. Lawton. There was a new gentleness in the eyes that were rather like hers.

"I'm not shy, father," she murmured, but again blushed.

"No? Then will the little girl say Cambrrr to her father?"

They laughed together. Her father! Her grandfather rather. I looked across to Muriel, who was still wrapped up in Edward Kent. That was a girl! and suddenly I thought of Maud, her bold brown eyes. I wished she could see me then, " among the upper ten," as she would have said, and I felt a little disappointed because these people spoke slowly, in modulated voices. They knew gaiety, not ragging.

Mrs. Lawton again turned to me. Did I like London? Of course I had seen all the sights, the Tower? Not that she had ever been to the Tower, she owned. Did I like the English? I replied. I had plenty to say, but I could not talk of the things I cared for, the office, my schooling, my home, the Hoopers. Mrs. Lawton made no comments, and her questions were not indiscreet; she seemed to want to know only what I thought in general, not what I thought in particular. I wanted her to lay hands on my private life. I invited her to do so.

" I am quite happy in my rooms," I said, irrelevantly; " the people are very nice to me, and it is amusing because there are two young girls in the house."

" Oh, yes," said Mrs. Lawton, " and it's very handy for the Underground. Don't you think it's easy to get about in London? "

" Very easy," I said. " Yes, I like it very much; and the City too. I like the men I meet. There is one of the clerks, Mrs. Lawton, whose clothes are an education, they are so good, though he does buy them in the City; he——"

" Ah," said Mrs. Lawton, " the City is a wonderful place. Have you seen the Lord Mayor's coach? "

The conversation went on in that way, I struggling to figure my own life, Mrs. Lawton inertly bent on compelling me to sink it in the life of the crowd. I wanted her to tear at my personality—but that isn't done: she didn't do it. I was angry because I was baulked, I sulked, allowed Mrs. Lawton to say what she liked, interposing a minimum of "yeses" and "noes." She did not mind. She was there to talk to me from half-past seven to nine; if I was silent she would talk a great deal; if I had a great deal to say, she would gracefully listen; if I made unusual or improper remarks she would misunderstand them and suavely lead me back to the safeties of the Royal Family or the London police. While she talked I examined the furniture. The dining-room was what is called handsome, for there was a red paper over a white dado, a splendid mahogany sideboard; I could feel a thick Turkey carpet under my feet and see expensive-looking oils on the walls. But—the revelation came suddenly—it was the Hoopers' dining-room; the wallpaper was the same, except that it had probably cost four and sixpence a piece instead of two shillings, and the sideboard was the same. True, there were no cruets nor salad-dressing bottles on it, but there was the tantalus. And the oils! There were bad oils on the Hoopers' red walls! I seemed to understand the Lawtons, the Lawton breed, the "Terraces" and "Places" and "Gardens" and "Gates" which are full of Lawtons, Lawtons all alike, who buy the same things at different prices. As I looked at this furniture and those who sat among it I understood: they had tried to be like everybody else, and they had brought it off. That was why they were Good People.

"In the house I live in," I tactlessly said, "they have red paper in the dining-room."

"They say brown is coming in," replied Mrs. Lawton. "I have seen it up at Egerton Jones'. What do you think of our big shops?"

I told her vaguely, and as I did so, listened to the conversation of the others. Kent was telling the story I have since heard in many forms, of the judge who was rude to the counsel for the defence and at last pointed to his ear, remarking:

"It doesn't matter what you say, it goes in here and comes out on the other side."

" ' No doubt, my Lord,' " Kent narrated smoothly;
" ' there is nothing to stop it.' "

Half the circle began to laugh, and before the laughter
subsided Kent was talking mixed hockey; he did not spoil
his effect. I heard Muriel protest against a charge of
whacking the men's shins, Mr. Lawton gravely remon-
strate with Louisa, for whom the Steinway wasn't good
enough.

" Oh," she said, " I couldn't give a recital in that little
place. What's the use of having studied with Marsay if
I can't have the St. James's? "

I gathered that Louisa was a professional pianist, or
about to become one. As Mrs. Lawton had turned towards Kent, I addressed Edith.

" I see Miss Kent is musical," I said.

" Oh, yes, she's very clever," said Edith; " she's been
to Dresden and she's studied in Paris under Marsay. Now
she's going to give her first recital and I'm sure she'll be a
success, though she says nobody cares for the piano. She
looks so well, too, on the platform; don't you think she's
very pretty? "

" Very," I said. " And you, do you play the piano? "

" A little—oh, it's nothing."

Edith had blushed and stammered. Curious, she could
chatter of Louisa Kent without a trace of shyness, but a
single reference to her own affairs deprived her of all self-
possession. I went on talking to her, gently, as to a child,
and little by little she became able to speak to me, not
freely but adequately.

" I like it in Brussels," she confided. " I'm going
to stay at least two years, to be finished as they
say."

" Well, I hope they will not finish you completely, as
you are only just commenced—begun, I mean."

" Begun! " Muriel almost screamed across the table, and
then exploded into giggles. " What did I tell you about
the Ancient Briton, Edith? "

" Muriel, my dear," said Mrs. Lawton reproachfully, but she smiled.

Mr. Lawton laughed.

" Your laurel-wreath as a student of Gothic is on your head, Cadoresse."

" Mr. Kent," said Muriel, faintly; " never say fork again—say prong."

" I will say prong—I will say ' Je prong ' to please you."

I glared fiercely at the red paper, which was no redder than my ears. They were laughing at me, all of them, English pigs, because they couldn't speak their own language. I did not reply to Mrs. Lawton's gentle apologies and requests that I should not mind chaff. Chaff! they call insults chaff! Under that calm, that decorum, lies a desire to wound; hypocrites, they never lose their self-control save when the foreigner gives them an opening. I ate my ice angrily, barely replying when Mrs. Lawton asked me questions; Hugh had smiled, and Louisa had giggled when Mr. Lawton explained the joke.

" I think it's rather a shame," said Edith's gentle voice, but I did not warm to her. I hated them all.

I had barely regained my composure when Mrs. Lawton rose; there was a scuffle of chairs, a rustling of skirts as the conversation suddenly ebbed away. As I thrust my chair aside I had the mortification of seeing Kent dart past me and open the door, next to which he stood with bent head while the ladies filed out. I was gloomily conscious that I, who was nearest to the door, should have done this, but the realisation did not prey upon me, for I was too interested in Kent's sudden act of courtesy, following as it did upon his indifference to the women during dinner. But then door-opening is done.

We drew together at the table; we were already drinking port when the coffee came, and after the coffee we returned to port. The conversation was languid. Mr. Lawton asked me whether I was getting used to London; this question was beginning to be wearisome but I took it up.

"Yes," I said. "I don't feel a stranger. Everything is so easy here, for you don't have to know people long, and the fog is so amusing."

"Oh, I say, that's a bit thick," said Kent.

"Kent! Another one of those and I throw you out," said Hugh.

I went on, unaware of Kent's detestable pun. I said that London in the fog was romantic, that the buildings were lifted up in it until they looked like Laputa floating in the clouds.

"You're a poet," said Mr. Lawton. "This 'll never do in Fenchurch Street, Cadoresse; you'll be seeing romance in a bill of lading if you go on. Now a real Englishman like you ought to like nothing but hard fact, know facts, thousands of them——"

"Five thousand," I cried. And after I had laughed I told Mr. Lawton about Mr. Hooper and *Five Thousand Facts and Fancies*. He listened to me, faintly smiling, no doubt because I had laughed; he did not seem to think Hooper so very odd.

"Oh, well," he summed up; "you don't know whether his facts won't come in handy one day."

I suggested that Hooper would be better off reading the paper and acquiring political views. This did not displease Mr. Lawton, and soon he was talking suavely of the Conservative Government, to which he was opposed. At first he did not interest me much, and I listened with one ear to Kent and Hugh, who discussed with gravity the correct strapping of skis. What their difference of opinion was I do not know, but they seemed full of intensity.

"Of course, no one can tell how long this will go on," said Mr. Lawton. "A Government which comes in in the middle of a war may do anything it likes when the war's over . . ."

Hugh and Kent were still engrossed, disagreeing as to the respective merits of Norwegian and Swiss ski-running, but I did not hear the end of their debate, for Mr. Lawton had gripped my attention.

"This Education Bill, for instance. Well, I don't mind religious education, far from it; but I don't think it fair that the Nonconformists should share the cost of keeping up Church schools."

I asked for an explanation and received it. It was a clear, moderate exposition; without a gesture, without raising his voice, Mr. Lawton figured for me the dual system of English education, the Church schools and the Board schools, made me understand the grievance of the Dissenters.

"So you see, that is all the trouble. I think it wrong that people should pay to have taught a creed they do not practise. And I can say it, I think, as I am a Churchman myself."

"What!" I cried. I could hardly believe him! How could a man who professed a creed grant that other creeds had rights?

"Yes," said Mr. Lawton. "I am a Churchman, and I am ready to pay for Church teaching, but I cannot see that Nonconformists should pay for it too. They are free to believe what they choose."

"Should not your religion dominate? Why don't you burn them?"

"We did, once upon a time," said Mr. Lawton gently, "but we're wiser now. And we never burned them enthusiastically. After all, a man may believe what he chooses."

"I can hardly understand it."

"You couldn't, you're French. I suppose you're a Roman Catholic and——"

"I'm an atheist," I said, roughly.

"Oh . . . of course, you're free to believe what you choose (the fetish phrase!). There are lots of agnostics in this country."

True, in moderate England the atheists are all agnostics.

Mr. Lawton continued mildly to dilate on religious freedom. I was amazed; he seemed so ready to allow people to save their own souls; he seemed so devoid of rancour. He was certain of nothing except that men should be free. I did not, before I met him, understand that for the English there were several ways of reaching heaven. And he could discuss politics without excitement; he did not interrupt me when I opposed him, he did not anticipate my questions, or shout, or call anybody a traitor or a hireling. Hugh and Edward Kent heard us, no doubt, but did not seem to want to thrust their views upon us; they talked indolently now of the hotels of Vermala and Caux.

" Have some more port, Cadoresse," said Mr. Lawton. I accepted, poured out another glassful, then returned the decanter to him.

" No, no—not that way—give it to me, Cadoresse."

There was a shout. The three men had burst into animated protests; they were almost excited. I looked at them, dumfounded, the decanter in my hand. Hugh had risen to his feet, while Kent, with outstretched hand, seemed taut with excitement. And there was a flush on Mr. Lawton's face.

" Not that way, not that way," he said in a loud voice.

But what had I done, what had I done? All three explained together, interrupted one another, offered explanations, seemed ready to consult history books to seek out the origin of the tradition.

" The way of the sun, the way of the sun," said Mr. Lawton; " give it to Kent."

As we rose to go to the drawing-room I was still trying to understand: politics, religion, these things could be viewed temperately, but there might be a riot if the port went from right to left instead of left to right. (I am not yet quite sure which way it does go.) And these are the sons of John Hampden!

We lingered in the hall, looked at the hunting pictures. Kent asked Mr. Lawton where he had picked them up, while Hugh offered to show him the two new ones he had temporarily hung in the morning-room. I was impatient, for I wanted to join the ladies. But we lingered again on the stairs, and Hugh resumed his argument with Kent as to the Swiss hotels. At last we sauntered into the drawing-room, as if we were indifferent to the women. The three men certainly seemed careless; they smiled but faintly as each one moved towards an empty seat, idly sat down; it was cruelly significant that Muriel and Louisa Kent should both have in their eyes a gleam of interest for Kent and Hugh who so languidly came to them. And it was, perhaps, their languor partnered me for a while with Muriel, while Louisa succeeded in capturing Hugh. Mr. Lawton had deliberately chosen Edith, and soon I could hear Mrs. Lawton laugh at Kent's jokes? Were they jokes? or was it some artificial quality? I exclaimed as I sat down, for the seat was very low.

" Did I leave a needle there? " Muriel asked.

" Oh, no, but this chair is so low. But it's quite comfortable, very soft."

" Don't you have soft chairs in France? "

" No, hardly ever. Fine straight chairs—Louis XV, Louis XVI, Empire—you know what I mean."

" I don't," said Muriel. " I'm awfully ignorant." She laughed again, and I had to admire her dark hair, her white skin, her extraordinary triangular eyes. " Tell me what a French drawing-room is like."

I described our graveyard, Empire sideboard, garnet footstools and all.

" It doesn't sound comfortable," said Muriel. " Don't you like this better? " She nodded towards the chintz-covered settee, now occupied by Kent and Mrs. Lawton. I examined the detail of the room and found it singular. With the exception of three mahogany chairs, Chippendale I believe, there was not a piece of furniture into which one could not sink. The settee looked like a swollen bed covered with pink-flowered chintz; Mr. Lawton half disappeared in a similarly covered grandfather, while the others lounged on padded tapestry. Under my feet I could feel a thick carpet; I could guess that the green velvet curtains were very soft. But I liked the room, the white walls, the water colours, the small gilt mirror over the mantelpiece, the flowered cushions. I liked it and yet felt shy of it.

" Yes," I said, " much better, but . . ."

" But? "

" But . . . a drawing-room, you know . . ."

" Oh, it's hardly a drawing-room; we sit in it half the day."

" Well, that's it," I blurted out; " it doesn't feel official. Now if you had white and gold walls . . ."

" And kept it neat? " said Muriel, and smiled rather wickedly.

I found my eyes straying to a little stool on which was a piece of unfinished fancy work, to the brass fender against which the evening papers had fallen in a pink and green heap. Muriel followed the direction of my looks, threw herself back in her chair; her slim white shoulders shook as she laughed.

" Mother," she said in a loud voice. " Mr. Cadoresse says we're untidy. He says we leave the papers about and spill cigarette ash on the floor; he says——"

" I did not," I cried in much distress. " I assure you, Mrs. Lawton."

" I'm sure you didn't," Mr. Lawton interposed. " I never believe Muriel, and no more will you if you're wise."

I recovered my ground, apologised for nothing, quite honestly reviled the French gilt chairs, our stiffness and stuffiness. I warmed, I converted myself, I felt almost sure that a drawing-room need not be a holy. I tried not to be angry with Muriel, to remember that the English chaff, and succeeded, for she was charming now, though her eyes often roved towards Kent.

" I am bored with the theatre," said Kent; " it's so

uniform. If only the frivolous plays were deep and the serious plays were skittish I'd go and see one every night."

" Don't you think Mr. Kent very clever? " said Muriel.

" Very amusing," I said, observing that this was the first personality I had heard that evening, and wondering what it implied. " What does he do? "

" He's a barrister. It's a pity. I'm sure he would have preferred a fellowship at Cambridge."

I obtained a vague idea of the meaning of " fellow," gathered that Kent's capacities were mainly academic. It was intolerable that this pretty girl should praise another man to me. So I spoke of my own career, of my courses in economics, political finance, international law.

" How very clever of you," said Muriel, respectfully.

" You must have been a swat," said Hugh.

" A swat? "

" A mugger. A hard worker."

" I suppose so. I was seventh of my year." I pretended to be modest, but I happened to know this formula; I was very proud of the achievement.

" Good for you," said Kent; " when I was at Harrow I only wanted to be a blood."

" Out of two hundred and eighty-five," I added, without even feigned modesty.

There was a short pause during which everybody seemed to be looking at me. Then Hugh laughed a little shrilly.

" Lord! I was sent down."

" Hugh! How can you? "

There was a chorus of protests through which I gathered that Hugh had not been sent down, that he had come down with an adequate degree. I wondered why he should belittle himself. I did not do so. While Muriel continued to talk, of a play I think, a very distant memory came to me, a memory of a handsome middle-aged man who stood in a Bordeaux drawing-room in front of a small black-clad boy, and told him that in England people didn't know anything. He, too, had belittled himself, and I threw side-glances at Mr. Lawton, the open-minded advocate of popular rights, wondered why he, too, hid his merits.

Muriel refused a cigarette from Kent, with an ostentatious " Not in public."

" Do you smoke in private? " I asked.

" Rather. Then father hasn't got to know."

" But he does know? "

" Oh, of course, but he's not supposed to."

To know and not to know. Well, I supposed it made life easier. Muriel vowed it did, pleaded for peace against clarity. I was ready enough to be convinced.

" And, of course, I always have my whisky and soda in bed."

I looked at her, shocked; I could not believe that she was serious, that her lovely lips were soiled with spirits and tobacco: but the inner Frenchman in me spoke:

" Yes, I know, English ladies all drink."

It was too late to call it back. My remark was retailed all round, and at intervals I was made the butt of the evening, asked if I drank to my *fiancée* only with mine eyes, begged by Muriel to drain a bumper of wassail with her in the scullery, told by Mrs. Lawton that she adored methylated spirits.

I did not suffer as much as usual. I was getting hardened, I was beginning to understand the English; I was becoming ready to take as chaff a black eye or anything they fancied.

Muriel sat down at the piano, played some Henry VIII dances, while Mrs. Lawton told me what plays I ought to see. Kent affected disdain of the music, assured me that " *blasé* men scored, for they expected so little that everything amused them." I talked to Hugh, exclusively of myself and uninterrupted. It was getting late when, at last, Edith was pushed to the piano by her father, made in my honour to sing a French song.

It was the pretty little lay of a conscript's bride, tripping, sentimental, where *village* rhymed with *courage, amour*

with *retour*. She was like a shepherdess of Dresden china.
Her blue eyes were misty and as she sang her neck swelled
towards me, a little as that of a slow-moving swan. I
looked at Muriel, at her slim shoulders, her strange eyes.

II

I walked home slowly along Oxford Terrace towards
Edgware Road. The dull light of the gas lamps was
reflected in the black varnish of the wet pavement. As
I walked, undisturbed, save when a cab splashed through
the puddles, I tried in vain to relate these people to one
another, to analyse them and of their elements to make
a whole. They were all different, as half a dozen French
people would have been different, and yet had that something common for which the French group would have
had a national equivalent; Kent's bland brilliance, Hugh's
calm, the frankness and liberalism of Lawton . . . dis-
cords, and yet over all, a concordance of behaviour, manners, therefore morals. The men were linked to the
women, to the garrulous and discreet Mrs. Lawton, to shy
Edith, to gay, audacious Muriel.

I thought most of the things I could not see, of their
reticences. Yes, that was the link: they all held back.

At the corner of a side street I stopped to let a four-
wheeler pass. The old driver, who looked in the night
like a bundle of rugs, pulled up in front of me.

" Got a light, mister? "

I handed him my matchbox, and as he lit his pipe,
observed:

" It has been raining, has it not? "

" Mum," he grumbled, " yes. Not much in it for me.
Ain't a night for old ladies."

I made a polite sound. The old cabman puffed at his
pipe, declared that times weren't what they had been,
wondered what they would be soon.

" I suppose you're going home," I said, as he did not whip up."

" Shouldn't be hanging about if I wasn't. Been out since ten this morning."

He paused. Then: " Well, mustn't keep the missus waiting, or she'll have the poker ready for me." He clucked, shook the reins, and as the old horse leisurely strained at the harness, added humorously, " No, it wouldn't do; mustn't let the turtle soup get cold."

He, too, was an Englishman. But was he? And as I thought of the old cabman I felt less certain of his nationality. Heat and cold, money, food, a wife, those were his thoughts; was there anything to show that his moral outlook, his standard of art, his hopes for a future of ease and peace, differed from those of any cabman who at that time sat on his box in Bordeaux, Naples or Berlin? Those classes are all alike, can know nothing but the primitive: they have no time; they must eat, love, die, and that is a big business. Some may be gay and others dour, some bait the bull in the plaza and others back cocks for a wager, but the varnish upon their souls is very thin. And those others, the intellectuals, the artists, they are linked by the fineness of mental things as the lower folk are linked by the material; it is a Swinburne for a Baudelaire, a Spinoza for a Descartes, a Dostoievsky for a Stendhal. They, too, are alike, think alike.

Between the highest and the lowest lies the nation. The nation is made up of those who have leisure and money enough to think not too much of material things, and yet no spirit to transcend these. The nation lies between the plebeian and the intellectual patrician. As I walked away towards the Edgware Road, where the poor were making merry in as cheap and rough a way as they do in Belleville, I knew that behind me, in Lancaster Gate and its vassal streets, was the heart of England, beating very regularly, very slowly and for all time.

III

In the months that followed I found that the Lawtons
bred in Maud a feeling of disquiet. She took in them an
interest which she did not share with the other inhabitants
of the house who, I soon discovered, viewed my new intimacy with satisfaction. One evening Mrs. Hooper stood
at the foot of the stairs, watching me while I teased my
tie into a proper set in front of the hallstand mirror.

" You won't make too much noise when you come in,
will you? " she said, confidentially, for familiarity had
grown a little between us.

" No," I promised; " besides, I shall not be late. I'm
going to Mrs. Lawton's."

" Ah! " Mrs. Hooper paused; curbed by her manners,
she repressed a question and released a comment. " I like
to see a gentleman in evening clothes, Mr. Cadoresse."

" Yes," I said; " besides, one has to wear them."

" Of course, of course, when there's company. We're
quite homely here, but it's different at Mr. Lawton's."

I pondered for a moment on the curious sex-difference
which made me think of Lancaster Gate as " Mrs.
Lawton's," while Mrs. Hooper saw it as " Mr. Lawton's ";
then:

" They always dress, I think, for I've been there when
they were alone."

" Quite right too. So shall we . . . when our ship
comes home."

She smiled rather sadly and I thought of her and her
snobbish innocence, of the gradations, the people who
didn't wash before food, those who washed, those who
" changed," the great who " dressed." The Royal Family
on the top—not that it had anything to do with clothes,
but whatever it was Mrs. Hooper classified, the Royal
Family somehow always came to the top.

" I used to think I'd like it too, when I first married,"

she said, reflectively; "but Mr. Hooper thought in our position it wouldn't look well. Of course," she hurriedly remarked, "it's different for young gentlemen."

She threw me a glance of approval, rather a fond glance, which made me wonder whether Mrs. Hooper regretted that she had no son, whether she would have exchanged Lulu for me; yet she would not have parted with Maud, the artist, the infant prodigy. Maud was the centre of the house.

I had begun to understand Maud, her emptiness and the nature of her charm; very reluctantly I was coming to see that she would resist me to the end, not because she had anything to protect, but because she had nothing to give. Our conversations were seldom of love, infallible sign that there was no love; we spoke (I by compulsion) of the new musical comedy, of the new star on the halls, of record railway runs, the cost of London buildings. We also spoke a good deal of the Lawtons, or rather Maud questioned me as to their habits. She had none of the reserve I chose to think English.

"I 'spect they're pretty oofy? Does she have a carriage? No footman? Well, I don't think much of that, having to get out and ring the bell herself. How much do you think they've got a year?"

"I don't know."

"What's the good of your being in the business if you don't know? Ten thousand?"

"I shouldn't think so much."

"Five, then?"

"I don't know."

"Well, there's not much in it unless it's five thousand. What's the rent of the house?"

We were walking in the Park that Saturday afternoon, and as I had just arrived from the City it was still before two. Maud, intent on the Lawton rental, insisted on calling on a house agent and pretending to want a house in Lancaster Gate. He looked at us with suspicion, as we did

not seem the sort of young couple likely to set up there,
but opened his book, being too old in his trade to feel
things keenly.

" I can offer 99A. Two hundred and fifty a year," he
said, gloomily.

Maud had the audacity to say that was just a little
too much. We left with an order to view a mere hundred
and forty pounder in Connaught Square. We said we
would let him know. The estate agent smiled cheerlessly
and did not open the door for us; he knew life.

The episode was vulgar, and a bitterness crept into my
reward, which consisted in viewing the house in Connaught Square; Maud viewed it magnificently.

" Why is there no electric light? " she asked fiercely of
the haggard caretaker.

" I couldn't say, Miss. P'raps Marstons——"

" Pooh! Marstons don't know anything. And that
panel's cracked."

Maud examined the whole house, scowling at the caretaker, and, behind her back, grinning at me. At last I
entered into the joke. By Maud's instruction I loudly
addressed her as Lady Grace. The caretaker collapsed
completely; her earlier remarks were replaced by half
inaudible " Yes, your Ladyships " and " No, your Ladyships."

" There aren't enough cupboards," said Maud; then,
angrily: " Where do you suppose the second housemaid
will keep the brooms? "

The caretaker's attitude intimated that she didn't know
what a second housemaid was. Maud pranced and fumed,
asked me to remember Ascot, Hurlingham and (a slip)
the Tivoli; she abused the bedrooms, swore her maid
wouldn't stand the second floor back, declared that her
" husband " must have a bath fitted in his dressing-room.
While the caretaker shuffled to the basement to fetch a
candle, so that Maud could inspect the inside of a hanging
cupboard, we both laughed, and I loved her for her gay

insolence, her cheek, and I kissed her, still laughing, while the old woman slowly climbed the stairs.

But not all our talks were enlivened by such pranks. Often Maud commented bitterly on Lawtoniana.

" They're only a set of prigs. There they are, all over starch and you'd think the butter wouldn't melt, talking about Eton and the different kinds of port, and thinking all the time of us, Mother Tinman's little girls who'll be at the Gaiety in another two years. I know the sort."

Not far wrong as an impression. But could it be that the Hugh Lawtons of London nursed far-back thoughts of the Mauds? "

" See 'em hanging about when we come out," Maud summed up. " But I'm not taking any. No fear."

For Maud the " toffs " were a race apart, whom she hated and admired because she knew that, in this land of caste, she would not be accepted of them save by chance of marriage. Though English, she understood them little better than I did, for she knew nothing but their external habits, the addresses of their tailors, the restaurants and clubs they frequented, the location of their winter and summer pleasures. She admired their good looks and perfect clothes, the easy, cold manners which she angrily affected to despise.

" I'll be the Honourable Mrs. before I've done," she confided to me one day; " anybody could do it now that Betty Bell has got the old earl."

Then she would recite the list of the latest prizes captured by the privateers of the stage, and towards the stage her talk would drift. Hers was a double instinct: she wanted social position because she would like to have it to humiliate her old associates, to rise, and she probably nursed a dim equivalent of *lex talionis*. To marry a " toff " would be social revenge. When she said, " Ain't I good enough? " she spoke with the voice of all the girls of her class whom the aristocrat has preyed on, and almost said, " An eye for an eye, a tooth for a tooth." I could not

protest, for I could not offer marriage; I could only say:
"But, darling, I love you," and she, "You *can* tell the
tale, Froggy." She was sure that the Lawton girls made
up their faces, and she was darkly jealous of the admiration she had convicted me of feeling for Muriel and her
triangular eyes.

"You look out," she said; "triangular you call it, as
if a girl ever did have an eye like that. Shape of a danger
signal, anyhow, so you look out."

Then she would scoff at my sincere protests that she
was much prettier, repel my advances, later woo me
back and, when successful, repulse me again. She feared
Muriel, for she had to confess she "sounded all right,"
but laid no stress on Edith. She knew the sort: been sent
to the cleaners too often, like Lulu, and got all the colour
washed out.

Maud annoyed me when she attacked the Lawton girls.
I was not in love with either, but they were apart from
Maud as from me, and when she sneered at their "quite
the lady" manners I felt like a devout Catholic who
sees an irreverent tourist try to enter a mosque with his
boots on.

IV

Maud had matter for her questions. As the months
passed and the English summer shyly sidled into the country, I went more often to the Lawtons, on Sunday afternoons, on Mrs. Lawton's at-home day, not then abolished
by fashion, a little to the houses of their friends. For I
was still a curiosity and, as such, well received.

"One never knows what you'll say next," said Mrs.
Raleigh, the comfortable wife of Colonel Raleigh. "When
you begin to talk, Mr. Cadoresse, I'm always afraid that
it's going to be quite dreadful."

"Do you mind it's being dreadful?" I asked, auda-
ciously, for I resisted Mrs. Raleigh no more than I resisted

any other woman. I must, loving them all, suggest to all
women that I love them. Audacity is the path to love."

"Well . . . no," said Mrs. Raleigh, "perhaps I don't.
It's refreshing to hear you talk of the latest society
divorce as if it were an everyday sort of affair, but you
oughtn't to."

"Why?"

"Oh, how can I tell you . . . we don't do it. Of
course, we know these things happen, but——"

"But you think they only happen in the papers?"

"You're too sharp for me, Mr. Cadoresse," said Mrs.
Raleigh, with a mock sigh. She leaned back in her chair,
smiling at me with her very good teeth; she was forty-five,
but her wavy brown hair, her fine skin and bright blue
eyes were still attractive. If only she had worn proper
stays! But those Englishwomen are always unconsciously
insuring against temptation.

"Still," she added, "you oughtn't to talk like that. It's
silly of you to say we think those things only happen in
the papers. We know all about them, but we don't think
it necessary to discuss them; there are lots of things we
don't discuss——"

"For instance?"

"If you think you're going to entrap me into discussing
things with you by telling you which are the ones I won't
discuss, you're wrong, Mr. Cadoresse; I'm not to be caught
like that. No, there just are things we don't discuss publicly—we don't see why we should; they're quite unnecessary. Why should we trouble about the unpleasant things?
They do none of us any good and they may do harm, while
there are so many pleasant ones."

My conversations with Mrs. Raleigh generally ended in
this way. She was not narrow, she was almost racy
sometimes, but there were things she liked to have illusions
about. This led me to talk seriously to her, which generally
made her laugh and say, "Oh, of course, you're a Frenchman, you can't understand." That phrase always exas-

perated me. I didn't want to be a Frenchman, so I tried
to understand; it was not easy, even with faith to help me.
On those occasions I generally lost my head and shouted.
If Colonel Raleigh and Gladys were present I made myself
rather ridiculous, for my careful pronunciation failed me.
On one occasion Colonel Raleigh tactfully intervened and
tried to change the subject by making me talk of the army;
he asked me whether I still had friends there, and in my
excitement I managed to tell him that I knew "a buggler
at Tours, in a regiment of dragons."

Colonel Raleigh left the room, declaring that if he stayed
his heart would give way, while Mrs. Raleigh and Gladys
apologised. But I was quite unnerved, and that was the
day I referred to the "tablecarpet." They did not chaff
me mercilessly, and indeed Gladys, whose precise, pale face
and quiet manner had designed her for a schoolmistress,
promised to drill me in the mysteries of the words which
end in "ough." I think they liked my absurdity, the
occasional incongruity of my frock-coats and brown boots,
my unexpected accents and the general strangeness of my
point of view. And yet I did not want to be strange;
I had done everything I could to be an Englishman; I
knew London well, had even explored several suburbs; I
had learned to like English beer, to open the door for a
lady, to say that Fiona (the Lawtons' Scotch terrier)
ought to be shown at Cruft's. I had even begged a
morning to see the Boat Race, which was very dull,
and had taken part in Boat Race Night, which was very
mild.

I was an oddity, outside them. "You are not one of
us," said every lineament of Colonel Raleigh. I admired
the old soldier, knew the tale of the fort he had held near
Chitral, knew that he could not cheat at cards, or give
a woman away, or wear the wrong hat: but I could not
connect him with my own old colonel, who was fat, took
snuff, and whose amorous adventures were the talk of our
regiment. Colonel Raleigh was not very human, or rather

he was no longer human. He was an officer and a gentleman.

There were others, too: Bessie Surtees, dark and madonna-like, except when she was in Switzerland and purposely fell into the snow when a curate or a schoolmaster was near enough to pick her up. And Dicky Bell, tall, upright, bird-like, who was ashamed of his grammar school, and Archie Neville, who dressed on nothing a year. They whirled about me, all of them, amiable, dignified, and well-washed, asking me general questions about French customs and tolerating the answers, revealing themselves but slowly and reluctantly. Chaos still reigned in my mind.

It was many months before I knew that Bessie Surtees was trying to make me propose to her because this was one of her habits, and that she had a brother in the army for whose sake her father had mortgaged his life insurance. They refused themselves, and even Dicky Bell, who talked, gave me little more than a hint of severely regulated affairs of the heart. They wanted to talk of theatres, games, politics (a little), France, but not of themselves and me.

And yet I loved them, because, in their own word, they were " decent." I might inwardly rage and long to ask questions, though I knew they would evade them, but I knew that Bessie Surtees never told a lie, while Dicky Bell spent half his evenings drilling boys at a settlement for the fun of the thing. And Archie Neville, who was not sure that twenty-five francs went to the pound, was poor because he had shouldered a dead father's debts. Simple and simply fine, they were hard to themselves, these Romans.

These people made me think of their own houses, houses of the Queen's Gate type. No man can live in those houses unless he has five thousand a year, and yet no man gilds his door, which he could well afford to do. They take it coolly, all of them, and never talk about it. That sort of thing gives one the measure of the English quality.

V

Into the midst of England fell, every week, a letter
from my mother, a letter she wrote every Friday and will
write every Friday until one of us dies. It was written
in the fine sloping hand the French call English and the
English Italian, with violet ink on cheap white paper. She
always filled four pages, no more, no less, as if she kept
on those shelves which I like to put up in her brain, a
diary marked " News for Lucien," and every week took
out just enough notes to make up my ration. Her letters
followed a settled plan: 1. Hopes that my health was
good. 2. Her health and Jeanne's. 3. Hopes that I was
doing well in business, comments and warnings (against
Socialism, answering back and loud clothes). 4. Miscellaneous. On New Year's Day and my Saint's day the
four sections were reduced owing to pressure on space,
for congratulations were included. At Easter I received
a flaming heart, or chromolithographed angels. On the
anniversary of my father's death came the yearly reference
to him, a hope that all was well with his soul, and this
formula: " I shall go and lay flowers upon his grave
to-morrow. As this is the month of May, the flowers are
beautiful."

Dear mother, I know you bargain with the flower seller
for those flowers, try to make her abate her price by
telling her that they are for the dead; you loved my father
economically, but you loved him dutifully, for he was your
husband and could not do quite wrong, as you love me
cautiously, for I am your son and cannot do quite right.
Your letters are written in another planet, where people
do extraordinary things, where Jeanne goes up for her
Brevet Élémentaire, where the vine has bad years and
M. de Pouvonac stands as a Catholic Republican for the
Bordeaux Town Council. In those days you were incredibly
remote by the side of this English knowledge I had so

greedily been sucking in; I began to see you and the
things that surrounded you as toys with which little foreign
children played. For the English held me by maintaining
me in the middle of their whirlpool. Their faces flash
past me as I think of them, and I cannot remember where
I saw them, these people; some of them are dead, some
gone, some merely older and friendly; one of them will
endure for ever, and for ever beautiful and young. Among
them is even the black face of a dog. It is the face of
Fiona, the Aberdeen, whom I saw for the first time as she
sat on the mat outside the dining-room door when I entered
the house of the Lawtons. As I took off my coat she
surveyed me with unemotional calm, as befitted her staid
portliness; she winked round brown eyes at me from under
her shaggy eyebrows; she did not growl, or stand up; she
moved so little as she watched me that the dull sheen
on her coat seemed fixed. Fiona was Scotch, therefore
more closely allied to the true English than the soft people
of the South. She seldom hurried; when she wanted a
door opened she scratched it with indomitable obstinacy;
if she required sugar she sat up and monotonously waved
her front paws. She never barked except for a purpose.
She never loved anybody nor hated anybody, but she
could show her liking by a small wriggle of her twisted
tail. Amiable, self-centred, resolute, limited, brave enough
to fight three cats together, Fiona was an English dog.
Other scenes and people too, dinner-parties, Sunday
afternoon calls, Saturdays at Ranelagh, the River, all
splotched with white, and pink, and blue, the Strangers'
Gallery, and restaurants and English taverns, the horse
guards, the meet of the Four-In-Hand Club, the inside of
the Stock Exchange (a dangerous expedition), the ritual
fish lunch at Simpson's—these things rise up and all blur
together into chaotic early impressions of slow, steady men,
youths with all the purpose of their lives in their strong
arms and legs, and girls with lily-petal skins. I love them;
I like to think of them because they can live without care

for age or fate, because for them life is so like cricket that an ugly deed is "not cricket." Cricket! I was bent on being English and mastered the rules of the game; I grew so enthusiastic that I ran out of the office on certain afternoons to buy a paper and see what was the state of the score at Lord's. I watched football matches, sagely preferred Rugby to Association (at the beginning; later I thought more of soccer than rugger). I found with melancholy that I was too old to take up the game, was by Muriel tactfully directed towards tennis.

One tennis-party, a very early one, I remember best. The Lawtons and the Raleighs belonged to a club near Hounslow, where they played rather ostentatiously on Sundays. They rejoiced in the sin until a little guilt crept into their pleasure. Admitted as a guest, I figure myself, looking very dark in my white garments, collarless, unfortunately sashed in blue silk. Partnered by Muriel, I played Hugh and Gladys Raleigh, rather badly. I think Hugh and I were a study in contrasts, for he seemed slow, almost lazy, struck swift and very low balls towards the bottom of the court, while I leapt into the air, struck wildly and savagely, aiming straight at Hugh's feet or at Gladys's left. I am sure I would have fouled if one could foul at tennis, for I wanted to win, to extract admiration from the little crowd, Colonel and Mrs. Raleigh, Edith, Mrs. Lawton, who seemed amused by the performance. With them was a girl I have never seen again, a Miss Fox-Kerr.

But the game was going against us. Having led off by winning my service and Gladys's we began to lose ground, were beaten four times in succession. Muriel ran in vain, begging me at times not to hit *all* the balls into the neighbours' court. I recovered a little, made a few lucky shots, looking every time towards the spectators to see whether I was watched. I felt angry because the relaxed look on Miss Fox-Kerr's long face told me that her attention was fleeting. But she was watching me all the same, for she smiled, said something to Edith which made her giggle.

My wounded pride translated itself into wilder hitting, while Hugh's long arm worked like a machine. At last came the crucial ball of the last game, a swift return from Hugh. . . . I heard a cry of " Back! " from Muriel. . . . I struck, heard the sharp " splack " of the ball against the net ribbon. I also heard a contemptuous " Pff " come from Miss Fox-Kerr, saw her lips purse up. I said nothing in reply to the cry of " Game and," for my soul was full of hatred, I could not trust myself to speak in presence of this girl. I have learned to be a sportsman now, to take my beatings and my chaff, to win without strutting, but I think I hate her still, this dim girl, before whom I was a fool, who knew I was a fool and did not conceal it. She is in my little museum, by the side of Chaverac who saw me exposed as a coward.

And all goes fleeting; Edith, who in those days appeared only three or four times a year when the Brussels finishing school made holiday; Muriel, with whom I had a timid flirtation, who good-humouredly accepted innocent kisses when Edward Kent's superior fascination palled on her. Maud even, that continual irritant, is less vivid, for her attractiveness wore a little thin as I grew accustomed to the exasperation her presence and her inaccessibility provoked in me. Besides, a new feeling was born in me, a curious feeling towards women which had no roots in my Latin temperament. Very slowly I had ceased to look upon women as toys; England was beginning my sentimental education. I had been prepared for my evolution by Barker's lecture on good women and bad, by his analogous but less strict division of men into good and bad. He had not shaken me at the moment, but he had sown in my mind the seed of a new flower called purity, which blooms more readily under the pale English sky than in our own fierce sun. He did not influence my conduct, but he made it possible for my conduct to change; I was ready to modify my standards, then, when Hugh suddenly opened to me.

We sometimes, in search of exercise, walked westwards from Fenchurch Street to Marble Arch, an incongruous and not unfriendly couple. I liked Hugh, and though we never had much to say to each other when we had exhausted skysigns, the play, and the contents of the evening paper, it pleased me to walk with this handsome figure. One evening, as we jostled through the press in Cheapside, I broke off in a sentence to exchange smiles with a young girl as she passed us; I even turned to look back at her: it was harmless, even from the English point of view, for all I wanted was to gratify my own vanity, to see whether she, too, looked back. But, after this, I had for some minutes the conversation to myself; Hugh did not say a word until we reached Holborn, when he suddenly interrupted my comments on *The Chinese Honeymoon*.

" Look here, Cadoresse," he said, haltingly; " you know, you oughtn't to do that."

" Do what? "

" Look at girls in the street. I wish you wouldn't."

I threw him a quick glance. The admonition had displeased me, but the second sentence had surprised and moved me a little, for Hugh had never before connected himself with me, and now he was trying to express personal interest, to drag himself out of his unemotional Englishness.

" Why? " I asked, gently.

" It's not done. But it's not that only," he added, hurriedly, as if dimly aware that this reason was not enough; " it's not what a decent sort of chap does. You see, that kind of thing's rather cheap; if you get snubbed you feel very small, and if you don't, well, you ought to."

" But how is one to know people one wants to if one can't get introduced? "

" Oh, you know I don't mean that," said Hugh, rather acidly. " Those aren't the people you might get introduced to; I don't set up for a saint, but a man's got to keep away as much as he can from that sort of thing. He wants to forget all about it, keep his head clear for the things that matter. He can't be big unless he's straight."

"Galahad," I said, ironically.

"Who's Galahad?"

"A man in a book." Hugh was Galahad *sans le savoir*, then. "Never mind, go on."

"Oh, I'm not going in for pi-jaw, but believe me, Cadoresse, I'm right and you're wrong, even if you are cleverer than me."

I protested, though I did think myself cleverer than this fine fellow, whose clear blue eyes seldom held the animation of an idea. But he did not pursue this side issue, for he apparently knew that he was not very clever and accepted the fact without demur, while he was bent on reforming me.

"That sort of thing," he began again after some minutes of silence, during which I waited anxiously for what he would say; "it's all right for . . . well, all sorts of people . . . the fellows at the office. . . . They do that sort of thing on the pier at Hastings . . . by the bandstand, all that. But somehow a fellow like you can't. Of course, I know you're French and it makes a difference, but you're in England and you've got to choose . . ."

We walked along Oxford Street and I said very little while he floundered, trying to say what he thought, drawing back because he was afraid of preaching, and sometimes quite unable to express himself because he so seldom did express an idea. But his lecture came down to

THE CREED OF A PUBLIC SCHOOL BOY

"I believe in the gentlemen of England. I believe that I must shave every morning and every morning take a bath, have my clothes made to order, in such wise that no man shall look at them twice. I believe in the Church, the Army, the Navy, the Law, and faithfully hold it to be my duty to maintain myself in my caste if Fate has called me to a walk in life other than these. I believe that I must have a decent club. I believe that I must not drink to excess, nor be a teetotaller. I believe in my father's politics. I believe that I must not tell lies, nor cheat at cards, nor apply the letter of the law in games. I believe that I must perjure myself to save a woman's reputation, even if she has none, respect all women, except those who are not respect-able, for they are outlawed; I believe that I must hold my passions in check, feel shame when they master me and yield only in secret, because I am a gentleman of England. And, above all, that which I believe I must never tell."

It moved me very much to hear Hugh telling, violating for my sake the canons of his reserve, compelling himself to interfere, because it was "the straight thing," "the handsome thing." When he had done I was silent for a long time, so long that we did not exchange a word until we reached Marble Arch, where our roads diverged. Then Hugh suddenly spoke again:

"You know . . . I don't want you to think . . . well, I say all that sort of thing, and you needn't believe it if you don't want to . . . perhaps I'm wrong. I can't be sure of being right, only I've always taken all that for granted . . . so I don't want you to feel . . . hurt . . . or anything . . ."

I shook hands with him, hard.

"That's all right, Lawton; I understand. It's very good of you; I feel . . ."

"Good-night, good-night," he said, hurriedly, and walked away from me.

He could not bear my thanks, for they made him see that he had "given himself away"; he disliked the idea of preaching, disliked the half-apology his heart had dic-tated, disliked my quick, over-emotional response. He

walked away, very fast, as if he were escaping from some
menace. Perhaps he was afraid that I was going to kiss
him outside the Tube Station. Unaccountably, much of his
spirit entered into me; the samurai began in my heart to
struggle with the voluptuary; I saw more grace, less seduction, I saw grounds for respect, and self-respect, decencies,
knightlinesses, all kinds of lofty but appealing fetishes.
The samurai did not triumph, and has not yet triumphed,
perhaps, but he fought hard for the dignity of my soul;
he was often beaten, on those nights when I paced my
little room, avoiding the sickening sight of " In the Garden
of Eden " and " The Jubilee Procession," on others when
a sudden gentleness came over Maud and she was all allure.

But I tried, for you can be a Frenchman and just be
a Frenchman, a German, and that is enough; but what's
the good of being an Englishman unless you can be an
English gentleman too?

PART II

CHAPTER I

EDITH LAWTON

I

SUDDENLY I became aware of Edith. I had been in England just two years. Across the dissolving view of my impressions she had flitted from time to time, a fair, gracious little figure. Flitted! Hardly; while bolder actors held the stage she had stood in the wings, watching the play, shyly peeping from behind the scenery, showing in the shadow her pale golden head, her tender blue eyes. And if ever I looked at the figure it blushed, soon withdrew, as a dryad might shrink away from the gaze of a satyr.

I had seen her only during the short holidays of the Belgian school, at that first dinner, then again at the tennis party, some afternoons at her mother's house, not ten times in all. She had never mattered; she had been agreeable, like the white walls and the flowered cushions of the drawing-room; she had talked to me a little more readily after the tennis-party, for she had resented the contemptuous " Pff " with which Miss Fox-Kerr branded me. I knew this, for we had exchanged a few words later in the afternoon.

" I'm sorry I play badly," I said, gloomily watching Miss Fox-Kerr's overhand serve. I sat, mortified and hunched-up in my blazer, the colours of which I was not entitled to use.

" You don't play badly," said Edith; " you only want practice."

" No doubt," I replied. I was curt, for that was not the remark I wanted.

"You play quite as well as Miss Fox-Kerr, anyhow."

I threw Edith a side-glance. Why had she picked out the girl who had insulted me? But Edith's reply to my next sentence made her attitude clear.

"She does not seem to think so," I suggested.

There was a pause. Then Edith said, inconsequently: "I think it's rather a shame." I made no comment, but I understood her; I looked at the slim white fingers that grasped the racket, thought I should like to kiss them, to kiss them not so much because I wanted to kiss them, as because such a gesture would express my gratitude. But one does not in public kiss the hands of shy English girls; I said nothing, because I should have said something emotional, and I knew already that this was not done. But when Edith returned to Brussels, and whenever she came back, I did not forget. Now and then, when I sat in my room alone, Hecate sent me a graceful empusa. The ghost always said the same thing: "It's rather a shame."

I must not exaggerate: I did not so very often think of Edith while she was at school, for the claims of new common things, of England, of my business, of Maud, of others, of Muriel, tended to fill my mind. My relation to Muriel was peculiar, for the girl did not set out to fascinate me, being more drawn towards Edward Kent and, in his absence, to others amongst whom I did not greatly count. Yet she was friendly, and, while treating me as a friend, treated me as a man: that is, as a creature susceptible of becoming a lover. She did not admit me as a lover, but she did not consider it impossible I might become one, for she was light enough and, so far, untouched enough by love to make no emphatic distinctions between men. Ours was a comradeship, an *amitié amoureuse*.

"Hello! what's to-day's tie? Valenciennes? Point d'Alençon?"

"It isn't lace," I said, roughly.

"It looks rather like it. Now, Mr. Cadoresse, if I were you I'd go in for Irish; it's more solid, more manly."

"You know quite well I never wore a lace tie. A little insertion——"

"I'll be fair. It isn't lace to-day. It's more like the Mediterranean."

"Do you want me to wear black?"

"No, of course not." Muriel grew serious, ceased to chaff me. "Don't be obstinate; go to any place you like in Jermyn Street and ask them to sell you the tie they've sold most of during the past month, and you'll be all right."

It was Muriel, in her kindliness, anglicised my clothes as soon as she became friendly enough to criticise me to my face. She also gravely taught me the things to do.

"You've got to be smart," she said. "A man's got no right not to be smart. It's the only way he has of looking pretty. Now he mustn't look like a mute, and he mustn't overdo it. You did overdo it with that suit of yours, the teddy-bear, Hugh called it——"

"Well, I saw it in the window," I said, flushing.

"If a suit is exposed for sale, the buyer is exposed to ridicule."

"I will bet that sentence is one of Kent's."

"What if it is?" Muriel threw me a rather spiteful glance, then relented, not displeased by my suggestion that Kent condescended to be brilliant for her sake. "It's true. Now listen, Mr. Cadoresse. . . ."

I owe a great deal of my education to Muriel; she was fundamentally dashing; she classed people by their voices, names and places of residence. In her own words, "she had no use for people whose fare to the City was over threepence"; she did not despise these people: she merely ignored them. It was Muriel explained to me that Earl's Court wasn't right, but that the Welcome Club was, that I was not to go to the seaside on Sunday League trips, that I must either pay my shilling for tea in Bond Street or go without, that I had better have no club than join one which had no waiting list.

"And don't show off," she said. "It isn't done. You mustn't tell people how well you did at school, or what a lady-killer you are, or that you can pull twenty miles without feeling it."

"Well, I can," I said, sulkily, as I thought of a wonderful Sunday with Maud between Hampton Court and Staines.

"There you go again. Don't say it."

"I suppose you think I'm a bounder."

"If I did, I wouldn't say so. I wouldn't talk to you."

I unbent. I even took her hand, told her she was very sweet to me, tried to kiss her; she resisted me at first, but soon surrendered, with a serene indifference which ought to have told me she valued me no more than the others. Like most English girls Muriel did not care very much whether one man or another made advances to her; if she invited his attentions it was to satisfy her vanity. She liked me, was amused by my Frenchness, the uncertain temper she so often had to soothe; she found an obscure maternal pleasure in training me. She was not in love with me, and I could not fall in love with her because I knew she did not care.

Thus my heart was free when Edith returned for good. This was in October. I had not seen her for six months, for the Lawtons had settled at Ostend in August, and she suddenly struck me as new. She was eighteen and had grown a good deal; this I judged early, for I did not know I would find her as I entered the drawing-room on a Sunday afternoon, when the air was still warm and glowing. She stood at the open window, and had evidently not heard the maid announce me, for she had one hand upon the window bolt and was looking out towards the Gardens. As I came in and stood watching her, Fiona turned, came towards me, faintly wagging her tail, stopped a yard away and, lying on her back, gazed at me with unebullient friendliness. I could see Edith's profile, the pale gold of her hair, now " up " and dressed in soft coils, the low forehead, the small, straight nose, the little pink mouth with the serious air. Upon the bolt lay her slender, white hand; as she stooped I observed, detached as if I looked at a statue, the long curves of her arms and shoulders, the noble straight line of her back. Upon the carpet Fiona lay and rubbed herself, grunting a little with content; very lightly her tail went " swish, swish " across the pile.

Edith turned round, saw me. But she did not blush bright as I expected; a faint flush, no more, rose to her cheeks. She smiled, came towards me, her hand frankly outstretched.

" How do you do, Mr. Cadoresse? I didn't hear you come in."

" How do you do? "

I released her hand, which I had held just that fraction of time which expresses significant instead of emotional salutation. She did not seem disturbed, sat down on the settee, indicating a chair with a movement so gracious that it chilled me a little, until I realised, which I did within a few minutes, that Edith the child had become a woman. She was a woman, though but eighteen, having been forced towards maturity by association with the bolder Belgian and German girls. She was conscious instead of self-conscious.

" What were you looking at? " I asked, as I bent down to tickle Fiona behind the ear.

" I don't know. The motors, and the people in the Gardens. They're sitting down, some of them, as if it was midsummer."

" As if it was " grated upon me. How those English speak English! But I resisted the impulse to correct and patronise.

" I too," I said, " like looking at people. They're all so different."

" Yes," said Edith, softly, " they're all different. All doing something different, wanting something different."

I watched her. This interest of hers in people, it was not every one's interest. Edith was not pricing garments, as Maud would be, or gauging elegance, which Muriel could not help doing. There was a gentle reflectiveness in her preoccupation.

" So you realise they have lives? " I suggested; " that they're not ready-made goods produced by the hundred million? "

" Of course." She laughed. " I like to think they have wonderful lives, and some of them dreadful lives—" She paused abruptly. " Oh, well, it's none of my business. Mother'll be down in a minute."

I think she had broken the spell with intent, for she seemed embarrassed, hurried. You too, Edith, you were afraid in that first minute of " giving yourself away." Or instinct watched over you.

Mrs. Lawton did not come down for some time, as I was an early caller and she was not ready. So I went on talking to Edith and scratching Fiona's ear. Edith had become a little aloof after she had expressed more of her soul than she intended, and now I did most of the talking; at times she interjected a leading question.

" I suppose you had a good time this summer? "

As it happened I had been to Pontaillac, where my mother had taken a small villa for the season. I described Pontaillac, the haunts of the Bordeaux smart set, the little woods, the vine-clad hills.

" And you see the Gironde," I said. " It's lighter than the sea; it looks grey, while the sea is green. Across the estuary you can see the cliffs, and it is so hot that sometimes there is a mirage and another line of cliffs seems to sit upside down on the top of the real ones."

" How lovely! " said Edith, without excitement. She induced me to talk of the open cafés, the *petits chevaux,* which had not in those days been superseded by *la boule;* of the extraordinary clothes, notably the red trousers the Bordelais like to wear at the seaside. She said it was

rather like Ostend, asked whether I did not think all
seaside places were alike.

"Hardly," I said. "There's nothing like the English
ones, nothing so dull. Worthing, for instance." Then I
plunged, looked her straight in the eyes and said, "I've
been to Worthing, on a Sunday League trip."

"How jolly!" said Edith. And her smile meant that
she thought it jolly.

It amused and pleased me that she did not snub me as
Muriel had done when I mentioned this inexpensive
pleasure.

The keynotes of this and of other conversations I had
with Edith were always the same: frankness and freshness, mixed with sudden reserves. She was the young girl,
who is modest and bold, not *la jeune fille,* who is curious
and furtive. She was afraid of the things she did not
understand, and became shy and silent whenever I spoke
of anything that verged on the "naughty," as the English
say. Naughty! you have to be English to be "naughty";
if you are French and "naughty" you are bad.

II

I talked a good deal with Edith during the next few
months. Ours was a paradoxic relation: absolute but limited frankness; that is to say, the things we could discuss
we discussed without reserves, while we ignored the others.
She frequently fell to my share, for Hugh was being more
and more closely hemmed in by Louisa Kent and watched
by Bessie Surtees, while Muriel, who was not jealous, was
quite equal to enjoying simultaneously Edward, Dicky Bell
and Neville or any men she could detach from Gladys
Raleigh. Muriel made no piratical efforts: she was an
Autolycus—she gathered rather than stole. So very often
I found that I talked to Edith for an hour at a time, and
there was about her a fragrance of youth which slowly
began to charm me. I did not love her, not yet, but I felt

pleasure in her society, a gentle, unemotional pleasure. As we talked I found myself analysing her mentally as well as physically, realising her grace and her toy-like daintiness. But I suspected that under the toy-like exterior was some strength, not that noble strength of action which is given to so few women, but the strength of uncomplaining endurance. She almost expressed it once when I asked her whether it did not bore her to drive in the Park with Mrs. Lawton's aged mother.

"Well," she said, " it's not very amusing; she's funny, she's always losing her spectacles, or her handkerchief. Or she wants to stop and look at the children feeding the ducks, or playing. She made me get out yesterday and tackle five dirty little boys who were picnicking——"

"Picnicking!" I cried; "in December."

"Yes. Small boys will do that sort of thing. They had a sham camp fire and a sentry to watch for the parkkeeper—anyhow, Grannie made me ask them all their names and whether they were Hurons or Iroquois, which, of course, they didn't know, and give them a penny each to buy rifles. We had quite a little crowd before I had done. I felt——"

"Silly?" I suggested out of mere mischief.

"Of course I felt silly," said Edith, with sweet severity. "One does hate to be looked at. Still, she likes it, and what does it matter?"

I gave vent to a little Nietzscheanism.

"Well, perhaps you're right, but one has to bear a few things in life, hasn't one?" Edith looked at me with so soft an expression in her blue eyes that I wanted to agree with her, but as I did not reply she went on: " It wouldn't be good for one, would it, to do everything one liked?"

"It would be very pleasant."

"Yes, I suppose it would be nice. But if one always did what one liked one would become so selfish, one wouldn't remember how to do anything for anybody. Perhaps it isn't good for one to be too happy."

" Puritan," I said.

" I wonder whether I am? " Edith looked reflectively at her slim hands. " I don't think so, though; I like to enjoy myself, only I want other people to enjoy themselves too."

Edith was not telling the truth: at heart she distrusted pleasure; she loved it, but she was never sure that it was not sinful. Ten generations of Protestant ancestors had given her an attitude almost incomprehensible to a Roman Catholic, that is a Pagan, such as I. But the gentle severity of it, her rectitude and simplicity, appealed to me as the pretty Quaker maidens have ever appealed to the most hardened adventurers. And I was far from being hardened; I had loved often and lightly, but seldom grossly; that is, I had always managed to introduce into the most commonplace adventures a strain of romantic idealism.

I wondered, after this conversation, whether Edith were more capable of idealism than of enthusiasm. I was not sure, for it is not often a human creature can feel intensely in one way only; I ought to have known her better, to have understood how fettered and canalised is the English faculty for romance. I ought to have guessed that Edith sometimes thought of love and marriage, if never of love alone; that she had visions of a very respectful lover, very strong and very gentle, very brave, very generous, upright, God-fearing, and reasonably addicted to the virile habits of tobacco, oaths and drink. A sort of Launcelot, this, not Hugh's Galahad; a Launcelot with a commission in the Guards.

It is true that Edith did not help me much. She was all implications; she never revealed herself, never tore her body off to show me her soul. But that is not the way of the soulful. Besides, I had not often the opportunities I needed to cross-examine her, to drive her by

syllogism and inference into positions which would compel
her to confess; though we talked long we seldom talked
alone: rival conversations intruded upon ours or threatened
to do so, so that I could not produce the atmosphere in
which men and women tell one another the things that
matter. Curiously enough, in those days I never wondered
whether there were anything to be drawn from Edith;
already, no doubt, I suspected that Edith must be as other
women, an extraordinary field where grew flowers of impression, desire and reticence; I must have suspected that
she wanted certain things desperately, and none the less
desperately because dumbly. Edith, it is true, was not
alone in my thoughts, for I still pursued Maud with the
hopeless obstinacy a man can exhibit only if he live in
the same house as the one he favours. I had then as
a somewhat cynical motto that there were many good fish
in the sea, and I would have forgotten Maud when another
woman crossed my path if I had not seen her every day.
She had not altered much. On the night of my arrival,
when she granted me that bold but deceptive kiss, she had
been young for seventeen. Two years later she was young
for nineteen. Her training was finished: she never would
have had any training if the Hoopers had not faintly
hoped that by wasting time they could gain time, prevent
her from going on the stage and safely marry her off.
They would gladly have married her off to me.

"Yes, she's getting a big girl now," Mrs. Hooper said,
ruminatively; "she oughtn't to be on the shelf long.
Not," she added with compunction, "that I want to lose
my little Maudie, though—" (proudly) "—with all her
education—well, well, I suppose it'll always be the same;
young gentlemen are already paying her attentions;
there's Mr. Saunders, he's doing well in the Estate office.
And Mr. Colley—though a dancing master, Mr. Cadoresse
—well——"

"Exactly," I said, my masculine pride being exasperated
by any idea of rivals.

" Yes, that's just what I think. Still—of course, it's not like Lulu."

Mrs. Hooper sighed, for Lulu at seventeen had fulfilled the promise of being plain which she made at fifteen. She had maintained her one characteristic of reading penny novels, and acquired no others. I think I saw Lulu the other day (she must be twenty-five now); she was stouter and wore good, dowdy clothes: some paper-backs were sticking out of her muff.

" You've never thought of getting married, Mr. Cadoresse ? "

I parried, alleged youth and lack of money.

" Oh, well," said Mrs. Hooper, encouragingly; " young people can't expect to begin where their parents left off."

Mrs. Hooper began to enlarge once more on her daughter's accomplishments, her dancing, her singing. " Comes in so handy in society," she said. Evidently she thought that the teaching of Mother Tinman could be made into a refined asset, that in days to come Maud would, thanks to Mother Tinman, shine in, say, Kensal Green circles. Perhaps charity concerts—or graciously political socials.

Maud was franker.

" Oh, I let the old dear talk. I know what I'm after. You don't think I swallowed old Bella Billion neat and her tooraloo and keeping the limelight on your pearlies. I wasn't going to start up as a third line girl on a quid a week and work up to the first and wait ten years for a line: No! I'll start up in the flies, old dear, give you my solemn ! "

She had changed, I suppose, though she seemed young for nineteen. The vernacular of the stage had gained on the cockney. But she remained hard, invincible, ready to play me off against Saunders or Mr. Colley. Their cause advanced no more than mine.

" Of course ma sits dreaming (dreams of love and dreams of you)—every time she thinks she's spotted a winner. Why, the old dear can't say rice, or slipper, without making a goo-goo sort of eye at me—you know, the ' Bless you, my cheeild,' sort of eye. But I'm not taking any, I can tell You. Don't say I wouldn't look at a Duke if there's one going cheap, or even an Earl, but she's backed a wrong 'un if she thinks I'm going to warm Saunders's slippers for him or prance round with the grocer for the sake of the Signor."

I laughed, for Maud had gauged " Signor " Colley's affection, but the subtle quality of " spotting a winner " and a " wrong 'un " tended to show that Saunders, the " sport," had made some headway. I was not indifferent, indeed I chafed, for the brown eyes had never been so bright, the small pointed hands so firm and cool, but I had learned prudence, dared not be called sulky, as Maud applied sulkiness in return and always beat me at the game. If I did not allow myself to be wooed back after having been practically insulted she sometimes refused to speak to me for several days.

" Such a spirited girl," said Mrs. Hooper, fondly.

When this happened I fell back on Mr. Hooper, who had completely failed to educate me in the tenets of Conservatism, though he had taken me to his club, in a back street off the Harrow Road, to be properly grounded by his fellow members and occasional speakers from the headquarters of Unionist, naval and military societies. I had no precise politics in those days, I had nothing but an unappeasable thirst for information which made me read, in the Tube, at lunch and in the intervals of work, indigestible chunks of oratory, emasculated Liberal ideas in the Tory papers, and garbled Conservatism in the Radical press. For two years I had every day been reading the paper, skipping sports, murders and law reports; I had abandoned foreign affairs, for was I not going to be an Englishman? Tariff Reform and Free Trade pamphlets, booklets on the land question, licensing, the iniquities and virtues of the House of Lords, the rights of Chinamen, all this jostled in my head, slowly ordering itself, mixed with the history politicians use, tags about Magna Charta, Cromwell, Burke, Phœnix Park, Gladstone and the paper duty, Disraeli and primroses. I suppose I knew as much about politics as the ordinary man, perhaps more, for I wanted to know, while he merely had to. But Mr. Hooper failed to move me, no doubt because the Lawtons were Liberals; if Lawton, Hugh and their women had been repellent to me I should have been a Tory Democrat, which is the rough equivalent of the French *Radical* I was. But the Lawtons were the great English and could do no wrong.

I did not, however, despise the Conservatives, for they too were English and could not be quite wrong. Thus Mr. Hooper retained hopes of saving my political soul. Sometimes, at the club, he spoke. I can see him, a thin, bald little figure, with a melancholy blue eye. He stands upon the low platform, holding tight the lapels of his frock-coat:

"—The Free Traders are always saying—er—that the tariff would raise prices. Now, gentlemen, I don't think anybody can say what will happen—er—under—under the new system. Of course they might, the prices I mean —but then if we were getting more for our work it wouldn't matter. Of course, there are all sorts of ways, like Layshell Mobil——"

Then Mr. Hooper would throw back his mind to *Five Thousand Facts and Fancies,* or some other book of the kind, and expound *L'Échelle Mobile,* that cunning reciprocal scale of prices and duties, becoming eloquent and secure as soon as he abandoned ideas for the firm ground of fact. But at last he would tail off again into references to "Joe" (for whom there was a large cheer and a faint Unionist Free Trade hiss), beg the audience to give the tariff a fair trial. A fair trial! that is what impressed me in the dingy little club, which had as a president an undertaker and as members some fifty shopkeepers, workmen and clerks. Even here, in a dusty back room,

which always smelled of pipes, the tendency was to examine the new idea suspiciously and yet to try it.   I
never heard anybody talk wildly of high protection, or
call the opposition leader a liar, a traitor or a hireling in
Germany's pay.   The members seldom interrupted: if they
did the undertaker stroked his grey whiskers and said
"Gentlemen!" with an air of shocked mournfulness, possi-
bly professional, which at once restored peace.   They were
sane, moderate; they believed in the decencies of debate.
Perhaps they were too sane.   Often I longed to jump up,
and though I was nominally a Liberal, roar: "Down with
the Little Englanders!"   I wanted to wake the little club
up, but I felt dimly that it would not wake up.   The club
was neither awake nor asleep, it was sleep-walking.   If
I had shouted I should not have been thrown downstairs as
an interrupter ought to be thrown; the undertaker would
have said: "Questions will be allowed later."   Still, it
was good to think that tempers could be so well kept—if
there were tempers.

III

But my political days were only dawning.   They were
near, but Edith was nearer, and as I turned away from
the glare of Maud's footlights I began to see the soft
glimmer of Edith.   One startling fact stood out: I had
not kissed Edith under the mistletoe.   I was a guest at
the dignified Christmas dinner on which followed a dim
rowdiness of games; I had dragged Muriel, Bessie Surtees
and laughing Gladys Raleigh under the iconoclastic berry
and publicly kissed them; I had seen Edith kissed by
almost every one of the men, from the collected Edward
Kent to the self-doubting Neville.   But I had not kissed
her; I could have done so and, for one moment, I wanted
to; then I hesitated and knew that I was not lost.   Some
unexplained impulse prevented me from treating in
sportive wise the Dresden Shepherdess, something tremu-

lous that made my heart beat. I was not in love with her,
I told myself, but I could not bear to think that I would
have to wrench her slim shoulders round and force upon
her a caress which she would not permit if the idiotic
license of Christmas did not compel her to do so.

It was a long time before I knew that I wanted Edith's
lips consenting, and not conventional.

But soon accident was to intervene and to drive us
further towards intimacy. I had not seen Edith for a
fortnight when, one Saturday afternoon, as I walked down
Bond Street, where on that day I liked to shopgaze though
most of the showcases were sealed by iron shutters or
holland blinds, I saw her slowly coming up the hill. I
knew her at once, by her long measured stride, the rigidity
of her carriage and the un-English steadiness of her arms.

Almost tall in her tight blue coat and skirt. Her little
feet shone in patent leather. Upon the high, boned neck
of her plain white blouse, the flower of her winter-stung
face, crowned with a small blue velvet hat, round which
circled a light blue feather. Gently she came with downcast eyes, easy, slow-moving and slim, like a fishing smack
under little sail. She saw me, stopped, and as she smiled
I mumbled of the fineness of the day, for I was stirred
by the surprise of the meeeting. I, Cadoresse, man of the
world, hero of thirty affairs of the heart, stood almost
abashed because a Dresden Shepherdess was prettily
smiling. She said she had been lunching with two girls
who had that morning been examined at Burlington House,
and now she was going home. I detained her, talked
quickly and idly, of Hugh, the big poulterer opposite,
Fiona, anything that came to me, so that I might think
how to prolong a meeting which Edith was very sweetly
but firmly trying to cut short.

Then an idea struck me.

"Look here," I said; " I suppose you are in no hurry.
Have you seen the Claude Monets? "

"No—you mean the painter? "

"Yes, Monet, the impressionist. They are showing him just there." I indicated with a nod a gallery over the way. "You must come. He's wonderful."

"I'd love to, but——"

"The show will be closed in three days," I lied; "now you have nothing to do, have you?"

"No, but—" Edith paused. Evidently she wanted to come, and evidently she was afraid. But it would not do, I knew, to let her see that I knew. I grew fervid, urged educational value, the dulness of Saturday; then I was inspired to say:

"Besides, I want to go myself, and I hate going alone."

"Very well, then," said Edith, moved by this argument. In the cause of human charity she followed me across the road, and I glowed with my victory, for was I not experiencing a new sensation: taking one of the house of Lawton to a public spectacle? This was not like the familiar, jostling, arm-in-arm strolls with Maud, for we stood away from each other, dignified, careful that our elbows should not touch. It was a cold companionship, akin to that of a king and queen who sit on a common throne, but on separate chairs; but, after all, we were only paying for our quality.

It was a small show, the series of twelve (or is it twenty?) rustic bridges spanning the reed-grown rivulet. I have forgotten the details, remember only the atmosphere of the pictures, for all represent an absolutely similar subject, and all differ in lighting and weather. Their colour, though, I remember well, their faintness and suggestion of transience and the baldness of that suggestion: for in those days, when Post-Impressionists had not yet slain Sisley, when Futurism was swathed in the veils of the future, the Impressionists were still impressive. We stopped in front of the third. There the bridge stood in the grey morning, a black shadow on a sky which, a few minutes earlier, had been as black. The reeds hung dejected and damp in the whitish mist that rose from the river.

"What do you think of it?" I asked.

Edith did not reply for a moment, then said: "It looks very cold, doesn't it?"

"Yes, but do you like it?"

"Yes, I suppose I do, because it makes me feel cold—melancholy."

I listened with a mixed feeling. This was not exactly stereotyped art criticism, which of course interested me, but it was, I thought, too subjective.

"But don't you think it beautiful?"

"I don't know. Yes. It *is* pretty."

"I think it beautiful," I repeated, emphasising the adjective. "Why, look at the light, so pale and so watery. I've seen it like that, very early, when I was mounting guard on the fortifications."

"You mean when you were on sentry-go," Edith corrected. "Of course, I've never been up so early, but that doesn't matter, does it? If it makes me feel it must be like that?"

"I suspect, Miss Lawton," I said, after another reflective pause, "that you know a good deal about pictures."

"Oh, no, no, I don't," cried Edith, with an air of distress. "When we were at Brussels they took us to the Wiertz now and then, but I don't really know anything. I really don't. Only, I want to feel something."

We wrangled amicably over the next two. I had an expert air, I liked to use the words "background," "foreground," "masses;" I liked to hear myself say "*éclairage*." Suddenly I saw myself as I was and said (to myself): prig. Edith, I felt, was the truer appreciator of us two, for she wanted to feel, not to judge. She did not measure pictures by a standard of quality, as do the men who cannot understand them; while they have for them a set of units, equivalents of pints and yards, such women as Edith, who know nothing and understand every-thing, have a standard of emotion.

"That one," she said; "it's lovely."

"Yes," I replied. "It looks as if it were painted with crushed opals and with the powder of those mauve pebbles, like old, dull glass, that you find on the seashore."

Edith said nothing, and I went on criticising the picture, enthusiastically, for it held all the flush of a wet dawn. I was literary, a little artificial, but at the bottom of the artifice was some truth, and I wondered whether Edith lacked artifice because no admiration was in her to inspire it. I doubted her especially when, suddenly, she said:

"Muriel has a dress just like that."

"Perhaps she has seen the picture," I spitefully suggested.

"Oh, no, Muriel wouldn't come here." Edith gave a frank laugh and, as I joined in, my chilled feeling passed away, for here we were in the domain of the very little things which matter so much. Accomplices.

"Isn't she artistic?"

"No, I shouldn't say so. Her dressmaker's rather clever."

"I suppose her dressmaker is your sister's salvation."

"Very likely."

Edith looked at the next picture as she spoke the two curt words; she had turned away from me a very little, a significant couple of inches, and a slight rigidity had come into the set of her shoulders. I felt I had said the wrong thing. I still had to learn what family loyalty means, but at that moment I began to realise dimly that Edith could have said "Muriel is a beast," while, if I had said "Muriel is a beast," Edith would have replied: "How dare you speak of My sister like that?" Con-scious of the snub, I talked more briskly, compelled her to stop in front of the other studies, delicate fantasies in blue, and others, full of twilight, where the leaf was heavy and green. Little by little Edith seemed to forgive; she answered me, and, at last, when we stood before the last picture, we were once more side by side.

"That's the best," she said, decisively. "I like all that colour; it's sunshine. It's pretty—" Then, her eyes twinkled as she added: "Beautiful, as you say."

"It is beautiful," I said, aggressively. "But why don't you say 'beautiful?'"

"I don't know—it seems——"

"What?"

"Well, you know—exaggerated. We say things are pretty, or lovely——"

"Or nice?"

"Yes—nice—I mean, at school we used to say 'nice' a lot, but they say I mustn't now. Like 'horrid.'"

"But do they say you mustn't say 'beautiful?'"

"One mustn't exaggerate," said Edith, with an air of gentle obstinacy. And further than that I could not draw her.

Apparently "beautiful," save when it was used by a long-haired pianist, was the word of a gushing schoolgirl which womanly Edith ought not to be. I was inclined to pursue the subject, to get to the bottom of this modesty of Edith's ears.

"I know what you mean," I said; "it was like that at my school. If anybody tried to recite poetry properly everybody laughed at him."

"One mustn't show off. Still—I don't mean one ought not to recite properly."

"But not like an actor?"

"No, of course not. That would be showing off."

"But do good actors show off? No, of course not. Then oughtn't one to recite Shakespeare like an actor?"

"There's something between," said Edith.

I knew what she meant, something between Kean and a gabbling child, something moderate, English. And I therefore felt that she was right. We were still standing in front of the sunlit picture; there were only four people in the gallery just then: another young couple, who whispered in a corner, so near the picture that they certainly could not see it, an old gentleman who painstakingly looked at each study through a handglass held in front of his speectacles, and a quick, angular woman with a notebook. She was too busy to notice us; a journalist probably, making notes for an article. We were not looking at the picture, but covertly at each other.

"Yes," I said, reflectively, "that did bother me at school. But, of course, you remember better; you haven't left it so long ago."

"No," said Edith. "I liked it, you know." She began speaking of the Belgian school, some girls, Caroline de Woesten, a certain Henriette, who recurred. "We used to see the Prince, riding in the Avenue Louise, in the morning."

"Did you smile at him?"

"Of course we did, all of us, he was so handsome. Caroline bought a picture postcard of him and hid it in her desk; she did get into trouble when Madame Beaujour found it, with a poem on the back. It began:

"Prince Albert, je vous adore,
Pour la vie et pour la mort. . . ."

We laughed together. And Edith looked almost melancholic, though her head, thrown back, showed a white throat that swelled with laughter, as she thought of the good old times that were not so very old.

"They weren't good verses, were they? But then Caroline's only a baby, only sixteen now."

"Well," I said, "you're not much older."

"I'm eighteen," said Edith, very staid. "And what about you?"

I paused before I replied, for the question pleased and surprised me. "Not quite twenty-five."

"I suppose that does feel old," said Edith.

We were silent for some moments. Then we heard the chimes of St. George's Church. A quarter past four.

" I must go," said Edith, hurriedly.

" Yes," I said, " but not yet. It is time to go and have tea."

" Oh, no, I couldn't—I really couldn't."

" Well, you might ask me to go back to Lancaster Gate to have it."

" You can if you like. Do come."

" But do you know if anybody else will be at home? "

" No, I don't think so. Still——"

" Well then, you may as well come with me to the Carlton."

" Oh, no, no; not the Carlton."

Edith seemed frightened, as I expected, and I watched the success of my ruse, for I guessed that, by giving her the shock of the Carlton, I could make any other place appear innocent.

" No," I said, smilingly machiavellian; " we'll go to Mrs. Robertson's. Come along."

I think I took her elbow for a moment to urge her on, and at once released it so as not to frighten her. She was blushing a little and did not speak much as we went through Mrs. Robertson's passage and up the stairs, but she seemed unnaturally self-possessed when she sat down, so self-possessed that I realised she was nervous. I could see her, as I ordered tea, look quickly to the right and left in case some one should know her. But the week-end calm already hung over the dignified tea-shop, which has now followed many Victorian dignities into the grave; there was nothing to disturb her, for one couple had so arranged their seats as to turn their backs upon us, while the family up from the country seemed too busy with topics of its own to trouble about us. A tall, melancholic young man, who was evidently waiting for somebody, broke the tedium of his watch over the door by frequent, if discreet glances at Edith, but on the whole we were unobserved; besides, I made some business of ordering the tea, complications of toasted scones and their degree of toasting, so as to give Edith time to settle thoroughly into the faintly compromising slough.   And then, as we rather silently drank our tea, I looked at her, established in the large chintz-covered armchair.

She sat up very straight.   The blue hat and the pale golden hair stood out against a green curtain.   The moon of her face looked like a delicate rose, soft by the side of those vivid roses which sprawled over the chintz.   Her open coat showed her plain white blouse, revealed by the slimness of her that the child had not long been expelled and the woman installed.   One ungloved hand lay upon the table, and the rosy finger-tips played idly with the lace edge of the teacloth.   She looked up, and suddenly was mischievous:

"I shan't be able to tell anybody I came here, you know."

"Of course not," I said, smoothly; "though I don't know why."

"You do know why, Mr. Cadoresse," she said, and I found her severe.   "You of all people, a Frenchman. Why, French girls don't even go out alone."

I agreed.   I attacked the French system, was all for freedom.   Edith did not differ from me; she, too, thought it silly that girls should be watched.

"But then, perhaps the French know what they're doing," she added.   "They may be right and we wrong."

Her liberalism charmed me, and I repressed the desire to tell her that she had not faced the question, that Frenchmen and French girls could not be allowed English liberties, lacking English innocence.   We spoke guardedly of chaperonage, of marriage in France, and Edith showed some indignation when I told her that my sister Jeanne had but poor chances because her *dot* was only fifty thousand francs.

"Two thousand pounds," she said.   "It seems a lot—

but don't you think it dreadful? One doesn't want to marry for money."

I agreed, though in my heart I differed. I did not state the case for the French marriage, the restfulness of it, its ease and secureness. I did not want to oppose Edith, to shock her, annoy or frighten her; she was with me so simple and so frank that I did not want to lay hard hands upon her dreams. And, thanking my star for so much good fortune, I did not try to detain her when she rose to go. We parted at Bond Street Station.

"Good-bye," she said, as we shook hands; "thank you for a very pleasant afternoon." My spirit rebelled against the conventional phrase, but again came the mischief: "I don't know what I shall say at home if they're back."

I still had in mine the hard-impressed illusion of her firm, gloved hand. And in my mind was the consciousness that we shared a secret, she and I. A guilty one. I carried with me the feeling that I had had an adventure by the side of which coarse realities did not seem real, for visions are sometimes keener than concrete things; a dream may be more vivid than a material object which the eye can overlook. She had been so simple, had confided in me as readily as her reserve would let her; she had become a significant figure in my life. She was imprinted upon my brain no longer as the younger Miss Lawton, but as Edith.

In her home she was not the same; she did not avoid me, but she did not deliver herself into my hands; she was, like Muriel, my good comrade. As I grew familiar with the house and its tenants I accepted this comradeship so foreign to my nature. Before three years had passed I was then so anglicised that I was able to look upon women less as women than as human beings. My thoughts no longer leapt so quickly to their pretty faces; I found in their society the mixed and purely English feeling which makes of girls and boys gathered together a large family. I could still admire Muriel, her challenging eyes, and

Louisa Kent's rosy skin; I meant what I said when I told
Bessie Surtees she looked like an Italian Madonna, but
an element had been obscured in my imagination; I was
less disturbed, less preoccupied by these young women than
I would have been in earlier days. I came to England
ready to pursue even a Lulu Hooper, to accept her ridiculous taste for novelettes, unable to look upon any woman,
young or old, beautiful or ugly, without keen consciousness
of her womanhood. But now some strange scales had
grown upon my eyes, for I could chaff and bear chaff from
the graceful and the fair without being provoked by conflict; I could let Muriel re-tie my black bow into a more
modish shape without leaning forward to breathe the
suavity of her dark hair.

They were comrades, all of them. It was comrade
Muriel pushing past me into the drawing-room, butting
me with her shoulder as she passed and telling me good-
humouredly to get out of the way; and comrade Gladys
(though precise) fearlessly touching my hand as she helped
me to set up a ping-pong net; it was comrade Bessie with
the deep eyes, comrade Edith too. There were no rough-
nesses of contact between us, for I feared to touch her,
just as if she actually were a Dresden Shepherdess, so much
that, at a cinderella, she had to beg me not to hold her
as if she were a meringue. There was comradeship even
between me and Maud, when there was not sulkiness or
fierce allure, an incomprehensible capacity for wrangling,
contradicting each other, for throwing small objects
at each other under the meek, protesting eyes of Mrs.
Hooper.

Was the English fog getting into my blood?

I carried with me no disquiet as I went to my work,
which I did well enough, inspired by the comparatively
speedy rise of my salary to a hundred and sixty a year.
I was still foreign correspondent, but I was now framing
my letters and submitting them to Mr. Lawton instead
of merely taking his instructions. I enjoyed a hearing

when I had something to say. Merton and **Tyler** no longer presumed to chaff me, and sometimes I lunched with Barker in the chop-houses I affected because they had bills of fare and not menus. It was in the chop-houses, and especially in the Meccas and Caros where I drank my necessary coffee, that Barker criticised my criticisms of England.

" You silly old josser," served him usually as a beginning. " You don't know what you're talking about. You're always gassing about our being cold and never letting ourselves go; one might think you never read the police news, or that you'd never seen anybody tight. You should come down our way, you should; I'd show you something when they turn 'em out of the pubs. They come out like a lot o' sheep, laughing and singing like— jackasses, and kissing and going on anyhow; there's always a fight going on round the corner, all about nothing, only to let off steam, which you say we haven't got. And if you like to come on a bit further I'll show you Clapham Common about eleven; that'll open your eye, Froggy; you haven't got a monopoly of that sort of thing in gay Paree. Now I'll tell you something. One night I was walking home across the Common——"

Handsome, gay Englishmen like Barker always end by telling one stories in which they have figured as frightful dogs. The stories are too disgusting to be true. Englishmen so much dislike bragging that they can brag only of the things they have not done. I put up particular instances of English coldness.

" Well, what about it? " Barker commented. " What do you want old Purkis to Do? Want him to run round shrugging his shoulders and singing Mon Dew? And what about it if he does work in the garden? "

I tried to put into words the immense contempt I felt for gardens, for this sordid growing of smutty flowers; it was difficult to express, for I did not know how to say without seeming a prig that men should keep their brains

busier than their muscles. The innocent priggishness of
the early days was smothered in self-consciousness.

"Dunno what you're driving at," said Barker at last.
"I like a bit of a garden; *I* indulge in geoponics," he
added, playfully. "You talk of old Purkis! Why, his
place at Penge——"

"Sydenham," I suggested.

"Bit of swank, Sydenham. It's Penge I tell you, but
what was I talking about? Oh, yes, old Purkis's garden.
You should see it in the summer time, it's lovely."

"But oh, in the winter time, in the winter time," I
quoted from Maud.

"Never you mind the winter time. In the summer it's
all over honeysuckle, and sweet peas and crimson ramblers.
Why, he's got a pergola . . ."

Barker talked on inexhaustibly of gardens and garden-
ing, for which he had early acquired a taste by working
in his landlady's flower-beds. When "Mrs. Right came
along" he was not found unready. He bought a dog and
began to satiate, on a space of ten yards by twenty, his
English passion for the land. Barker was the *raisonneur*
of the English play; he explained old Purkis, his crabbed
love of his garden; he mitigated Farr by representing
him as a decent man, fond also of his garden, sound in his
politics and proud of his son. He had a broad tolerance
for the futile "sprees" of Merton and Tyler, their shilling
poplin ties and their shock-socks.

"Dunno what you want," was his continued grumble.
Then he would expound the creed of the plain man living
beyond the four-mile radius:

THE CREED OF A MIDDLE-CLASS MAN

"I believe in the suburbs of London. I believe
they are enough for me. I believe that I must shave
every evening and take a bath every morning, unless

I have overslept myself, wear dark suits as is seemly in the City. I believe in drawing-rooms for the use of callers, semi-detached villas, nasturtiums in season and dogs with aristocratic, if distant relatives. I believe that public-school boys, University men (who must not be called Varsity men), and commissioned officers are snobs. I believe that the West End is a gilded haunt of vice. I believe in sober worship once a week, regular payments to the clergy. I believe in temperance, saving an occasional bust, a spree, a night on the tiles (when the wife is in the country), but even then I believe I mustn't go too far. I believe in a bit of fun with a lady now and then, being a dog and all that, so long as there's no harm in it. I believe that I am a gentleman and must be genteel, not too tony though, for it must not be said that I swank. And I believe enough to be saved with. I believe that my wife loves me and that I must reward her by insuring my life; I believe that my sons should be clerks and that my daughters should wait until clerks marry them. I believe that, when I die, the neighbours must approve of my funereal pageant. I believe that I must be honest, that I must not swear in mixed company, that I must visit the upper classes whom I despise. I believe that I am the backbone of England. I am a middle-class man."

Barker loved to expound his creed. It seemed ridiculous that this well-groomed young fellow with the delicate mouth and the fine grey eyes should be a Puritan, but the blood of the Covenanters still flows through the English veins: that is really blood, not water. Still, there were impulses in him upon which I played; he liked to hear me brag of and unveil my conquests, invent adventures

for his benefit; this exercise filled him with subtle, sinful
delight.

"Shut up," he would say at last. But Barker's "shut
up" meant very little more than a woman's "don't."

Sometimes, not often, I talked to him of the Lawtons,
for whom, as represented by Mr. Lawton, Hugh and
shadowy "young ladies," he harboured mixed feelings:
envy, admiration and hatred. A sort of mental sandwich.
But I never spoke of Edith.

IV

For Edith was stealing upon me, gently, softly, as the
dawn steals up into the wet English skies, so subtly that
one hardly knows it has come until one realises suddenly
that the sun has risen. She came a little nearer when
Hugh's engagement leaked out, for love is contagious
among the young. If this engagement of Hugh's were
love, of course, for I say advisedly that it leaked out;
it was not proclaimed by an interested family, nor did
it burst forth outrageously and irresistibly like a water-
spout from the sea. Muriel told me, between an appreciation of the art of George Alexander and her plans for
Easter on the South Coast. When I ventured to ask when
Hugh would marry Louisa Kent, Muriel said:

"I don't know. Year or two."

Evidently nobody had made any plans; those two
had not been affianced, they had "got engaged." The
Lawtons did not seem much more moved than if Hugh
had contracted the measles: measles and engagements gave
a little trouble in the house, but in due course, as the
measles would have been cured by lying in bed, the engagement would be remedied by marriage. I did not find
Hugh much more emotional.

"I hear I am to congratulate you," I said.

"Thanks, awfully." He paused, then added, shame-
facedly: "Don't let it out at the office."

Before I could promise a discretion which seemed unnecessary he was talking of his father's chances at Hambury, which he was nursing in the Liberal interest. As he talked I wondered whether he cared for Louisa, when and where he had proposed to her. He had always seemed so aloof or so good-humoured when she was in the house. Yet he was making a love match; he must be, for Mrs. Kent's house in Thurloe Place suggested comfort, not wealth. I priced Louisa Kent's allowance at a hundred a year, perhaps less. But then—what was this love, this equable attraction? Was it not affection? I should have expected from Hugh some splenetic fits, some attitudes of devotion, some rages. But no. If a postman knocked at the door when I was there, Hugh did not start up. He was attentive to Louisa, but he seemed equally attentive to Gladys Raleigh or to any other girl. And Louisa? A shade more triumphant, perhaps; she was a trifle more proprietorial in her attitudes, more secure in her " I say, Hugh " than she had been in her " What do you think, Mr. Lawton? " I wondered whether she had proposed to him. As I looked at the steady eyes, the firm-set rosy lips, I grew almost sure that she had not felt the cost of the first step.

I soon had an opportunity of finding out. For now Edith was beginning to haunt me. Her picture did not obtrude itself upon me, as did sometimes the dashing figure of Maud; I did not walk with an ache in my heart, but I was disturbed by " something " that was about me, a vague, enveloping atmosphere, like an undefinable scent I might have brought with me in my clothes and suddenly perceived when the wind blew towards me, then forgotten, then noticed again. The Dresden Shepherdess did not follow me, but I could never be sure that, when I looked up from my desk, rested my pen, I would not see her slim figure before me. I might, at immense pains, be explaining to a French merchant that the bottomry bond he held on the brig *Augustine-Thérèse* was irrecoverable,

the unfortunate ship having gone down with all hands off
Vigo, when the slim figure would appear. I would lean
back, look unseeing at the grey frontages of Fenchurch
Street, evoke her, dressed in light blue or faint pink . . .
with little knots of roses frilling the skirt . . . a palely
pink face, tender blue eyes, smooth hair of very old, worn
silvergilt. I would try to dispel the vision, mutter fiercely
" bottomry . . . bottomry . . . *nous regrettons.* . . ." But
my thoughts would wander. I found myself saying, writing, " barratry " instead of " bottomry," thinking of her
gentle presence, until it so insisted that I surrendered, gave
myself up to an imprecise day-dream. Little Dresden
Shepherdess, your hands hung idly by your sides, long
and lax as sprays of fern, and when you smiled the bud
of your mouth bloomed so sweetly as to be sad. Your eyes
were like the mist in melancholy, when the sun is about to
pierce it in merriment.

My heart did not compel me to seek her, but I wanted
to find her, and soon it was not enough to speak to her
while Louisa played Bach to soothe her ridiculous brother
and the indifferent Hugh, or while Muriel threw spells
over Bell or Archie Neville; I wanted Edith alone, to
speak to her of herself. I surprised myself in a big Oxford
Street shop, at six, throwing quick glances at every fair
girl—on the chance; I began to walk home along the
Bayswater Road, which meant a quarter of an hour's
delay—on the chance, but I never met her. I grew exasperated; I began to be angrily conscious that my office
hours, ten to five-thirty, cut me off from the possibilities
of intercourse. At last Edith precipitated the crisis; in
reply to a question she said:

" Well, I don't think women as good as men."

" Why? " I asked.

" I'll tell you some other time," she said. And I could
drive her no further, for Muriel, Hugh and Louisa came
to claim me, to make me play bridge, a new accomplishment of mine. When I was dummy I looked at Edith;

seated upon a large cushion she looked up at her father, who talked to her in low tones. Her blue eyes were full of sweet seriousness. I decided to make an opportunity to come closer to her, to haunt the neighbourhood until I could force my society upon her.

And so I became a familiar of Lancaster Gate and the Bayswater Road, on weekdays between half-past six and seven, on Saturday afternoons, at odd times on Sundays. Waiting bored me, but racked my nerves, for I had to be careful as I hung at the corner of the street lest I should be seen by other members of the household; sometimes I saw Hugh or Mr. Lawton come home, or the brougham stop at the door and disgorge Mrs. Lawton with Muriel; twice I saw Edith, but her mother or her sister accompanied her. I became naturalised to the district, knew the mews, the public-house; I expected the postman, the boys who deliver the late editions of the papers; the servants of other families seemed like old friends, and one housemaid began to look forward to my appearance, to smile up from the basement with an inviting air. And if the policeman had not often been changed I should certainly have been cautioned against loitering with intent to steal. I was ready for him, however, with a confession and half-a-crown. I had hardened, and though I hardly knew what I wanted, I was determined to have it if I had to wait for weeks.

I did not have to watch for more than ten days. I knew I should not have to, for Easter had come; thus I could watch for two and a half days, during which Edith would certainly come out alone, for the family had not left for the South Coast; Muriel had gone on a visit in the country, while Hugh and his father went out early to golf. Edith would not always be with her mother. I was not wrong. At ten o'clock on Easter Monday the familiar door opened and Fiona came bounding down the steps, leaping at sparrows and barking as the sharp air sizzled through her coat. Behind her came Edith; she paused on the step, and I could feel my heart beating. The presence of Fiona meant that her mistress intended to walk in the Park; I felt exultant, as a poacher who, approaching his trap, hears an animal rattle it. She turned to the right; I followed cautiously, allowed her to cross into the Gardens, which she did slowly, for she carried Fiona across the road by the scruff of her neck. I ran a hundred yards westwards, entered the Gardens by the little gate, doubled back. For one deadening moment I thought I had lost her. Then, suddenly, I saw her coming towards me, who sauntered on as coolly as I could.

"Hullo, Fiona," I said, bending down to the little beast, who snuffed my trousers and burrowed at my hand with her wet nose. Then, successfully affecting surprise: "Good morning, Miss Lawton."

"Oh, good morning. Isn't it fine?"

"Very. And so cold! I don't appreciate it as much as Fiona does."

"Oh, she's Scotch; she likes it."

I talked of the habits of Aberdeens, and, having turned by degrees until I faced westwards, moved step by step, drawing Edith on. By imperceptible gradations we began to walk side by side, slowly, then quickly, as if we had set out together. Edith, realising her entanglement, but finding nothing to urge against it, was embarrassed and rather silent.

"Tell me," I said suddenly, "what did you mean the other night, when you said that men were better than women?"

"Oh, I hardly know," she reflected. "It's so difficult to find words. I feel somehow that we're so small, so busy doing nothing, that it's men who are making the roads in India, and fighting, and inventing things, and writing books, while we . . . we sit at home and wait." A slight weariness was in her young voice.

"That does not make them better," I said.

"Oh, yes, it does. They're doing things."

"Working in offices, ten to five-thirty."

"Well, even that. I couldn't. Father wouldn't have me as a typist, would he? I'd make too many mistakes."

We laughed together, and I wanted to say that it would be sacrilege to connect her white fingers with copying ink, but I knew better than to pay compliments, even sincere ones. Besides, I understood her attitude; it was achievement this English girl admired.

"Are you bored with life?" I asked, bluntly.

"What funny questions you ask! No, not exactly bored. There's plenty to do; I skate and read a lot, and we go out. Still . . ."

"Still?"

"What's the good of it all?"

"Pessimism is suitable in youth," I said, rather sententiously. "What do you want to do?"

"I don't know. Something different from what I do."

"Fall in love?" I said suddenly. I had not planned that remark.

Edith flushed, called Fiona, who came to us, bright-brown-eyed, quivering with excitement as she guessed that her mistress was going to throw a stone. The stone was thrown into the rough grass, and Fiona went searching; as she nuzzled among the crisp blades her tail wagged rhythmically, upright, as if translating all the excitement of her little black body. I watched Edith covertly, for the loss of the stone had defeated her object. The flush was not yet dead on her cheeks.

"What else is there to do but fall in love?" I said.

"I don't know. Well, I suppose I shall get married some day."

"Married!" I cried. "But that's not love."

Edith began to laugh, at her ease again now that I seemed absurd.

"Of course it is. Oh, you are odd, you Frenchmen; you have such complicated ideas. We fall in love here and we get married, and there you are."

"And there you are!" I said, a little bitterly. "Yes, and there we are in France. Of course, I don't say one shouldn't get married, but marriage is only—well, registration of a fact. While love——"

I think that for several minutes I spoke of love, and I spoke of it as never before; the old, gross shell had fallen away, and I seemed to know love as the angels may know it. I painted for her love so fine that the lover could hardly bear it; I said it was not good unless it was forbidden; that it was shy, mysterious, secret, that it fled if grasped too hard.

"It comes . . . like a shadow, and it lies across your path . . . and if you obscure the sun it is gone. . . . You do not know that it is there, until it is, and if you have seen it once you never forget it. Love is the only thing that matters: we make money to gain the one we love, we want fame so that she may be proud, and we are pure so that she may have peace."

"Peace," said Edith, softly.

"Love is not the bird that rides in the storm—I do not know its name—the bird that flies over the waves. It is more like the beautiful peacock in the garden that struts and flaunts its tail. It does not lose its feathers if they are real and not placed upon a jay. It is the only thing that lasts and makes things last. . . . For you may have everything, and yet you have nothing if you have no one to whom to give."

"One does want to give," said Edith. "I always feel with my mother . . ."

But I would not be turned, I let my speech blaze into rhetoric, I said of love things I do not believe, but they seemed true in that quiet avenue, as the wind hissed in the bare branches. We walked slowly, she silent and I stirred. The people that passed were not people, but shapes; young couples and old couples, and family parties, a few soldiers with their girls, they went by as unobtrusively as the scenery round the revolving stage at Drury Lane. As if by common accord we stopped near the Dutch garden, where a shower of almond blossom had fallen into the grass among the crocuses.

The crocuses stood erect, white, yellow and purple, as spangled wreaths of iridescent tears. I bent down, picked up some of the fallen almond blossoms, gave them to Edith. She looked at the soft, almost fleshy flowers as they nestled in her grey-gloved hand. I was not to see them again for many long years, and then they were dry, crumpled, as if they had been crushed, and I thought that they carried a faint scent of suède glove. Silently we walked towards Kensington, then to the Achilles statue, when Edith tried bravely to talk of some friends of hers, who were staying at the Hyde Park Hotel. But her words were rambling, her sentences disconnected, as if she knew their artifice. We had not spoken of ourselves, but we had spoken of immortal things, and we could not return to the everyday things. The consciousness of the unspoken, which perhaps we could not have expressed, stood between us, separating and linking us, a little ironic in its resolution never to be set aside. And, strangely enough, there ran through my embarrassed ravishment a strain of anger; I called myself a sentimental fool, told myself that I had been inflated, rhetorical; I threw glances at Edith, who did not raise her eyes, and hated her because she made me idealistic, romantic, because she made me slough gross tastes, gross desires, filled me with a religious worship for abstract loveliness. Ah, if it had been her loveliness, it would have been different: but her influence upon me was not to draw me to her; she inflamed me for what she represented rather than for what she was.

And then I wondered whether I had been clumsy, frightened her by the sudden violence of my impersonal romanticism. I tried to talk, and as we walked towards

Marble Arch we almost succeeded in discussing whether Mayfair were not stuffy.

"All those mews . . ." said Edith.

"Yes," I said, "mews . . . everywhere."

We had nothing else to say, for we dared not talk of the only thing we could talk of. We separately patted Fiona, disturbing her in her favourite occupation of snuffing the soil, we looked at watches, we commented on the cold. But I think neither of us was unhappy when, on reaching Marble Arch, we parted. The phrase I had in my mind would not come.

"Good-bye," said Edith. She raised to mine blue eyes in which was no anger, but a shyness new to me. And in my own, I think there was shyness too.

That night in my room I looked at "In the Garden of Eden," clerk and typist in the Park. I tried to scoff at myself, but my sense of humour failed me.

I spoke the phrase a month later, driven to it by my obsession of her, by my certainty that I must see her, if only to be sure that I wanted to.

"Will you meet me to-morrow at three?" I said in a low voice.

She did not reply. Louisa played a minuet, a minuet for the Dresden Shepherdess. I repeated my question.

"I can't," she whispered. And I saw fear in her eyes.

"You're not engaged. Are you?"

"No—but——"

"To-morrow—three o'clock—at Prince's main entrance —nobody ever goes there on Saturdays."

She did not reply. I saw her fingers tremble.

"Don't you want to?" And it was I trembled, for fear she might say "No."

She looked at me, still with frightened eyes, as if saying: "Why do you torture me—frighten me? I am such a little girl, please, please don't." But I was in no mood for mercy: indeed, I began to understand it was her helplessness, her delicate weakness made to me this incredible appeal. I hardened my gaze, suggested, commanded now with a harsh voice that sued no more.

" To-morrow," I said, assured of victory.

Edith looked down rather than nodded, as if I had laid a yoke upon her neck.

CHAPTER II

I

Even aliens felt it coming, and I sooner than my fellows, for I longed to shed my alienage, this election the result of which everybody foresaw. Even the Germans who, in the City, paint their brains with khaki, knew that the Liberals would win, and went loudly boasting, but conscious that they would have to eat the leek and the thistle and the shamrock too, while the rose wilted by the side of the primrose. And I am sure that my Liberalism was enhanced by the knowledge that my side would win; had the result been in doubt I do not suppose that, at twenty-five, I could have taken a judicial view. I should have been for armies, for Imperial Preference, because it was imperial. The Englishman of my dreams was not the Radical with whom I began to mix; I distrusted his whiskers, or his smooth legal cheeks, his fondness for oppressed nationalities and his taste for ginger ale; I did not feel that the real Englishman could care much about Chinamen, and I was sure that the last thing he would do would be to close the public-houses.

My wonderful Englishman was short, stout, ruddy; he had plenty of grey hair, a Roman nose, stubby hands and a fierce look in his blue eyes, when it was not a tender one. He insisted, this phantom, on wearing a low, glossy top-hat with a curly brim, comfortable for driving, breeches and top-boots, a riding coat and, over his capacious paunch, a red vest. He never said much at a time, and then it was " Bless my soul! " or " Tally ho! " or " Damnation." In those days he often said: " The country's

188

going to the dogs." He ate enormously, beef, boiled potatoes and Yorkshire pudding, also "greens" (said to be vegetable); he drank beer in imperial pints, and plenty of crusted port, which was bad for his toe and impelled it towards niggers, Germans, reform feeders, revivalists and artists in general. He was ruined every year by bad crops, but rode to hounds; he denounced the local authorities if they suggested he should be rated five shillings to feed school children, but sent two guineas and a tear to free-meal clubs. He suspected halfpenny papers and read them, believing every word they said, and grew very angry in a general, bullish way.

Bullish! it was John Bull I was in love with, and no wonder, for he was the most absurd and charming person I had ever met. I delighted in his gross joviality, his childish glee, his irrepressible brutality and his shame-faced emotion. He seemed, in that crucial year, to have waked up and to be trying to get into the skin of the English, to remind them that Falstaff was not dead: he was having a bad time. For old John Bull had been asleep for many years, and he could not believe these were his grown-up sons: Bullenstein, on the Stock Exchange, and Mr. Bull-Bull, K.C., who had taken a hyphen with silk; and he particularly disliked General Cannon Bull because the warrior was always hanging about and shouting: "Hullo, Bull! wake up. Can't you hear the bugle? You're wanted in the barrack square."

John Bull had gone to sleep comfortably in 1886, a Tory. Twenty years later he found that the prodigy of Rip Van Winkle had been "speeded up" by his Americanised papers and that he was a mere Unionist. He also discovered that he owed two hundred and fifty millions, which had piled up somehow while he snored, that he hadn't got much in exchange if all those tales about Chinamen in gold mines were true; to make confusion complete he heard they were actually going to introduce tariffs, nasty foreign things, which might interfere with his trade. That

made John Bull's blood boil; its boiling point is not low,
but when it boils it seldom stops until the hunting crop has
been broken on somebody; if the hunting crop acts as
a boomerang, recoils on John Bull's nose, he growls and
strikes again. His trade! He wanted to protect his navy,
his religion and his women, in order, and to keep cool
about it, but he wasn't going to have them monkeying with
his trade.

So John Bull threw savage glances at Bullenstein, Bull-
Bull, K.C., and General Cannon Bull, flung them a few
Elizabethan adjectives and substantives and looked about
him for a body in which to materialise. He had to materialise if he wanted to vote, and he passionately believed
that there was a vast difference between blue ballot-papers
and buff. I think he glanced at the Socialists and Labour
men, but made few remarks; indeed, nothing is recorded
of these save scattered words: " Sharing out—loafers—
sandals and nut-sandwiches—free-love——" He had then
but one place on which to lay his bullet head, for elimination left only the Liberals. Elimination was his way of
deciding; he picked out and discarded the worst, then the
bad, then the inferior, and developed enormous enthusiasm
for the survivors. This is what John Bull called " com-
promise " or " making the best of a bad job." He was
not getting what he wanted, though he never asked for
more than he wanted, and was quite willing to take less
if allowed to grumble; the Liberals were not giving him
his desire, and he hated them, but they were not trying
to give him what he did not want, and he began to love
them. He discovered in Edwardian Liberalism the creed
he was longing for, the great creed which is called Letting
Well Alone. The Liberals were Not going to interfere
with Free Trade; they were going to put back education
where it Was when he went to sleep; they promised also
to restore in South Africa labour conditions as they Had
Been. " Not! Was! Had Been! " said John Bull, cheerfully; " I like those words."

He had heard rumours he did not care for: "Home Rule," which aroused troublesome memories, and "Land," which always made him very angry, but these words were only whispered, while the roar of "Not! Was! Had Been!" filled his ears. As he liked the roar very much he did not trouble about the whispers and beamed upon those who roared, his youngest sons, Ebenezer Holyoake Bull, and Bull (of the Watermeadows); he told Macbull that he had always thought him a clever fellow, O'Bull that he had a sense of humour, and went so far as to shake hands with Llewellyn Bull, after buttoning up his pockets as a matter of habit. He went over to the Whigs. It is true that there were no Whigs, but something of their subtle essence hung about the Liberals, an essence which, snuffed by John Bull's broad nostrils, reminded him of Cromwell, Hampden, ship-money, democratic arson at Bristol; he had been fond of the Whigs once upon a time, of their way of letting well and ill alone, of their factories, counting-houses and (a long time ago) public-houses. Their tricks in Egypt, South Africa and Ireland had annoyed him, but he was so afraid of the Tories, because they reminded him of sheep suffering from the rabies, that he said: "I'm for the Whigs." When told there were no Whigs he flung himself into a terrific passion and declared, characteristically enough, that even if there were no Whigs he'd vote for them all the same. He wasn't going to argue about it, he was for the people who were going to let things be, the Whigs, and he was going over to the Whigs.

And I with him. I did not take them quite as he did, for I was a Frenchman and believed that people intended to do things when they said they were going to do them; I had no desire to let bad things alone, nor, for the matter of that, good ones, and I had rooted in my mind that, as anything that was must be bad, one could not go wrong if one broke up institutions. I was for the new law because it was the new law; I would have accepted reaction if it had been presented as progress. Thus Tariff Reform did not seduce me because I had been used to it in France: I had not been born under Free Trade, thus worshipped it; had I been a natural born Englishman I might have shouted " Down with it ! " but I was a Frenchman, so that it made no appeal to me, for I was a crude revolutionary. I wanted to smash, not to build.

It was not the cry of " Not! Was! Had Been!" which appealed to me then. While John Bull folded the Liberals to his arms because he took them for the Conservatives, I hailed them as the iconoclasts. I read the pamphlets which poured upon me when I became a subscriber to their official publications; I chuckled over cartoons where Cabinet Ministers appeared as foxes, rabbits and mad hatters. The Liberals were the people for me: they were going to " give one " to the capitalists, and another to the Church (*à bas les calotins!*), to take votes from the powerful—and there was a rumble in their machine, a rumble I could just hear: in those days the rumble sounded faintly like: " Down with the Lords ! " I did not know that the rumble would eventually develop into a mighty roar, that I would stand on a cart near Peckham Rye and be cheered while I referred to the Lords as " the gilded scum of the earth, titled ruffians, hangers-on of the chorus—" as is our political way down South, but even as a rumble it thrilled me.

The Liberals had a bold air of activity which pleased me; they were against abuses, they did not dislike foreigners, they were going to turn the country upside down and make it a better place: I honestly wanted it to be a better place, and as it could be made such by smashing all the old things I decided to be a Liberal. I wanted votes, land, houses for everybody, but I mainly wanted to take the votes, the land and the houses from somebody. It was, I felt, going to be a great big rag. Besides, Mr. Lawton and Hugh were Liberals. And Edith was a Liberal. I had to be loyal.

II

I joined a Liberal Club, which proved a temporary
cause of estrangement between Mr. Hooper and me. He
made no remark when I aggressively told him that I had
abandoned the primrose; he sighed, as if to say that good
grain often fell on stony places. Sometimes, when he
returned from his own and purer political association,
he found me obstinately reading *The Life of Gladstone,* or
a booklet on land taxation: then he would sit down in
the armchair by the grate, and do nothing for a while,
as if this sight took the strength out of him. If I looked
up I found his mild blue eye fixed upon me and unmis-
takably signalling: " The pity of it." This filled me with
malignant joy, and I went so far as to murmur " hear,
hear," and " good " as I read the poisonous gospels. Soon
I provoked him sufficiently to make him attack me.

" All that sort of thing," he said generally, " it's all
talk. You People, you only want to upset things; and
you don't want to do what the country's crying out for.
Why, look at the unemployed! How are you going to
find work for them? With all our home market swamped?
and everybody leaving the land because they can't make
anything out of it. No wonder they emigrate, all the best
of them; they're not going to stay here and starve.
There's much too many of us, that's what it is, but we've
got to feed them somehow."

Mr. Hooper rubbed the bald part of his head with his
handkerchief, peeping at me from under it, and I was
struck by the pathos of his attitude; here he was with a
whole bundle of problems: trade, agriculture, overcrowd-
ing, and the conflict was so complete that he regretted in
the same breath emigration and the increase in the popu-
lation.

" Well," I said, " tariff reform won't settle all that.
What will it do? "

"Work for all," said Mr. Hooper, delivering a swift blow.

I quoted Austrian and Italian figures of appalling unemployment.

"Oh, we don't count *them*," said Mr. Hooper, airily. "What about Germany?" He quoted most reassuring figures of German unemployment.

Then I quoted absolutely enormous figures of American unemployment, calmly picking out a period during which there had been a great strike and confining myself to the building trade.

Mr. Hooper, shaken for a moment, retorted, "What about tinplates?"

"Well, what about tinplates?" I asked, angrily.

"Going," said Mr. Hooper, gloomily.

"Oh? Cotton is going too, I suppose? and wool is gone?"

"Yes," said Mr. Hooper, with ghoulish delight.

Then there was a rumble of figures and I grew excited, Mr. Hooper talkative.

"It's all been stolen from under our noses, and the foreigner's coming in and taking our markets. Now I was talking to a man I know, he's a traveller in brasswork, he is, fenders and fire-irons, that sort of thing. Do you know what he said? Well, he said that in half the places he used to book orders they said there was nothing doing, that they were buying in Germany—cheaper!" cried Mr. Hooper, with restrained passion in his voice. "Cheaper! do you hear? And there's all your Liberal lot going round and saying that if we have Tariff Reform everything'll cost more. It's a shame, that's what it is."

"But how do they manage to make them cheaper in Germany?"

"Sweating," said Mr. Hooper, with infinite contempt. "Why——"

"Then Tariff Reform means sweating?"

" It means nothing of the kind. In America a brick-layer gets a pound a day."

" In France he gets three shillings."

" I'm not talking of France," said Mr. Hooper, with a stately air.

" No, you were talking about Germany, where you say there's Tariff Reform sweating——"

" I did not, Mr. Cadoresse."

" Now, Mrs. Hooper, I appeal to you," I said.

" Oh, don't ask me," said Mrs. Hooper, without raising her eyes from her fancy work; " I don't understand politics. You tell Mr. Cadoresse, Alfred."

We " told " each other with increasing energy, we feinted when cornered, we found figures and we tortured facts. We proved Spanish theory by German practice. We whirled in the midst of tariffs, Socialism and credit; we completely tied each other up in the payment for imports by exports; our talk became simultaneous, expanded, sucked in the waste of money on drink, housing, the hiring of barristers by the poor, tramps, betting—we touched peers, skimmed the divorce court—we slung heavy names at each other. I shouted " Gladstone," Mr. Hooper fluted " Disraeli." I laughed as I observed Lulu, a novelette in her lap, and her mouth so wide open that I could see her palate.

We grew silent suddenly, and I saw Mr. Hooper wipe his head again, very carefully, as if he had sworn to leave none of it unwiped. I pictured him again, pathetic, like a wretched little cork tossed on a stormy sea, rather a river in spate; nothing was so near our debate as a turgid river, flinging refuse into the air. Mr. Hooper took thought, then closed the discussion:

" All that sort of thing," he said, generally; " it's all talk. You People, you only want to upset things; and you don't want to do what the country's crying out for."

He delivered an exact replica of his opening speech !

We had argued in a circle, then. And for one moment I wondered whether I, too, had argued in a circle. But this did not trouble me long, for I felt sure I could break out of any circle, however charmed.

I felt strong, primed by the literature issued at my club. The library we owed to a pious founder, Clogg, sometime a Borough Councillor. The aged pensioner who kept it, a veteran who had "fought under William Ewart," practised among his shelves an extraordinary religion, Cloggolatry, of which he was high priest and sole adept. He seldom took a decision without conferring *sotto voce* with Mr. Clogg's spirit. When I came to him and told him I wanted books on Liberalism, he smiled, a gentle, thin-lipped smile; under his white eyebrows his blue eyes sparkled.

"Good boy, good boy," he said to the young generation, then with a rapid change of tone: "What would you like to begin on, sir?" And before I could make a suggestion, he murmured: "No, Mr. Clogg, really no, we can't start a boy like that on *Progress and Poverty*—now, come, Mr. Clogg, really—well, if you think so, Mr. Clogg——"

He interrupted his conversation with the ghost and offered me a disreputable-looking copy of *Progress and Poverty*. Evidently the shade of the Borough Councillor had prevailed. The old librarian's name was Smith, but the club called him Cloggie behind his back; he was well over seventy and would have been very tall if his back had not been bent as a bow; his stoop compelled him to thrust his brownish face forward as he talked, which he always did at some length, for he had the rapid, yet mellifluous flow of the practised speaker. But, alas, Cloggie was no longer as lucid as on that great day in 1882, when he had stood at the back of the orchestra in the Grand Theatre (which he sometimes located in Birmingham and sometimes in Wolverhampton) and held Gladstone's hat and overcoat.

"There I stood," said Cloggie, "for one hour and a half, and I could hear Him rolling away like a trombone,

and I couldn't hear what He said 'cos they were cheering
every five minutes, but it was splendid, I can tell you—
and I couldn't feel my legs any more, what with standing
up and what with the excitement, and people shoving me
to see Him. And then the cheering at the end. I couldn't
hear myself shout, though I could fetch a good howl then,
being a bit of a boy. And then He came along, quick, you
know, with His eyes all alight, and His chin waggling
up and down in that collar of His, and laughing because
they were all crowding round Him, all Birmingham, and
trying to get hold of His hand. 'Where's my coat?' He
shouts, and I can tell you I was proud when I stepped
along with it, saying 'by your leave,' and seeing them
make way for me as if I were the King's messenger. And
then, when I was putting it on Him, trembling all over I
was, He turns and looks me in the eye—looking like an
eagle. He says to me: 'What's your name?' He asks.
'Smith, sir,' I said (and I nearly said Your Majesty).
'Smith?' says William Ewart; 'that's a good name. Go
and tell all the Smiths of Wolverhampton to hammer
privilege on the anvil of democracy.' You should have
heard them shout when He said that."

The old man stopped, choked with emotion.

"Yes," I said, "that must have been fine."

"Fine! Why, Mr. Clogg and I used to talk about Him
for hours and hours. Don't believe me if you like, but
Mr. Clogg knew Him. Yes, he had dinner with Him in
1887——" Cloggie worked his psychic switch, and suddenly I heard him wrangle respectfully with the dead:
"I remember quite well, Mr. Clogg—it was 1887—when
you were standing for St. Anne's Ward—oh—um—well,
yes, that was in the spring of 1886—well, perhaps you're
right, Mr. Clogg." Cloggie switched Mr. Clogg off and
announced, with an air of relief: "1886, I mean."

The adorable Cloggie did, however, more than amuse
me; he liked my being a boy, that is under sixty, for
he was himself always "a bit of a boy" in any story

anterior to 1890 or so; he decided to educate me, so that
I often forsook the smoke-filled clubroom to go and sit
with Cloggie, and be catechised. Cloggie was bent on my
being thorough; it was he lent me Morley's *Life of Cobden*,
the speeches of John Bright, Mill on *Liberty*. He failed,
to his great chagrin, to make me take away the four volumes
of Sir Spencer Walpole's *History of Twenty-five Years*.
I was, said Cloggie, wilful and would do no good. But
the blue eyes, that twinkled under the white eyebrows,
said he didn't mean that, and that the old man, whose
family was either dead or in distant colonies, had found
in me a sort of grandson. So he let me browse in the
succulent pastures Mr. Clogg had left behind him, nibble
at Bagehot, Adam Smith and Mazzini (who was almost
equal to Him); and he forgave my flight from Walpole
when I appeared with a compact but orthodox J. R. Green.
And sometimes he would press upon me, almost mysteriously, a very old pamphlet.

"Read that," he whispered. "It's grand, grand." It
was usually some contemporary of the Repeal of the
Paper Duty. But Cloggie felt it would strengthen my
faith. He was not wrong, for I read with fierce enthusiasm
in the Tube, at home, when Maud was out, while I dressed,
in the street as I walked. I could not read while I shaved,
but soapmarks on my *Life of John Lord Russell*, show that
I read while I lathered my face. And sometimes Cloggie
would emerge from his book-lined bunk and sit in the
clubroom, cheerfully blinking, while his wonderchild hurled
the principles of Liberalism, in almost faultless English
marred by a fairly strong foreign accent, at an unoffending
speaker who had come from Headquarters to expound
Franchise or Poor Law Reform.

III

And that is how it came about that I contested Hambury. That is, I soon began to feel that it was I, and not

Mr. Lawton, who was going to stand for that shapeless slice of country where the old merchant suburbs of London, the villas of the clerks, workmen's dwellings and a few scattered farms have made an evolving little world of their own. Hambury, which I could reach from Euston in twenty minutes, began in the south by being urban, grew neo-urban a little further, then died in the fields; here and there it burst into smokestacks, while a pest of building plots, sown with sardine tins and old boots, had spread to every corner; even the elms, judging from the notice boards, were to be let on lease. And, not far from brooks and hedges, when one stood on a hillock, one could see companies of navvies breaking the roads so that the tramways, whose terminus was still in the south, could crawl nearer to the fields and strangle them with snaky steel tracks. It was on such a hillock that we stood, Edith and I, on a Saturday afternoon in November, for we were both of us " nursing " the constituency. We were not nursing it very loyally that afternoon, for I had not called at the office of the Liberal Association, while Edith had pleaded a second engagement and escaped from Mrs. Murchison's garden party in time to reach, by devious ways, this place where there were no votes and therefore no risks.

It was warm, for the Indian summer still lingered, as if reluctant to forsake the peaceful fields; the sun, veiled by faint mists, coloured tenderly the western sky, and there still was heat in its oblique rays. Indeed, something of the gladness of summer enfolded us, though the heavy dews had risen, blunted the sharp outlines of the branches; a faint but pungent smell of dead leaves was carried on the light wind, and, in a hedge, I could see a large spider, moving very slowly in its web, spiritless as if it knew that winter and death were coming. But we were alive, full of that quiet life which sometimes assures us of an immortality of which we are not aware in our more hectic turbulences. We stood, very content with each other, for

I knew that everything of Edith, her sedate grace, and the repose of her small gloved hands, filled me with a sense of rest: she stroked my soul, and it purred. And I had begun to gather as she looked at me, now a little more eloquent, that my dark face, my alert black eyes, my moustache and its audacity suggested to her something lurid which my words did not belie; for her I was the unexpected, the danger, the creature without rules or canons, who was exploring her world and daring to question it. She was, I felt, deliciously afraid of me. I liked to feel she was afraid of me, and to think she enjoyed her fear.

"Isn't it jolly?" she said.

"Isn't it?"

We remained silent for some moments, registering impressions; and I wondered whether in her mind I mingled with the landscape as much as she did in mine.

"You know," I said suddenly, "I like you better here than in London."

"Thanks." She smiled rather archly. "Am I so dreadful in town?"

"You're charming. But here, you're different because the place is different. You're sensitive, you see, like the chameleon. You take the colour of the place. And I like this colour better than that of London. It's all so restful and so simple; life seems so easy; I think of milkmaids, and calling the cattle home. Listen—that's a cowbell."

"I'm sorry," said Edith, resolutely; "it's a tram."

"Tush!" I was angry. "How can you talk of trams? Trams! They murder the world—they and the railways. It isn't like sedan chairs, and chaises, and hansoms; even motor-cars and motor-buses are better; all those things don't leave a trail of steel lines and posts and signals to remind you what a beastly world we're making. Trams! If I go to hell when I die and they want to do their worst, they'll put me in an L.C.C. garage. Oh, you laugh—but don't look that way, Edith, where there are men. Look there, towards the skyline, where the sky's blushing and making the cows look black."

I took her by the arm, and she yielded, turned towards the west. On the crest of the long, low hill, a cow stood outlined, snuffing towards the sunset with her raised snout. She was flat and, though dun-coloured probably, black against emptiness.

"She's lovely," Edith murmured. "What is she doing, I wonder; do you think she's saying her prayers? Perhaps she is, saying: ' Oh, sunshine—send me green fields and let the hay smell sweet—and let my baby calf grow up until it's too late for him to become veal —oh, sunshine, give him long life, so that he may be beef.' "

We both laughed together, but grew serious again, and I held her arm closer, moving my fingers slowly, taking in with all my hand its delicate, but firm outline.

"That's not the end," I said. " She's also praying: ' Oh, sunshine, let my hide be golden and glossy, my eye deep as a pool and my muzzle soft as velvet—so that the black bull with a gaze like hot coals, who paws the ground and throws steam from his nostrils, shall look at me while I stumble by—and make me shiver and yet draw nearer as I pass——' "

Edith drew her arm away with a jerk.

"You are silly. And I've already told you not to call me Edith."

"Why not? You can call me Lucien if you like. You did, once."

"That was an accident. And then you laughed at me because I pronounced it Loosian."

"Call me Loosian. I love it, please, Edith."

"No," said Edith, firmly. " It's wrong. What would people think, if I called you Lucien? And I don't want to call you Lucien."

I managed just in time not to tell her that she liked calling me " Lucien," that she had done it twice in her last sentence, for the pleasure of it. For I was not sure of her, I was not quite sure that I wanted to be sure of her. " Nobody would know," I murmured. " Any more than they know we're here."

" But if they did? " Edith looked at me with appealing eyes. " Wouldn't it be dreadful! I know I oughtn't to meet you here—if father knew he'd be so angry."

" But he doesn't know."

" He doesn't. But don't you see that because I know he wouldn't like it I can't feel it's right. A thing doesn't become right because it isn't found out, does it? "

I was compelled to own that it didn't, then turned on her.

" But you wouldn't like him to know, would you, if it made him unhappy? You'd hide rather than hurt him."

" I suppose I would," said Edith. " Of course I couldn't hurt him. I see what that means; I mustn't meet you again."

" Edith," I said, reproachfully, again laying my hand upon her arm; " but then you'd be hurting me."

" But what am I to do? " she cried out, and there was real misery in her voice. " If I go on meeting you like this, I feel—a pig—and if I tell, they won't let me—and if I don't come you say you'll be miserable."

Edith could not bear to hurt her father or me, and it never came into her mind that her father might not care or that I might not suffer. She took us as we seemed, and in this, I think, was her attraction: she simply believed in what she saw; unflinchingly honest, she believed others were honest, and now she suffered because her life was no longer without a secret. I tried to comfort her, for I had at every meeting to dispel her scruples and her fears; I reminded her that we did not often come together.

" Why should you worry? We've only met four times, by arrangement I mean; once at Prince's, and twice in Battersea Park, and once at Kew."

"And once on Primrose Hill—five times," she said softly; "you've forgotten, and——" She stopped abruptly, and we looked at each other. She blushed, and at once we knew that the quality of our relation had changed: it was she, not I, who had remembered, and she had unguardedly acknowledged that those meetings—mattered. We began to talk feverishly, both together; she interrupted my protestations with commonplaces, and the forced tone in her voice told me that she was holding back an emotional impulse. And I, Cadoresse the adventurer, was afraid. I helped her, and soon we were talking of Mrs. Murchison, and Chike, the progressive grocer. We laughed; I even recited a limerick. The strain ceased, and quite gravely we were able to discuss my rôle in the election.

"Father's awfully pleased with you," Edith confided. "He says you're frightfully keen; he hasn't told you, I suppose, but he's going to ask you to come down and help for ten days when the election comes. You'll come, won't you?"

"Will you?"

"Of course I will."

"Then, of course," I said, significantly.

"Oh, I don't want you to put it like that. You really are keen, aren't you?"

"Of course I'm keen. I don't say I believe in the programme, the whole of it, but I think on the whole it's the best."

"I'm so glad," said Edith. "I wouldn't like you to do it because—because—on account of me. I want things put right, you know."

Edith became sociological. The end, not the means, interested her; she wanted everybody happy, sober, working, each man in his little house, with a garden and some flowers in front.

"I'd give anything for that," she murmured, and as I looked at her pure, rosy face, I knew she was speaking the truth. We had left the hillock and walked through a field, then into a straggling wood. We climbed the low hill and looked over the crest where the cow had stood, towards the clustering villas of Hamburyville, the new suburb of the old town. Little streamlets of bluish smoke rose from the chimneys. A mile away we could see the tiny station and its model engine, and dots on the high road: the return of the Stock Exchange.

"They're coming home," she said; "it's getting late."

"Oh, not yet, not yet," I murmured. I drew her away, made her walk homewards by a devious way. It was half-past five, and the sun had set. We hardly spoke, but slowly, reluctantly went towards Hambury. We stopped for a long time, leaning on some palings, while invisible cows in the valley sent towards us, as they shambled towards their stable, the music of their bells.

"Bells," I said. "I was right. There still are cow-bells."

Progress, which has now engulfed Hambury, had not yet stamped them out. And so, softly, as we waited, the bells tinkled, some crystalline and gay, and others mournful, and yet others deep and portentous. I looked at the slim girl, her serious eyes fixed on the sky; I imagined her dream of impracticable hope for all those poor and misled, who had soiled their lives with cupidities and envies. And there was such wistfulness in those eyes, such undefined, greedy love for all those creatures that breathed, that I leaned forward, with words upon my lips that, repressed, made my mouth twitch. But Edith looked at me.

"Come," she said, "we must go, for the night is coming."

We parted outside Hambury, where a few lights shone in the windows.

"You will come again," I said.

"I oughtn't to."

"But you will? You will, Edith—little Edith, you will?"

"Perhaps." The eyes were veiled under the delicate, veined lids.

"Say ' I will write next time.' "

She laughed nervously. "Oh, I couldn't write."

"Then how shall I know? How shall we meet?"

She was silent. Then at length, very low, as if frightened:

"Very well."

I took her hand. "Good-bye, Edith."

"Good-bye."

"No, not good-bye. 'Good-bye, Lucien.' "

She looked towards the ground, obstinately silent.

"Good-bye, Lucien," I repeated.

She shook her head. "No." I held her hand, pressed it without speaking. At last she looked up, and I saw her lips tremble, form "No"— But, quite suddenly and spontaneously, I think, I heard her blurred, hoarse "Good-bye, Lucien"; her slim fingers pressed mine, while I bent down, and with my lips touched the glove on her unresisting hand.

IV

I had two whole months to think of Edith, to define my intentions to myself, for I heard, ten days later, that she had caught a chill and was in bed, then that she had been sent to Brighton for a month, in charge of an old aunt, for the Liberals had come into temporary power and the election was upon us: her mother could not be spared. Mrs. Lawton and Muriel were almost every day in Hambury, canvassing, smiling and making friends by means of condescensions and expensive furs. But I think I knew that I wanted my slim English girl only when I thought of her as ill, of her golden hair flowing on the pillow, of her little listless hands. My pity kindled my love, for

Edith had not the strong body which arouses contempt when it is sick; so like a flowering white convolvulus was she that I loved her first in her greatest weakness, as I might tenderly have raised the fallen plant and helped it to cling once more to the more robust ivy.

I loved her. I loved her in spite of myself, for love of Edith involved marriage, and my old tradition held me enough to urge that a Frenchman does not marry at twenty-five; also it reminded me that Edith would have no *dot,* that my income was a hundred and sixty a year: it laughed at me. But I laughed at it, for England had breathed her spirit in me, wiped out some of my grossness, some of my mercenary spirit. I was ready to take Edith poor and weak, to be poor and weak with her, to bow before her, the beautiful and pure, if only she would take my humble forehead between her smooth white hands. If I had thought of her, in the very early days, when she ceased to be a figment and became a woman, as the road I might follow to a partnership in Barbezan & Co., I had now forgotten such imaginings. My quest of the Golden Girl was at end, that sorry, delicious quest during which the knight upon the road meets such as Maud, Lottie and their like, and knightly speeds on. While the months oozed away, my love crept back upon itself, for I could not see Edith, or write to her, and dared but seldom question Hugh; I was reduced to such expedients as to alternate between her father, mother, sister and brother, so that my interest might not arouse suspicion, to question casually even Louisa Kent, who stung me with the remark that Edith was " a dear little thing."

I think I hated Louisa that day.

I suffered that madness of isolation which always overcomes me when I have lost the treasure I had or do not yet see the treasure to come. I fastened on the Lawtons, but they eluded me, all of them too busy with Hambury to listen to me; the clerks of Barbezan were intent upon Christmas holidays and had no eye for the alien; and

Maud preferred to me, to Saunders, the auctioneer, and to " Signor " Colley, a new friend, " a real gent who'd been introduced to her at Tinman's," a certain Bert Burge. I had not seen Bert Burge, but I knew he had something to do with the halls: as Maud was " on him like a bird," while he was " gone on her," she found a reason to be out of the house nearly every evening.

" So high-spirited," said Mrs. Hooper, with her air of mournful pride.

I was thrown back on Hambury, for now four weeks only separated us from the test. I had conceived a passion for Hambury, and, ten days before Christmas, I solemnly informed Mr. Lawton that I intended to devote myself to " The Cause," to give Hambury every night and every Saturday.

" Thank you," he said; " it's very decent of you."

Bare thanks! English thanks, or rather recognition of my sense of duty. I wanted more, and I wanted tribute. I did not have tribute, but a more precious gift was waiting for me that night: it was a letter in an unknown hand, addressed in good round writing, almost childish in its carelessness. The Brighton postmark made my heart pound against my side, and I could feel it still as I read, feel it long after I had finished learning the words:

" DEAR MR. CADORESSE,

" I thought you would like to know that I am much better. I suppose you know I have been ill. Only a chill, but I had a *high* temperature. I oughtn't to write to you but—(several words scratched out)—I didn't want you to think I had forgotten to write before we met again. I *do* want to come back, but they won't let me until next month, or they won't let me canvass—and I do want to canvass; it'll be *such* fun. You would like Brighton (but how silly of me, you know it), for the sea is so blue, it's like turquoise; you'd think of something much prettier

to compare it with, but I feel stupid. How is Mr. Chike
and have you converted Mrs. Chike?

"Yours sincerely,

" EDITH LAWTON."

" P.S.—Of course you mustn't write to me.   It isn't
safe."

I went to my room to read the letter again.   I read
it five or six times; the letter was Edith, shy, affectionate;
it tried to say what she meant and shrank from at the
last moment.   It thrilled me, its spontaneity and the fact
that it was spontaneous; I kissed the letter and rejoiced
because it carried no scent.   The innocent underlining,
the literary timidity which made her eschew similes, all
this was Edith.   It was all she, the boyish anticipation of
the election rag, the mild scoff at the progressive grocer,
the fear lest her silence should have hurt me; that was
Edith, and exquisite, but more precious to me was the
Edith in relation to me implied in the scratched-out words,
which I made out with a magnifying-glass to be " I wanted
to."   She had wanted to write to me, and she had dared
to do it, but she had not dared to say she wanted to—
just as her postscript implied that she wanted me to reply,
though she dared not let me.   Sweet fugitive, I knew what
you meant, though you did not say it, and I, who ever
loved the bold, loved your shrinkings.   And I thought of
her by the turquoise sea.

Poised against the western wind she stands upon the
white stones, little girl for whom the blast is too rude.
Hands muffled in white wool, she rules the straying gold
of her hair, and the wind furls her skirts about her, clings
to and presses her against its soft, cold bosom.   The wind
kisses into vividness the roses of her cheeks and tints with
purple her mouth that pouts as a split cheery, and as she
laughs her eyes are dim with fine spray; she looks at the
turquoise sea and it is jealous of her eyes' blue depths.

V

And on again to the comedy of elections which so recalls the fights of dirty little boys who roll in the London gutter; to meetings, canvassings, lies, proofs and smart retorts; to charges of unfairness and appeals for the playing of the game; to fine prejudice too, to noble fanaticism, to generosities and unselfish hopes; to impracticable cures for evils, to truthful promises and self-abnegation; to all that incoherence and turbidness of purpose out of which comes, after all, stumbling and halting, some mercy and a little justice.

Every night at half-past six, I reported at the central committee-room. I came out with a bundle of canvass cards, sometimes alone and sometimes as escort of Muriel or Mrs. Lawton, when they had to visit certain quarters of the old town reputed to be " dangerous." For Hambury was getting on in the world: the merchants had deserted the old houses for modern detached residences, so that Hambury had had to turn the early-Victorian homes, among which was occasionally a fine, square Georgian house, into tenements. It was among these tenements I had to take Muriel, who wrinkled her nose at the smell of man—food—washing, to stand by her side and look confidently at the big, truculent navvies who were laying the tram-lines towards the blessed fields, while she recorded their opinions, and said the weather would improve if the Liberals got in.

We were splendidly efficient; we wasted no time on argument, for Hambury was unmanageable: since the redistribution its electorate had grown from about eight thousand to twenty-seven thousand. Thus all the canvassers could do was to ascertain where was the strength, so that it might be polled.

" It's simple enough," said Muriel; " we found that out when father stood for Bowley. In these big divisions it's not worth while arguing: poll your strength and you win; at Bowley we polled seventy-nine per cent., which was jolly bad; if we'd polled eighty-five we'd have got home. You don't want to turn a vote. Just poll your own."

Whether this was or was not democratic government did not seem to trouble Muriel much; I remember her during that month as a completely cynical girl, intent only on winning; her dash had been transmuted into a ceaseless and businesslike activity, her talk of theatres and dances into a rhapsody of half-a-dozen words: " doubtful —removed—ours—theirs—meeting—canvass." We raced each other along opposite sides of a street, waving ironically across the road when we had gained a couple of canvassed houses; we learned to work at top-speed with a blunt pencil, slippery canvass cards and uncertain electric lamps; we talked only of elections, and we never kissed. Tacitly Muriel had abandoned me to Edith, and I, being now so little of a Frenchman, accepted her attitude.

Hambury was a centre of chaos, for I seemed not only to be always canvassing, always rushing into the committee-rooms for further supplies of cards, to find there a buzzing group of women, who checked lists of voters, addressed envelopes, scrapped the dead, always catching trains and omnibuses to lose myself in Balham or Richmond while I tracked removals, or stewarding at meetings, or whirling in a motor-car in an aimless, distraught way, going to a place I didn't know, with a message I didn't understand, to meet a man who did not appear. The fog of the election was like the fog of war, and I, a private, did not know what I was doing. But one thing I could feel: the splendid English organisation. The professional agent showed amazing mastery of the registration law, of the Corrupt Practices Act and of the topography of Hambury; the constituency was covered, area by area; canvassers were allotted and marshalled; meetings were held in six places at a time, speakers changed, speeches toured, men imported from London, carried off in motor-cars, dropped at

scheduled points, emptied of their speech and whisked off
again by other cars to do service twenty miles away. Our
colours were everywhere; our cars, decked with red ribbons
and posters, let their engines race and roar in the market-
place, so that Hambury should know we were there, mob
us, stand open-mouthed and mentally promise votes to the
authors of the fine to-do.

And figures crowd about me: Hepson, the agent, who,
on being informed that one of our cars had killed an old
woman at Broughton, remarked: " That's all right. Broughton's a quarter of a mile over the boundary "—and Mrs.
Mill, a sweet-faced old piano-teacher, a Roman Catholic,
who burned a candle every morning at the shrine of her
favourite saint while praying for our triumph—and Wing,
his friend Mayne, both Young Liberals, who 'ad a bit on
ole Lawton and 'ud give three to one agin the other
blighter. They crowd, some of them just names—Rennie,
Morrison, Miss Festing—and some nameless faces, ascetic
faces of old men with side-whiskers, and the sly, fat muzzle
of a publican who saw the point of being the one Radical
innkeeper, and very young, boyish and girlish faces, rosy,
blue-eyed; faces of children who wept for favours and
occasionally paraded with our poster pinned on their backs.
And others: Lady Bondon, the wife of Sir Thomas Bondon,
our opponent, a large, red lady, with an enormous black
silk bust and a voice which Sir Thomas must have learned
to respect in his—no, her own house.

There is Hugh lecturing me because I had called Sir
Thomas a blackguard.

" He's not that—he's on the other side, but——"

" If we're right the other side must be blackguards."

" Oh, no—he's entitled to think as he likes, and one
mustn't mind. You know, Cadoresse, in England political
enemies can be personal friends."

" Hypocrisy."

" Not exactly; of course an M.P. may feel a bit sore
when he's being slanged in the House by the chap he plays

golf with, but he mustn't say so. One's got to play the game and keep a stiff lip when one gets one in the eye."

It struck me as a little artificial, but the Englishman always plays the game, and thinks everybody ought to do so. I think Muriel carried the attitude to its extreme development when she told me that fox-hunting was all right because the fox had a chance to get away.

"Not like pigeon shooting," she said scornfully, "or hunting carted stags. That's not sport, but the fox has got a chance—he *likes* a run."

Well!

And there is Chike, the progressive grocer; five foot two, or three at most, marvellously active and apologetic, running like an overgrown rat about the streets, with his little brown eyes racing towards the point of his long nose, and a general air of timid, incredibly swift scuttle.

"Hullo, Chikey," screamed the urchins as he ran; "look out, 'ere She is."

And then Chike would leap as he ran, and shake wild, futile little fists at the boys, for She was Mrs. Chike, Primrose Dame, thirteen stone in weight, and determined that her husband should not disgrace himself with our low lot. Everybody knew that she thrashed Chike, that she locked him up as soon as the shop was closed "to keep him out of trouble." But Chike was much more than nimble: he developed extraordinary cunning, once dived right under her vast person, when she barred the door, and rushed out more like a rat than ever, like a rat that a cat is chasing. He had his revenges too.

"I got even with her yesterday," he excitedly related. "I was trackin' removals 'cos I 'ad time, bein' early closin'. So when I got me first, I ses to meself, 'ere's a chance, ses I: I'll telephone the ole gell to cheer 'er up. So I telephones 'er, an' you should 'ave 'eard 'er. And I telephoned 'er again: 'Got another, Maria,' says I. 'Where are yer—yer dirty tyke?' ses she. 'Ah, wouldn't yer like to know,' ses I. And I telephoned 'er agin, when I

got another—an' she 'ad to answer, 'cos she couldn't tell it
wasn't a customer—so I telephoned her agin', jest for luck.
Cost me eightpence altogether, but it was worth it, but "—
Chike rubbed his head significantly—" she did go on awful
when a' got 'ome."

Yet the contest seemed to breed no ugliness. We did
not always tell the truth, but I seemed to miss the
atmosphere of violence in which French politicians breathe;
I looked in vain for the inspiring red, white and blue
posters which, when Frenchmen are polling, stare at us
from every wall:

LIAR!

> Voters! Do not be deceived by a Candi-
> date whom I do not condescend to name, a
> Man who has sold to the Jews such honour
> as he derives from his illegitimate par-
> entage. . . .

or—

I CHALLENGE

> That Hireling of the Church to say he
> did not suddenly receive Eighty Thousand
> Francs. (Did you say Panama? Hush!) . . .

That is what I called electioneering, and I told Hepson
so, but he merely laughed and said that in England no
man was a traitor until he was in office. I felt that my
attempts to " ginger up " our leaflets were coldly received.
Reluctantly I decided to help win this election like a gentleman: our French way is a much bigger rag.

VI

And at last Edith came. In ten days the people of
Hambury would go to the poll. She came, and in the

first handshake she gave me, which lingered a little, she said: "Here I am." And her blush, her quickly averted glance repeated: "Here I am," added, "what are you going to do with me?"

I did not know what I was going to do with her. Perhaps I did not know what I was going to do with myself, unless I intended to place myself in the hands of the Providence of Lovers, beg it to make or mar me as it would. All I knew was that the shy girl thrilled me because she was no longer so shy with me: I was as Christopher Columbus landing on the shores of America; I had not explored a continent, but I had set my foot within its boundaries.

This inner life of mine was one of storm, for the tender bordered ever on the businesslike; we perpetually drifted to the personal while we canvassed, and then again we would be driven away from the open gates by the preoccupation of an illegible name on a card, the facetious howl of some small boy, or meetings with other canvassers. Those other canvassers! How intolerably bright and metallic was the surface with which they coated their jadedness, their sickness of the whole affair; they made jokes out of cold feet, lost pencils, electors removed to another corner of the borough, things that are quite tragic in January. We met Dicky Bell, his brown eyes beady with excitement because he had found a street of seventeen "Fors," one "Against" and one "Doubtful." He announced the result at the top of his voice, shouted "Hooray! Hoo-blastedray," apologised to Edith with a "Beg pardon, election fever," and ran away to the central committee-room for new cards. An Englishman excited! And sometimes we saw Neville, patiently plodding from door to door, doffing his hat to the suspicious wives of the railwaymen, and gaining promises by the sheer pathos of his innocent blue eyes. Neville could suffer rebuffs in silence, cover his close-cropped curly fair hair, and squaring his weak chin as well as he could, go on to the next

house, humbly, stodgily, as if he were still at work on his
father's debts. They whirled about us, calling for cards,
leaflets, window-cards for our supporters, notices of meetings, all of them, Louisa, with Hugh in her train, and Kent,
who had given up epigrams because " when you were polite
the poor knew you were being rude," and Gladys Raleigh,
and Bessie Surtees, and the local enthusiasts, Wing, Mayne,
all red tie and three-inch collar; Mrs. Mill, always a little
prayerful; the sly, fat Radical innkeeper, and Chike, scut-
tling past, with a glance of apprehension for every big
woman. We talked, we argued, we contradicted, we told
each other the way, we clamoured for notes to be made
that Thompson wouldn't come unless we sent an electric,
that O'Kelly wanted Home Rule for his vote, and would
Mr. Lawton go and blarney him? that Smith was engaged
up to five minutes to eight, that Emmett could speak and
wouldn't, while Morrison would speak and couldn't—Fog!
And in the midst was Mr. Lawton, neat, not too smart, in
perpetual conference with Hepson, gravely forbidding us
to give the children pennies, cautioning us against treating
when treated, reminding us that to give favours was a
corrupt practice—I see his tired, handsome face as he sits
with Hepson.

"Ward four is very bad, you must double the open-
airs there, Hepson—and I can't speak at the Drill Hall
at eight fifteen if I'm to be at St. Catherine's Schools at
nine—you must recall that poster, it's too thick—the Bur-
glars' Cabinet, I mean—Lord Wynfleet will lend two cars
for the day——"

Fog! And then Mr. Lawton, in the market-place, on
a dray. He speaks slowly, hands clasped behind him,
without notes, his face lit up by a naphtha flare. I hear
his steady voice:

"And because we are free we intend to remain free.
We will not have to lead us the men who have stolen our
schools, who have placed our women and our children in
the hands of the liquor trade, who have sat upon the

fence when we asked whether they would tax our food, who have not even had the courage to lie. No, Englishmen, you must never again trust them, never allow them to enslave your trade any more than to enslave Chinamen——"

And I hear the roar that rises from hundreds of faces, white, ghastly under the flares, stained by the hundred black holes of their open, roaring throats. The sound rises, beats upon the four façades of the market-place, drowns the feeble oratory in the other corner where Sir Thomas Bondon is being heckled, for Lawton has hit home. They sing, these open throats:

> "There is a golden Rand,
>   Far, far away.
> Millionaires say they can't pay
>   More'n a bob a day;
> There Chinese toil all day
> And, toiling, sadly say:
> Chinee-man he likee be
>   Far, far away."

VII

But one night we were lost, in that fateful ward four. Having set out with hazy ideas of our destination we could not find Molton Street; questions to the natives increased our confusion, for the Hamburyites did not know their way, they found it by instinct. We were told to bear to the left for Granby Street while the Granby Street plate showed opposite in the light of a gas-lamp; we missed turnings, retraced our steps, sought for villas in dark little streets where flickered the window lights of stationers, tobacconists and cheap confectioners, of public-houses which Liberals dared not enter. Directed towards a square, we suddenly arrived on the banks of the Ham.

" I'm sick of this," I said, stopping. " Aren't you? "

" Well, I *am* rather tired," said Edith. " Still——"

I looked at her, smiling, her eyes black in the bad light, so slight, so delicate and yet wistfully determined to go on.

"Only one day more," she said, bravely trying to laugh; "and then——"

"Victory," I said. I detected a hoarseness in my voice. Victory? Yes, for Lawton—but did the word mean anything to me, Lucien Cadoresse?

"Let us give it up for ten minutes. Shall we? Let's go along here."

"All right," said Edith.

We walked along the tow-path. The night was dark; between the gas-lamps we could not see each other's faces. The river flowed very slowly, and, here and there, where rubbish had accumulated, a film of dust made sheets of shimmering grey satin. We went silent, and very close together, elbows touching and intimately conscious of solitude. Then, near a light, we found an old stone bench. "Rest in Peace, Wanderer, and in Peace Depart. 1787," said the inscription. We both smiled; Edith traced the letters with her finger.

"Come," I said. "Let us sit down for a little."

Edith did not reply, sat down, and as she did so, shivered, for the night was cold.

"I'm glad you've come back," I said at last. "It was a long time since you wrote."

"I ought not to have," she said, in a low voice. Her face was averted. "But——"

"But you wanted to," I suggested.

And so gently had I spoken that, after a while, she sighed and said:

"I suppose I did."

"I wanted you to come back, Edith, dreadfully. Without you it was dark. But now—everything is different. When I'm with you I feel alive, I want to be great. Oh, I know, I'm nobody——"

"You mustn't say that," replied Edith, "or you'll never be anything. And I—I want you to be something."

"What?"

"I don't know—I want—oh, I can never talk to you, Lucien, you—you talk so queerly—you frighten me."

She shivered.

"You are cold," I said. And for the first time I laid my arm across her shoulders, held her gloved hand. She did not resist; indeed, I fancied that she rested against my shoulder, that her slim fingers clasped mine. And later, as I drew her closer, I found her cheek against my shoulder, light as a leaf upon a stream. As I looked down I could see some loose strands of pale hair, the blunted edge of her foreshortened nose. She was so near that I could feel her breathe, so near that an inclination of my head would have brought my lips to her eyelids, and the desire of it began to hang behind me, urging me on, pressing my head down with soft, ghostly hands. But some other instinct held me back, some obscure æstheticism which forbade that I should spoil with a concrete caress this minute most exquisite, because it was the first.

"What am I doing?" said Edith, at last, to herself rather than to me. Then: "I ought to be away, out there, where the lights are——"

"No, no," I said thickly; "stay here, stay here. There is nothing out there. If all Hambury were to become air we should be here both of us—little Dresden Shepherdess, that is what I call you; when I hold you like this I know that life is good."

"Life is good," said Edith. And later:

"I'm not so frightened as I was. I was frightened, you know."

"Of what?"

"I don't know. You're so dark—you seem so fierce —you look at me with your black eyes. They glow like coals—and you're French. I hardly know what you mean sometimes, when you talk about pictures—and you're cynical. One doesn't know what you mean."

"But you know," I murmured, holding her now so close

that I could feel against my side the hurried beating of her heart.

" I try to understand. But you're not like the other men I know; they say what I expect." She laughed nervously. " It's so easy with them, while with you, I'm always afraid that I'll not understand, when you say that kings are at their best without their heads—or other things—about women—cynical things."

" I never say cynical things about you."

" No—you think I'm a baby."

" Sweet Edith, do you not feel like a child, as I hold you so close? "

" You oughtn't to," she said, weakly. Then: " Yes— I suppose I do . . . And I don't mind."

The light grew, for the heavy clouds that shrouded the moon were slowly drifting towards the east. A white glow oozed through them where the hidden planet hung. I released Edith's hand, let my hand glide along her arm, to the slim shoulder that trembled, until my fingers touched her cheek. A shiver, a long shiver that shook her whole body passed through her, and as she pressed her head on my shoulder, while I caressed her cheek, soft and smooth as the flesh of an orchid, the cloud became as a film of grey gauze, let the deathly pale rays of the moon silver the hair of my beloved. We sat, thus linked, for a long time, I think, and I was so ravished that I listened to the chimes of Hambury Church with such indifference as may feel a prisoner for life, when the hours ring out. We did not speak, we had nothing to say, but I knew, as I felt my knees tremble, that everything had been said, that nothing was left for us to do save to put that everything into words.

" We must go," she said, without moving.

" We must go," I repeated.

But at last the chimes sounded ten o'clock. We started up.

" Oh—what shall we do? " cried Edith.

I was holding her hands, drawing her towards me. "Edith—Edith—my darling——" I murmured, in a voice so thick, so muffled that I could hardly form my words.

"Oh, we must go—we must go——" she whispered. She let me draw her against me, clasp her close, but she averted her face, buried it into my coat. As she freed herself I knelt down and, holding palms upward the little hands, pressed two kisses into the openings of the gloves— two long, tremulous kisses upon the scented suède and the smooth, cold palms. Together we turned back, and our hands did not unclasp until we saw before us the glaring naphtha lamps of the market-square.

VIII

And the next night I spoke. Canvassing was over, so I hung near the most eastern of our two Roman Street platforms, while Edith exchanged dignified and compulsorily democratic pleasantries with Mayne, who was now giving four to one agin the other blighter. He could afford to, though we had to pull down a majority of sixteen hundred and to reckon with a new vote of six thousand, mainly in Hamburyville; for our canvass showed that we ought to win by at least fifteen hundred, and on this night, the eve of the poll, a jovial, singing, hear-hearing crowd was perpetually expanding from our platform into the High Street, then swirling back as the tramways cleft through it to a fierce accompaniment of bell-ringing. Twenty yards away a struggling mob was shouting down Sir Thomas Bondon's men, and a shrill crowd of children, decked out in our red favours, screamed and whistled them into inaudibility.

"Isn't it great?" I said.

"Great," said Edith, excitedly.

We were against the platform and, over our heads, the Headquarters man, Federation, I think, boomed out practised, eloquent phrases that stimulated the crowd into cheering, fired off the morning paper's epigrams, spurted personalities to which the crowd responded.

" The Tories scuttled when we talked Tariffs. Shall they scuttle Free Trade? "

" NO," roared the crowd.

" Will you have Hambury boots made by Chinese slaves? "

" NO, NO—to 'ell with 'em."

Phrase by phrase the speaker lashed them, striking again and again at the Chinese, until at last the mob broke out into the song:

> " There is a golden Rand,
> Far, far away. . . ."

But something was wrong, for he bent down to the chairman:

" I can't go on—voice going," he said, hoarsely.

" Oh, try, sir, try," said the chairman. It was one of the ascetic-looking, whiskered old men.

" Five minutes," said the speaker, " spoken six times to-day." He wiped his face with his handkerchief. I heard the old man muttering, " What's to be done? What's to be done? " Then my heart began to beat, a little vein to shiver in my left temple. The blood was thick in my head—I remember imposing my help on the old man—and Mayne advising me to " give 'em 'ell," and Edith, with a mouth that trembled and tried to smile. And then I was on the platform, speaking in a raucous voice that did not belong to me, terrified, excited—saying things I did not know I knew, to a great, white sheet of faces full of black mouth-holes—and when the wind blew the stench of the burning naphtha. I spoke. I heard a roar of approval. What had I said? Ah, yes—I had forgotten the election, plunged into the future—I had said that dukes were not two a penny, but certainly two for a fully-paid share—I began to describe Protection in France, my country—sugar at fivepence halfpenny a pound—suits cheap at sixty shillings—bread at twopence a pound—I saw Edith, deadly white, with three black stains for eyes and mouth—and Mayne, grinning.

"Down with 'em—down with 'em," roared the crowd. I spoke, and on, and on, growing clearer, calmer now, smiling back at Edith, pointing an excited finger at her.

"They say that England's going to the dogs—it will, if we get the tariff, for then we'll EAT the dogs." (Roar.)

For twenty minutes I spoke, and I saw Edith clap her hands with the others, though the old chairman put up a deprecating hand as I ended on my "rouser." "I've come all the way from France, boys, a thousand miles, to tell you that England's the place for men—(cheers)—that England is your privilege and your trust. (Blank silence.) To ask you not to let it be chained and starved and enslaved by a gang of blackguard manufacturers allied with drunken squires. (Roar.)"

When at last I came down into the crowd, flushed, mobbed by the friendly, hot bodies, I was glad, if a little ashamed of my violence, for was not this violence the only expression I could give to my love for this land of freedom and silent passions, seldom unleashed? And Edith had slipped her bare hand into mine, gripped me convulsively. I heard her voice:

"It was splendid—splendid——"

Was it splendid? Was this not Darkest England I saw? This England of elections where men yawned if you said "Principles of Liberty," and shouted if you said "Pretty Fanny?" England, must you wallow in the mud sometimes, because you are a buffalo? But I crushed down my suspicions, told myself this great force could not be fine or gentle; I pictured the progress of England as that of some Roman warrior on a chariot, racing the wind, brutal but conquering, and magnificent, winning the race, winning. I filled my ears with the thunder of the hoofs.

And in the midst of chaos we polled. Twelve hours of terrific noise, the hooting of the cars, the songs, the bands. For there were bands to bring up the two hundred Tories on the blue-decked vans of Hardafort's brewery, bands to lead the Liberal reds from the boot-factory, and the band of the Ancient Order of Elephants, doubtful that one; the temperance interest wore red for the day; eighteen Irishmen followed to the ward four schools an orange-decked drum and interrupted polling for twenty minutes while they settled the Home Rule question with the rest of the Irish interest.

One day of almost continuous din, for the tramways persisted in running, crammed to the doors with people who speechified in defiance of bye-laws, a day when splendid sunshine lit up Hambury, so that a passing airship might have taken its quilt of posters, streamers and favours for the robe of Harlequin. I seemed to be running all the time, perpetually calling at the same house to make sure that Thomson had polled, or helping bed-ridden old Carvell into a car; also I bundled our people into the Bondon cars, having stripped off my favour and bluffed the Tory chauffeur. I ate standing up in the central committee-room, beside Edith, who trembled with excitement, and Hugh who smoked, with splendid calm, consecutive pipes, while Louisa in vain tried to hustle him into activity.

Some little things jut out, like church-spires out of a fog. Cloggie, who came up at six, saying that he had polled his share, Cloggie, anxious, bright-eyed, whispering of the Repeal of the Paper Duty and the greatness of the late Mr. Clogg—and Neville, as resigned and mild as ever, progressing saintlike in ward four, escorted by two score dirty little boys who threatened to put him in the Ham—and Chike.

Chike! I did not see him until ten minutes to eight. I stood wearily with Edith at the entrance of the schools in ward three. Only ten minutes more! There was nothing more to be done, for we had either won or lost.

A few yards away, watching the door, was a very big

woman with a red face, over which fell some rumpled grey hair.

"Mrs. Chike," I whispered to Edith. "Watching for him."

Edith laughed merrily, then murmured, "Poor Mr. Chike. What a shame!"

"He won't poll," I said; "she's locked him up in the coal-cellar, I expect, and she's watching to be sure he doesn't escape."

We laughed again, both of us, looking into each other's eyes; I was full of the intimacy of love. And I knew now that Edith felt that intimacy. Yet I left her, for I wanted to go into the station and, for the first time, see the actual voting. An excited crowd surged in it, mobbed the clerks, snatched the slips and filled them in at the desks, maintaining the secrecy of their choice by ostentatious hunchings of their shoulders and squarings of their elbows. It amused me, this seriousness, and it enhanced the splendour of hard, steady England.

There was a swirl in the crowd, caused by four big men and a load. I heard protests, an "all right, guvnor." In a cleared space lay a large case marked HARDAFORT BREWERY COMPANY, LTD.

"What the devil——" said one of the clerks as he stood up.

There was a breathless moment as the lid slowly rose and there peeped out the long, ratlike nose and beady eyes of Chike. Then a roar of laughter and cheers as the progressive grocer unfolded his little limbs, proudly strode up to the table and proclaimed: "Chike, Thomas Albert, 5 Fullerton Street."

"She kept an eye on me, she did—but she didn't think of looking inside the empties when my pals came for 'em —she thought I was in the store-room gettin' some more when they carried me out. Lor'!"—he removed some straw from his hair,—" it was 'ot in there."

"It'll be 'otter outside, ole man," said Mayne; "you bet

she saw the van and twigged it—she'd 'ave stopped it if the police 'adn't been there."

" Lor'! " said Chike, apprehensively, and peeped out of the window into the night.

" Any'ow, a've done me little bit for ole Lawton."

" Four to one agin the other blighter," said Mayne, automatically.

CHAPTER III

BETROTHED TO AN ENGLISH GIRL

I

"ARE you going to the count?" said Edith.

I shook my head. "No, they'll only let three people in. Your father is taking Hugh and Kent."

"Then there's nothing to do but wait."

"Two hours and a half at least. Where shall we go to?"

"Oh, we can't go anywhere—I'd better find Muriel and mother. Mother's at Roman Street, I think."

"Edith!" I drew nearer, spoke in a whisper, though the voices of the crowd would have allowed of ordinary speech, in a deliciously guilty whisper. "Don't go—come with me. We have time; you won't be missed; everybody's so excited. Come with me—we'll go to the old bench near the Ham. Look, there are the stars all over the sky, like silver-headed nails."

"I mustn't," she said, but weakly.

"Go and find your mother," I suddenly commanded. "Tell her you want some air, that you're going to find Bessie and that you'll be back in an hour——"

"But——"

"But of course you won't find Bessie. You'll take the tram to Four Trees Corner; it's quite near the river, and I'll wait for you there. We can't go together; everybody knows you. And—if you've got a thick coat, wear it."

Edith looked at me, still hesitating; I drew closer to her, gripped her hand.

"It may be our last chance for a long time, little Edith."

I left her before she could reply, and as I sat in the tramway among the men who were returning from the poll, I was barely conscious of their computations of chances, their stories and oaths; even the obsessing song:

> "There is a golden Rand,
> Far, far away. . . ."

formed but a background to my thoughts. For I knew that this was the Day.

As she looked up at me, with a little fear in her misty eyes, a tremble in her mouth, I knew that Edith had come to me—no, that I had snatched up her light frame and sat it in my heart upon a throne. She would come, I knew it, she would have to come, for she could not help it, I wanted her so much that she could not escape. I ached for her.

Half-an-hour later we sat together on the stone bench. She was buried in a thick motor-coat; her head was hooded but hatless, so that under the rough blue frieze and the pale hair her face was in a shadow, broken only by the depths of her darker eyes. I held in mine her unresisting hand. We had been sitting in silence for some minutes, at first linked and peaceful, then restless, for as I flung glances at Edith I wanted suddenly to seize her, crush her in my arms, mutter into her frightened ears an avowal so fiery as to frighten her more. For I knew the quality of this love of mine; it was infinitely tender and worshipping and yet it was cruel, it wanted to conquer and to hold. I loved her for her fear of me; I wanted her to lay upon my altar a broken and contrite heart so that I, I and no other, should heal it and make it glad.

" I wonder whether we've won," she said, mechanically.

" Oh——" I surprised myself by the anger in my voice. " What does it matter? What does anything matter except that you are here, you, with me? I've forgotten everything, except you, you, my sweet." And now I surprised myself by my own gentleness.

"My sweet, my sweet," I murmured, and without conscious intention laid my arm across her shoulders, drew her closer to me, pillowed her hooded head so that my cheek rested on the harsh stuff. She did not resist. For a very long time, I think, we did not speak; both, I feel, were assured that the irremediable, the delicious irreparable was achieved. Then again:

"Edith, my darling—I said it might be our last chance for a long time. It isn't true, it could not be true. For you haven't come to me just to go away. Have you, my sweet?"

The hooded head shook on my shoulder.

"I've found you—you're precious—you're like the scent of violets——"

Edith raised her head, looked at me, and our faces were serious.

"Lucien, I——" She faltered, then hurriedly: "Oh, Lucien, don't look at me like that, I'm afraid—I—I too——"

"Edith," I said, very slowly, detaching the two syllables, tremulous, wondering.

"Oh—you don't know what you're doing—other men have said things to me, things—nice things—but you, Lucien, oh, I don't know, I don't understand. When you look at me like that you make me tremble and yet I'm glad. What am I saying? What am I saying?"

There was a ring of sorrow, shame in her last words. It stirred me so deeply that I suddenly turned her towards me, sat almost face to face to her, my hands on her shoulders, looked into her eyes, and mine, I know, told my need of her. The hood fell, her upturned face shone white in the light of the moon, and her eyes were veiled.

"Edith," I said at last; "my little girl. My beautiful —I love you."

I saw a little tremor convulse her lips, but she did not move.

" I love you," I said hoarsely. " I've loved you for a year. That day when we stood among the almond blossom, I wanted to ask you whether you'd be my wife—my darling, my darling."

Still she did not reply. My insistent hands drew her towards me, and I trembled as she yielded, trembled as she lay close against my breast. I inclined my head, laid my cheek upon hers. And my phrases were broken now by the intensity of my emotion.

" My darling, my love—say you will come to me—say you'll not leave me—I love you—I can't be without you—my Edith, my little girl——"

She did not speak, but I felt our faces move, yet without parting, as if they clung together, as if they could not bear to part. Slowly they moved, and I trembled, as my lips brushed the smooth cheek. Then I was looking at her lowered eyelids, while my hands knotted round her and, as if answering, she held up for my kiss her parted lips.

Soon I had drawn her across me, seated her upon my knees. And now she lay, nestled in my arms, with her head upon my shoulder, silent but breathing fast. I could feel upon my face her warm, fragrant breath. My kisses travelled from her forehead, where a few golden threads clung to my lips, to her cheeks, hot and feverish, to the soft whiteness of her neck, to her tender, yielding mouth. As I caressed her I could feel her draw closer to me as if some instinct bade her lose herself in the void my love had dug in my being.

" Will you, my beloved? " I asked.

Then, at last, she opened eyes that seemed immense, so grave were they and as if awed by some incredibly joyful prospect. Her hands climbed to my shoulders, trembled against my neck and, as she whispered, she lightly touched with hers my hungry, dry lips.

II

Nine hundred and eight! Market Square was full from wall to wall. Right and left, the High Street was blocked with tramcars that rang their bells. There was cheering and booing, and some blew tin trumpets, some played the Chinamen's song on mouth-organs, and those who had no instruments whistled or shouted. Here, on the balcony of the Town Hall, was Mr. Lawton, the victor, smiling broadly as he proposed the vote of thanks to the returning officer; Sir Thomas Bondon, doing his best to smile as he seconded; Lady Bondon, monumental and smiling sadly as an insulted Juno; Mrs. Lawton, Muriel, both dead-white with weariness and excitement, their smiles were wan. I saw them, I heard them, but they were a Punch and Judy show, a study in smiles, not a group of human beings. There was nothing real, even in the vast crowd about me, save Edith, pressed against me, save her bare hand gripped in mine.

" You're hurting me," she whispered.

" Do you mind? "

" No—I don't mind anything——"

" I adore you."

III

Subtle is the air when Eros flies and tell-tale the beating of His wings. Maud understood. As I reached the gate at St. Mary's Terrace she crossed over from Fulham Place, and I felt a spasm of contempt when I realised that she had been a half of the couple I saw from a distance, publicly embracing.

" Hullo, Caddy. You're in the nick: I haven't got a key an' I don't know where I live! Got yours? "

" Yes."

" Is that all you've got to say for yourself? " she asked

in the hall, as she pulled the chain of the incandescent burner. I looked at her contemptuously. This girl—this was the girl who had inspired a passion in me! This bold, aggressive girl with the sulky mouth, the tumbled, crimped hair, the hat that carried too many flowers. I read in the loose curls the embrace at the corner of the street—I tried, in my unjust revulsion of feeling, to see the traces of drink on the lovely skin, for I hated her and hated myself for ever having cared for her.

" S'pose you saw me with Bert," she blurted out. " Well —and what about it? "

I made no reply, and she lashed herself into anger.

" S'pose I've got a right to go about with who I like. Why, you must be barmy if you think I've got nothing better to do than hang about until me noble lord pleases. I'm not so gone on your face as you think, I can tell you."

My eyes strayed about the hall, and I thought how well vulgarity sat on Maud in this setting of red-papered wall; there were dusty hats on the stand; the buffalo horns were dirty. And still she raged at me, angry because I was not angry, because she could not hold me whom she did not want.

". . . I've had about enough of it, I can tell you, Mr. Frenchman, what with your airs and graces, and ma turning up her eyes, and pa trying to get me off with the milkman. I've had enough of the whole blooming shoot and I'm going on the halls. What do you say to that? "

" I don't care."

" Oh, you don't, don't you? Well, it's Bert who's going to get me a show. How's that? "

" I don't care what Bert does."

" Not so much of your Berts. Mr. Burge, please." She pushed hair and hat away from her eyes and, for one moment, looked intoxicated. " Bert may not be one of your extra-superfine A 1 quality toffs, but he's a gentleman, he is, and there's no flies on him. No, don't you try that on," she cried, barring the passage with outstretched arms as I tried to go upstairs; " you've got to take it from me this time. I've had enough of your old buck, all your French gassing about stars, and flowers, and all your beastly goings-on. D'you think I don't know what's what? "

And then, for some terrible minutes, I saw that Maud did know what was what, that she knew it with a terrible clarity which had so far been spared me, that she had leapt to the heart of fact while I wandered over London in my desperate loneliness, that nothing was too pitiful for her to make it ugly. But—but, what was this?

" I know all about you, Caddy; while you've been messing round me you've made goo-goo eyes at the Lawton girl. I know her. The one with a face like a dry-cleaned sheep——"

" Silence! "

I was deafened by my own voice and, trembling, I stood in front of Maud with a raised, clenched fist. And she stood there too, afraid but laughing, hysterically, as if she could not stop. Then I heard a mild voice, felt at last the cold air from the open door, realised that some of her words and my reply must have reached the ears of Mr. Hooper, who stood at the door. I heard stirrings in Lulu's room, and Mrs. Hooper, in a red-flannel dressing-gown, appeared at the top of the stairs.

" What's this? " Mr. Hooper was saying. " What's the meaning of this? I can't have you quarrelling with my daughter in the middle of the night."

" Quarrelling! " screamed Maud. " I'm just telling him off, the——"

" Maud! " cried Mrs. Hooper, as if she had been stabbed. " Oh, Mr. Cadoresse, what have you been doing? "

" Mind your own business, ma," said Maud, savagely.

" I cannot allow you to speak to your mother like that," said Mr. Hooper.

" I'll say what I like. And if you don't like it you can do the other thing."

Maud stamped, again gave her hair and hat that intoxicated shove. The door of her room opened, and, very
cautiously, Lulu put her head out. I saw her vacant,
frightened eyes, discovered that she put her hair in curlers.
And, suddenly, irresistibly, I began to laugh, and I laughed
more as I looked at Mr. Hooper, severe and shocked, at
the tearful figure in the red dressing-gown.

"You seem to be enjoying yourself," said the tragic
Hooper.

"Oh——" I gasped at last, "it's just like one of Lulu's
novelettes."

There was a crash as Lulu slammed the door. Maud
threw me a sulky look.

"Oh—so it's Lulu too, is it? Not even Miss Lulu?"

"Maud," said Mr. Hooper, with sudden force. "Go
to your room. I'll settle this with Mr. Cadoresse."

"Shan't."

"Do you want me to put you there and lock you in?"

Mr. Hooper took a step forward and Maud, after throwing him a look of defiance, shrugged her shoulders and
walked away. There was another slam.

"Alfred, Alfred," moaned Mrs. Hooper, "shall I come
down?"

"No. Go to bed."

"Very well, Alfred." Then, as he opened the dining-
room door, "You might turn down the light, Alfred, if
you're going to be long."

But Mr. Hooper was past economy. In silence he lit
the gas, shut the door. We stood face to face on either
side of the table.

"Now, Mr. Cadoresse, I am waiting for an explanation."

I considered the dining-room, the common sideboard,
bad oils. The only remark I could think of was: "Why
do you keep the salad dressing in a bottle?"

"Well?"

"There's no explanation."

"No explanation? When I find a gentleman quarrelling

in the passage—in the hall, with my daughter—at midnight? I heard her say things which, I trust, are not true——"

This little shocked man in the shabby frock-coat, whose blue eyes were no longer mild, did not seem ridiculous. I had an English impulse:

" I am sorry we made such a noise," I said.

" Yes, yes, but why was there a noise? I am entitled to know."

" Well," I said, hotly, " if you do want to know, Maud is jealous."

" Jealous? My daughter jealous of you? May I ask what your relation is with her, that she should be jealous? "

" There's no relation."

" Indeed? "

Mr. Hooper was not ironical. I saw, as he stroked his bald patch, that he was honestly trying to understand the mystery. I determined to help him.

" Look here, Mr. Hooper, here is the truth. When I first came here, I—I admired your daughter, I told her so—and she did not seem to mind. But she did not—respond——"

" Respond? You mean that she did not care for you? "

" That's it," I said, realising that my original intentions would never occur to him.

" All this going on behind my back! But why is she jealous if she does not care for you? "

Then I lost control of my tongue. I, Lucien Cadoresse, betrothed to the perfect Edith, was not going to be catechised by this futile creature. In one breath I gave him my opinion of Maud, suppressed the details of my pursuit of her, but painted her as a philanderer, a harpy.

Mr. Hooper did not speak for at least a minute. Then:

" I accept your explanation for what it is worth. I make no inquiries as to my daughter's conduct. Goodnight."

But I was not going to let the matter rest there. If I had still been a Frenchman I would have spared him nothing; I would have given him every detail of my vain but degrading courtship—I would not have let him ignore the existence of Bert Burge; I would have flung into his face my knowledge of his desire that Maud should marry Saunders, or " Signor " Colley, or me, or anybody. Yet, some new cleanliness, decency invaded me; I had been French enough to attack Maud generally while defending myself: that was done, but now I was English enough to " play the game "—not to give her away.

" One moment," I said. " You will not be surprised, Mr. Hooper, if I say that I must leave your house."

Mr. Hooper looked at me with an expression of mingled dismay and resignation in his mild eyes. A compromised daughter and a lost " paying guest " in a quarter of an hour!

" Well," he said, reluctantly, " I suppose if you feel——" Then, with an access of dignity: " Perhaps that will be the best thing to do." A note of genuine regret came into his voice: " We shall be sorry to lose you."

And I respected him. He had found dignity. This absurd, elderly clerk, despite his shopman's frock-coat, his petty mind, found it in that wonderful reserve of the English, in their repose. Somehow Mr. Hooper could face the music even when it consisted in such a tune as " Pop goes twenty-seven bob a week."

" I shall pay a full week and leave to-morrow," I said.

We shook hands silently, and I think we were both sorry that our ease should be broken into by one whom even her father could not hold blameless. As I went to my room there intruded into my regret a feeling that I was not blameless either, that I had not played in the encounter the part of a Galahad. Borne on the pinions of my love, I hated myself for ever having pursued such a one as Maud, and others of her kind. I knotted my hands together; I felt self-contempt rather than remorse.

I looked out into the black garden, and as I raised my
clasped hands I was filled with the thought that comes
so seldom to men, so often to women when at last they
love and mourn the loss of the first freshness which they
long to give to the beloved: " Oh—why was it so? Why
could you not be the first, the only one? Why, my beloved,
could you not have come before, first of all, above all,
alone of all women, my Edith? "

IV

I threw myself face down upon my bed. Edith! As
I spoke the word into the pillow from which my breath
returned damply into my face, the ugliness of the past
half-hour disappeared as a dissolving view. I ceased to
think of Maud and her harsh vulgarity, of her irrelevant
mother and sister, of Hooper and his dignity. The
Hoopers became as actors on a stage; the ugliness of their
association receded until, on the black screen of my mind,
there was room for the ever-better defined figure of the
Dresden Shepherdess.

Little Edith, I saw you in that minute. The acute
clarification of my mind recreated you as you were, your
cheek upon the pillow, your mouth as an open rose, and
your hair spread about you as if a cornfield had been
turned to molten, flowing gold. I felt admitted. I had
penetrated all the arcana of England; I was as other men
and more, for I loved, was loved. Love had pointed the
way. And as I lay in my beatitude I felt something upon
my face, something fine that troubled me, clung to my
eyes and lips; I tried to brush it away, but it clung, almost
defiantly. I seized it at last. It was a hair. But, as
I negligently pulled at it, it seemed very long—and suddenly I knew whose it was. I leapt from the bed, gripping
the precious token with two fingers, lit the gas. I placed
the hair upon my outspread black coat, where it lay, very
long, glittering. Oh, wonderful golden hair, you were

She. Fine, pale and yet delicately brilliant, you were the North, its imagination, its melancholy and its shy tenderness. You came to me, to whom the South had given naught save the crude glare of the sun and the bibulous ecstasy of passion, you came soft and grateful as the dew, master of all beauty and wistfulness. You were fine as a razor edge, and as a razor edge you were the bridge over which I, the faithful, would glide into Paradise.

PART III

CHAPTER I

THE ENCOUNTER WITH THE SPIRIT

I

WHEN I look back upon the early months of my engagement I wonder how it came about that I accepted so calmly my new condition. These three and a half years of England must have anglicised me more than I knew: I had long intended to become an Englishman, to marry an English girl, and now that I had come closer to the English ideal the fact of being betrothed to an English girl was not so extraordinary as I had expected. True, my triumph had come, my efforts had been successful; I knew that I was going to do more than marry a daughter of the greatest race, but the feeling was not baptismal, as I had expected: it was confirmatory.

I think that several facts militated against the abstract triumph of England through an English girl. In earlier days, when the English girl was a hypothetical figure, when I knew only that she would be fair and pure, the marrying of her was coldly idealistic; in those days the English girl was merely one part of my broader career, the other being eventual naturalisation, a partnership—a seat in Parliament; the girl did not exist and was therefore amazing. But Edith came, and she was not the English girl I had dreamed; she possessed the pale pink cheeks, the blue eyes and the fair hair of the mental picture, but she also had what I had not bargained for: a soul. She was not an English girl, she was just Edith, whom I would have loved, I think, if she had been an American or a Russian, if only she had still been Edith. I forgot her great English quality because she ceased to be a representative of her country; she herself assumed the purple, and it was her I loved.

Moreover, three and a half years of upward strivings, of intercourse with the English, of attempts to speak, dress, think like them, of watching their games, reading their books and courting their votes, had worked a change in me. Though still a Frenchman with a marked foreign accent, I had gained repose. I spoke less and not so loud; I had my hair cut shorter, but not too short; I did not wear a bowler with a morning coat and no longer bought aggressive " teddy-bear " suits. I was beginning not to say, not to do: I was becoming English. Nobody will ever know how much concentration was required of me by the English attitude, for I was secretive; my labours were done in the dark, as I always wanted to emerge suddenly and surprise the English by my identification with them: the French frog wanted to swell in the dark until he became a John Bull.

The frog often thought he would burst in the process of swelling. I have still a black copy-book which might have been tear-stained if I had filled it as a small boy, so impossible did it seem to me to remember the English said asso'ciation, not ass'ociation, that villages had no mayors, and that St. James and Moses, when possessively inclined, were St. James's in the former case, Moses' in the latter. But I clung to my book, my passport to Eden, read it almost every day as a priest, eager for Paradise, reads his breviary; when it grew and threatened to become as all-pervading as Mr. Hooper's *Five Thousand Facts and Fancies*, I found it more precious, more necessary. For it was the record of my efforts and glowed with memories, memories of a snub due to my having pronounced Caius College " Kayus," of triumph when I alone, in a wide company, had known the status of a Bishop Suffragan. The black book was my record and I was proud to think that I no longer made everyday entries of new errors. One week I learned nothing, which was wonderful; the following I made one mistake, but I was human enough to cheat myself and to forget to enter it. I am still uncomfortable when I remember that occasion, but it is too late to atone: I have forgotten my blunder and can do no more than hope that I would not make it again.

So far did I go in my neophyte fury that I altered my voice. This had too long been high and, when I was excited, shrill; Barker and Merton would, on those occasions, compare it to tin whistles and bicycle bells, not very good similes, which humiliated and angered me. I began to study the English voice. It is deep, low, and there is about it a muffled quality, a quality of averageness that is national; it is neither so high, produced from the anterior palate, as is French, nor so throaty as German. I determined to lower my pitch, to produce from the posterior palate with a little "head" influence taken from Hugh's Oxford voice. A bad cold made the change easy, for I emerged from it with a new, low voice, which I ascribed to "a permanent lesion of the vocal cords." The new, low voice had nothing to do with lesions: it had been manufactured in seven evenings, after midnight, in quiet squares. After I had guiltily accepted the sympathy of everybody who heard me, I found that the new voice was popular; Muriel called it "wood-wind" and preferred it to my former "brass band," and Edith said that she didn't care what instrument it recalled so long as its tune did not alter.

For Edith was franker than she had been. She no longer feared me so much and could afford to laugh at me a little, nervously perhaps, as a man plays with his very big dog; though less articulate than I wished, she was able now to say what she meant, to be gracefully arch, to correct and criticise me. It did not hurt me overmuch when she criticised me, for she had always ready on my arm an anæsthetic hand. But these were infrequent occasions, for Edith's love for me was made up of shynesses and delicacies, of unconscious reserves and exquisite reticences; under the light of day it wilted like a violet in over-fierce sunshine, and it is literal to say that she feared the day; for once, when I tried to kiss her behind a great clump of lilac in the garden of an untenanted house, she whispered rather than said: "Oh, no—the day —the cruel day." But she found some sacredness in her love which it was reverent she should hide: once, in the coffee-room of an inn at Harrow, I came in suddenly to find her softly caressing the grey felt of my Homburg hat. As I came up behind her she wheeled about, and her face was flaming with shame when I took her in my arms.

Such moments are immortal, and I think that while I have a body there will be graven on some tablet of my brain the picture of the slim girl whose hair the sun made into his brother, as she caressed the hat which had covered the head she loved. It was significant of Edith that she should be bold with the symbol and shy with the object, for she did not with it have to fear judgment or response. She loved Love and she feared it. She was woman, she courted love, longed for it, and yet withdrew from it, eternally elusive, eternally desirous, assured of victory in capture, fearing capture and welcoming it in a turmoil of emotion. And along the windings of the rose-grown path I stumbled, adjusting the rougher male gait of me to the tortuous twistings of this woman-spirit, reading assent in its refusals, certainty into its doubts, bewildered and ever looking for a truth of feeling which could not exist until I created it. And over all this searching, this analysis and the cold blood thereof, over the thrust and parry of lovemaking, the jugglery of its subterfuges, I threw the golden mantle of Love itself, the mantle so thick that once under it one cannot see the world, so thin that the illumined eyes that gaze through it can see the world and beyond.

I loved her. I needed her. She was of my essence and should be mine.

II

For I had "intentions." I had not idly slid into the
relation which existed between us, though my intentions
formed after rather than before the night on the banks
of the Ham, when Edith for the first time offered me her
tremulous lips. The retirement of Escott, the chief
accountant, had resulted in a general post at Barbezan's;
Barker had been made second in the accountant's office,
while my own duties were split with a junior typist, so
that I became second in the Exports, immediately under
Hugh, retaining the foreign correspondence. My salary
was raised to two hundred a year: I had every reason to
expect that the admission of Hugh to partnership when
he married Louisa would result in my becoming head of
the Exports with a salary of three hundred and fifty or
four hundred pounds. Sometimes I encouraged wilder
dreams, dreams of a simultaneous admission to partnership
of Hugh and myself, of two weddings in one week; that
was uncertain, but after all I was a Cadoresse, the son of
the old founder, and betrothed to the daughter of Barbezan's master. Why not?

There ran thus a faintly mercenary trail over my love,
but I do not want to blacken myself: I saw that it was
a good stroke to marry my employer's daughter, but I
had never planned to marry her as such. Well aware
that "the little God of Love" cannot "turn the spit,
spit, spit," I knew that to marry Edith I needed money;
and was determined to make it, but I knew that I loved
Edith, not Lawton's daughter, that I would have taken
her as she was and asked her to share my two hundred
a year and my rooms in Cambridge Street. For affluence
had enabled me to gratify my growing desire for comfort.
I had now two rooms on the third floor, from the front
windows of which I could see the gay little public-house,
the busy Edgware Road and the sunset; as I had furnished

them myself they cost me but twelve shillings a week, including nominal attendance and the use of a modern bathroom. I had a sense of property, for the furniture, twenty pounds' worth, was mine, and doubly mine because Edith had chosen the chintz for my settee, my curtains and my tea-set. I think those purchases brought us closer than would have any avowal or any caress, so intimate are the things among which one is to live.

" I wish I were buying it for us," I whispered behind the shopman's unobtrusive back; " it would tie us up."

" Tie us up? " said Edith, genuinely puzzled.

" Yes—I hardly know how to say it, but things like chintz, which one has chosen together, which one lives with, which are—the witnesses—you see? "

" Yes, I see," said Edith, softly.

" The chintz is not you, and not me, it's We, it becomes We. It becomes so usual that one can't think of oneself outside it. It's like an atmosphere which two people need to breathe. If we had that chintz we could never part——"

" Until it wore out and I went to buy chintz with somebody else——"

" Yes—but never again the same chintz."

" No," said Edith, with sudden gravity; " never the same."

And, behold, as I write I see not the pink rosebuds on white of that very early purchase, but a newer chintz, green leaves on a black ground. Shall I rejoice or sorrow because one never buys the same chintz twice?

Edith enjoyed the furnishing even more than I did. We had grave discussions as to whether we should buy a new sitting-room table or the second-hand and ponderous Victorian tripod. The first was cheap, but the second was in the hands of a diplomatic German Jew who had drawn blushes into Edith's cheeks by persistently calling her " Madam." And she calculated cretonne widths for curtains, achieving unexpected (and invariably incorrect) results when trying to determine whether four-feet width at three and nine was cheaper for seven-feet curtains than three-feet width at two and eight. She sat at a table in a Clapham A.B.C., scribbling upon the back of a letter, and I laughed as she despairingly pushed the hair away from her wrinkled forehead. Her one regret was that she would never see the rooms. When invited to come alone, or to bring Muriel, Hugh, everybody, she shook her head.

"No—I couldn't. I couldn't come alone, could I? And if I brought the others, they'd think—well, they'd think it funny of me, they'd suspect. And you don't want them to do that?" There was a note of appeal in her voice.

"No, they mustn't, not yet; they shall soon."

"Not yet. Oh, please, not yet." There was appeal in her eyes now.

I asked "why?" but I knew. Edith had something to hide, felt guilty, and she hugged her guilt because of the romance it carried. Incapable of the dishonest she clung to the secret; if questioned she would have confessed, but, unquestioned, she liked to bask in private knowledge, to feed her imagination with pictures which her mother could not see. Her mind was in search of romance; starving, it seized upon anything that touched me, gilded it, and, having gilded it, hid it as a magpie hides a spoon. She hardly knew that she did this; I had to construct from my own inferences her delicate mental sensuality. "I don't know why," she said; "it wouldn't be the same if they knew. They mightn't like it—I couldn't bear that. And if they liked it——"

"You'd be glad, darling?"

"Oh—glad, glad." The blue eyes shone, but not quite gaily, and I suddenly felt a fear seize me that they wouldn't like it, that she knew it, that we were both blinding ourselves to the truth. "Yes, I'd be glad, but if they did like it, they'd—talk—make jokes——"

I closed my hand upon hers, crushed it, the pencil and the envelope within my larger fist.

" They shan't know, my sweet, not until you choose." I almost added: " Don't be afraid. I shan't stab the picture you have painted," but I felt that she would think this cynical, that she would be disturbed and begin gravely to question whether she were " being silly." " Be silly, little Edith," I thought, and, as I thought, grew old; " you will not always find it easy to be silly." No, I would tell them later, when my position was better assured. Should I, by haste, spoil the glamour of early days, the beginnings, when hands grope for hands? No; my precocious sybaritism told me already that this was the most wonderful experience in the world, that I must not urge on love to its fulfilment, for here was the time when it tried its wings. Rather would I let it perch upon my wrist, smile at its awkwardness and find it graceful; I would have everything love can give, its doubts, its timidities, its half avowals; I would have its romance, its sentimentality and its languor. When the time came for love to fulfil itself I would open my arms to it, but not an emotion should be stolen from me: an emotion marks for evermore, and comes again nevermore. I was no Goth to hurry it.

III

Reasons other than these rather neurotic delicacies helped to hold me back from a blazoning forth of my passion. I saw the Lawtons with new eyes: these people were not so strange because I could conceive of a time when they would no longer be strangers, and, as I understood them better, I found points of difference where I had found, if not similarities, at least an absence of dissimilarities. I knew them to be aloof, self-centred, " islands in an island," but I had not taken the measure of the hatred they felt for interference, of the protection they afforded to the rights of their souls. Muriel, perhaps, awakened me first from my dreams.

"I like Neville," she said; "he's a good sort."

"Yes, and rather handsome."

"Handsome? Well, I suppose he is, in a pocket Adonis sort of way. Wavy hair, blue eyes and not too much chin—it's a smart face, rather. But I don't mean that; he's decent, you know, having taken on his father's debts, the old rotter!"

She gave me a full history of the "old rotter," who was apparently not much worse than his "rotter" ancestors. Neville was the last of his line: great-grandson of a country gentleman who rode to hounds, diced and put up a hundred guineas for cricket matches; grandson of a fashionable Harley Street physician, who would have his horses and money to pay for his son's Grand Tour, and son of a commercial agent who lived at Brixton so as to be able to afford a car, he was on the step of the social stair below which is the working-class. The last of his line, loaded with its follies and devoid of the energy, the life-lust which had made them possible.

"That's just it," Muriel summed up; "they're going down, those Nevilles, and Archie's got nothing in him, except to be decent. He's got no spirit and he wants to do the handsome thing: that's enough to smash him up, for he's not strong enough to afford it."

"What will become of him?"

"How do I know? He might have a stroke of luck."

"He might get married to a clever woman," I suggested.

"He might. Of course, he'd be easy to manage, he's a pussy-cat."

The mysteries of feminine classifications were unveiled; Neville was a "pussy-cat," meek, kindly and pretty; the ugly, leering men were "toads," and I fastened the word on Farr; there were "worms" too, creatures as mild as "the pussy cats," but in every case nasty; creeping, mingy little animals.

"Well," I said at last, "why don't you marry the pussy-cat? You might turn him into a Blue Persian."

The "triangular," grey-green eyes turned away from me. Muriel replied, and her voice was thin and cold:

"Indeed?" Then, without any hurry, she began to speak again, but no longer of the thin ice I had broken. I think she seriously discussed the weather.

I was snubbed, too, when I asked Hugh where he would live when he married Louisa Kent.

"With your taste for sports I'd live in the country, if I were you," I said. "I'm sure you would like a ride in the morning and you could get up from Epsom or Leatherhead."

"I might," said Hugh.

"Yes, I like the town, but you don't, do you?"

"I'm sure I don't know," said Hugh.

"Of course, you'd like some parts better, wouldn't you? Kensington?"

"Got nothing against it," said Hugh.

"Or Hampstead, though it's far out."

"Perhaps it is," said Hugh.

"But I hear they're going to build a new tube. Have you heard that?"

"Can't remember," said Hugh.

I went on at great length, analysed the merits of Bays-water; "I'll tell you the name of a good agent," I volunteered, remembering the melancholy man who had given Maud and me an order to view.

"Thanks," said Hugh.

There was a silence, and I gathered that Muriel was looking at me coldly, that Mr. Lawton, who leaned against the mantelpiece, was staring over my head. On Edith's face I could see a very slight perturbation; I knew there was something wrong, but what? And the Lawtons did not tell me: Mr. Lawton was the first to speak again, asked me whether I thought the Licensing Bill went far enough. I might never have known what I had done, for the Lawtons never told: it was not for them to interfere with me by telling me. By degrees only, and from Edith did I gather what I did.

"You see—they're like that—if you're interested they think—well, I hardly like to say, only it feels like interfering." Edith, too, could not tell; it was only because she loved me that she hinted. Yet she helped me to see the English resenting my interest in their affairs, the influence I wanted to acquire over their course; she showed me that Hugh might not know where he wanted to live, but he didn't want me to tell him; he did not want my help to find a house-agent; he had far rather make a bad bargain and make it himself than suffer intrusion into his business. And that remark to Muriel was dreadful: it was, Edith regretfully confessed, enough to wreck the chances of the match, for Muriel was going to marry her man herself, not to be taken by the hand and given unto him until the wedding-day. Sometimes I grew angry.

"I think they're very conceited," I said.

"No, no, they really aren't," Edith pleaded; "it's not that. I hardly understand them myself, but they aren't. They don't brag, do they?"

I had to agree they did not brag, remembering Hugh's account of his career at Oxford, but maintained my position.

"It's not conceit," said Edith, "but they don't like to be corrected, told things. They want to be let alone; you should hear Hugh sometimes, not often, when he's alone with me; he says he's an awful duffer in business. He's not, is he?"

"Oh—no," I said. Then I found a very slight frigidity in Edith's voice. I had not been enthusiastic enough: therefore I had criticised.

"Of course he's not a duffer," she said. "But he says he is, and he means it; he doesn't think he's any good."

"Then why won't he be helped? Does he think I'm a duffer?"

"Of course not," said Edith, indignantly; "he thinks a lot of you. He says you're smart; he's said it several times."

"But then why won't he let me tell him something useful?" I asked, and was still in the fog.

"I don't know. He's like that, perhaps we're all like that. We want to be let alone—perhaps we don't want to be improved. Silly, isn't it?"

We laughed together, and the chill passed away.

"I'll tell you how I see it, Edith," I summed up. "The English are always saying, ' I'm not much, but, hang it, I'm as good as you.' "

Edith's chief preoccupation, in those days, was that I should make upon her people so good an impression that, when the time came, our engagement would be agreed to. She was always coaching me, at our stolen meetings:

"Now, mind, don't tell father that the Liberals are bound to break up into Moderates and Radicals. Oh, yes, I know it's true, that you've got a dozen parties in France, and perhaps it's true that we'll have them here too, but he's—well, I can't tell you, but he doesn't like it."

"Has he said anything?"

"He hasn't; you don't expect him to, do you?"

"How are you to tell if he doesn't say something?"

"Oh, Lucien, how silly you are." Edith squeezed my arm as we sat together in one of those secluded corners of Kew Gardens where lovers go to. "We don't say things, I suppose, at least not like you."

"I suppose not," I said, rather gloomily, and I realised that there were portions of the English psychology which I had not explored. I am not sure that I have even now explored it all, that I know the subtle reactions of national upon personal characteristics. In those days I was haunted by the problem: "How does one become popular among the English?"

"Oh, you're doing it very well," said Edith, cheerfully.

" I'm sure they like you; even if you do rub them up the wrong way sometimes. You see," she added, with a sweet, confidential smile, " they know you're French."

" Indeed? " I was rather angry. " They make allowances for me? You mean they don't expect me to behave properly? "

" Lucien! "

" I understand," I said, in a hard voice. " I seem to remember things—I remember what Muriel said when I told her that I didn't see why one might bet on a soccer match but not a rugger match. Do you know what she said? " I went on, more angrily than ever. " She said: ' Oh, you can't understand, you're French.' That is to say, she looks down upon me, she thinks I don't think as a gentleman——"

" She doesn't." There was a shrill note in Edith's voice, and I felt that I was on the edge of a quarrel, for the sweet face was inflamed, the lips were compressed. I had touched sacred things. " She doesn't mean anything of the kind. Of course, you can't feel like—being French, you——"

" Ah, you too, Edith! " I laughed bitterly; " you too. You feel I'm an intruder, you think I can't see things properly because I can't see them as you do." I knew I was hurting her, but I had to go on. " What am I, after all? I'm a stranger, a foreigner—a dirty foreigner, as they call us in the City. Do you think I don't take baths? I suppose you think I eat frogs—you're looking for my wooden shoes——"

" Lucien! "

But the pathetic note in her voice did not move me, I was too angry to respect the tears in her eyes.

" What do you want? A flat-brimmed topper? Or shall I shrug my shoulders and scream ' Mon Dieu '? Shall I? Yes—look—look, watch me shrugging my shoulders."

As I write I am two men. The writer is calm, almost taciturn, owns a bulldog and this morning's *Times*—but the other, the dead one, is a dark young Frenchman who stands in Kew Gardens, near the plantation; he faces a slim, golden-haired girl, blue clad against the grey-blue sky. And while she clasps her hands together, while tears roll down her flushed cheeks, he shrugs his shoulders again and again, waves his hands; he grins, he laughs maniacally, he is maddened by his sense of injury, by his sense of exclusion, he feels like a pariah dog driven away with stones and sticks from the homes of men. And all that because he is not an Englishman, because the English won't accept him for one.

"Lucien, Lucien," Edith wailed. She put out a trembling hand. My shoulders still worked convulsively; I could not stop, they shrugged naturally, and I laughed. I could not restrain the hysterical ring of my laughter. I thrust the hair away from my forehead, the movement of my shoulders became less, and suddenly I saw myself as ridiculous, became cool, then conscious that I had done a terrible thing: I had hurt her, for the first time made her cry.

"Edith——I," I faltered, " I—what have I done? "

The hand was still extended. I looked round hurriedly; there was no one near us. I led Edith towards a group of chairs; she followed, still weeping, but quite silently. There we sat for several minutes, while I held and fondled the little, quivering hand. At last she ceased to cry, looked at me with immense, tragic eyes.

"Edith," I said, gravely, " can you forgive me? Can you ever forget this; care for me again? "

She pressed my hand hard, but did not speak. A last sob escaped her.

" I don't know what seized me—I lost my head, I acted like a cad——"

" Dear, no——"

" I did. I lost my temper, and then I lost my head. I was so angry because the English wouldn't have me—and I did just the things that make them turn me away."

" I won't ever turn you away," said Edith, in a low
voice. " Never—Lucien."

We looked at each other sadly, rich in experience now,
and I vaguely felt that the hateful incident had united
as much as it parted us, for I had ceased to be the magnificent, romantic Lucien Cadoresse; I had shown myself
as a human and weak thing; because I was weak the
mother in Edith was coming out to fondle and heal
me.

" I understand what you feel," she said. Then, gently,
as if she reproved a child: " You mustn't let yourself go,
dear; I know it's hard, but you must be patient, you must
learn. If you want to be like us—I don't know why you
want to—you must be very quiet. You will, dear, won't
you? "

I pressed the hand. Then:

" I hardly know how to explain. You're the splendid
people of the earth, for me. You're the handsomest race,
you're strong, and yet gentle; you never swerve from
your purpose, you never know when you're beaten, and if
you are beaten you take it well. You're truthful, honourable—I want to be like you——"

" I know, dear—I know——"

" And I can't quite—I'm excitable, and a sort of despair
seizes me, for I feel I'll never be like you, never be one
of you——"

" Never mind, dear, if you don't. But you will, you
will."

I looked long at the lovely rosy cheeks, the glittering
hair, the blue eyes that met mine so indulgently. Then,
after a quick glance to the right and left, I bent down,
pressed my lips to the back of the smooth hand, pressed
them long, humbly, hopefully, as if by the act of worship
I cleansed myself of all those traits which made me an
alien. As if my feeling had passed into her body Edith
softly laid her other hand upon my head. Gently she
stroked my hair, and I was soothed; I wanted her to take

my head upon her breast and, with almost imperceptible caresses, smooth all my pain away. At last she spoke.

" Come, dear, don't think about it—let's go and see the orchids."

We went into the hothouse. Though the air outside was warm, here was another warmth. I closed the double glass doors and, for some moments, stood inhaling, taking in through the pores of my skin the heavy, hot moisture. Before my eyes were the palm trees, the bamboos, the fat, crawling and gliding plants with the thick leaves that were soft and dank as wet flesh. Climbing about a post was some tropical string hung all over with fierce, purple blossoms, and there were squat growths that wanted to burst out of their own bosoms, so congested were they with their cribbed energy. The yellow eyes of the waterflowers stared out of the pool.

We stood side by side in the steamy haze, at the foot of the bamboos that reared up like the gouty fingers of some Malay giant, and as we breathed our lungs were filled with the oppressive air, air hot and languorous, laden with the scents of herb that rots in the water, of blooms that fight for predominance. When the doors behind us opened, the air did not move: it slunk about us, softly pawing our faces with moist velvet, and as we walked it gave way like some deep cushion, closing behind and stifling us. The wildness of the jungle was in the scents of the flowers, while the swamp spoke, drawled out some contemptuous message through the reek of the wet earth. It was the most ancient earth, fed of the dead it had swallowed alive, and the wetness of its giant tongue lay over its black clots.

We passed a tree all edged with the fire of scarlet cones; about the base of another the moss was rising like a green and never ebbing tide; there was a mop of streamers so fine and so pale that no mermaid seen through shallow water could have trailed behind her as she swam a greener golden mane. We did not, we could not speak, though I heard the voices, the Cockney voices of other couples; we could not criticise, we had to feel, and the suck of the jungle was about our feet. At last we stopped in front of an orchid that stood alone. Upon a thick stalk it carried green sepals that glittered as painted metal, sepals that opened to hold the pale rose flowers. One I remember, large as a man's hand; its edges curled back to show that the rosiness of the rim melted by incredibly fine gradations into white absolute; from its heart protruded a long red pistil.

" Look," I whispered.

Edith gazed at the thing, then I felt her draw back.

" Oh——" she murmured. " It's lovely—but—I'm a fool, I'm afraid of it."

I understood what Edith felt, for I suddenly knew what this thing was; I remembered what I had read of the fly-eater. I saw that its lower edge hung like a lip, that its upper edge was without a curl; I saw that it was not a flower but a mouth, a white mouth, with a long red tongue. And as I looked at it I fancied that I saw it move, move with indomitable deliberation. I put out my hand, and, while Edith gave a stifled cry, touched the lower lip.

A faint shudder seemed to pass through the flower, the red tongue bent towards me, and under my fingers was some movement in the warm, white blossom. Edith snatched at my arm.

" It's alive, it's alive," she gasped; " come away, come away."

But the flower did not, as I half expected, follow my hand with its devouring white mouth. It sat upon its green throne like a sultana on a green couch, whose eyes do not condescend to consider the creature that must be her victim.

I would not move. The passionate scents oozed into my brain.

" Look," I murmured; " this is not England, this is the earth. I smell the scents of the forests that grow in the water, and there are snakes in the moss, poisonous insects, plants which it is death to touch. Look, they're alive, all of them, fighting for life——"

" Lucien ! "

". . . fighting for life, crawling and struggling and climbing, and snatching earth and gorging themselves with water, drinking one another's blood! It's India, Borneo! And look, how they embrace and roll, how they kiss as they kill. You—you're a begum—there's jasmine in your hair. Where are your brass armlets? "

I seized her wrist. She stared at me, and her skin was the colour of cream, all the rose had fled from her cheeks. My eyes, mechanically watchful, told me that we were hidden by the bamboos. I threw both arms about her, and as I drew her to me there was no violence in my grasp, but a slow, resistless pressure, as if my arms were long, green streamers, cast about some ready prey. As I kissed her warm, pallid lips, my nostrils were filled with the steamy scents that rose about us, swathed us in warm veils. As we kissed the jungle enfolded us, motionless and yet latently, violently alive.

Edith seemed to sway in my arms, did not reply when I told her to kiss me. My head began to swim, and I did not see her face, I saw a white blur like the pale mouth on the stalk. Then I saw her eyes dark as those pools, and I saw them as I bent down to kiss her again. As we clung together I moved, and something soft touched my neck. I leaped aside and, though it was only a fat, warm leaf had brushed me, found that I was shuddering.

" Take me away," Edith whispered. " I'm fainting—I must go."

IV

If I could have stayed with Edith in the jungle the spirit of England could not have touched me. The jungle would have been too primitive, too insidiously sensuous to allow any gross nationalism to thrive. But we had to struggle, in our delighted fear, away from the seduction of the universal earth, to go back to roaring London, to make of the jungle an episode. For I did not see Edith very often, and then only for a few minutes alone, or for longer periods under the eyes of those strangers, her family. Indeed, in that year of our engagement, we only escaped three times into the country, on Saturday afternoons when Edith came to me, staggering under the weight of a lie, an Eve driven out of Eden and carrying her shame. But those few afternoons explained her to me, her harmony and her variety. For me Kew had stated together her romanticism and that of her race.

Edith had been afraid of the hothouse and its silent inmates, while they woke in me a peculiar appetite; that which to me was acrid was to her merely terrifying; she saw life as a beautiful rolling plain (the life of every day), with high blue mountains in the distance (the life of romance), but she was disturbed if she met angry rocks, red with the blood they had lost as they forced their way through the earth, or torrents that respected not their banks. She wanted, as I did, adventure, not the adventure of the wild beast that snuffs its prey and, panting, hunts it down, but stately adventure, knights and ladies, sacrifice, heroism, verse, song and tears. Thus it is not wonderful that there was between us a clash, for I am not romantic: I am lyrical; I do not want beautiful things to make me glow, I want to glow when I see common things. But Edith's romanticism was very beautiful to me. It was the romanticism of Rossetti, or Burne-Jones, the romanticism of Dumas, Lamartine and Walter Scott. It was cold, but cold as are snowy mountains because they are high. Edith's coldness was her purity, and often I lay abased before that purity—though I loved it as a foreign, an impossible ideal. For it cleansed me when I touched it; after I had spoken to her I was absolved. Purity, which is so seldom informed by charity, so often narrow, ignorant, harsh, intolerably cruel, caused her not to turn away from pitch lest she might be defiled but to assume such an attitude that she did not know the pitch was there. Her quality was one of aloofness; it was the things she did not do which mattered, things that were not done by her people. Edith was Edith first of all, but she was also the English girl, and like other English girls she shrank from lies, from deceit, from boasting; she did not deny her Creator, she respected the things that are, except those which hurt. For her hands were open to the world. She was of her people, calm, sober and distant, yet tender and ready to love, because, like them, she placed love upon a pedestal.

" Why do you love me? " I asked her.

" How can I tell? " Her happy smile said she did not want to know.

" I know what I love in you—I've told you."

" Tell me again," she whispered.

" I will—always," I vowed; " but tell me too."

" Tell me," she repeated, like an obstinate child.

I bent over her, whispered to her the eternal love poem, full of the anxious cry of the desirous body, the greedy clamour for a blending of souls. But I, too, wanted to hear her voice raised for me. I wanted my song of songs.

" I don't know why," she said at length. " The first time I saw you I hardly dared talk to you, but I loved your black eyes."

" Why? "

" They glowed—I was frightened—I'd never seen eyes like that."

" Only my eyes, then? "

She hesitated, flung me a shy glance. " No, of course not. It was the things you said, things one didn't expect. And you talked about pictures, books—people hadn't talked to me like that before."

" I was different, then? " I said, greedily.

" Yes, you seemed to care for me—that was different."

As I closed my hand over hers I think I understood her and with her all those Englishwomen who are always seeking for something different. Noble Englishmen, I love you, and you are not quite unworthy of your women, but you don't love them enough. You don't tell them often enough that you love them, you don't tell them they're beautiful, you don't analyse and appreciate them as you do fine horses. Because you don't, inch by inch, praise them, because you cannot value every colour in their eyes, every shadow in their skin, because you can't see that their hands are like sprays of fern, because you can't even tell them that they are pure, gentle, devoted, they droop. The plant of love must be watered with praise, with flattery. The Englishwoman withers because you don't love her enough, and then, as Edith, she seeks romance, the new, the strange: if it does not come to her she dies without having ever known what she wanted. Edith, like her sisters, wanted romance: vows that might be false but were beautiful, high hopes doomed to disaster and high endeavour to achieve the impossible. Her soul cried out for wings, and because it thought I had wings it came to me.

Perhaps I had wings, but I was also of the earth. I confess without hesitation that the loftiness of my love did not transmute me into a new being. Though intolerably ashamed of past adventures, because they lacked the fineness I had come to know, the very quality of my love still urged me to the sources of further shame. An obscure sybaritism drove me towards the coarse, so that I might have contrast in my mind when Edith stood before me in her remoteness from all that is ugly; and on those heights of undefined idealism the air was rarefied: I had to come down to earth. If I had not loved Edith I could have looked at no other woman, and I attempt no paradox when saying that love inclines the heart to universality. I loved her, was so saturated with her that I radiated love. She became the intermedium between womankind and me.

V

If I loved Edith as a stranger, I loved her more as she became a familiar thing, as her mind responded to my efforts. I had guessed at its reserves, and now it began to unfold, for I had to win her trust to gain it. She was not expansive; her confidences were not akin to a light woman, whom any man may approach, but to some sleeping princess between whom and the knight a thick forest interposes. And now I began to see her, for I had ridden through the forest, climbed the castle stairs. It was July. We sat in the shadow of a hedge in a field between Harrow and Pinner. The rutty little path, broken by stiles, ran across the field, so that the many who passed, working men looking for a place to sleep in, hurrying daughters of the farmers making for home from the Harrow shops, and young couples, arm-in-arm or hand-in-hand, saw us only as a blotch of light blue and light grey. It was hot, the sun sat high, and over the hedges I saw that the sky was like a slate, for this was England, where a little mist always refines the brutal brilliancy of the air. So we sat limply, our warm hands touching but too listless to clasp. I noted details round me, the ugly railway bridge, a few fields away, and the glittering snakes of the railway line; the hedges tangled with flowering blackberry brambles; daisies, poppies, little blue and mauve flowers; a beetle struggling on its back, and the light patches of sunshine in the grass about us; the patch of light which gave Edith one burlesque red cheek.

"It is hot," I murmured. "How many miles to Pinner?"

Edith did not reply at once; she played with a blade of grass. Then:

> "How many miles to Babylon?
>   Three-score and ten.
> Can we get there by candle-light?
>   Yes, and back again."

I made no comment. It was not the first nonsense rhyme I had heard, but it stirred me, for the French have no nonsense rhymes, and this peculiar English form of poetry always struck me as wistful; it held the vague idealism of the North, it meant to me that here was a soul struggling with a brain. And then I found I was forgetting Edith, that the North was on me—Andersen —the red shoes—the North came to me out of the mist, wooing me with melancholic grey eyes before which my bold black ones shamedly closed.

" What are you thinking of ? " she asked, and now was smiling. " Do you think that silly ? "

" No. It's wonderful—it's like rain upon a loch."

" I don't understand."

" No more do I. But what does it matter ? We feel."

" We feel," said Edith, dreamily.

I took her hand, drew her down; we lay side by side, our heads pillowed on a grass-grown hillock at the base of an oak. When I spoke again I was inconsequent.

" I have done it again," I said, " and I don't care. It's too hot."

" What have you done again ? " asked Edith.

" Put my feet in the dish. I mean—oh, of course, you laugh. I've put my foot in it."

Edith apologised for having laughed. " It was so French," she said. Then she begged to be told what I had done with those idiomatic feet of mine.

" I've offended your family again—I always shall."

" Cheer up. But what did you do, anyway ? They aren't sulking, so it can't be much."

" Last Sunday your mother was there; she wore a blue silk dress and a large hat with a curling blue feather. She looked so pretty with her rosy cheeks and those triangular eyes—well, you can laugh, they are triangular, like Muriel's."

" I suppose mine are triangular," said Edith.

"No." I took her chin, turned her face to me. "They are just sapphires; you haven't got that narrowness on one side between the eyelids which makes the triangle. They're sapphires, my delight—don't be shy, don't hide them even with lids as delicate as roseleaves." I kissed her eyes, one after the other, gently, as if afraid to bruise the roseleaves. But my mind was filled with my misbehaviour. "Triangular, yes. But I didn't tell your mother her eyes were triangular; I don't know what she would have said if I had. What I did say was, 'What a beautiful frock, Mrs. Lawton! I'm sure you must dress at Worth's.'"

"Well, what did she say?" Edith was serious. She, too, did not like my remark.

"She hardly said anything. She said, 'I'm glad you like it,' and at once talked of something else, the Eton and Harrow match, I think. She didn't seem displeased, but then she never does, and I felt—I don't know quite what I felt, but what I do feel with English people—a sort of draught."

"Oh," said Edith, lightly; "you're making too much of it. Still——"

"Still what?" I looked her full in the eyes. "Come, tell me."

"She mayn't have liked . . ." said Edith, reluctantly. "You see, something like this. She may not want to be criticised."

"Yes," I grumbled, "I suppose I ought to know that by now."

"And then you spoke of Worth. Well, she can't afford Worth, you must know that——"

"I know, but how was I to express what I meant?"

"She didn't want you to express it. And perhaps she thought you were making fun of her when you spoke of Worth."

"Edith!" This idea shocked me. Make fun of Mrs. Lawton! And the attitude was incredible unless I accepted that in Lawtonian circles peaks of conceit rose up from a morass of humility.

But Edith went on talking, not very lucidly, for she was trying to defend her people and her family without attacking me and mine. She tried to translate feelings into words, failed because English people have no chance to practise this art; but I think I understood, because prepared by experience, the humility that lies behind English pride, the chronic belief the English hold that you don't really think much of them. The North! I thought of Murchison, one of Barbezan's clerks, a Yorkshireman, of his customary reply when congratulated: " D'you mean it? " The English soul holds two St. Pauls, the unregenerate and the converted.

As we lay there side by side and gazed into the hot heavens, I was just conscious of the burning glow in Edith's sunlit hair, for I thought of yet another recent scene. I had been talking to Muriel on the balcony, on Sunday afternoon. We were friends, we two, for a sexlessness had come to part us and was joining us as if we were boys. As she sat on the parapet she played with a little black bag, tossing it in the air and catching it. Once she nearly missed it.

" You'll lose it," I warned her.

" It doesn't matter, it's so old. I must buy another to-morrow, and I'm as broke as broke."

" How much do they cost? "

" I think sixteen and six."

" Sixteen and six! I know where to get one like that in the City for ten shillings net."

" Indeed? that's cheap." Muriel did not seem interested.

" If I were you I'd come down to the City. It's worth it."

There was a silence and I felt guilty, for I had not been able to repress the " If I were you " against which Edith had warned me.

" Oh, I might. Still it's too much fag——"

" Let me get you one," I volunteered, eagerly.

" It's very kind of you, but don't trouble——"

" It's no trouble. I'll get you one to-morrow."

" Oh, it doesn't matter——"

" That's all right. I'll leave it here for you."

I did buy the bag and it was certainly an excellent bargain. But when I told Edith, which at last I did, while I averted from her my uncertain eyes and gazed at the blazing brick walls and shimmering spire on Harrow Hill, she said:

" I suppose Muriel wanted to buy it herself."

" But why? why? when I could get it at half-price? "

" She wanted to buy it herself," said Edith, obstinately.

I stuck to my point, reminded Edith that there was no question of choosing a bag, that Muriel wanted one exactly like the one she had.

" She didn't want to trouble you." Then, in a rather desperate tone: " She wanted to do—to manage her own affairs."

Yes, that was it. I had an impotent little outburst, for I was moving in a crazy circle, one day offending English pride, and the other disturbing English humility.

Edith did not defend her sister; her attitude was disapproving and I knew that she was against me. Truly, blood is thicker than marmalade. At last she said:

" Don't let's quarrel, darling." She took my hand. " It's lovely here with you."

The touch of her hand turned my thoughts from bitter to sweet. I drew her into my arms, kissed her softly on the forehead, then just behind the ear. The spell of her youth and her purity acted upon me incomprehensibly in this brazen light. To me, the passionate, the adventurous, it was like getting drunk on spring water. But I could not be content, I had to kill the thing I loved.

" Kiss me," I said.

She looked up at me, smiling, but did not move. I

slipped my arms round her so that they were under hers.

"Kiss me—you haven't since that night at Hambury." As I whispered, slowly I raised my arms so as to lift hers; they responded to the movement, though I had to initiate; Edith's hands clasped gently round my neck, and my face was very near hers. We kissed, and there was no fever in the caress, but delicious, calm content. I still held her close in my arms, pillowed against my raised knee.

"Why don't you kiss me yourself? Don't you want to?"

She blushed. "Yes—I do—but, I'm afraid somehow. You might think me forward."

"My darling!" I laughed at the phrase which recalled the much more equivocal French: ' Comme vous allez me mépriser!' "No, I want you to be forward, as you say—I don't want you to be afraid of anything. Now you shall do more; you shall not only kiss me, you shall ask me to kiss you."

"Oh, Lucien, I couldn't——"

"Do you want me to?"

"Yes, but——"

"Then ask."

She hesitated, and my mind flew back to the dingy room in St. Mary's Terrace when I had failed to make Maud say "I love you." But at last Edith closed her eyes and murmured her request. As I kissed her I knew the savour of conquest; but she did not understand why I demanded tribute. What more did I want than her caress? Why should I wish to hear her say that she loved me? Why should I need to know that she wanted my kisses? Was it not enough that she should yield?

Poor little English girls—of course, for too many centuries your men haven't cared to know whether you loved them. They wanted you, not your love. They seldom wondered whether you loved them. Indeed, if the idea occurred to them, I think they set it aside as unladylike and repulsive, that they believed with Squire Western that marriage is well founded on a little aversion. It was this strange inquisitiveness in me that appealed to Edith while it frightened her, and yet it drew her out, for she had begun to feel that I would tolerate in her the things I did not understand. As we slowly walked towards Pinner, stopping at times to clamber over stiles, when I averted my eyes so that the exposure of her ankles might not make her ashamed, she talked. She talked more than I did, for I was glad to let her bare her soul. It was broken, this little speech, but precious.

" You know, Lucien, I'm two people, I think. There's one of them longing for excitement, for things to happen. You know what I mean, you call it adventure; but then there's another one, who's clinging to rules and principles, all that sort of thing. The first Me wants to be bold— it wouldn't be afraid to say anything, to say—There, I can't say it."

" What can't you say, darling? "

" I can't say——" Edith hesitated, then, with the air of a diver poising his body on the edge of the plank, " I can't say ' I love you '—the first Me wanted to, but the second was too shy."

" I love you both," I murmured. She pressed my hand.

" I'm afraid; I've got no courage, no candour—oh, I won't tell lies; no, I just say nothing. I can't talk. Even with you, though it's easier. You know it's somehow more difficult to talk to you than to the others, though it's easier. What I mean is, you say odd things, and I'm afraid because you aren't afraid; I'm afraid because I feel you're so obstinate, inflexible; you don't care for conventions. I'm like a child with a box of matches."

" My darling, if I asked you to run away with me and work for your living, you would. Wouldn't you? You wouldn't mind what they said? "

There was a long pause.

" I couldn't," said Edith, in a very low voice. " I'd

want to, but I couldn't. Oh, Lucien, you won't see it.
I couldn't give pain to my people, even if I knew they
were wrong. If one of them were ill I'd have to stay at
home and be their eyes and ears and arms and legs."

"What about you—and me?"

"I've got to—got to——"

"Got to play the game?"

"Yes," said Edith, desperately; "I've got to. Oh, I
want love and beauty as much as anybody, but there's
duty. Duty's the only brave thing to do. It's no use
kicking against the pricks; one's got to stand them, and
one does unless one's spoiled. Of course, I know I'm silly,
narrow——"

"My darling, you're wonderful."

I drew her to me, kissed her rather feverish lips, but she
had more to say.

"I care for all the little things. When we marry I'll
be happy, I'll be so glad, but I'll miss father and mother,
and Hugh and Muriel too—and Fiona——"

"I'll buy you a bulldog."

"A new dog," she said, slowly, "and a new house, and
a new—well, you know what I was going to say, but there
it is. It'll all be so new, and the past'll be dead; and
I did like it, and all the other little things—parties, birthdays, and Christmas presents. Though it'll be so good,
Lucien; you don't know how unhappy I was before you
came—lonely. In Brussels I used to wish there was a man
in love with me, anywhere, in Canada or China, even if he
never wrote, just to feel some one loved me."

"Yes," I said, gently, "one can be warmed by a distant
love as one is warmed by the incredibly distant sun."

She pressed my arm, began again. "I was afraid I
wasn't pretty enough—or clever enough. I was so lonely,
I wanted a friend——"

"And now you have a lover."

"Yes—it's good—but I wanted a friend above all.
Somebody to encourage me, to listen to me. That's why

I'm so grateful when you make me talk, though I'm frightened. I know it's weak to tell you things; it may bore you—yes, it's all very well, but it may, and it isn't right to unload worries; it's cowardly, selfish. But yet I'm grateful because you love me, while you might be amusing yourself, getting on. I wanted it so badly that—Oh, I couldn't tell you."

I pressed her with questions. At last came the stumbling avowal that, when she was sixteen, a Mr. Egerton, a married man, had kissed her, that loneliness lay so heavy over her that she had not resisted.

" Oh, it was dreadful," she said, hurriedly; " it felt so disloyal—I couldn't help thinking of what his wife would say, how it would hurt her. Poaching. And now—now that there's you, it's worse." She squared her shoulders, raised her head and looked me full in the eyes. " I thought you ought to know."

Some seconds elapsed before I realised that Edith had thought she ought to confess this scandalous portion of her past: the English girl is the lover's surprise packet. Though nervous, she looked happy; her conscience had been troubling her. I managed not to laugh when I thought of the absurd exaggeration—but then it was no more absurd to her than would have been to me the catalogue of my own episodes. Then it seemed pathetic and I was stirred when I said:

" What does the past matter? Here we are, we two."

As we walked on, silent and glad, I saw Edith more clearly, her passionate desire for love and friendship. These were for her almost synonymous. Lonely in her heart and her spirit, she held out her hands, begging that they might be filled. To love and be loved, two necessities. But she had never told me this before; she had not dared, and she was ashamed because she could not stand alone. Weak, she hated to be weak among the strong. Taught not to cry out when hurt, she despised herself because her soul cried out. And thus she was tortured on two sides, by her desires and the shame they entailed upon her; the things she wanted she feared: if she thought of passion at all she shrank from its effects, personal and social. Not once during our engagement did we use the word sex: I knew it was not for her ears, that it would frighten though it delighted her, and that it would have been cruel to frighten her thus, though I longed to frighten her. And some chivalry bade me refrain from using on her an influence which she together feared and welcomed.

When, in response to a very faint hint, I confessed that there had been other women, Edith did not say, as I hoped, as I had said: "What does it matter? Here we are, we two." She said, with serious lips, something much more touching:

"How they must have suffered when you left them."

I gripped her hand hard. She should not suffer, I swore. And I loved her because she had questioned me; that had been frank.

Yes, she was frank now. Frank as might be a violet if it reared its head through moss and then looked round in horror, saying: "Oh, what have I done?"

VI

We had tea in a little inn at Pinner, at an oak table surrounded by Windsor chairs. There was a grandfather's clock that ticked against the oak panels; the white walls were decorated with copper warming pans, blue willow-pattern plates. The landlady had smiled discreetly upon us as she laid down the rough-cut bread and butter, the jam into which some negligent farmer's daughter had put more stones than fruit. Then she had shut the door with much ceremony, after gloating over us: she was stout, very red-faced, and her crossed arms were enormous; she was one large gloat. We laughed when she tried the door from the outside to prove that it was quite closed, and we laughed when Edith dipped her finger into the jam and

I insisted on kissing the finger clean. We were practical, we decided the conduct of the " campaign," the " operations " during the holidays, for we were both fond of military metaphors; we proposed to " tell " if it were announced that changes were to take place at Barbezan's in view of Hugh's marriage in October. But, though we were practical, the charm of enlightenment hung over us. I looked at Edith, smiling over the teapot, so wifely in that attitude, formulated:

THE CREED OF A YOUNG ENGLISH GIRL

" I believe I must tell the truth, obey my parents and love them. I must conform to the rules of my caste, hold such ideas as it allows its women; I must respect, in order, my father, my eldest brother, my mother, my sisters; I must be kind to my grandmother, to my other relatives, to friends and servants: that is, be kind to those whom I do not respect. I believe in the Almighty as stated by the creed I have been taught to profess. I believe in courtesy, in good clothes, which must be neither much ahead of nor much behind the fashions, and such as befit my age. I believe in baths, clean linen. I believe that false hair, rouge, face powder are sinful. I believe that I must like, in order, music, books and pictures, but my liking for them must not be hysterical; also I must see to it that all my reading be not light. I believe in love and that, in the name of love, providing my conscience tells me it is holy, I may transgress certain of my rules; but I believe that love must be pure and noble, that it must be steadfast and true; I believe that it comes but once in life and that it must be sacrificed if it threatens the eventual happiness of the loved one. I believe that I must not tell the loved one that I love him but that I must wait his pleasure. All this I must not tell. I believe that I must wait for success, for love, for death, and that I must not complain in the waiting. I believe that I must listen, not speak; obey, not command; respond, not exact. I am a pure young English girl; my life is not my own. I believe that my business is to find its master."

CHAPTER II

THE ENCOUNTER WITH THE BROTHER

I

WORKING with all those abstract English forces was another, and curiously enough it was embodied in a man. I was surprised that this should happen, for I had not of late years found much use for men. At the higher commercial school three youths Gobot, Luzan and Lavalette had occupied my mind and stirred my emotions, but even then I knew that they were merely the channels of least resistance which my mind and emotions followed because they were the channels of least resistance. Some of our friendship was made up of youth's passionate desire to express itself, and thence sprang the antagonism of our views; we did not in fact differ, but we had to differ in order to force out of ourselves anything that might be there; we shouted, we snatched words from one another's mouths. It was good, but it was not what I wanted. Woman alone could give me that: thrilled sympathy, some admiration and gratitude for my condescending to think her worth talking to. I loved woman because she responded, because her mind leapt up to meet mine; and I hated man because he was my rival, demanded of me those things which I wanted myself. I tried, and a little because " it was done " in England, to make friends among men, and I succeeded in walking with Hugh Lawton, lunching with Barker; I managed to be interested in Bell and his slum boys, in Archie Neville, though I thought him too vapidly good; I let Merton take me to a football match, I asked Kent to smuggle me into a moot at Gray's Inn. But nothing availed: I do not like men; there is no thrill in

their speech; no passion lights their eyes when I speak.
I am a Frenchman, I cannot be parted from women, I love
them; I am uneasy when I love no woman, when no cheeks
flush as I enter a room. Even if she love me not she must
be there; I must see her gracious lines before me, hear
the music of her high voice, the rustle of her skirts.
Woman is the ozone of my atmosphere. I am a lover.
When I am too old to be a lover I will be friend, confidant,
match-maker, so that I may still be near her. When I
die I hope that my soul will reincarnate into the body of
a chocolate pom . . . or of any beast woman fancies at
that time.

And yet the man came. Charles Stanley, one of the
departmental heads of the Chinese and Peruvian Shipping
Company, sat rather rigidly at his desk between glass
walls beyond which I could see the clerks, some perched
on high stools, some standing to write at their desks. My
business was rather intricate. We had, acting for a client,
chartered the Company's steamer, *Ning-Po*, whose activities
were, as a rule, confined to the China seas, while she
lay at Liverpool on an empty bottom, to carry rolling-stock
which she was to shed at Colombo, Singapore and Shanghai; at Shanghai the *Ning-Po* was to load up an arranged
consignment of raw silk, land it at San Francisco and
terminate her journey at Panama, where she would be delivered to agents of the Chinese and Peruvian. It was an
admirable plan, for it converted the *Ning-Po* from a necessary carrier into a speculative tramp, while our clients
escaped the risks of tramping. Unfortunately, on that
morning the ship was steaming north from Singapore and
the captain did not know that the warehouses containing
the raw silk had been burned down. As wireless telegraphy
did not yet count commercially, there were no means of
instructing him to call at Manila and Canton on the chance
of booking American freight; thus the operation threatened
to end disastrously, for the *Ning-Po* might have to travel
to Panama in ballast, unless we could secure the carrying

of a large cargo of Japanese cotton goods, then lying in the Chinese and Peruvian's charge, according to our cable advices, at Yokohama.

I explained so much of the facts as was politic, for it did not do to reveal, when bidding for freight, that the ship would probably have to travel in ballast to accomplish her journey within the term of the charter-party. Stanley listened to me to the end, nibbling his penholder. He was tall, very thin, rather bald; deep-set in his dark face, every feature of which was irregular, his grey eyes seemed extraordinarily passionless and acute. He fixed upon me so concentrated a gaze that I seemed to lose my nerve, to grow voluble; my trained bass voice threatened to revert to its high pitch. At last, when I had finished my long speech, splashed with the sonorous names of quite irrelevant Eastern ports, he ceased to nibble the penholder he held in his strong, knubbly brown fingers and, after a pause, said:

" Why do you want us to charter our own ship? "

There had been no hesitation. The essential question had come out and I wondered by what devilry this man had guessed our weak point. I began once more my involved speech, mixing up " Canton . . . possibility of accommodating you . . . Yokohama." I struggled to keep him in ignorance of our casualty: if he found out he would offer a freight rate which barely covered our expenses. But as soon as I stopped Stanley was on me, swift as a boxer when his adversary gets up from his knees.

" You've no freight at Shanghai? "

" We might . . ." I faltered.

" The *Ning-Po* will travel to Panama in ballast. That is so? "

His question was hardly a question; it was a piece of information, and the grey eyes held mine as the magnet holds iron.

" There may be no cargo," I growled, " or not enough."

" Ah. Now we're talking. Well, we haven't fixed these

cotton goods from Yokohama. You can have them at twenty-five shillings a ton."

I pretended to cry out in despair. It was preposterous. It would not cover our expenses. It would . . . I shouted, I pleaded for thirty-five shillings, but Stanley nibbled on, made not the slightest effort to interrupt me. When I stopped he said:

"Twenty-five shillings. Or take her into Panama in ballast."

"We can pick up freight at Manila or Canton," I said, truculently.

Stanley did not reply. He opened *The Shipping Gazette,* ran a brown finger down a column.

"Steamer *Ning-Po.* Sailed from Singapore for Shanghai 14th. She's not calling at Canton or Manila."

I remained silent.

"You've got no freight at Shanghai. You thought you had, but now you're not sure. Something's happened to your cargo."

"How do you know?" I asked, angrily.

"Oh, something *has* happened?" A very faint smile creased the thin lips. "What was your cargo?"

"Silk," I snarled. I felt now as a man must feel who is slowly being dragged from a music-hall by the chuckers-out.

"Silk, was it? Burned?"

"Yes," I said, wearily. "How did you tell?"

Again no direct reply; then quickly:

"Well, take your chance at Shanghai. You may find freight . . . but don't wait too long there. If the *Ning-Po* doesn't reach Panama on the date, it's fifty pounds a day."

I gazed sulkily at my feet. When I looked up, humbly now, the grey eyes seemed kinder but still unflinching.

"It's a deal at twenty-five shillings then?" said Stanley.

"I'll tell them. I can't accept myself."

"Right oh," said Stanley, airily; "and tell them we put down our price sixpence every hour."

It was terrific; and when I left the office I was overwhelmed by my defeat at the hands of this man who had gone straight to the heart of the business. Nine-tenths of the interview had been taken up by my conversation, my evasions and verbal nimblenesses, one-tenth by his series of intuitive stabs. He had guessed everything, our empty hold, the ju-jitsu lock laid upon us by the fact that we had to render up the ship on a given date; he had even guessed that our cargo was burned. I do not know how it is done; Stanley says it is elimination, that in the case of the cargo he saw at once we would not have chartered the ship unless we knew there was return freight; *ergo* the cargo must have disappeared; a shipload of silk couldn't be stolen; *ergo* it was fire or water; no floods in the papers, *ergo* fire. May be, but certainly Stanley eliminates the unlikely as fast as a mechanical drier expels water.

II

We became friends. Stanley held out his hand to me the same day, when I returned in the afternoon to agree abjectly to his terms on behalf of our client. While he telephoned the cable room to make sure that the Yokohama cargo was still open, I studied his face; it was a monkish countenance, very long and emphasised as to length by the recession of his dark hair; his bent brow seemed enormous and was furrowed by a great number of horizontal lines; there was a break in his nose, a humorous twist in his thin mouth. His clothes were very dusty and seemed to have been made for a much bigger man; he had never been manicured. When he looked up at me I was again flooded by a sense of clarity rather than power.

"That's O.K.," he said.

I was dismissed, but something held me back. As he

looked at me I saw at once that he knew it, that he was analysing . . . eliminating, I suppose. It was intolerable; I was being vivisected.

"Look here," I blurted, "that's all right. But this morning I tried to bounce you."

"That was your duty. Besides, you enjoyed it."

"I did," I said, rather wonderingly; "how can you tell?"

"Sheer intellectual pleasure. Just like chess, you know. Do you play chess?"

"Yes." I did, not very well, but then in the City one has to play chess if one hates dominoes.

"Come and have a game with me. What time d'you get out to lunch? One? I go later; still, I can manage it. To-morrow at the Gracechurch Street Mecca? Right oh."

I went and was so nervous that Stanley fool's-mated me, then beat me in less than twenty-five moves, giving me pawn and move. There was no sport in those games which we now played at lunch three or four times a week, while the gravy on our plates clotted into grease, but they served a good purpose. Stanley confessed this to me a little later.

"I like your spirit; you never give in. Of course you're a silly ass, and you make it a rotten game by sticking to it and exchanging until I get down to king and rook or something . . ."

"I never give in," I said, sulkily.

"But why not? I thought Frenchmen didn't stick."

"They don't," I said. "But Englishmen do, and that's why I stick."

"It's a rotten game," Stanley persisted, "but then that's your way. It's like the day you came and tried to bounce me about the old *Ning-Po;* you came at me with a regular net of words. You said the same thing ten times, tangling and tangling. Yes, you came at me with a net."

"Well, you came at me with a rapier."

This was true. Stanley's mind worked like a sword; mine worked like the net of the retiarius, but I was going to be an Englishman, and therefore " stuck "; the English had always gained what they wanted by " sticking." Naturally subtle, I often tried to combine subtlety with obstinacy, for the English bull is obstinate. Our relation therefore contained a paradox: the Frenchman liked the Englishman for his quick Latin mind; the Englishman liked the Frenchman for his artificial English grit. The friendship was anti-natural, but it prospered, for Stanley did not refuse himself as do most Englishmen; though born in Northumberland he was not suspicious; rather he did not deign to be suspicious, as his Northern pride told him that his mind was so keen that no despised Southerner could injure him. Soon, therefore, I discovered him to be a human being, a rare species of Englishman. He still played cricket and was generally right when he gauged the chances of teams; he read enormously, economics, philosophy, verse, novels and newspapers; he never liked a very bad book, though his taste was not quite developed enough to keep him from the second-rate: he saw, but he did not feel very keenly, and for this reason could not love the greatest. He was very gentle, a little sentimental under the cynical varnish, and worshipped his absurd little wife.

I was taken down to dine at his small house at Esher. His wife, whom he overtopped by a foot, leapt at his neck in the hall. She was fair, plump, round. She had round wrists, round blue eyes, a one-year-old baby, the roundest baby boy I had ever seen. Stanley called her delightful and insulting names: " dumpling," and " toadstool," and " roly-poly." Though he had been married two years he still persisted in asking her whether she had come in handy at school when the teacher wanted to illustrate the use of globes.

" Isn't he silly, Mr. Cadoresse? " she asked (round-mouthed), " with his dumplings? You silly old hop-pole!

Do *you* come in handy as an alpenstock? You . . . hay-fork!"

She was no fool. Their conversation seemed to touch everything from religion to the rise of coal prices, and she was nimble enough, knowing his elimination methods, to " fox " him when he tried to guess her opinions.

" Ha," she would cry, triumphantly, " I knew you'd think I wanted a new bonnet for baby because I said his was shabby. Well, I don't; he's done with bonnets . . . he wants a hat. Got you!"

But Stanley persisted in mental analysis. He even tried it on the dog, an Irish terrier.

" I see your game, Pat," he said, severely. " You're begging for your dinner because you know the meat isn't up yet. Therefore you think you'll get a bit of sugar to keep you quiet. Wrong, Pat, wrong. There is no sugar."

" It's you who are wrong, Sherlock Holmes," said Mrs. Stanley. " He's begging for the cat who's sitting on the back of your chair."

I loved them. Nothing told me that I was going to need them, but a bridge was being made.

III

I was going to need the Stanleys, as I was going to need my own strength, the power of my optimism and my love. Before the end of that month of July, when Edith unveiled her soul, an atmosphere which I felt in the making began to define itself. Mr. Lawton was courteous to me in the office, but cold; he seldom now added general conversation to commercial instructions; he did not tell me, as he had done the year before, where the family was going for the summer or suggest that I might come down for a week-end. He did worse: Hugh was going abroad for a month in August and I, as second to him, expected to have charge of the Exports. Mr. Lawton, however, took an unexpected course.

"Oh, Cadoresse," he said, "I'll attend to things while Mr. Hugh is away."

"I'll manage," I replied, and there must have been something aggressive in my tone, for Mr. Lawton said very distinctly: "I—can—do—that." Then, as if a little remorseful, "I'm not too busy."

For a few seconds our glances crossed, but I could read nothing in those calm blue eyes. I saw merely a very handsome man of fifty, absolutely unruffled as to hair or clothing. And his steady, well-cut mouth told me nothing. The terrible English veil hung in front of his face. But, in later weeks, my impression was confirmed: I was not being pushed out, but I was not being let in. I was striving against something which did not yield, something which suggested, though it never said, "Oh, leave this to me, Cadoresse," or "You must ask Mr. Purkis for instructions." But what was it? what? suspicion of my relation to Edith? a hint that I could not hope for preferment? Who can tell . . . in England?

And the atmosphere thickened still more in September when the Lawtons returned. There was a coldness in the air; I called, but was not asked to call again. Muriel, when reminded that she was to teach me to play golf, pleaded vague engagements. Hugh did not again walk home with me; he had "a man to meet at the Club," or he had to go to the tailor's.

It was three months since the last of our queer, intimate little talks, which were for me rather like a game with a tortoise: one incautious touch, and in went the head. We had gone to his club for a drink before dinner and, very warily, I had drawn Hugh away from memories of Winchester towards his theory of schools.

"Of course they don't get swished very often," he said when I attacked corporal punishment, "but one has to have a cane about. Just for the look of the thing."

"Like the classics?"

We had a long, formless discussion, Hugh defending

Latin and Greek on the plea that they trained the mind (which mathematics or English literature couldn't do) and taught one to understand one's own language (much better than German, even though English was German rather than Latin). Hugh was going to maintain the classics, as a sort of introduction to Shakespeare.

" Do you read Shakespeare? " I asked.

" Well . . ." He hesitated, then, confidentially: " I do rather like Shakespeare, but . . . one can't talk about him, that would never do. . . . Side, you know, all that sort of thing."

I delighted in these revelations, and I missed them, but Edith could tell me nothing, for nothing had been said; we were afraid, so afraid that we almost decided to tell, to end the tension.

" There's something up," I said, " somebody suspects. The maids smile at me when I come . . . your mother, she's cool. Even Fiona . . . oh, laugh if you like, but a few minutes ago, when we sat on the sofa, she came and sat down between us, looked at us each in turn with that idiotic, sentimental air of hers. It sounds mad, but she's been different to me since you and I . . ."

" You're absurd," said Edith, irritably. The something was beginning to tell upon her.

Four days later we were caught at St. Bartholomew's. We stood hidden by the side of an enormous stone pillar, hand in hand, very happy. Suddenly I saw Edith stiffen; she grasped my hand so hard that her finger-nails hurt me. Her other hand, raised, stopped my exclamation. Two yards off passed a couple, Bessie Surtees and a middle-aged woman in country tweeds.

" Did they see us? " Edith whispered, tensely. " I'm not sure Bessie didn't."

" We were in the shadow of the pillar," I said.

We made light of it, though I had to hold down in Edith a terror that struggled like a weasel in a gin.

" I can't bear it . . . we must tell . . . we must tell.

Oh, if we were caught, it'd be dreadful. It's bad enough deceiving them . . . but to be caught. . . ."

I comforted her, kissed her in the dark, silent church, pointed out that we must wait a few weeks, for Hugh was to be married in November, the wedding having been postponed, and we needed to know whether he was going to be made a partner. Edith clung to me, trembled, agreed, but the afternoon was spoiled, for now we knew that some accident must happen if we waited; the struggle was going to begin.

It began, but not at our own time. On the fourteenth of October I was asked to dinner; I had not been invited to the house for three months and now wondered whether I had exaggerated the tension or whether the Lawtons were merely doing the decent thing. By a private arrangement with Edith I arrived at ten to eight, was shown up to the empty drawing-room, into which she tiptoed, breathless, as soon as the maid was out of the way. She ran into my arms like a little, frightened animal, and there she lay, quivering, while I covered with impatient kisses her mouth, her cheeks, her soft, white neck.

"Oh, Lucien, it's been so long, so long . . . a fortnight."

"My darling, my darling, have courage! Soon we shall be together, soon. Kiss me. Ah, kiss me again."

I crushed her against my breast. I hurt her, I wanted to hurt her, and she laughed weakly as I relaxed the pressure but still held her in my arms. For a moment we remained, eyes gazing into eyes. Then we heard a sound, parted as suddenly as the strands of a broken rope. In the doorway stood Hugh.

IV

For three or four seconds the silence was quite perceptible. The air of the room seemed to have acquired an extraordinary, blanket-like quality. Then there was a change; I heard with extreme distinctness a motor-car pass the house and stop a little further up the street, and the maids in the basement, laughing noisily. But the sounds, clear though they were, seemed foreign to the scene, as if they came from another plane, while we three stood in a plane all our own.

Hugh had closed the door as he came in, stood against it, his face expressionless, a tall, rigid body. Edith had retreated to my right and clutched the settee so tight with both hands that on every one of her finger-nails I saw a red zone surrounded with white. And her eyebrows were comically twisted in the middle over her strained eyes. I knew that my fists were clenched, that a stream of blood had rushed up into my head, burning my ears, and pains in my teeth told me that my jaws were hard jammed so that the bones stood out.

The seconds passed and we did not speak. A stranger who lived in my brain cried out that this was a stage . . . the West End stage . . . he cast the three characters without hesitation, picking out well-known actor-managers and the latest ingénue. . . .

Hugh moved, very slightly. The play producer vanished and a trainer shouted tips at me: " Don't look at his hands . . . watch his eyes . . . get him on the point with your left and bring the right over the heart. . . ."

At last Hugh spoke, and the effect was that of an unexpected pistol shot, though his voice was absolutely normal:

" Edith," he said, " you'd better go up to mother for a bit."

He opened the door and stood aside to let her pass. For a moment she had met his gaze, still clutching the settee, but his rigidity mastered her and she ran past him. I heard her draw in a great gulp of air as she ran. Then Hugh, closing the door, turned towards me, and I realised that I was a fool, that there would be no fight. He was too cool. I was glad, for I was a little afraid of this trained man who could give me three inches and at least a

stone, and I was sorry, for the excitement of the encounter
was such that, to allay it, I wanted to leap at him, tear,
bite, scratch. But Hugh, still collected, spoke very quietly.

"We'll have to talk this over, Cadoresse. The others'll
be here in less than a minute and we'll want more than
that. I'll find an opportunity after dinner. Is that all
right?"

"Yes," I said after a pause.

The door opened to let in a laughing couple, Muriel
and Louisa.

"What are you plotting, you two?" asked Louisa.

He smiled benignantly at the flushed face, the dimpled
little chin.

"We were talking of golf. Cadoresse says it's too much
fag to get down to the links and that he's going in for
marbles."

"I really shall have to take you on, Mr. Cadoresse,"
said Muriel. "I'm ashamed I didn't keep my promise.
But we'd better get Louisa to take us down to her club,
the West Repton; I have to manage with clay, worse
luck, while West Repton's sand. Now in October, when
it's wet——"

I listened with apparent absorption to a mercifully long
lecture on sand versus clay, which expanded as Muriel
talked into a disquisition on made links, on bunkers, on
hard lines. While I listened and managed an occasional
appropriate comment on the game, my mind worked round
and round, like a goldfish in an aquarium: "What was
going to happen? What would Hugh do? What should
I do? No reply. Then, the other way round: "What
should I do? What would Hugh do? What was going
to happen?" . . .

"Oh, yes," I said in a high voice, "you'd better help
me buy my clubs."

But I felt giddy. More people came in, Mr. Lawton,
Edward Kent, Mrs. Lawton, apologising for being late,
and then Edith, behind her, with two flaming patches on

her cheeks, a metallic gleam in her eyes and a quivering mouth. I could hardly bear to look at her. And other people, the two Bennings, and a man with no face, and a woman who, when she laughed, made a sound like a cockatoo's screech and . . .

Damnation . . . I don't know who came, what they wore . . . I don't know whether the dinner happened at all. I remember only an atmosphere, paradoxes somewhere, near Kent I suppose, and the cockatoo laugh, and Edith, just her face, red and white, not a face at all, but a painted carnival mask, and my voice, harsh, high . . . some dogmatic views, some laughing, ah, plenty of that, and champagne, plenty of that too and the sear of it on my palate. At last the women gone, and Hugh's voice, clear as a flute:

" Oh, Cadoresse, you wanted to see that new gun of mine. Come up to my room and have a look at it."

V

" Well? " said Hugh.

Before I answered him I took in a few details. His was a large room, the third floor front. Rose-bud wall-paper; good silver fittings on the dressing table; on the walls prints after Cecil Aldin and Tom Browne; above the bed a large photograph of a football team; in a corner a cricket-bat, golf-sticks. These objects marked my mind without my knowing it, for I remembered them best a few days later. My brain was busy with his " Well? " He had spoken almost lazily, as if the tragedy bored him. Apollo was languid and was evidently doing his duty because it was the thing to do; evidently too he cared, or he wouldn't have bothered, but his ease exasperated me.

" Well what? " I said. " It's for you to talk. Go on. Tell me what you think of me. Call me a blackguard. Say I've come behind your father's back to steal his daughter . . . say I've played you all a dirty trick. . . . Go on, don't be afraid."

" I wasn't going to say anything of the kind," said Hugh. " I wasn't going to say anything. It's for you to say what you're going to do about it."

" What do you want me to do about it? "

" My dear fellow," said Hugh, blandly, " you really must see that there's only one thing for a man to do when he's caught kissing a girl."

" Oh! " His ease continued to annoy me, but I did not understand him at once. Then, suddenly I understood: Hugh meant to suggest that I might not intend to marry Edith, but that now I was caught and must ask for her hand. That cast such a vileness over the kiss he had surprised that, for a moment, I could not find words. At last I said, hoarsely: " Do you mean to say that you think I don't want to marry her? Do you dare——? "

" My dear chap," said Hugh, as he raised a deprecating hand, " please don't say ' do you dare '; this isn't the Adelphi and it isn't done, it really isn't done. You'll be challenging me to fight a duel, like you did Farr . . ." His tone was almost worried.

" No need to drag that up," I replied, savagely. " Say what you have to say."

" Well," Hugh went on in his tired voice, " it's simple enough. It looks as if you were gone on Edith, and, mind you, I don't see anything against that; she's a decent little kid. I suppose you want to marry her: then there's only one thing to do, as she seems willing; you've got to go to my father and ask for his consent."

I was surprised, so surprised that I forgot to be annoyed by his familiar allusions to my " being gone " on Edith, " a decent little kid." Edith! . . . a decent little kid! What I could not at once understand was the coolness with which he received the fact that I, an unrecognised suitor, had kissed his sister without having beforehand gained a right to pay my addresses to her. I knew that this was the English way, but knowing did not make it much less wonderful.

"Do you mean to say you don't mind?" I asked.

"Mind? Why should I mind? Edith's got as good a right to marry whom she likes as I have."

My mind flew back to his father, the Churchman, pleading for the rights of the Nonconformists. This tall, rather commonplace fellow suddenly seemed splendid.

"I say," I remarked, rather wonderingly, "it's awfully decent of you. You see, I thought there would be difficulties; I haven't much of a position——"

"Nothing to do with me," said Hugh. "If Edith wanted to marry the cobbler round the corner I mightn't like it, but it'd be her look-out."

"Ah, so you don't like the idea," I cried, my pride at once scenting insult.

"Don't be a silly ass; I wouldn't have you up here if I minded. But I'm not going to take sides; if my father agrees that's good enough for me. You can have her if you can get her, but things have gone far enough in a hole-and-corner way; you've got to finish them off fair and square."

"Well, I will tell him. Of course I'll tell him; I've wanted to for months."

"Good. Let me see, those people won't stay long; they know there's something up. Oh, yes, they do; the talk was pretty jerky at dinner; not one of them'll stay later than eleven. Not one. You'll have an opportunity then; I'll see to it."

"But—but——" I gasped, "you don't want me to tell him to-night?"

"Why not?"

"It's so sudden—I——"

"You're going to tell him soon. You may as well do it to-night."

We crossed eyes and I realised that Hugh, having decided without much consideration that I was to settle the matter that night, would not budge. He might know he was unreasonable, but then he was English: he had started and must go on. Then I reflected that it did not suit me to speak that night; it was important that I should know whether there would be changes in the firm. I thought of confiding in Hugh, but prudence held me back; if I mentioned business he would think me mercenary: the English know, but never like to think that marriage has anything to do with money.

"I shan't," I said. "Not to-night. Soon, but not to-night."

"Why?" said Hugh.

"I can't tell you. I'll ask him soon, but not to-night."

"I can't agree to your putting it off, Cadoresse." Hugh's voice was polite but a little hard, and some wrinkles appeared between his eyebrows.

"I shan't do it to-night," I replied.

There was a pause during which we measured each other's powers. Vaguely I knew that the cool one was winning because he was cool, but I could not regain my composure.

"You must," said Hugh in a low voice.

"I must? Oh . . . I understand, you mean that if I don't go to-night you will, that you'll——"

"Chuck it!" He was angry. I had scored a point then. No, though; Hugh did not raise his voice much, despite the passion in it. "I'm not going to give you away. I'm not a sneak, Cadoresse, though you choose to think so. What I mean is that I can't have a man hanging round my sister and making love to her without his having the pluck to do it openly. You've got to break cover some time: any way you'll get a run for your money. You want Edith: well, go and ask for her, don't beat about the bush, don't hide, or squirm when it comes to the point; face the thing out, and if you do get whacked take your licking like a man."

There was fire in his eyes; the sporting jargon excited

him, expressed him and his passion for the right, that
English form of right which has no subtlety or qualifications, which has less bend in it than there is in a battle-
axe.

" Well, suppose I won't," I said.

He ignored my answer.

" You will," he said suavely.

" Will I? How do you know? "

" You will, Cadoresse. You're going to play the game.
Oh, I know, you wouldn't have done it four years ago . . .
and even then I'm not sure, but anyhow, now you've been
here four years you know what I mean. You're going
to bell the cat to-night because it's the thing to do, the
decent thing. I'm not going to give you away, of course;
I couldn't, but if you don't do it I'll put it into the mater's
head that Edith's looking peaky; I'll have her sent down
to Brighton; I'll set Louisa to keep an eye on her; you
shan't write to her either; I'll grab the letters first post;
and if you do manage to get hold of her again I'll tackle
her and make *her* tell. . . . It's the decent thing to do."

I listened, less angry now than amazed. Here was a
brother ready to torture his sister, to spy on her, to have
her persecuted by others, briefly to do the rotten thing
because he wanted her to do the decent thing! And apparently it did not matter what Edith suffered provided nobody
sneaked and everybody did the decent thing. He was for
the letter of a gentleman's law.

A spasm of anger stirred me.

" Damn the decent thing! " I shouted. " Why, there's
no decent thing, not in love . . . you all say that ' all's
fair in love and war.' "

He hesitated, for he trusted proverbs and quotations as
much as he doubted epigrams. He withdrew into the keep
of his obstinacy.

" The decent thing is the decent thing, and you know
it."

" I don't, I don't pretend to know what's the decent

thing; or at any rate it isn't bullying and persecuting a young girl and making a man do by threats a thing he thinks undesirable. The decent thing isn't a live thing, a real thing; it used to be, when it was invented, but you've let it get out of date. Good heavens, Lawton, the decent thing you talk about came in with the Crusaders. It's dead, dried up; it's a mummy."

"It's all the better for having come in with the Crusaders," said Hugh; "if it's still going on, that shows there was some good in it."

I had an unwonted attack of Frenchness, raised my hand in despair. I had touched the rock bottom of England, her conservatism. It was all over, I was beaten, I felt limp, and I did not mind, for here was a splendour of sorts, this attitude of narrow purity, senseless honour. I knew that he had won as he came at me with those simplicities which stirred me like fine music, those splendid English views which are as unimaginative as a cask of English beer and as strong:

"Even if you think it may not do the trick, play fair. I've got nothing against you and I tell you this: there's only one right way of doing anything; all the others are wrong. There's the straight road, and a hundred crooked ones. If you want anything go and ask for it, that's the straight road. If you can't get it like that, you've got to take it, that's the next step on the straight road. Let it all be fair, honest fighting, with no dodgy ways and no messing with the rules; let it all be fair and square, so that if you are licked you may feel you did your best. And you're going to do that because you're a decent sort of chap——"

He faltered, for his last words made him shy. Then he went on. "You will; I'm not going to take sides, and whether you win or lose I won't take sides, for it isn't my business. It's yours and Edith's and my father's. But I can put my father up to it before you see him; it may help you, though, mind you, I shan't take sides either way.

All I'll do is to wish you luck. Shall I do that? You'll bell the cat to-night?"

I hesitated; he was smiling; never had he looked so handsome, so unutterably stupid and yet splendid.

"All right," I said rather gloomily, "I'll bell the trick."

"Bell the cat, you silly fool," Hugh roared as he opened the door and pushed me out; and again, as he smacked me on the shoulder:

"Not the *trick* . . . the *cat!*"

CHAPTER III

THE ENCOUNTER WITH THE FATHER

" What's this I hear about you and Edith? " asked Mr. Lawton.

Hugh had prepared him, then. I did not at once reply. I stood, one hand upon the corner of the dining-room table, looking past Mr. Lawton's well-brushed head at the clock which said ten-past eleven; I was nervous, and, as he leaned against the mantelpiece, the whole scene of our first meeting in my mother's Empire drawing-room passed through my mind. I saw myself as a small, bare-legged boy, inquiring and confident, much more confident than at this moment; and " young Lawton," who had not changed so very much. An immense interval of time seemed to elapse while I looked at him, described him to myself as a very well-groomed man of fifty, with fair, straight hair streaked with grey, regular features, a firm mouth and eyes as unflinching, as blue as those of his son. He seemed immensely tall, and his absolute immobility was impressive. Why did he not roar at me? I wondered; surely the occasion justified it.

" It's true," I said at length. Then, defiantly, " Quite true. I'm in love with your daughter Edith."

" Oh—hem——" He was embarrassed; I guessed that " in love " was too stagey for an Englishman, that I ought to have said: " I want to marry your daughter Edith."

" Well," he said at length, " what do you expect me to say to that? You can't expect me to say that I approve, give my consent to your marrying her. I suppose that's what you mean."

" Yes, I want to marry her, and I ask for your consent."

294

Mr. Lawton did not move. Suddenly I wanted to make him angry; it was proper he should be angry if he refused his consent.

" I'm going to marry her," I said, defiantly.

" Oh? " He remained perfectly calm. " You say you are going to marry her? Without my consent? "

" I did not say that," I replied, more cautiously, addressing the head of the firm.

" You suggested it. Still, I will let that pass, though I may as well tell you that Edith will refuse to marry you if I forbid it. Let that be quite clear."

I had doubts as to his power, but said nothing.

" Let it also be perfectly clear that I do not consent. You will want to know my reasons. They must be obvious to you. In the first place I think Edith is too young to marry just yet; she is only twenty, and she is too young in mind, too childish——"

" Excuse me," I interrupted. Edith too childish!

" One minute, and allow me to give my opinion of a girl whom I have known rather longer than you have. Edith is a child; she is not very strong; she is full of romantic notions, and I'm sure that that's why she—why—well, anyhow, I understand from what Hugh said that she considers herself . . . attached to you . . ."

Mr. Lawton stumbled on for a few sentences. Obviously he was not used to talking of love: he soon abandoned the subject.

" She will get over it; every young girl passes through this kind of affair, so I'm not blaming her. You, Cadoresse, I blame. You're not very old either, but I happen to know something about Frenchmen; a Frenchman of twenty-five——"

" Twenty-six," I corrected.

" Well, twenty-six, is at least as old as an Englishman of thirty. The sort of life Frenchmen lead. . . . But I'll let that alone, you know what I mean. Therefore you must have known perfectly well that as I was not

likely to let you marry Edith you were not entitled to
make—to propose to her."

" I did not know that," I said.

" You did not? What position have you to offer
her? "

" It is a rising position."

Mr. Lawton smiled, and I could not help liking him
because he was so calm in tragic circumstances. He had
not yet taken his hands from his pockets.

" Rather a tall thing to say to the senior partner,
Cadoresse. Still . . . yes, I see what's surprising you; it's
that I've said senior partner, isn't it? "

" Well! " I said.

" This is hardly the place to discuss the matter, but
I want you to understand that I have nothing against you
in general, and for that reason I will tell you, in confidence,
that my son will become a junior partner next month,
before his marriage. As for you, as I have said, I appreciate your services; you will take Mr. Hugh's place, and
we're going to raise you to three hundred a year at
Christmas."

" Thank you," I said mechanically. But my mind at
once set aside this good news. Edith alone occupied me,
and I was trying to adjust my ideas as to this man who
could be so judicial, blame my private behaviour, and yet
promote me according to my commercial merits. These
English gentlemen!

" That, however, has nothing to do with the business
we're discussing. What makes you smile? "

" Nothing," I said. I could not tell him that I was
not English enough yet to look upon our difference as
" business."

" As I say," Mr. Lawton went on, " it's got nothing
to do with it. You cannot marry Edith on three hundred
a year, nor on four, and there's no idea of giving you
four. You know the life she's been used to; to marry her
on three hundred a year would be preposterous. Edith's

not the girl to rough it in the suburbs with a day-girl."

" How much do you want? " I asked.

" How much I——? What——? " My bluntness about money disconcerted Mr. Lawton as much as his awkwardness about love disconcerted me. " You mean how much do I think you need? Say a thousand a year. Eight hundred at least."

" Not so much as that," I said, but I felt he was right; I was summoning courage to say boldly: " Make me a partner then, I'm as good a man as Hugh," but he interrupted me.

" Every halfpenny of it. The business can't afford that—and besides, there are other reasons."

This time there was a long pause. My bold phrase receded and receded into the back of my mind, while I conjured up the other reasons. Black eyes and blue eyes met now with a more dangerous air.

" Other reasons? " I said, politely; " would you mind——? "

" I had much rather not, Cadoresse. It's quite unnecessary; you have my answer; I decline; though, as I say, I have nothing against you."

Evidently he was trying to spare me, to do the thing nicely, but I was going to know.

" No," I replied, " you must tell me, Mr. Lawton. This is not fair."

I had chosen my last words with intention. An Englishman will do anything if you can make him believe it is " fair " to do it. I was right.

" I don't know about it's not being fair, Cadoresse, but if you think so, as I don't want you to think yourself unfairly treated, I will tell you. I don't want Edith to marry a foreigner."

" Why not? "

" I don't want Edith to marry a foreigner," he repeated, obstinately. " If you really want to know why I'll try and tell you. I've got nothing against foreigners, but they're different, they're fundamentally different, they're . . . foreign."

"Oh!" I said, very angry but quite cold, "I understand. Foreigners are foreign, and because they're foreign they're foreigners."

"Don't be so damnably logical," said Mr. Lawton, testy at last. "That's just it, Cadoresse, that's just like the foreigner; you've got to have sentences made like razorblades, and you're angry if you cut yourself with them. There! I'm making epigrams now; as if I were a foreigner myself; it's catching, I suppose. But look here, just try to understand a little. Here you are, a Frenchman; you've been four years in England. That's right, isn't it? You've done pretty well, but you're still a Frenchman."

"I'm sorry——" I began. He interrupted me.

"There's nothing to be sorry about. There's no harm in being a Frenchman; I've met lots of them—your father, a very fine fellow, and lots of other intelligent, honourable, sober people, but they were French. Now just try and think how different you are from us. They educate you differently, in a way better; they cram you with all sorts of things we never hear of, even at the 'Varsity, things like European history, and science mixed up with translations of the classics. That's one of the things; in England we don't go in for mixtures; a man's a classical scholar or he's been on the modern side. You may not think it matters, just because I can't be sure of the meaning of the inscription on a coin though I gave Latin six years— but it does."

I looked at him. Did it? Perhaps. These people do specialise.

"That means that you don't grow up like us; oh, I know, plenty of people say we run in a groove, but that has nothing to do with marriage. You may be better men, but what does matter is that like must marry like. You're streets ahead of a Kaffir, but you'd make a Kaffir girl a bad husband." He smiled. " I'm putting the case rather strongly, but I'm trying to explain; you're too different. Especially, you don't play games——"

" Excuse me," I said, " we did, and especially at Bordeaux. I played tennis when——"

" Tennis! " said Mr. Lawton, and his scorn was immense. " Again you give yourself away, Cadoresse. Tennis doesn't come in at all, except for girls. By games we mean football and cricket."

" You play other games," I said, aggressively.

" Yes. And we like a man to be handy with an oar, a racket or a golf-club, but those aren't the real games. Football and cricket have made us, and again, I want you to see that we may be nothing much, but we're different. Personally I think games have made us a great nation. They've taught us courage, discipline, obedience; and especially they've taught us to be unselfish."

" Unselfish? " I asked, puzzled.

" Yes. If you'd played Rugby and had passed to another man the ball with which you were racing to the goal line, given up your chance to score so that your side might score—you'd know."

For several minutes Mr. Lawton developed his subject, and though I was unshaken in my determination to gain Edith, he forced upon me the fact that I was different, fundamentally. A new misery crept over me, for I loved England almost as much as I loved Edith. It was not only my education estranged me.

" There are other things," said Mr. Lawton. " You don't dress as we do, even if you try. Your pleasures are different; you go in for art, not in reason as we do, but in a funny way; you won't mind if I call it a bit neurotic. Your ideas—your standards—they're all different."

Misery turned to anger.

" Then," I cried, " all this means that you don't think me good enough, apart from money."

" I did not——"

" Would you consent if I had a thousand a year? "

" Well, that's hardly fair. I might, but I shouldn't like it."

" Then it is true I'm not good enough. You wouldn't like it. That is to say that because I'm different I'm inferior. Oh, yes, it does mean that; if difference meant superiority it would not bar me. You despise the foreigner. But—but what am I to do? How can I cease to be different? I'm more English than I was, for I've tried, I've wanted to; you don't know how fond I am of England and the English, that I want to settle here, to live here, to be an Englishman." There was a shake in my voice, but I repressed a desire to weep, which would have been most un-English. " It isn't right, it isn't fair. You let us come here, work here, settle here—and then you won't recognise us as human beings, you won't have us as equals. You'll eat and drink with us, and play with us, and have us in your clubs—but you're only tolerating us, looking down on us all the time. It's horrible, it's making outcasts of us—pariahs."

I stopped, breathless, wet-eyed now in spite of my efforts. An idea began to gnaw at me: Edith? Did she too look down upon me, though carried away by a passing fancy? Mr. Lawton was speaking again, begging me not to exaggerate, pointing out how—foreign that was. I hardly listened, in my new misery. Now it was my nominal faith he attacked.

" You're a Roman Catholic," he said, " now——"

" I'm an atheist."

" Yes, yes, I know, an agnostic. But still you've been brought up as a Roman Catholic; we're Church people, and you know very well that I think a man has a right to believe what he chooses. There are lots of Roman Catholics in England, and I don't know that I like mixed marriages, not only on account of the children, but . . . but, I hardly know . . ."

Mr. Lawton hardly knew, but, little by little, his tangled sentences managed to convey his meaning to me because my mind had become as sensitive as a raw wound. Better than he did himself, I grasped the hidden fear and hatred the Protestant Englishman feels for Rome, the Jesuits, the sumptuousness of the mass. It was a plea for simplicity, for freedom from theocracy, for democratic government. Through the mouth of Mr. Lawton spoke the ancestor, two hundred and fifty years dead, who had shouted " No Popery! " and marched to Newbury with the Parliament men, or sailed on the *Mayflower* to escape the Stuart— the popish, foreign Stuart. Religion, even nominal, was vital. He believed in the imprint of Rome. He thought that it must have made me sly, crafty. He thought it must have filtered into my moral standards.

" You don't live as we do. Your attitude to women —well, I don't set up to be a saint, but still you know what I mean. It's not my business to inquire how you behave, but you'll not deny that Frenchmen generally lead loose lives, get entangled, lose respect for women . . ."

I tried miserably to make him see how my love for Edith had opened my eyes to the meaning of purity, the handsome thing, the decent thing; how I had made fetishes of chivalry and honour, and would uphold them because I had adopted them at a mature age. He disregarded my plea; I felt that he doubted me, suspected me; that at bottom he did not believe a foreigner could always be trusted to tell the truth, to refrain from sharp practice, to shield a woman, to play the game—all this because he was a foreigner.

" No," he wound up, " you'll see one day I'm doing you a good turn. You wouldn't be happy."

" What! " I cried.

" You wouldn't. Edith would displease you because she's not so keen, so assertive, so . . . showy as the French-women. And you'd jar on her, oh, for all sorts of reasons —your accent—your clothes. If you boasted, you don't do it often now, but sometimes, she'd shiver—and there's other things, being faithful—well! "

I did not reply. It was all over, from his point of view.

" Don't let us say any more about it," said Mr. Lawton, kindly enough. " I've spoken plainly, but you would have it, and perhaps it is best to understand one another. Of course you can't come here for a time. You see that? "

" Yes."

" Later on, when Edith is more sensible. And don't let it interfere with business; we're very pleased with you there. Now promise me that you will not try to communicate with Edith in any way."

" I can't do that."

" Oh, you must."

There was a mental tussle; we were man against man for a moment, no longer employer and clerk. Mr. Lawton was too generous to use his advantage.

" No," I said at length, " not unless she says so."

Mr. Lawton thought for a moment. Then—

" Very well. I don't mind. I will give you an opportunity; I shall tell her I forbid it and she will obey."

I looked defiance at the father. Oh, I could rely upon the Dresden Shepherdess; she was not strong, but armed with my love I trusted her.

" Good-night," said Mr. Lawton, " have a whisky before you go."

I shook my head. It was past midnight. Mr. Lawton opened the door, started back. Against the wall opposite, rigid, still in her evening clothes, Edith stood, her face flushed, her eyes downcast.

CHAPTER IV

THE ENCOUNTER WITH THE BETROTHED

WE remained all three as motionless as a *tableau vivant*. I was in the hall, face to face with Edith; behind me, in the doorway, I could feel Mr. Lawton. Details crowded upon me, Edith, as rigid as if she had been petrified, in a gown of white muslin, with little knots of roses circling the hem—the flowered wallpaper—the big, modern Lowestoft bowl full of visiting cards.

Then Mr. Lawton spoke.

" Edith! what are you doing here? "

She did not reply.

" Go up to your room at once." Mr. Lawton spoke in low, hurried tones, and a diabolical pleasure filled me as I realised that the fear that the servants had not gone to bed hung heavy over him. But, then, we were in England: the first thing to do was to avoid a scene. Edith was not, on her part, going to make a scene either; she looked up and said, quite calmly, in a strained voice:

" I wanted to see you, father, so I came down. All the others are in bed."

" You can see me to-morrow morning," said Mr. Lawton, rather harshly.

Then I joined in. A sense almost of the theatre urged me to have the matter out at once.

" Look here, Mr. Lawton," I said, " we both know what this means. Edith knew that I was asking leave to marry her; she came down to know your decision. There's nothing very wonderful in that. Well, I can tell you, Edith; your father refuses. He does not think me good enough——"

" I have told you that that is not the point, Cadoresse,

but I'm not going over it again. Now, Edith, go to your room."

Anger filled me, and I spoke quickly, fearing that Edith would obey: she might, for most English girls have been kicked into the gutter by their fathers and told by their mothers that it is ladylike to sit in it.

" No, Edith, don't go. Let's have it out. Your father refuses his consent, and I have refused to accept that as final. I said that I would take my dismissal only from you. Come, let us both go into the dining-room—and if you tell me it's over—very well." I turned to Mr. Lawton, and I think my tone was ironical: " I promise I won't make a scene."

" Impossible at this time of night," said Mr. Lawton. " I said I would give you an opportunity, and I will. Be here to-morrow morning at ten and you shall have it. Now, good-night. Edith, go to your room."

" Don't go, Edith," I said.

The girl looked at us in turn. Ah, my spirit fainted: she did not go, but she did not look like a rebel; her father's will and mine held her motionless as the handkerchief in the middle of the rope when there is a tug-of-war. I might win, but, if I won, would I win?

" Go upstairs, Edith," said Mr. Lawton, rather louder.

" Edith, stay," I murmured, in the low voice of which I knew the power.

" Don't you defy me, Cadoresse," said Mr. Lawton, with at last a hint of the theatre.

" I am not defying you, Mr. Lawton. All I say is this: our engagement has been discovered to-night. I have had it out with your son. I have had it out with you. Now I am going to have it out with Edith, and we shall know the end as well as the beginning. I refuse to go because I have a right to know. It is not fair . . . (ah, faint flicker of hesitation, Englishman!)—to condemn Edith and me to a night of . . . well, to suspense. We have done no wrong, it is not fair we should suffer. Now, Mr. Lawton, allow us to go into the dining-room for half-an-hour. When we come out, if Edith sends me away for ever, I'll "—(my lips twisted into a wretched, wriggling smile)—" I'll take it like an Englishman."

Mr. Lawton hesitated for a moment, looked at me so angrily that I felt he would not have hesitated to throw me out of the house and to carry Edith upstairs, but for the probable scene. Then he gave way.

" All right," he said. " Perhaps you're right. Go in, you two, and I'll sit here and wait. Take your time— it shan't be said you didn't have your chance, Cadoresse; put on your coat and take your hat: when you come out of that room I don't want to speak to you again to-night." He stepped away from the door, held it open after we had entered the dining-room. " Edith, understand this: I forbid you to marry Mr. Cadoresse. I forbid the engagement, I forbid you to communicate with Mr. Cadoresse after to-night. I have legal rights which I will not use, and other weapons which I will not use either. All I tell you is that I forbid the engagement, and order you to break it off at once. Now you can give Mr. Cadoresse his answer." He closed the door.

For some moments we did not speak. With downcast eyes we faced each other, as if we already knew that we were joined in an incomprehensible battle. And when at last I looked up I found in Edith's face a rigidity which revealed fear rather than excitement; though my blood was hot, as it always pleasurably is when I am going to try a throw with Fortune, I too was not without fear, for I was looking upon the girl who loved me, who was still affianced to me—and I could not know whether, in a few minutes, she would still be mine. Perhaps because of this, I did not speak, bade the moment tarry and, instead, went up to her, took her in my arms. Edith did not resist me; indeed, with a sudden movement, she flung both arms round my neck and clutched me to her, silent and trembling, and pressed her body against me, burying her face upon my shoulder, all taut with an anxiety that increased my own. As she grasped me, and as my hands knotted about her, as I felt her fingers, cold as any stones, upon my neck, and the burning of her cheek upon mine, the whole essence of us blended, and a formless, passionate prayer came out of me that I might absorb this girl I needed, that we might be made one, henceforth dwell in the same body. During that moment I believed in God, threw myself abased before One who might give me my desire.

We stood, close-locked, and our breathing was heavy, heavy with sobs rather than longing. And, truly enough, the sobs were very near. Edith's breath came quicker and quicker; she choked a little, faint sounds rose from the back of her throat, horrible, repressed little sounds that tore at me, brought tears to my own eyes, for I knew she was trying to be brave and finding it difficult, then impossible. Now she was crying, almost silently, but as if she would never stop; I could feel her tears upon my cheek, and, as I half-led and half-carried her to the big leather armchair, my eyes were dimmed by my own tears. There I held her upon my knees, until her weeping became less violent, remembering bitterly that once before only had I held her upon my knees, that night when I told her my love. At last her tears ceased to flow; with an uncertain hand she made a movement which showed she wanted her handkerchief; I gently dried her eyes, while she lay in my arms, exhausted, her head thrown back on my shoulder. When I had done she gave me a little, cheerless smile and said:

" My dear, you must let me go. We must talk."

" No, no," I murmured, and clasped her closer. Instinct told me that if I loosed her I lost her. I was right, for she struggled to her feet, and at once the sense of nearness, of fusion, was no longer there. Without contact we were not one, but two. Edith also felt it, wanted it so, refused me her hand, as if she guessed that, hand in hand with me, she would not be free. Indeed, it is hard to reason when hands are linked.

" Do you still love me? " I asked.

" Can you ask? " she replied.

I made as if to seize her, but she put out her arm; at that distance, now that we stood in front of each other, she already seemed lost.

" No," she said, " wait, Lucien, we must talk. We must decide what to do."

" But if you love me," I said, " there is nothing to decide. I love you, I need you, I can't do without you . . . I'll wait for you all my life if I must——"

" I too," said Edith, softly, " I'll wait, Lucien."

" Ah—my darling—yes, we must wait; oh, not long, I hope. You will tell him you can't give me up, that you'll marry nobody else—you will tell him you'll wait for ever——"

" Yes, Lucien," said Edith, gravely, " I'll tell him. But —but you know what he said—he won't let us be engaged——"

" He won't let us be engaged! Well, what does that matter? We are engaged, we remain engaged until—oh, my darling, my love, you're not going to give me up? "

" I can't," said Edith, weakly, " you've got me. But we can't be engaged if father won't let us."

" Oh, but we must, we must. You can't be trodden down like this, you will be twenty-one in a few months; then you can marry whom you please. You won't need to obey anybody. You will, my darling, you will? "

" I can't," said Edith, and she shook her head.

" But why? why? "

" I can't. I can't defy father. I can't. I'm not—oh, I'm a coward, I'm no good, but I'm afraid—I can't."

" You can if you love me."

" Oh, don't hurt me like that, Lucien. I can't—I can't bear everything that will happen if I do that. Father will

be angry, and mother will be on his side, Muriel too—
she'll say you haven't got enough money——"

" I shall, don't be afraid."

" Oh, that's not what I mean. I know it's weak of me,
but I can't think out whether they're right or wrong, I
just can't stand their all being against me—I know father
doesn't understand us, no more does mother, she's forgotten all about love—and I know Muriel's hard, and that
Hugh doesn't care—but they'd all be against me, and I
can't bear it. I can't live here like that——"

" Don't live here, my darling, come with me. Promise
me you will, and to-morrow I'll leave the firm, find another
billet, marry you. Oh, it won't be long. You love me,
don't you? you wouldn't want me to earn much? "

" It's not that, it's not that." Edith shook her head
wearily. " You know I love you, Lucien; you know I'd
marry you and live in one room, but I can't. Oh," she
added quickly, " I know what you'll say: if we go away
together soon it won't matter their being against me, for
I shan't live with them, but they'd still be against me, and
I'd know it: it'd be almost the same thing."

I did not reply, for no concrete argument avails against
the imponderable. I was frightened, too, for this height-
ened my sense of difference: no French girl could have
thought such a thing, have been . . . mystical.

" You see," Edith went on, " I can't disobey father. It
would be wrong."

" Wrong," I cried, " but, Edith, when one loves . . ."

" It would be wrong," she repeated, obstinately. " Perhaps he doesn't understand, but he's my father. Besides,
he's so fond of me. Oh, Lucien, you don't know how fond
he is of me. When I was at school he used to write to
me every week, to send me extra pocket-money hidden in
the lining of ties, because we weren't allowed to have much
—and it's still me he likes to take out alone. He's so fond
of me, I couldn't hurt him, I couldn't . . ."

" He's being cruel to-night."

" Yes—but he thinks he's doing his best for me . . . it's because he's so fond of me. Oh, Lucien, don't make me hurt him."

" But it's me you're hurting," I cried. I seized her hands, clasped her against me. " You're hurting me, don't you see that? I love you, I want you, my love, I need you . . . and you want to give me up. Oh, yes, you do, you wouldn't obey if you didn't. No, it's not true, forgive me, my darling, forgive me." I pressed kisses upon her bent neck. " No, I know you love me, and it's only because you're full of the sweetness, the tenderness that I love, that you think of giving me up. But you mustn't, you mustn't . . ."

Clasping her hard in my arms I covered her face with kisses; in broken phrases I begged her to cleave to me, to defy the world for me; I strained to give her some of my own energy, to exasperate, to inflame her; I was all artifice and yet all my artifices were spontaneous, for I was trying every door as may, without much thought, a man who is seeking for an outlet from a burning building. She lay passive in my arms under the hot stream of my words, too weak to cry, to respond to my passion. Despair seized me, for I realised the quality of her love for me. It was absolute, would shrink from no agony of waiting, but it had no activity, no courage. It could bear everything, but do nothing. It was all yield, devoid of aggression. Edith would love me all her life, but, overlaid by education and tradition, she might be lost to me.

" Ah, Edith," I murmured, " don't give in. Fight for me."

" I can't fight," said Edith, in a low, tired voice.

" But you must, you must. Everybody must fight." I released my hold of her, retaining only her hands. " You must fight, that's life, or die. Fighting is the destiny of man, and nothing good can be had of life, unless you fight for it. You are born with everything against you, the law, your parents, your family, conventions, fashions;

there's the law telling you what you mustn't do, your
parents telling you what to do, your family asking you
to consider their feelings, and conventions saying that they
must dominate you because they are there. Oh, don't,
don't," I cried, passionately, " don't give in. It's nothing
but a conspiracy—it's a fraud—it doesn't exist. You only
think it exists, all that. If you say you won't obey, it
all falls down. The world doesn't want to give you the
good things; my darling, there aren't enough good things
for everybody, and if you want them you must take them.
Oh, don't give me up; be bold, be free. Take your happiness, my darling, take it by force. Force is the only way,
force is the only thing that makes you fine. Until you've
fought you're no good, and it's better to have fought and
lost than not to have fought. Fight for me, fight for love,
and you'll win, you can, you can——"

" I can't fight," said Edith, miserably. " I can't."

There was a long pause. I dropped her hands, looked
with new eyes at her white face, her downcast eyes round
which were appearing shadows which would, on the morrow,
be purple rings. My plea for contest had excited me,
and an impersonal fury seized me when I thought of the
soft people of the world who could not or would not
fight. For I am a fighting-cock, and I despise the barn-
door fowls; I know that the barn-door fowls do not think
much of me, call me braggart, and creature of bombast,
and seeker of brabbles, but that does not trouble me: I
know that I am made of hard, sharp stuff. And, as I
looked upon myself in hateful complacency, my impersonal
fury became personal, for the softness of Edith galled me.
Ah, I had wanted that softness when I was strong; now
that victory seemed less certain I wanted to find in Edith
a useful hardness.

What do we want of women then? Vanity that is
humble, courage with a hint of cowardice, purity soaked
with passion. It is too much to ask. And now I, who
had stretched out hungry lips for honey, raged because

there was no vinegar in the precious store. She could not fight for me. Ah! then she would not. She did not love me. I was no lover of hers, but merely a schoolgirl's dream. Cadoresse, you strutting gallant, you had thrown yourself away.

"You can't," I said in an unexpectedly harsh voice. "You can't? Indeed. Then you do not love me." . . .

Edith did not reply, but sat down in the armchair and hid her face in her hands. I was too angry to care; I wanted to break my Dresden Shepherdess, as a mischievous child, untaught by experience, smashes a toy to see whether there is anything inside.

"You do not love me," I repeated. "You have not got the faculty. You are like the rest of your people, you do not know what love means. Answer," I cried angrily, after a pause, "but no, I suppose you won't answer. You're like the rest of the English—you're not going to defend yourself—you're too afraid of making a scene. Oh, I know you now, you and all the rest, and your damned discipline, your damned hypocrisy. You don't feel much, and what you feel you'll hide—you'll let me say what I like, but you'll keep your temper—you'll hurt me because you're too proud to speak—and you'll hurt yourself because you're too proud to cry out. You're not human beings at all, none of you—you've had it fogged out of you; you can't scream, and cry out, and rejoice, you can't thirst and hunger and rage—it's all gone, all the humanity, all the fine beastliness of man. Civilised, dried-up, mummified. Where's your blood gone to? Speak, I say . . . or did you go to Winchester with Hugh?"

Edith's hands trembled upon her face.

"I see, you won't speak. I suppose it isn't all pride and education then. Perhaps it's not worth while? Perhaps you see, after all, that I'm not good enough—too different, as your father says. Perhaps you won't fight because you don't want to, because I'm not worth fighting for. I see now—I understand. North is North

and South is South, and never the twain shall meet. I
ought not to have left my country, and the women who
are like my mother——"

Edith's hands dropped into her lap, but my anger had
given way to a bitterness so cold that the twist of her lips,
the dilation of her eyes inspired in me no pity. Indeed,
her pain filled me with an incomprehensible delight. I
had hurt her, I must hurt her again.

"I suppose you think I'd better go back to them," I
sneered. "Perhaps you're right, perhaps you're giving me
good advice. Well, I am going. I am, I am——"

Edith's features did not move; they were set in their
strained lines, but I heard her whisper: "Lucien!"

"Too late," I said, sombrely. "It's good-bye."

I seized my hat and coat, and, before turning to go,
looked at her again. She did not rise, but held out her
hands:

"If you come back, Lucien," she murmured, and a knot
of furrows formed between her eyebrows; "if ever you
come back——"

"If I come back!" I cried. "Oh, indeed, if I come
back——"

I can hear myself laughing as I opened the door,
laughing as I did not know I could laugh.

CHAPTER V

AFTER THE ENCOUNTERS

I

I do not remember very well what thoughts occupied me as I went down the steps of the house at Lancaster Gate, except one: " I shall go home, back to France." What else, indeed, was there to do, now that I knew the English to be marshalled against me in phalanx? And though I did not actually go back to France for some time, though I preferred to go to the devil, the thought clove to me. For home-sickness insists. In France, I felt, they would know me, understand me so well as to take no notice of me: and I did not want to be noticed just then. I wanted to slink away into a corner where I should see nothing, where nothing would see me. I did not want to read English papers, to speak with Englishmen, to interest myself in English things; I wanted rest, mental sleep, as if my mind had been exhausted by its three terrific bouts. I found sleep, for it comes all too readily to the young alien who lives in furnished rooms; he has but to abandon effort for society to forsake him, as a publisher who abandons advertisement sees his circulation fade away.

When I had closed behind me the door of my bedroom, having found my way home as instinctively as does a pigeon, I experienced a great sense of relief. The struggle was over, and I was too tired to feel my defeat, even to regret Edith: I was numbed; I pulled off my clothes, which felt heavy and complicated, threw myself on the bed, too tired to put on my pyjamas; I must then have instinctively crawled under the bedclothes, for, when I woke up, late next day, I found I had slept in my under-

clothes, leaving the light switched on. I made no effort
to go to Barbezan, allowed my landlady to think me unwell
and to bring me my lunch in bed. I was still torpid,
and when I tried to think, while the setting sun fell on
my window, I could not pull together any mental threads.
I was contented, contented as one is when the surgical
operation is over and pain has not yet come.

It was in the night I decided to go back to Barbezan
the next day. I found in myself no hatred for Lawton
and his son; my work waited and I saw no reason why
I should rebel against it. Indeed, I think I surprised my
masters when I returned, coolly excusing my absence by
a plea of illness which they had, tactfully enough, fore-
stalled on my behalf. Neither commented on the happen-
ings of the fourteenth. Mr. Lawton handed me a sheaf
of bills of lading, so that I might apportion them among
the available Lisbon boats; later in the day he sent for
me to reprimand me for having arranged an illegal deck
cargo from London, which should have been taken at
Antwerp; and Hugh began to settle with me the details
of the transfer of his work to me, which was to be made
at the end of the month. We did not discuss our private
affairs; we did not want to, and I think the Lawtons were
so relieved by my attitude that an unwonted courtesy born
of remorse stole into their speech.

That is all I remember. In the office I seem, for a
fortnight, to have gone about my duties as efficiently as
usual, subject to the errors into which my imagination
precipitated me from time to time. Out of the office I
lived my ordinary life: occasional games of chess with
Stanley, long walks at night (purposeless now and proof
against temptation), evenings at theatres or music-halls;
on one of the Sundays I sculled all alone from Hampton
Court to Staines and back; I was so calm, so ordinary
that I deceived Stanley, at whose house I went to dine.
I did not quite deceive him, for he said:

" Don't know what's up with you, Cadoresse; you're
quieter than you were. I suppose you're turning into an
Englishman after all."

That stab should have roused me, but the time had not
come: my emotional chord had been strained and did not
vibrate. It needed time to recover its sensitiveness, and
little by little, I found it did, that grief was stealing upon
me, slowly as a cloud on a light wind across the moon. I
did not yet suffer acutely, but I began to feel an atmosphere,
a peculiar one, for it affected me in the office. Perhaps
Barker first stimulated me when he asked me, elaborately
casual, whether I'd been to the Lawtons' lately. I replied
by a curt negative, but I was put on my guard; soon I
discovered that I interested the staff, that Tyler and
Merton came to talk to me of " life in the West End "
in a way which suggested impalpable raillery; Farr, who
seldom addressed me, took the trouble to tell me that there
was nothing like a decent country girl. When asked to
define " country " he fell back on the girls " down his
way." I managed to hold myself in, but I realised that
all this was not fortuitous, that they knew something, if
not everything, that the facts of my struggle had leaked
out. How? I shall never know, for facts leak through
crevices as small as those which, on board ship, will let
out steam. From Mrs. Lawton to a friend, from her to
some husband in the City, thence to his head clerk and
on to our own . . . thus, perhaps. I was not sure that
the clerks knew, but I suspected that they did, and I began
to hate them, to fear them as a weak thing fears a strong
one that may hurt it, and to hate them more because I
feared them. The fear was good for me, strong alkali
which made me wince but revived me; by hating I began to
regain my strength, my manliness. But, because I did
not know, because the English did not boldly come out
and laugh at me, I could not have the rough-and-tumble
I needed to make me active again.

Then the thing came. One morning, as I sat down

at my desk, I found a sheet of paper pinned on my blotter; on it stood:

> " A FROGGY WOULD A WOOING GO,
> A CADORESSE, A KNIGHT JUST SO.
> BUT THE ENGLISH ROSE SAID ' OH, NO, NO '
> TO CADORESSE, THE KNIGHT JUST SO."

I think I read the doggerel five or six times to make quite sure of its application to me. I felt my face burn. . . . Yes, they knew, not everything, for they evidently thought it was Edith had refused the Frenchman. A spasm shook me, a spasm of rage so violent that, had I not then been alone, I should have fallen on the first man I saw and tried to tear out his windpipe. But it was early, and I was able to contain myself when Barker came in, to say nothing to the others, though I covertly glanced at their faces to surprise in them the irony which would expose their guilt. They remained impassive, so English in their attitude of aloofness that I had to repress my desire to go to each one of the staff and suddenly show him the rhyme, asking him: " Did you write this? " I did not do it, for I was now English enough myself to shrink a little from scenes; to this day I do not know who the author was, for there was no clue. The doggerel was typed on one of our machines and on our own paper; it might be the work of any one of the staff of thirty, for nothing proved that my affairs did not interest those with whom I did not associate every day.

For several days I lived with the thing; having learned it by heart I found myself repeating it to myself over and over again, some other self forcing it upon my sentient self and repeating it to me, insistently, monotonously, maddeningly. A little tune composed itself and a demon began to sing it to me as I walked, even when I stopped my ears with both hands and concentrated so hard that sweat started from my forehead; sometimes the demon became fanciful, introduced variations:

> "A FROGGY WOULD A WOOING GO,
>   A WOOING GO, A WOOING GO,
>   A FROGGY WOULD A WOOING GO,
>   'HEIGH HO!' SAID EDIE . . .
>   A CADORESSE, A KNIGHT JUST SO,
>   A KNIGHT JUST SO, A KNIGHT JUST SO,
>   IS NOT A MAN QUITE 'COMME IL FAUT,'
>   QUITE 'COMME IL FAUT,' QUITE 'COMME IL FAUT' . . ."

I could not get rid of it. It rumbled at me from the wheels as I rode in the Tube, it tinkled out of barrel-organ tunes, it screamed itself out of the wind . . . and when I woke in the middle of the night, it came, low and obstinate, out of the innermost Me. It was at night I learned to bite my pillow so that I might not shriek out what I was beginning to believe: " I'm going mad . . . I *am* mad. . . ."

One effect of the rhyme was notable. My hatred of the clerks did not fog my brain, but cleared it; I ceased to see them as magical Englishmen, began to watch and analyse them, to find a queer, malignant pleasure in seeing the ugly where I had once seen the splendid. Farr gave me the first indication by suddenly asking me to come to Hornsey and see his wife, the most wonderful woman in the world, his son Norman and the roses of his garden while they were still blooming.

" You'll find it all right," he said, " in the Edgerley Road. ' Farrfield ' is the name of the house."

I refused, almost rudely, for I suspected that this sudden outburst of friendliness from my old enemy meant that he wanted to gloat over my downfall or that the most wonderful woman in the world wished to find out all about it. But, as he explained that he had called " Farrfield " after himself when the house was new and nameless, I saw him and his class. I watched him and his fellows, engaged them in conversation so that their accidental confidences might swell the total of my hatred; everything that was despicable and snobbish in them cheered me, for it convinced me that my race was not, after all, inferior to theirs. I know with what delight I observed that Barker reproved the new office-boy for sticking two halfpenny stamps on a letter instead of a penny one. "It doesn't look well," said Barker. Dull, conventional fool . . . as if it mattered to a free spirit!

Another day it was Tyler, who was about to be married, telling Merton while I listened that he was going to have a Turkey carpet . . . that is an Axminster Turkey; and a grand piano . . . an upright grand. I smiled as I pretended to write; I smiled more broadly as Tyler boasted of his best man to be, for the latter was quite the gent, a medical student . . . dental. Whether it was Farr suspecting Mayfair of every vice and kneeling at Hornsey in idiotic adoration of Regent's Park, or old Purkis expressing disapproval of a system which paid Harry Lauder a wage superior to that of the Prime Minister, but accepting the situation when he found that his wife appreciated the comedian, I felt surrounded by a hateful group of snobs, frauds, men of the villa breed. So much to the good: if I could not be an Englishman, at least I was no suburban.

But the emptiness grew round me as my aloofness increased; I paid the penalty of the new status I was acquiring in my own mind. Unable to call on the Lawtons, shunning the Raleighs, the Kents and their circle, afraid to go to Stanley lest he should vivisect me, I fell back upon myself, upon my bitter loneliness. Neither work, nor the facile pleasures of the London streets, from which too often I now returned unsatisfied, availed me. For I could not drink; the third whisky stupefied instead of exhilarating me, and I was unwell the next day; and the light flirtations of omnibus tops and London parks had been spoiled for me by my great adventure.

Edith had reconquered me, and now I suffered as I had never suffered before. Her light, graceful body, her clear laugh, the soft look of her eyes when they rested upon me, her voice, suddenly low when it spoke of love, everything of her rose up before me now that I had lost her, more precious and rarer than ever before. Too desperate and too proud to resume in Lancaster Gate the sentry-go of my early gallantry, I was not able to resist looking anxiously into the faces of girls as I passed them in the street, hoping a little it would be Edith I saw, and fearing that it might be Edith, and hoping too that something, the arch of an eyebrow or the curve of a lip, would recall her to me. Sometimes I tried to drive the image away, reasoned with myself and told myself I was sentimental, neurotic, that I must forget her and make another life; but I reacted very soon from those moods and, leaning back in some comfortable chair, gave myself up to a daydream with a delicious sense of foolishness and guilt. Whether I loved her then, I am not sure, for so much hatred mingled with my passion, but certainly she occupied and filled me as she had never done before, and often she called to me, faintly and wistfully; sometimes my mind clothed her in a white pannier skirt, all flowered with pink roses, dressed her hair high and powdered it, set a patch upon her delicate painted cheek and then bade her curtsey to me as an actual Dresden Shepherdess dethroned from her pedestal. In other moments she was neat and shirtwaisted, in others yet, all languid, in gold-flecked gauze, upon a bank of peonies. And often I ended by weeping, by digging my nails into my palms because I did not want to weep: for the joy one has not had turns to bitterness; it may be that St. Anthony suffered more after than during the temptation.

One dream never came to me, a dream of reconquest. Edith had fled back into the ideal land whence I had called her to me; no longer Edith, she had rejoined the phantom English girls among whom I had thought to find my mate. In those days she seemed, in her dream-land, to belong to another world, to live in some Eden from which I had been driven, never to return, because being foreign I was unclean. And yet I longed for her, wanted, needed her; deeper and deeper I sank into gloom and isolation, and I wanted her with a more insistent ache. For time does not heal a wound when both heart and pride are sore: that is too great a complication. I needed her hopelessly, well knowing that whosoever hath drunk shall evermore be thirsty, but resigned myself to everlasting thirst.

II

The year was dying. But four days before, on Christmas Eve, I had been handed an envelope in which, together with a Christmas box, was a typed notice to " No. 12 " that his salary was raised to three hundred a year, for Barbezan & Co., who wished to allay jealousy among the staff, concealed from the typists the names of those fortunates who benefited by rises. And now, gloomily enough, I was substituting pleasure for happiness; I had been to the theatre, in the stalls, as I could afford a stall on three hundred a year, and now sat before some cold chicken and half a bottle of Moselle in a big Strand restaurant. I had thought to find there gaiety, and there gaiety lived indeed, for the air was filled with excited babble, with the band's impartial selections from " La Bohême " and " The Country Girl." Much light, a red glow on the velvet seats, glitters on the gildings of the walls and about the crystal of the chandeliers. A general impression of movement, easy and fleeting adventure, and for me a feeling of separateness, almost disembodiment. I had not felt my loneliness in the theatre, but I felt it bitterly in this room where everybody had come in twos or in groups, where such as came singly nodded carelessly to friendly supper-parties and wandered on to some appointed table. I had no appointed table, sat at my own as a dog before its platter, and a sourness filled me as I looked at the couples, the dozens, the scores of couples, the parties of four which

were only duplicated couples. Young Englishmen in perfect evening clothes, with girls who were not of their class,
but lovely in their excitement; swarthy foreigners showing London to handsome London girls and ignorant of the
contempt the English felt for them; middle-aged men,
some with beaming, some with irritable wives, and some
with the obvious unwed, divided in their allegiance between
woman and wine, I hated them all. I hated their gaiety,
their freedom from care, the security of the English, the
ignorance, boldness of the foreigners; I hated them because they were not alone, because they had at least the
illusion of love, because the bubble of their self-esteem had
not been pricked. And in the horror of my solitude I felt
ready for any expedient, for any adventure, however low,
if only I might be gulled with pretty speeches, hold some
falsely friendly hand . . . if only I could cease to be alone.
. . . And still the double door revolved in its glass case,
hiding and revealing these ghosts that went in and out
endlessly. Ghosts! yes, they were ghosts to me, ghosts
whom my touch would dispel. . . .

Two girls seemed to have forced themselves into one
compartment of the door, for there was laughing and shrill
giggling as they bundled together into the room. I looked
at them carelessly, hating them too because they laughed.
But one of them interested me. Her clothes held my attention, for their fashion had anticipated the taste of London,
recalled a picture I had seen a day or two before in a
French paper. She was small, slim, wore a Nattier blue
coat and skirt over a white lingerie blouse which ended
in a large jabot; her hat was just larger than anybody
else's, and its Nattier blue satin bows stood out like
enormous wings; as she came towards me, slowly, followed by her friend, who was taller and dressed in more
commonplace khaki, I recognised her, and my heart began
to beat as she walked down the aisle between the marble-
topped tables. Just before she reached my table our eyes
met and, for a moment, she looked at me incredulously, and

I had time to see warm colour rise in her cheeks, her brown eyes sparkle. Then she took two quick steps forward and, smiling broadly, held out her hand.

"Lor!" she said, "it's old tea-caddy. Fancy meeting You."

I took her hand, which was bare and warm and, as I held it, recognised the familiar breadth of the palm, the sudden tapering of the pointed fingers; the red mouth, redder than in the past, for it was skilfully painted with lip-salve, smiled over the perfect teeth, and there was an air of artifice about the brown hair, now done in a score of curls. Maud looked rakish, almost defiant, but also genuinely pleased to see me, and as I smiled at her I knew that I too was glad, that I was no longer alone. She laughed nervously, freed her hand and turned to her friend:

"Allow me to introduce," she said, solemnly, "Miss Serena P. Huggins, of Chicago, where the pork comes from . . . Mr. Cadoresse."

"Pleased to meet you, Mr. CaDOR'ess," said Miss Huggins.

I smiled as we shook hands, for this was the first time I heard the American accent, and to be called CaDOR'ess amused me.

Also Serena was very attractive, much taller than I had realised at first, slim but absolutely straight; her perfect tailoring exaggerated her length of bust and limb; on her long neck she carried a small, aggressive head, round which were coiled endless plaits of thick, glittering black hair. A mat skin, warmed with pink and some yellow, a thin, defiant mouth, so dark red as to appear brown, unflinching black eyes and almost straight black eyebrows, all this was so pronounced, so assertive that I thought of Diana, the fierce huntress, as I said:

"I too am charmed, Miss Huggins; indeed, if anything could increase the pleasure of meeting Miss Hooper again, it would be making your acquaintance."

"There! Serrie, old dear," said Maud. "What did I tell you? There isn't another can tell the tale like him. But don'tcher care, Serrie, he told it to me before he told it you and it's the same old tale. Still, I'm not going to be hard on you, Caddy; you can stand us supper and we'll kiss and be friends . . . that is, if you're all on your lonesome."

"Yes," I said, "I'm alone. Sit down, both of you, and order what you like."

"What I like!" said Maud, staring at me. "My, you're up in the flies, Caddy. What'd you say if I made it fizz?"

"I should order fizz."

"Well, I never! Have they made you a bloomin' partner? or what?"

Before I could reply Serena had interposed:

"Say, Maudie, what's the matter with fizz, anyway? We ain't on the water wagon, either of us. What's the good of makin' a poor mouth about it?"

As I called the waiter I swiftly contrasted the humble attitude of the English girl with the cool, proprietorial tone of the American. But I had little time for analysis, as Maud, who seemed to have forgotten the quarrel on which we parted, had a great deal to say: having to explain me to Serena while she gave me some account of her last year's history, her conversation was a little mixed.

"Well, no, I'm not exactly on the halls. I did do a turn, eccentric dancing and, my word, it wasn't half eccentric, and I was on the road for a bit after I gave Bert the chuck. You remember Bert, don't you, Caddy? Oh, don'tcher care, it's all over, absoballylutely. You see, Serrie, this is my long-lost fiasco and love of my youth; he got the pip because of Bert, and as I wasn't having any of his old buck we said a tearful farewell, I don't think. . . . Oh, yes," she replied to my question, "it was pretty rotten, being on the road, but a shop's a shop and don't you forget it. I got the bird one night and that's what put the lid on it . . . though if you want to know it was the boss. What d'you think he said, one night, the. . . ." I was enlightened as to the morality of managers in general. "Fetched him one on the koboko," Maud summed up, "and hooked it. What am I doing now? Nothing extra, walking on in the second line; it ain't all 'oney, eh, Serrie?"

"It's a rotten dope," said Serena, fiercely. "Two shows a day, sixteen changes, an' ninety-four steps to climb each change. I'm goin' on the jag next week. Lookee here," she added, as Maud protested that drink wouldn't mend matters, "this show don't go on; do you know the money, Mr. CaDOR'ess? Ten dollars a week, an' there's a dollar for the agent, an' a shillin' for the dresser, an' sixpence for the callboy, an' sixpence for the doorkeeper—do you get me, Steve?"

My explanation that my name was not Steve was received with shrieks of laughter, during which Serena forgot her grievance and, little by little, as I learned to translate these girls' extraordinary language, I gained an idea of Maud's adventures. She had "eloped" with Bert Burge a week after I left St. Mary's Terrace, and she did not conceal that the word "marriage" had never been pronounced. She had gone on the halls as an eccentric dancer and singer, had been the partner in a knockabout with Bert; then, tiring of him or deserted by him (I never found out the truth), she had gone on tour with a third-rate musical comedy company. After the episode of the bird and the smack on the manager's koboko, provoked by her faithfulness to her temporary companion, the low com., she had been out of a shop for two months. There was a little break in her story which I did not try to bridge. Then she came to London, made friends with Serena in a teashop, and was through her engaged in the variety theatre where a mongrel entertainment, made up of singing, dancing, acting and parading occupied her twice a day. Now she was happy enough, could count on thirty-four shillings a week, and lived in freedom with Serena at Harewood Avenue. She had come into the restaurant on the chance of " getting off " with "one of the boys."

All this came out swiftly, with a metallic rattle of gaiety, sprinkled and spiced everywhere by the theatro-Cockney ironies of " tain't so likely " and " never let it be said." Maud was gay, fiercely, defiantly gay, and fiercely, defiantly cynical. Also her language had changed: here was no longer the mild slang picked up at Mother Tinman's, but a blend of the vilest Cockney phrases and of theatrical tags, sprinkled here and there with oaths; I had yet to learn that no words were too foul now, when Maud was angry: the Mile End streak ran right through her. She was vulgar, and became vulgar, vital, in a way which clashed with her cynicism, made me think of those sophisticated hot omelettes in whose heart is concealed an ice. That night cynicism was in the ascendant; curls, paint, the " pussy-cats " of make-up which still stuck in the corners of her eyes, accorded with her new attitude, her new name, " Maudie Devon." I asked her why she had adopted it.

" Fetches the boys," she said, " least I hope it will; got a newspaper chap in Dudley to put me in as ' Maudie D.' It'd be worth twenty quid a week to be Mordedee . . . and I can't get a line in this show," she added, viciously.

Serena did not speak much. She ate and drank voraciously, replying only by short sentences to the remarks I made to her out of politeness. I wanted to talk to Maud, who attracted me now more than ever, perhaps because the good looks of the girl had turned into the brazen beauty of the woman, perhaps because in my loneliness and misery my heart was as susceptible to temptation as is a weakened body to disease. And Maud's frankness, her aggressive boldness, fascinated me; the insolence with which she dropped hints of her various companionships; her fierce and open taste for a good time, all this was so easy after the reticences of another class that I found myself sliding, and gladly. Maud told me in plain words that she had gone to the devil because I didn't care for her, and when I publicly took her hand, did not resist. Apparently she didn't care what happened.

"Say, honey," Serena remarked, yawning as if the story bored her, " it's twelve-thirty; we've got to beat it. You're the sweetest thing, Mr. CaDOR'ess, and that's why you'll drive us home in a taxicab."

The fine black eyes commanded as they wheedled. In the cab the American lay back as if asleep after inviting us to " canoodle " all we wanted. And Maud, after declaring that spooning was O-R-P-H, orph, allowed me to take her in my arms and kiss her lips as the full lights of Piccadilly Circus streamed into the cab.

III

What did I feel? I wondered, as the cab took me to Cambridge Street. I often asked myself that question as my companionship with the two girls grew closer, and found it difficult of solution, for I had emerged from my ten weeks of insensibility without having thoroughly recovered my capacity for introspection; some of it had returned to me after the incident of the rhyme, for I had been stung, but I was not yet a sentient animal; those mental chords were still strained. I had a vague idea that, after Edith, I needed not a lover, but a soul into which to pour my soul, a woman with whom to mix tears. And yet I knew that I was glad of the girls' society, that their curious talk pleased me, and that I could be amused by stories of what Gwendolen Harcourt said to her boy, by descriptions of the " bucketing " Tozer gave his company at rehearsal, and the perpetual spicy stories which

found their way " behind " from Throgmorton Street.   It
was easy, for these girls were used to the foreigner, the
rich Brazilian and the German Jew, distinguished little
between the Honourable John Helbert (the candidate for
Serena) and old Mosenberg, who cast over the whole of
the chorus a favourable eye; here were no insults for the
Frenchman; so long as he had a decent coat to his back,
money to pay for a supper or a cab, and was not too dull
company, the Frenchman was just a man.

That was good.   I could fall into gallicisms now, and
merely be called a " date "; there were no more imper-
turbable disapprovals, no more classifications.   So, as I
let myself slide, surrendered myself to Maud's heady
charm, I felt as happy as a criminal who has confessed,
for I was not pretending any more; I was myself, a lover
in search of facile adventure.   It came, for I found that
Maud had preserved something of the faint taste she had
had for me; grafted on those remains, on the sentimentality
which inclined her towards me because she had known
me a very long time and in other surroundings, was the
boldness and the looseness which had come to her as she
draggled her way from sordid, mercenary companionships
to complaisances dictated by policy, and to indulgences in
which sensuousness played a lesser part than indifference.

Maud was a creature born again; she had seized her
politic morals and hurled them behind her.   She was
abandoned, not because she wanted to be such, but because
she didn't care.   One evening I was to fetch her at the
stage door at six, to take her to dinner and bring her back
in time for the evening show.   I waited some minutes
under the porch of the theatre opposite, for fine rain was
falling.   With me was a little crowd; there were two
obvious mothers, elderly, tired and wonderfully vigilant,
as if they feared that their girls would be kidnapped at
the door, several " boys " in fancy waistcoats and birthday boots; there was also somebody's girl pal, rakish and

still powder-flecked. Every time the door opened, to disclose in a cube of light the doorkeeper, who sat in his box, and to let out a stage hand or some principal, there was a slight stir in the crowd. Hungrily they watched the theatrical folk, the dressers, members of the band, and smart girls who furled their skirts and ran under the drizzle. But the tenseness of it amused me, showed me how little I mattered now, for nobody seemed to wonder with what member of the chorus I might be entangled; the tenseness was purely individual. There was nobody now to criticise me, my morals, manners or standards. Indeed, the attitude went further than I thought, for the door was opened suddenly to show me Maud, in tights and spangled bodice, beckoning to me to come in.

I crossed the alley, followed by the envious eyes of the "boys," entered with hesitation the cube of light. It was a dingy little place, no more than a corridor between the two stone staircases that rose to the right and left. The doorkeeper threw me so hostile a look that, in response to a wink from Maud, I handed him a coin, half-a-crown I think.

"This ain't allowed," he grumbled; "'urry up."

Maud seized my arm and drew me two paces away, but I did not notice her first sentences, so striking did she appear in her full make-up. Her face was marked with red and white patches and lines which made her look like a clown; both her upper eyelids were painted deep blue; she had moulded her mouth into a bow with thick red salve, while every one of her eyelashes was clothed with black grains at the base. She wore pink tights, and a close-fitting shell entirely covered with gold crescents and multicoloured paillettes; glittering wire and gauze wings stood out from her shoulders, and smaller wings rose from her piled brown hair.

"Couldn't let your youthful heart get sick with hope deferred, old dear," said Maud. "We've had a call to put a new girl through. Old Pinky-Gills gave Dora d'Esterre the sack this afternoon to put in a new girl he picked up at a night club. That's the third call we've had this week to please his lordship. You wouldn't think he was a thing of the past, the——"

"Maud, darling!" I protested, for another couple stood whispering at the foot of the second staircase.

"Oh, don'tcher care. Anyhow, I can't go out, and I can't stop."

"Can't you say you're unwell?"

"Rush of brains to the feet! Tell that to old Pinky-Gills! No, I'll meet you at the Bank to-morrow, at half-past twelve, as per use, and you can take me to lunch. Now don't be sulky."

I looked down at her, and vividly realised that the little creature was charming, that she was lovely. The tights moulded her slim limbs, and the shell, cut very low, leaving her arms and mobile breast bare, revealed by suggesting more than it hid. And, curiously enough, she was gentle.

"Must go," she murmured. Her hand was still on my arm. "Frenchy mustn't be sulky. Baby frightened." Four years streamed away as I remembered those words, spoken before our first kiss. Was there magic in them? Perhaps, for Maud laughed, threw a glance towards the doorkeeper's back and the whispering couple, then coiled a warm, bare arm round my neck and, drawing my head down, kissed me swiftly but so violently that the scent and taste of the grease paint still clung to my lips when I woke up next day.

"Ta-ta. Be good," she said, and ran up the stairs.

I went out, stood in the drizzle, and observed, impersonally, that the others still waited, that two flashy, Jewish-looking men had joined their group, that a motor-car stood at the end of the alley in readiness for the star. As I walked away I pondered a good many questions, notably, did she love me? Did I love her? I think in

both cases I answered " No." She had melted to me, as
she had done a score of times before. And I? I could
not tell, for one may love and despise; but I knew that
I could not drive her image from me, her fierce, aggressive
beauty, and the fumous intoxication of her. Soon, too,
I was to know myself a little better. Maud did not at
once melt to me again; when, next day, we lunched at
the stately Great Eastern Hotel, she said that she didn't
know why she had kissed me, and that after she'd done it
I looked as if I were going to have a fit on the mat. Her
hard surface had formed once more.

She was still hard over a week later, on Sunday night,
when we dined at the Trocadero, anxious only to point out
the well-known of her world, to catch and return smiles and
nods, to talk loudly to me so as to show that she had a
man. And hard again, when she took me with her to the
Fleur de Lis Club in a small street off Shaftesbury Avenue,
into which we were passed by the Honourable John, who
was there with Serena, slowly drinking himself into stupe-
faction. We formed a little party, to which were added
Sterry, a great success in the red nose and broken umbrella
line, and Rhoda Delamare, the immensely long, fair and
languid girl who stood against the target into which
Signor Viccini pitched his unerring knives. The Fleur
de Lis was almost exclusively a drinking club, though per-
functory dancing and singing sometimes took place on the
little stage; as but few members were allowed to pass into
the room marked " Private " I suspect there was also a
little gambling, faro or chemin de fer, but as the place
has not, so far, been raided I cannot be sure. Mostly
people sat in large parties of ten and twelve; newcomers
were at once absorbed, or discovered without difficulty that
another solitary man or woman was an old friend.

As we sat down at Helbert's table we became isolated,
for Sterry had nothing to say to us; leaning against
Rhoda's thin, white shoulder he spoke to her in the low,

throaty tones that were worth a hundred a week. Serena had few words for us. She smiled and said:

"Gee, you're some style in that gown, Mordedee; I wouldn't be seen with her 'cept in a tuxedo, Mr. CaDOR'ess."

The Honourable John gave me a fishy look, and weakly ordered the waiter to give me a whisky and soda and to bring him another.

"Listen right here, Jack," said Serena, seizing his arm, "this show don't go on. You've had four now, and I'm not stayin' here for you to get a bun on. See? That's all there is to it."

"Waiter, another whisky and soda," said the Honourable John, ponderously. "I'm all right, Serrie."

"I've a hunch you ain't," said Serena. "Waiter, you're the cutest thing, you'll bring the gentleman ginger ale."

And, strangely enough, the Honourable John accepted the ginger ale, and disconsolately sipped it in spite of the party's delighted chaff. Serena held him, played with him; I think he liked to be bullied by her, to find himself first encouraged to stroke her thin, dark arm while he told her a story she voted "cunnin'," and then suddenly to be repulsed, fiercely told to "put a lid on" and assured he was wrong if he thought he was the goods.

Meanwhile Maud picked out for me the celebrities of the Fleur de Lis: Walstein, owner of Walstein's Royal Halls, and Puresco, the Roumanian conductor, whose friendship with a middle-aged duchess was by now too stale to be worth discussing in detail. "That's Hopp," she said, pointing to a monstrously fat man, who sat between two shrimps out of some ballet, "and there's Sara Mallik; she used to do a Sheeny turn with Sam Davis, down Mile End way. Now she's rolling. That's her man there, just come in, Bobby Mornington, Lord Mornington's son. D'you know what he said the first time he saw Sara? He looked her in the eye for about a minute and said:

> " ' My name is Bobby Mornington,
>   So, Sara, hurry up,
> For when I grow Lord Mornington,
>   Your little game is up.'

Not bad, eh? She was on him . . . like a bird."

All the evening, and it was nearly two before we thought of leaving, Maud gave me the biographies of the members, the history of their alliances and appearances in the divorce court, also an inventory of the women's jewels. I had, mixed with disgust, an extraordinary sense of ease as I surveyed these people, English and foreign, equal, careless, more or less disreputable; this queer cosmos inside the cosmos, where the peerage and the wealth of management drank, jostled and grossly flirted with the chorus and the aged but skittish stars. One had to shout to be heard, for forty people were all talking together; ah, what an easy world, for the quality of the speech didn't matter; if one shouted one was heard. And we could do what we liked. Sterry had drawn upon his knees the careless Rhoda Delamare, and was telling her in a loud voice a story he could not have told on the stage. Helbert, who had outwitted his keeper and was intoxicated, was laughing the feeble, childish laughter of the sot as Serena, cool and hard, but pleased because he had promised her a ruby ring, described for his private information a new "vordevil turn" with which she was next day going to Bedford Street. Maud, too, had ceded to the ambient looseness, lay back in the crook of my arm and let me kiss her soft neck, merely remarking at intervals: "Stop yer ticklin', Jock." But as I held her I was pleading with her; softened by the ease of the atmosphere, all my English chivalries and purities had slipped away from me. I was like Maud, I didn't care.

"Maud, my darling," I murmured. I tried to tell her that I wanted her, that I had always loved her and still loved her.

"Tell me another," she said, lazily. But still she let

me caress her, carried away by the power of the place, half aphrodisiac, half drunken. Round us the scene was orgiastic. Helbert, giggling and hiccuping, was trying to force champagne on Serena, who played on him the trick of seizing Rhoda round the neck and guiding the drunken man's hand toward the other girl's mouth. Rhoda swallowed the champagne as if she were too lazy to resist, while Helbert glared at the girls and remarked at intervals: " Funny thing, Serrie . . . you got two heads . . . ver' funny . . . mus' have had too much." Sterry laughed so uproariously over this joke that his face had become purple. I, too, had had too much to drink for my weak Southern stomach, and it was in a mist I saw Hopp with the two ballet-shrimps on his knees, and an enormous crowd, thousands of people, men in tweeds and evening clothes, and women in red, green, purple low-cut gowns . . . and smoke, torrents of tobacco smoke.

I gripped Maud by the wrist. " Let's go," I said, thickly.

She obeyed, carelessly, as if her brain were soddened with alcohol and tobacco. In the cab, against the windows of which the rain spattered and flowed in silvery sheets, I clasped her to me, desperately, hungrily, and she did not reply to my rhapsodies, to the heady, broken phrases that came to me; but she did not resist me, and at times laughed. I remembered the high ring of her laughter, the " Who cares? " of her . . . and the beating of the rain on my face as I stood on the doorstep at Harewood Avenue . . . the black void of the hall . . . and then, in a dream, the harsh seduction of the voice as she said:

" Come in, then, you silly kid."

IV

Riot! Nobody cared. Not Serena, the immaculate, the juggler, the mysterious one who could touch pitch and not be defiled; nor Helbert, vapid when he was not drunk; nor those others, the Sterrys, the Hopps, the Rhodas, accomplices and partisans of mine; nor Maud; nor I. Serena stood as the perpetual goddess of "Who Cares?" or, as she put it, of "Don't give a damn." Fierce and pure, she had the art of giving nothing for everything, of tempting and exploiting the Helberts of her world, and preserving, in the midst of its foulness, the pride of her own purity. Serena could not fall, for her insolence held her up, served her as dignity; the strangeness of her beauty allowed her to draw behind her an unending trail of lolloping men-rabbits, for there were no weaknesses in her mind, no little windows through which a man might reach at her heart. Serena was on the make; trained to look upon man as a purveyor of candies, novels, ice-cream and flowers, she gave nothing because she had nothing to give. No man touched her because, in her sexlessness, she wanted no man to touch her; when she condescended to let Helbert take her hand, if he tried to kiss her she eluded him, thrust her hair straight at his face; to court Serena was like making love to a hedgehog.

So Serena watched unmoved the progress of our affairs, had no word of approval or condemnation when she found me with Maud at hours evidently ill-timed for formal calls. Serena had no views on morals; she tolerated everything that did not affect her evilly, nothing that did. In her view Maud was my bestest girl, and that's all there was to it.

In Maud I found a peculiar sweetness, wayward moods when she would suddenly seize my head with both hands, and feverishly caress me, and then repulse me, try to strike me, while the whole vocabulary of the streets flowed up to her lovely lips. And I loved my shame, shouted myself down when I asked: "Me that 'ave been wot I've been . . . what's going to become of you?" In Maud I found something that responded to my desperate mood, delirious moments when she actually loved me, and was

all a soft allure of inertia; splendid, drunken moments
when we sang, as we danced, the ditty of the day, when
a great, golden film hung over the world; and frightful
moments of reaction and savagery when we quarrelled and
found words that cut, when I shook her frail body as
a terrier shakes a rat, and mouthed at her insults lately
learned, when my fists clenched and my eyes became
blurred by a terrible, seductive picture of her face when
she screamed under my blows. . . .

And all through, for six long weeks, it was riot. My
day was naught but a somnolence, a round of duties carried
out with mechanical efficiency. The hours between Maud's
shows alone counted, when we walked the streets, or ate
and drank, made love and fought at street corners; and
the hours at night clubs, and those others when we were
half lovers, half enemies. She dragged me behind her in her
careless course, defiant, head in the air, into public-houses,
into the waiting-rooms of agents, on Sundays to Brighton
and its hotels, into the scented reek of the week-end trains
. . . I followed, drugged, narcotised, half-intoxicated, for
my head was stronger now, and I knew how to drink
without becoming drunk. . . . A pantomime was taken off
in the South of London, and there I was in the syren's
wake, at the supper on the stage, . . . lobster salad, I
remember, and cold fowl, and flat beer . . . the fat chairman, the personification of a grin, toasting " the lidies,
bless their little 'earts," and breaking down when the
career of Walstein's Royals was alluded to, weeping
drunkenly when cheers were given for 'ole Bill and 'ole
Jim. . . . Faces float up, like a " movie," as Serena said
when I told her what they looked like, a great nosegay
of faces, bloated male faces over the wrong collars, painted,
haggard women's heads with yellow hair in their eyes,
and pretty, round, baby faces with pouting lips. They
rise in the mist of alcohol, and there rises, too, the memory
of me, sodden and resentful, my soul still struggling with
me as I repeated again and again, " Me that 'ave been wot

I've been . . ." but I was too far from the past and the splendour of its ambition. Cast out by those others, the charm did not touch me.

V

For I hated myself in the degradation of which I was the more conscious as I plunged deeper. Ten weeks, and the slough up to my neck. March, green buds pricking their sharp points into the freshness of spring, but dull pains in my head and bones, spots before my eyes, liver blotches upon my cheek. The round of drink and dull orgy amid the coming of spring. Maud held to my lips no cup of elixir: the draught was either fiery or dulling, as suited her fancy, but never rich in hope or life. We lived for the day and by it. For a month she was out of a shop, as her next engagement, at a North London hall, did not coincide with the end of the current one, and during that month I seemed to saturate myself with the emanation of her gay, base and harsh personality. She found in me, the new me, exactly what she wanted, a shrill, cheerful despair; she liked me when I broke into the oaths she had taught me, admired me when I found tales to tell that made even Sterry uneasy, loved me when, of nights, at the Fleur de Lis, with my dank, black hair plastered over my wild eyes, I could sneer at the holinesses.

" Cheer up, we'll soon be dead."

So said all of us. And I didn't care who knew. Sunken in my passion, I wanted everybody to know I was enthralled; I boasted of Maud at Barbezan's, showed her photograph to the clerks, so that they might reprove me and envy me and despise me, and yet be subtly drawn to ask me questions. I made her come to the City to lunch, bringing Serena, who always went where somebody else paid. And one night, as we came out of the theatre, where I had taken Maud on pay-day, in the crowd under the veranda I laughed because there rested upon me the eyes of a theatre-party, Colonel and Mrs. Raleigh, Mrs. Lawton and Muriel. They would tell Edith. Well, let them tell in their superiority. I openly took Maud's arm and drew her against me; I smiled, I strutted, and though an incomprehensible pain shot through me as I thought of Edith, I bent down with my face close to Maud's heavy curls.

Let them tell it in the houses of superior England, for I had found England out. I knew those English; they were not a nation, but a caste, and I no longer wanted to enter it: Brahmins of the West who would not have me save as a pariah, I'd not try to be aught to you. English who despise Europe, whom mistaken Europe envies, I'd have the luxury of despising you. I knew what your virtues were: English virtues were not virtues but voids; instead of fine, ruddy vices the English had nothing. Their tolerance was indifference; their fairness was convention; their calm was coldness, their aloofness, stupidity. I drew Maud closer, crushing her to me.

" You French devil," she said. But now I minded no adjectives. The acidity of our love-making served me well enough, even when Maud refused herself to sweetnesses for which my buried self sometimes clamoured. She was hard. If I wanted to take her home after dinner, to sit with her for long hours, and to hold her hand, unconsciously to seek quietude, she did not: she wanted to go to a music-hall. Always Maud had to be active, to laugh, weep, clap or hiss, to see plays and turns, to drink, to smoke and to talk. In April I took her up the river, but she tired of Shepperton in an hour.

" One-eyed sort of place," she said, " let's go to Skindles."

And it had to be Skindles, Maidenhead, Boulter's, the sunny, crowded lock and the transferred blare of the town. Maud could not dine save among a hundred others, take her pleasure save with others, talk except against a restaurant band; hostile to the community, she needed it, was held by it, as if her envies and her hatreds linked her with her fellows more closely than would have her loves.

I was like her, wanted so to be, for now I carried my insolence, and now the inevitable crisis was coming. I had become a hero at Barbezan's, a person to whom juniors came timidly to tell tales, before whom they stood as might village beaux before Don Juan. Not a word had been said by Hugh or Mr. Lawton, for no fault had been found with me . . . or I had been tacitly excused because of the things that had happened. They were not going to be unfair to me, I think, and for that reason were ready to be unfairly lenient. They knew in what atmosphere I lived, for I cannot believe that Farr, my enemy, and the others, my envious friends, omitted to enlighten them. But nothing was said, and I hated them the more for their tolerance. " Damn your tolerance," I thought, much in the spirit of the proud beggar who says: " Curse your charity." Their tolerance jangled my nerves.

One morning I went into Hugh's room. He looked up at me, faintly smiling, and for one second I was stirred by the sight of him, young, beautiful and so emphatically clean. I suddenly felt an impulse to pour out my flood of pain and desire before this creature, so splendid and akin in its motionlessness to a statue of Apollo. But, as suddenly, I hardened, and rage filled my soul, for I was swift to take offence now, and I had found insult, subtle, biting insult: Hugh had sniffed.

" What are you sniffing at? " I asked, angrily.

Hugh looked at me with a very little surprise in his quiet eyes.

" I suppose you smell scent," I said. " Well, you do . . . and you know where it comes from. It's not I who use scent, it's the company I keep . . . it's Maudie D., Maudie Devon. You know how I stand with her, don't you? "

"It's no business of mine——" Hugh began.

"No business of yours!" I shouted. "Ah, here it is again, your damned tolerance, your damned liberalism . . . you don't care, you don't condescend to care, like the rest of the English. A man may go to the dogs, I suppose, if the dogs don't live in your kennel. You're not going to interfere, to help a man——"

"Anything I can do——" said Hugh.

"I'm not asking you to do anything," I snarled, though I knew that I ached for somebody who would do something; "I won't have your condescending help. You couldn't give it if you wanted to, for England's heart is in cold storage. You've got no hearts, no feelings, no enthusiasm: where the French keep their passions, you keep a slide-rule. I don't want help, I don't want sympathy. I just want you to respect my personality, I want to be recognised as a man."

"I'm sure I recognise all that," said Hugh.

"You don't. In France we value a man for being a fine man; in England you value him for being an Englishman. Oh, I know what that sniff means. You smell scent, you suggest I use scent, that I'm effeminate, disreputable —foreign. Why don't you tell me that I'm on a level with the barber, the waiter, the musician in the band? with the rest of the dirty foreigners as you call them, when you don't use a stronger adjective. Why can't you be frank about it? why can't you massacre the giaour, like the Turk? or torture him as the Chinese do the foreign devils? Tolerant Englishmen, you're only barbarians, xenophobes——"

"You do use long words," said Hugh, lazily, as he inspected his finger-nails. "What do you mean by xeno . . . what's its name?"

Then I lost my temper. The original little insult of the sniff receded, and it was indicative of my state of mind that such a trifle should raise such a storm—unless it be always the trifles that matter. I told Hugh what

I thought of him, his fashion-plate clothes, his superior Pall Mall club, his futile, brain-wasting golf, his liking for musical comedy, his sham Liberalism, his stupid satisfaction with the material world, his suspicion of art and letters, his dull, smug public-school standard. As I ranted, I hated him, and I hated myself because a devil in me made me shout and gesticulate, because I was a Frenchman, because like Kipling's big beasts, he wasn't going to notice the monkey. And I ranted on when Mr. Lawton came in from the next room to see what was the matter. I turned on him, charged him with being as his son, with having conspired with England to make his son like him, like his father, like his father's friends, so that all of them, caste, class and nation, they might sneer at different men.

" I hate your society of convention and artifice, I hate the boat-race, the meet of the Four-in-Hand Club, the Cup-Tie Final, the Academy. I hate your bourgeois dinners, your salmon, your saddle of mutton and your port. I hate your big police and your stupid life-guardsmen—we'd have made short work of them, my regiment. I hate your paid soldiers and your slavish worship of aristocrats and monarchs. I hate your sham fair play, which is only a habit. I hate everything that's English, and I'm going to leave it; I'm sick of it, sick of you, sick of your stupid, romantic women and your dumb, bloodless men; I'm sick of you all, sick of all you think and like, and I'm going back to France, going now, going at once——"

They looked at me with calm, faintly surprised faces.

" Can't you speak? " I shouted; " can't you defend your country and yourselves? No," I said bitterly, " I suppose you don't condescend to say what you think, or perhaps, you can't because you've never learned to. Well, I'm going now."

I turned as I opened the door and said:

" I give you no notice; you can keep my month's salary.

You can have the money: nation of shopkeepers, you understand that."

Then I slammed the door.

VI

Half-an-hour later I was at Harewood Avenue. Maud was still in bed. She was awake, though, and reading a halfpenny picture paper; on the little table by her bedside stood the remains of her breakfast, the skin of a kipper of which the whole room reeked. But her brown hair, tumbled upon the pillow, proved that it curled naturally, and her skin, devoid of rouge or powder, glowed white and warm pink, like the most delicate peony. I flung myself down on my knees, snatched one of her hands.

"Hullo! what's this blown in?" she asked.

"Maud, my darling," I said, fervently, "I'm going to take you away with me."

"Oh, my godfather! You're going to take me away, I don't think."

"I am, I'm going to marry you."

"Well! things *were* cheap! But tell us some more; let's hear all about this rush o' brains at eleven in the morning. Has your long-lost uncle come back from America, or what?"

"Maud," I said, solemn now, "you don't understand. I've had enough of this country, I've had enough of those people. I want to go back to France, where there is sunshine and flowers and wine. I want to go back because the people there say what they think, and mean what they say, where it's all simple and easy because people don't judge you by what you pretend to be, but by what you are. I want to go back, and I want you to marry me and come with me, because you're the only woman in England who has understood me, who has been kind to me. I want you because I love you—and you, my little

Maud, you love me, you do love me? Don't you, darling? It's been the real thing, hasn't it, all these months?"

Maud looked at me with distended eyes which showed that she did not in the least understand me. Her hand struggled in mine, for I was crushing her rings into her fingers. "Ouch, yer hurtin'," she said, and continued to stare at me. While I went on to explain that I had left Barbezan, that I was going home, that I would take her to Bordeaux, or rather to Paris, and make a good life for her there, I knew that I was struggling for her sake, too, trying to overcome some meanness in her, because she was the least mean of those English. I was clinging to her, pitifully, because she had loved me in her fashion, and because I could not face the idea of going back lonely to a place where I would be alone, I filled my greedy eyes with her beauty, tried to believe that I loved her, and that she loved me, for it was necessary we should love; if I had to go alone I thought I would commit suicide.

"Well, I never!" she said again. Then, mechanically: "Do it again, Ikey, I saw di'monds!"

I restated my case, and Maud took it in. She freed her hand, sat up, ravelled her curls and looked at me with an air of pity.

"You are a cough-drop," she said. "Why, you must be barmy, chucking up a good job like that, and I'm blowed if I know why. Oh, yes, you needn't go over it again, you've been chewing the rag long enough. I take it you're going home on spec., that you haven't got a job over there? No, of course not—and you come along and ask me to marry you when you may be on your uppers next month! Well, 'ere's me love to you, and it ain't a business proposition, as old Serrie says."

"Do you mean that you won't marry me?" I asked, incredulously.

"Oh, sit on a tack," said Maud.

"But I love you," I said, with pathetic obstinacy.

" Everybody loves me . . . nearly," sang Maud. Then, seriously: " Look here, you old tea-caddy. You've backed a wrong 'un if you think I'm going to throw in my little all with you, and walk out with you ' 'and-in-'and into the crool 'ard world.' I didn't ask you to marry me when I took up with you? No fear, I knew what I was up to; s'pose I was gone on you, and then you were ready to give me a good time, but marry you—'tain't so likely. I'm not going to marry anybody. Oh, yes, I know, you say you're going to get on, and all that, but that's Your version of the part. Take it from me: I shan't marry you, and if you don't like that you can hop it."

I did not take up the challenge flung down by her cynical brutality; I knew now what I had only suspected, that Maud had never loved me, that she had slid into my arms as she would have into those of any man who could give her a good time. She was not as sexless as Serena, but so undiscriminating, so light as not to care what man she favoured. Lightness! oh, yes, I had met it before. A man can choose among English girls: heavy as lead or light as air. But I was too broken to fight; all I wanted was to crawl into the sheltering arms that had not always been unkind. So I took up, faltering, the tale of my love.

" Oh," cried Maud, at last, " you give me the fair sick." She glared at me, and suddenly the flood of truth rushed from her lips. I understood that she had played with me for her own pleasure, exploited me and flattered me to keep me in a good temper, that she had never loved me, looked upon me as aught save a diversion, that she didn't want me, indeed, that she wanted to be rid of me, that she was glad I was going, and the sooner the better.

" Serrie, Serrie," she screamed, " come in and have a look at this nutty prawn. Serrie, Serrie!"

Serena came in from the next room, severe and beautiful in black. In a few sentences, broken by spasms of laughter, Maud explained the position.

"It ain't a business proposition, Mr. CaDORess," said Serena.

"What did I say!" cried Maud, triumphantly; "marvelooze!"

"Say, honey," Serena remarked to me, "you're a four-flusher, ain't you? You've got no money an' you've got no job, an' you want to marry Mordedee. That's getting down to brass tacks, ain't it? Wal, I figure out she can please herself, but if she says she won't that ain't enough to start you walking."

"What d'you take me for?" asked Maud, angrily. "Think I'm going to be your skivvy? or d'you want me to keep you? I'm not so stuck on your face as all that——"

Each in turn the girls shot their arrows at me. First it was Serena, languid and polite, conveying to me in that most concentrated form, American sarcasm, that, equally with Maud, she had no more use for me now that I was not likely to be able to give any girl a good time. Then it was Maud, more direct, spatterdashing her speech with disjointed music-hall Cockneyisms, invigorating it with adjectives. While Serena leant against the wall in an attitude which suggested that she would have put her hands in her pockets if she had had any, Maud leant forward, resting on her beautiful bare arms, her brown curls tumbled about her face, her shapely lips spitting insult at me. The American flicked me with a whip, the English girl used a bludgeon. In collaboration they painted the picture postcard versions of love and marriage. A man drinking too much beer, a wife sitting with a poker in front of a clock set at three A.M., twins howling in the night, a flirtation with the lodger: marriage. A dandy girl (according to Serena, a "Fluffy Ruffles") sitting at a little table before a bottle of champagne, a man "detained by pressing business," with a typist on his knees, six feet of femininity, firelit, "thinking of you," and a couple falling into acquaintanceship on the rink: love . . .

" No, I'm not taking any," Maud panted, " not if they make you a bloomin' Duke. So "—she broke off and sang: —" so, good-bye, Dolly, I must leave you——"

" Say, honey," Serena began again, sweetly, " you've got to take your medicine. I'm just crazed about you myself, but it's dollars to doughnuts we couldn't get fixed without you had the ooftish, as me friend Mordedee says. You better slope, for there's nothin' doin' here——"

" That's right, Serrie," Maud shouted. Then to me: " Get out. Hook it. I'm fed up with you, fed up with your beastly French ways and your high and mighty French talk. Hook it, I say, hook it, or——"

A red flood rose to her cheeks. Her trembling hand fumbled at the plate, seized the knife. For two or three seconds we looked at each other tensely. But she did not throw the knife. I turned, very weak and too numb to suffer. I left the room and walked downstairs. For some time I stood in the street, hatless, abstracted, and a butt for little Cockney boys. Now I was quite alone.

VII

For the next seven days, when I stayed in my sitting-room, among those pretty chintzes that Edith had chosen, I did not, could not suffer. I was driven out into the streets: I went to them seeking variety, society, that is the sight of my fellows, as I could not have their friendship. I was alone. I ate with extreme regularity at a restaurant in Soho where I could talk French to the waiters, bought French papers at the Monico, French cigarettes in Coventry Street. I did all this without violence; by natural reaction I was slipping back to France; with a new coldness, which was only French cynicism, I even allowed myself to be drawn into an ugly, unemotional adventure because the unseductive, seducing voice addressed me in French.

But these pale flickers of France did not warm me. I was uneasy, rather than suffering, and knew that my discomfort came from my loneliness. When again I began to wander the streets at night, seeking companionship, or to sit long hours in the parks, watching the children at play, and the business of the waterfowl, I knew that loneliness it was I carried upon my shoulders. Adventure did not call me: it had lost its thrill; I thought of drink, but I had drunk so much during the past three months that my stomach turned from the idea. One night I thought of drugs, but the chemists refused me laudanum, cocaine and veronal: I was not clever enough to go to a doctor and complain of insomnia, and thought myself inspired when I decided to have an orgy on tobacco, to smoke a hundred cigarettes before I went to sleep.

I did not do that, but my loneliness appears to me to-day when I remember what I did: with a crafty smile I decided to buy my cigarettes at ten different shops in packets of ten, so that I might talk with ten men.

But the end of that period is marked by something else, by an uncanny clarity of mind. Now that I was idle, had hours in which to think, and no woman to occupy my mind, I saw the English even more distinctly than I had done in my earlier fury. I saw them dispassionately, which does not mean I did not hate them, but I hated them calmly, as a judge may hate an atrocious criminal whom it is his duty to hang in proper legal form. The deathly London Sunday lay heavy on me now, for no houses were open to me, and the streets, wet or sunny, repelled me because they led me nowhere. I found the Sabbath out, dissected it into its simple components: conventional worship, Church Parade, roast beef, sleep, a large tea, nothing, cold supper, nothing, then sleep. For the impious, a little bridge. No billiards anywhere. Public houses open long enough for the nation to get drunk. Also sacred concerts and more love-making than usual.

Drink hung heavy over England. I saw that the rich drink to kill time, the poor to kill care.

I thought of politics, and suddenly remembered Gobot. Heavens! how many years ago that was! when I thought the English so fine. I could see Gobot's fat, red face, hear his loud voice as he shouted: "Who stole Canada? the English. Did the English help Poland? Did the English help the Balkan Christians, or did they give them to the Turk? Did not the English fight China to maintain the opium traffic? Hypocrites, liars, Bible-mongers——" Good old Gobot, you were not a fool.

I thought of the splendid figure of John Bull, of whom I had been so fond at Hambury. He appeared in a different guise: John Bull became a dull, offensive brute; I disliked the aggressive bridge of his high nose, the coarse paunch under his red waistcoat, his hairy hands, his top-boots, and his general air of lumbering health. I felt that no idea would ever get into that thick skull, though there was certainly room enough inside. The caution of the fellow was, I now knew, mere lack of imagination; John Bull was always letting the pot simmer—until the fire went out. I hated the grandiloquent way in which he addressed his colonies, the ostentation with which he treated them to an army and navy. Imperialism, for-sooth! Rather Imperial outdoor relief. I think I hated him deeply because I had loved him so much. Else I could not have felt the ghoulish joy I found in the Dutch song Querido quotes in *Toil of Men*, the song where the peasants stigmatise the English concentration camps of South Africa:

> "Women and children, see them lie,
> To the murder camps sent to die.
> Oh, my God, what a bitter shame!
> Come, let us spit upon England's name!"

My personal rancour vanished, and this song rang in my ears, expelling the terrible little bit of doggerel which had told me what I was. No longer was it "A Froggy Would a-Wooing Go"—held me, screamed out of the wind or rumbled out of the railway tracks, but this new song, this four-line summary of English beef-beer-and-blood-fed savagery. I knew what lay under the coldness and the polish; it was sheer, sullen brutality, unredeemed even by the subtlety of cruel China, the glorious, sunny ferocity of Spain.

Big counts, little counts, all added to the indictment of this country where parks had to be closed at sunset to arrest the grossness of the people, where no man might drink in the open air because the skies were of water and soot, where no flowers grew, where no fruit matured, as though the hateful coldness of the islands were such that even trees and shrubs acquired nationality. English daffodils, and English lilac, you bloomed in vain that April, for I knew the first to be Dutch, the second to be French. And English women, you flaunted in vain in the fresh, salt wind, the cream and roses of your cheeks; I saw your cheeks no more, your red, smiling lips that had smiled upon me with such tolerance; I saw only your unloveliness, your cheap beads, your machine-made lace, your soiled white gloves, your ill-cut stays, and the tragic draggling over your boots of the torn, muddy edges of your petticoats.

I was going home. In vain Stanley had come to me with a startling piece of news. I had seen very little of him during the last five months of misery and orgy; instinctively I had shrunk from his inquisitive eyes, knowing that he would soon discover my secrets, drag into his mental limelight the story of my love and its wilting, force me to see as it was my following shame. I had not been back to the little house to hear the round wife call him affectionate, abusive names. Now and then we had played chess, and I had resisted scrutiny by feigning a new absorption in the game; I must have deceived him, on the whole, for I did attain such absorption as to beat him now and then by moves which he did not think me capable of, but I discovered suddenly that I had not deceived him throughout. He arrived at Cambridge Street early one Sunday morning, when I still lay in bed. I would have refused to see him if the landlady had not shown him straight into the sitting-room. He came in and sat down near my bed.

" In bed at eleven? " he said, cheerfully. " Had another thick night? "

" I don't have thick nights," I said, emphasising my actual sulkiness.

" Oh, you've reformed then? I thought you would."

I threw him an interrogative look, and, as I met the unflinching, grey eyes, knew that he knew, wondered whether he knew every detail. I pressed my cheek into the pillow and let out a faint sound.

" Cheer up," said Stanley, gravely. " Cheer up. It's never too late to mend, old chap. I know all about it. Oh, yes, more than you think."

" I don't care," I said. " I'm going back to France."

" Are you? Well—— Anyhow—listen to me first. I'm not going to talk about your affairs—it's none of my——"

" Don't say it, don't say it," I screamed, as I started up; not his business—no Englishman's business—their phrase—I couldn't bear it. Then a heavy blanket of indifference smothered me. " Go on," I said.

" I won't say it," Stanley went on, as he mistook my meaning. " Let's bury it. You had a hard time and you went on the bust. No one can blame you, but it's all over, and you want to begin again. Don't shake your head: you do. If you didn't you'd have drowned yourself."

" I pretty nearly did."

" But you just didn't. That old fool Schopenhauer would tell you that you didn't because you still saw something in life; still, never mind Schopenhauer. What I want to say's just this: I'm leaving the C. and P. end June, because I want to set up for myself; I'm thinking of doing some shipbroking and chartering, same as Bar-

bezan. I've saved a bit of money these ten years, enough
to start the thing properly and run it for a year or so,
and I've got a few pals who'll enable me to pay expenses
if they give me all the work they promise. Now will you
come in as my partner? You'll get a good share, bar the
capital interest, of course."

I looked at him curiously, wondering why the opportunity did not thrill me, but it did not.

" I'm going back to France," I said.

Stanley stuck to his point, said frankly that he thought
I had push and that the sort of bounce I had tried on
him would often come off. He gave a still better reason
for wanting my help—namely, that the word Cadoresse
still counted in the Port, and that he had an idea it might
count in Bordeaux too; I was to have all the French business, and wasn't that as good as going home?

" I'm going back to France," I said. I made no effort
to tell him I was broken and spiritless, that I wanted
only to shake free from England. I was too broken to
explain. In vain did he re-state his scheme, break through
his English reserve and try to make me see that my
wounds might be healed, assure me again that it was not
too late to mend.

" It's too late," I said. " I'm going back to France."

" Well," he said at last, after an hour had elapsed, " I
shan't start for two months, and I shan't ask anybody
else. If you think better of it . . ."

I shook my head.

VIII

The English Channel—oh, no, not that, but " La
Manche." The Dieppe cliffs and, behold, a lesser green-
ness above them than in the land of everlasting rains;
the billowy fields of Normandy that dried into still paler
green as we entered the Ile de France. Ah, it was good,
Paris, the clatter of the carts and cabs on the cobbles, the

queer "oaty" smell, but it was better the next day when
the *rapide* hurled itself towards the South. For here were
Orléans and Tours, and now Poitiers—here were soldiers
wearing my old uniform, and there went a postman in a
linen *blouse*—of course, it was hot; this was not the weak
English May, it was French May, like an English July.
Faster, faster towards the South, Angoulême and the
cathedral on the hill, and Coutras, red and white, sun-
glowing Coutras—and suddenly the blue, burnished blaze
of the Gironde waters—Bordeaux, my town, the good
sweat on my North-paled brow, the good, heavy sun.

IX

I had a fortnight of happiness. Frigidly received by
my mother, who considered that I had disgraced her as
well as myself by leaving "the house," after proposing
without her consent to a girl who had no dowry, I found
that I was English enough not to mind very much whether
she disapproved of my behaviour. Besides, we settled our
relations on the morning which followed my arrival. We
stood in the drawing-room, which had changed in no
particular in five years, I against the black mantelpiece,
my mother near the Empire couch, her hand upon a garnet
cushion, and as she spoke her mild-severe speech I saw
that she had not changed either, that no streaks of grey
appeared in her tight black hair; I guessed that in five
years her point of view had not altered, that it never
would alter. She spoke of her disappointment, blamed me
for not asking her leave before I left London, informed
me that I had wrecked my life, inquired by what right
I did what I chose. I think I would have answered in
the hot, disrespectful English way, but I caught myself
analysing my mother, wondering whether, in the chest of
drawers, there still were the little high-heeled shoes, once
too large for me, near the black silk dress of the great

days. What was the use of quarrelling with the living past? It was about me, the full breadth of it—for did not the room still exhale the strange, familiar smell of decay? The smell sickened me now; I went to the window, threw it open and was rebuked. But my mother became more precise, wanted to know my intentions.

"At present, none," I replied, curtly. "Later on I will look for a position here. I shall not cost you anything; I will pay you a hundred and fifty francs a month——"

"I did not ask for money," said my mother, crossing her small hands on her black frock.

"I have some. I have saved about two thousand francs."

My mother did not reply for some time, but she was impressed, for eighty pounds is a large sum in the South, and she liked my having been thrifty. What would she have said if I had told her how much more it might have been if Maud and I had not sometimes spent ten pounds in a day and night?

"Very well," said my mother, "since you can afford it . . ." She was plainly relieved to see that the prodigal son had brought home a calf. Then she requested me to be secretive as to my affairs, which should be described as healthy, so that I might not injure Jeanne.

"We have had difficulties, great difficulties," she said. "Mademoiselle is not easy to please, and she has only fifty thousand francs. It is not as if she were very pretty, and she has ideas—*excentriques*."

I pitied my little sister: it is hard in France when you are *excentrique*.

"She has had some good opportunities, and she has not taken them. There was Monsieur Vachol, the engineer; of course he had an old *affaire,* but that could have been *arrangé*. And Monsieur Corzieux, you remember his son at school——"

"Old Corzieux must be fifty," I remarked.

" *Oui, oui*—still, he was very fond of her." My mother sighed. "She is twenty-three. We must see, we must really see . . ."

Something displeased me in the interview: the drawing-room in which was no comfortable seat, the formality of it all. But outside was pure joy; I could look out of the dining-room window and see the street that led to the Quinconces, the sun gleaming on the white tables of the *café* at the corner. And I liked to hear Jeanne, in the drawing-room, practising Chopin, Mozart, occasionally breaking out into Lalo or Fauré. Jeanne gave me nothing; we had never had much in common and, as soon as she found that I would not tell her anything about "low life in London," of which she had made a mental picture from *Les Mystères de Londres,* she joined my mother against me. What her wild ideas were I never found out; I suppose the ideas of English girls were so unmaidenly that I had lost my sense of wildness. Jeanne went alone once a week to a course of French literature at the Faculté. It may have been that; I had to drag myself back to the view that young girls should not go all on their lonesome, as Maud would have said.

No, the joy of that first fortnight was outside the house. There was the sun ever and fiercely glowing; the black shadows with the purplish penumbra lay across the white blaze of the paths when I went into the park to see the magnolia. It was just blooming, and its flowers were small; not one was yet as large as the big, fleshy creature upon which I had pressed the kiss of a lover. "Wait," said the magnolia. "This is your city and your sky; wait and I will bloom, arouse your old, wild passion."

I found some of my old friends. Lavalette had gone to Paris, and was now a barrister, a great success in the *Highlif* of the town. Gobot I saw only two or three times, for he lived some twenty miles up the river, on his father's vine-clad hills; but Luzan, who worked in a bank, I met every day at half-past five. Together we sat under the awning of the Café de la Régence, in front of a vermouth, watched the local dandies pass and smile at the spruce, dark work-girls with the ugly faces and the splendid figures. My old friends did me good, for we soon passed out of the " Do you remember? " conversation into a review of more actual things; I told them my story, colouring it up a little, shedding over myself Wertherian glamour (when I spoke of Edith), Byronic gloom (when I told the way in which the English had treated me). And I made up as Don Juan when it came to Maud.

Gobot was kind; he was stouter and redder than ever; he was married, had one child, intended to have two, to drink a good deal of claret, to sell a good deal more, to become *maire* of his *commune*, grow older, yet stouter, jollier, and to save his soul in the nick of time. Gobot, you're nothing but Pantagruel; you jolly brute, I love you. But Luzan helped me more, for Gobot was not exactly the listener a broken-hearted young man wanted. When you are miserable you need to be made still more miserable; then you touch bottom, rebound and feel much better. That is where Luzan came in; he was now so cynical, so gay a sceptic, so devoid of illusion as to success, woman and salvation that it was good to tell him my story. He laughed, vowed that my imagination would play me the same old trick: that is, I would love again. He almost made me believe that Edith had never loved me. His talk seared me, cauterised me.

Edith . . . I thought of her when I was alone, when I looked favourably upon my bold, broad-hipped country-women. I swore I would love them, turned away from the frail ghost of the Dresden Shepherdess. I cursed the ghost and its gold hair, the gleam of which was in the sunshine.

I won, for the sun was in my bones. I loafed along the wharves, smoked immensely, played billiards in the evening with Luzan, read a number of light novels. I did not look for work. I was settling down.

X

As I have said, the first fortnight was happiness; then came a fortnight of disquiet. This was so vague that I only realised it at the very end, decided that I wanted occupation, began to seek it. I did not find a post at once, though I should have if I had not been nonchalant, as my qualifications were high; but salaries were lower than in England, and I disliked the idea of living on a reduced scale; besides, I had money enough to keep me for a year: there was no hurry. Yet the disquiet grew, and I felt offended; accustomed things grated upon me: I looked at them again, and found them normal; then they worried me again.

I began to look for work more feverishly and found at once a post as foreign correspondent in a very good firm, at the high salary of three hundred and fifty francs a month. Enough to marry on, I thought, bitterly. And why not? I added. I began to consider the idea much as one may consider absolutely painless suicide.

But I was not to commit suicide, nor was I even to occupy the post of foreign correspondent. I could elaborate the mental processes of those two months—but what for? It is a chronicle of the dead, or the tale of the slow setting of a broken limb. Rather will I say that I was bored, chafed, and put down the revolution to accident. The accident was simple. One afternoon as I came up the stairs, I crossed Monsieur and Madame Luzan, he in a frock-coat and silk hat, she in modish brown velvet. We smiled, exchanged comments on the weather, but I guessed by their clothes and Madame Luzan's smiles that they had been on a solemn errand. I suspected she would have kissed me if we had not been on the stairs.

I found my mother in her black silk frock, smiling and rather stately, Jeanne very demure and self-conscious. I was not surprised when informed that her hand had that

afternoon been granted to Luzan, more exactly that her
fifty thousand francs had come together with a salary
of twelve pounds a month, and a parental allowance of
forty pounds a year. The fortunes having dovetailed, it
had been decided that the young people should go through
the formality of marriage. I congratulated Jeanne, kissed
her and my mother, went to my room. The affair sickened
me; I liked Luzan, but he had undeceived me as to his
ideals; also I knew that he had an old affair; also that he
had never been alone with Jeanne. Love her? absurd.
Then I called myself a fool, an English fool. Then I
swung back and decided to have it out with Jeanne.

I found her calm, cynical even.

"I do not dislike him," she said. "What more do you
want?"

I mumbled something about love.

"Oh, well, that would be *charmant*. Still, one cannot
have everything."

I went on, found she did not think it disgusting that
she should be sold in marriage; all that she could see
was that Luzan was much nicer than Vachol and old
Corzieux. Marriage was a contract, and she was twenty-
three. I looked in vain for sweetness in her small, dark
face, her splendid black eyes; there might be passion
there, if those heavy eyebrows and the faint down on
the upper lip meant anything at all, but not love. Still
I pleaded.

"Oh, well," Jeanne suddenly spat out at me, "love
played you nice tricks."

For some seconds I could not speak. Once, when I tried
to learn to box, I was hit over the heart: it was like that.
Then a cold rage seized me.

"It did. It will play them on you. I suppose you
intend to marry without love—and to make up for lost
time after."

We looked at each other with clenched teeth, hating
each other. She was livid, and I suppose I was too.

XI

I saw the French as they were, now, for Jeanne had torn me out of my dreams; I saw them, hated them. With English eyes I saw the big, vulgar sun, the men's absurd, tight clothes, the mongrel dogs; I saw the painted, simpering, sensual, lying women; I found the French furniture uncomfortable, the French table appointments fit for a prison. I went now oppressed by the stuffiness, the closed windows in summer, by the sensation that these people did not take baths.

I went into the park. But near the magnolia tree were two young men in flashy clothes. They laughed and talked very loud. Then one of them ran, leapt a three-foot railing, alighted with an air of triumph; I saw him look at the nursemaid he was fascinating by his nimbleness, at me, to see whether I was admiring him.

Showing off! said my English mind.

And France did not pretend she was going to take me back.

Through the mouth of a cabman who stopped his horse in front of the little table where I moodily sipped absinthe and tried to drive out of my head the thought of whisky and soda, she shouted at me. "Hi, Angliche!" cried the cabman, and in broken English offered to drive me round the town. I smiled bitterly and said nothing, while this Frenchman drew conclusions from my clothes and my silence.

The cabman was not alone in his opinion. My mother quarrelled with me, because I had sniffed at Jeanne's conveyance, I mean marriage. It was a mean, provincial little brawl, when my mother flung at me in lieu of argument a strange mixture of French social theory and financial fact. Stung by my silence, she said at last:

"Well? Have you nothing to say? No, I suppose not; you do not talk much nowadays. I suppose you have become an Englishman." Quickly she added, as if she expected me to interrupt her: "One has only to look at you, at your broad boots, that ridiculous hat that falls over your ears, and to smell your clothes. *Pouah!*" she said, pointing at my tweed coat; "you smell like a fire when the wood is damp."

I did not reply; I pulled at my pipe and thought that I had never smoked anything so disgusting as this French tobacco. No, I reflected, I am not an Englishman, but what the devil am I among all these things that gall me?

Cobbles in the streets, how you made the old cabs rattle behind the wretched French horses! Trams, how you roared! And people too, how you roared, wrangled and boasted! I hated you, hated you—mean, avaricious, petty, boastful people; overfed, sensual, brutal people—hated your cynicism and your hedonism, hated you because you had no illusions and no ideals—I was rejected of the French. I rejected them.

Away, away—anywhere—or where the buds are fragile, the blossoms tremulous, the air blue.

Stanley wrote, asking me to come back. . . .

To England, yes, to England, anywhere, only to get away.

XII

I stood at the peak of the steamer. The cliffs of Dover slowly rose upon the skyline, swathed in grey mist. My face was wet with soft English rain.

PART IV

CHAPTER I

STANLEY, CADORESSE & CO.

I

I LEANT back in the office chair that swung under my weight, looked out across Gracechurch Street. January, rain spattering on the windows, rain, rain, and above the glistening roof opposite, a blade of yellow-white, water-soaked sky. Behind me the fire spat and crackled, and there was a little crunching rumble as the lumps of coal crushed down the burning wood. I was idle, looked at the brilliant cuffs that protruded from my well-pressed sleeves; I was pleased with myself, with the sleek back of my head when I stroked it. Still interested in my new possessions, I looked at my roll-top desk, its choked pigeon-holes, at the filing cabinet against the wall and its drawers marked " Forward Shipments," " Outward freight," " L.C. Private." It was " L.C. Private " delighted me; behind its label was my all-important personality. L.C., twenty-seven, junior partner in what I knew to be a rising firm.

But idling did not do, at least not yet. I drew myself up, rang the bell. It is a queer little scene. Miss Condon comes in, stands obedient by my desk, very quiet and ready to take down my money-making phrases. She is pretty, with her brown hair braided over her temples, with her eyes that puzzle me because I never know whether they are grey, blue, green or yellow. But *noblesse oblige* when you are a partner. I reprove Miss Condon; I tell her that I am not " Yours sincerely " to Mr. Bent and that it must not happen again. Also I will not have " traveller " spelled with one *l* until we open an American branch. Then, to comfort Miss Condon (who does not

really want comforting after years of this sort of thing)
I tell her jocularly that Shelley spells " traveller " with
two *l*'s; I say this because Miss Condon is addicted to the
poet and has been known to say that she wished she'd
been his secretary. But Miss Condon is not to be chaffed:
she moistens the point of the pencil and waits her employer's pleasure.

"Dear Sirs," I begin. "With regard to the delivery of
50 tons of copper ex-s.s. *Iquiqui,* we beg to say——"

The telephone rings. Somebody who calls me "Sir"
says that an all-powerful bank craves an audience. Let
the bank wait. Stanley comes in and listens while I dictate,
his sharp eyes on me, his knubbly fingers on the edge of
my desk. When I have dismissed Miss Condon with my
passionate protest against a deduction, he says negligently:

"I've got Smith Brothers. They're going to let us do
about eight hundred tons of printed calico for the West
Coast if we can get the rate down for them. It's a cut
rate . . . still . . ."

Eight hundred tons of cargo! I don't suppose we would
do much more than curse those small orders if eight
hundred tons came in to-day. But then . . . the rapture.
My insistent, introspective self asks me whether there is
a kiss in the world so good as eight hundred tons of printed
calico.

II

We were bloated, but it must not be thought that we
were the talk of the London docks. *The Syren* and *Fair-
play* made short, if flattering references to the reappear-
ance in the Port of the ancient name of Cadoresse; good
wishes from Hugh Lawton came to me in a roundabout
way and evoked no response. For I did not want good
wishes; I was going to "give them one." I felt I was
"giving them one" when our offices opened one sultry
July morning; it was already a victory to have a share in

an office, in the concentration Miss Condon stole from
Shelley and the vast inefficiency of Baring, our bookkeeper-
cum-invoice clerk and handy man.   All this state had
been provided out of Stanley's capital, a bare thousand
pounds, for I was only the junior partner, taking forty
per cent. of profits after capital had been remunerated
on a scale varying with those profits between five and
fifteen per cent.   The firm lived in three small rooms,
one for Stanley, one for me and one where Baring received
inquiries, kept the books, the tea-set and the copying-press,
and made out bills of lading while Miss Condon drew
from her typewriter sounds that made one think of a Maxim
in action.

But we were proud of our office, of our stationery, of
our heading: "Stanley, Cadoresse & Co."   I think we
rather overdid our heading, for we put it on followers,
on the books, on the inquiry office blotting pad; we even
had our stamps perforated with our august initials.   We
loved our office; we would have patted it if we could,
though it was our master as well as our love.   For those
early days were hard enough; business came swiftly, thanks
to those faithful friends who believed in Stanley and to
the few in the Port who wanted to deal with us because
the word "Cadoresse" reminded them of my father and
of the 'eighties, the 'seventies, when they were young.
I traded shamelessly on the reputation of the old sea-
captain, abased myself before my angry mother so far as
to ask her to give me the names of his old friends.   She
gave them, and a few who were still alive and very,
very aged, received me well.   One of them I remember best,
a merchant with a face that might have been carved out
of yellow wood, seamed with hundreds of criss-crossing
wrinkles, and a toothless mouth closed very tight.   Alone
in the dead face of the old man, who was, I think, nearly
ninety, the eyes lived, luminous and pale as water.

"So you're young Cadoresse," he said.   "Young
Cadoresse."   He said this seven or eight times.   "I knew

your father very well. Let me see, if he had lived, he would have been . . ."

He could not remember, and I tried to help him, but at once his mind wandered, and he began once more his aimless " So you're young Cadoresse . . . young Cadoresse . . ." He lived in the past; his stories were of my father as a shipmaster, and most of the stories were unrepeatable, for they showed what a " frightful rip " the old merchant had been; he had not noticed the Boer war, but he remembered very well consigning foodstuffs to Paris after the surrender to the Germans, and his Paris still had its Emperor, its Taglioni. The luminous old eyes saw far beyond me, into an England devoid of Board schools; further yet, beyond even 1832 and the Reform Bill agitation . . . they were still talking of Boney and Waterloo when he was a little boy.

But he gave me business. " I couldn't have refused your father," he said. " Heavens! how funny he was sailing his ship in a frock-coat and a top-hat—tea-caddy I used to call him . . ."

My eyes filled with tears. Oh, heredity, that you should have chosen such an instrument as Maud to brand me as my father's son! The old man introduced me to his grey-bearded " boys," who treated him a little rudely, as if they knew he did not matter in the office, where he solemnly sat behind a newspaper and gazed at the wall and answered the leading questions of the chief clerk. The questions were manufactured and affected nothing, but the old man answered them with immense, concentrated interest, in the midst of respectful silence. This time he decided we should be given a show, and we were, for his sons liked our methods.

This was not very wonderful, for my mind was French; that is to say, I was hard, logical, punctual and contemptuous of no detail; I was very sharp and ready to take advantage of anybody, to bluff and to lie over a deal; but once the terms were made and my word given my quondam antagonist could be sure that I would not fail him and that I would carry out my contract to the letter, even if I were bound only by word of mouth. I despised the kindly old merchant, the stupid English sentimentality that made him promise us a show because he had known my father, and I respected but little more the sons who allowed their suspicions to be overcome by his senile amiability. But that did not concern me; I took the order and, by aggressively flaunting before the African & Asiatic Steamship Company a non-existent cheap rate quoted by the London and Burmese, which I knew these careless Englishmen would not trouble to check, procured so cut a rate that we completely captured the firm's business.

Our rates went up after we had caught them, and I do not think Stanley quite liked my methods.

"You work like an American trust," he said. "Bluff, bounce, make a loss, cut it, capture the market—and when you've captured it, sweat it."

"Well? What's caught?"

"You even talk American," said Stanley, laughing. "We dropped nearly sixty pounds over that *Otranto* business."

"And we've got pretty well every ton of coal Morrisons 'll send to Oporto this year—there's hundreds in the brokerage alone, and we may make a bit if we chance chartering a ship ourselves."

"They will find you out," said Stanley. "One of these days they'll realise you're not cutting rates so fine as you used to."

"They won't," I said confidently. "Englishmen are careless of detail; if I were a merchant I'd put my business out to tender. But not they; they're English. Lazy brutes."

Stanley did not mind my abusing the English. "I'm not English," he sometimes said, "I'm a mathematician." His attitude was one of indifference to trifles that involved no philosophic generalisations; his rôle was to collect facts and sift them; he made himself a master of the movements of ships all over the world; he knew who sailed in ballast and bluffed that it was timber; he knew who quietly took in guns and ammunition for the coast of Tripoli and Somaliland; he knew what master drank and what merchant would place an order with a white man and kick a Bengali clerk down the steps of the veranda; who it was could not forget tiny Sariti and her little paper house at Yokohama, and he knew why there was a sound like broken glass and a strong smell of spirits when the *Emily Mary* had a funeral in Boston roads and reverently lowered the coffin while a guileless American gunboat dipped its pennant.

Stanley looked upon the shipping trade as an exercise in psychology, a game of chess where you played with men (and a little with women); by that queer, flashing process of deduction of which I had once been the victim he discovered exactly what a man keenly wanted, but hid behind a careless mask and a cigar, and he knew how to stroke vanities, to stab jealousies to the quick. It was I, though, generally went out into the offices, to bluff, to strut, to advance and kick the weak, to fawn before the strong. I loved it, I exulted in it. I did not want to know my man, as did Stanley; I liked to come at him as he seemed, to cheat him, to bully him—until it was all over and, my contract in my pocket, I shook hands with my antagonist and decided to treat him fairly.

" I go in for honour," I said to Stanley; " it pays."

It did, for our efficiency was terrific, and we flaunted it. I made a practice of never fixing appointments for " eleven " or " three "; no, I fixed " ten past eleven " or " twenty to three." And I was there exactly on time, for I always arrived a little too early, and waited outside until I had only thirty seconds to climb the stairs. We drilled Baring and Miss Condon to make out documents " while you wait "; we always, in presence of some mer-

chant, wanted some undefined (but agreed) paper, so that
Baring might find it on the card-index in fifteen seconds.
" Fifteen seconds," we would say, proudly, to the impressee.
But if our efficiency was terrific, so was our labour; every
letter and document was checked four times; we refused
to take information from the *Shipping Gazette,* but compared it with Lloyd's *Weekly Index.* We took nothing
on trust; if we had needed Greenwich time we would have
correlated it with Paris time and checked by measuring
the difference in minutes on the map. In seven months
we did not make a single mistake—but for the first three
we stayed at the office every night up to eleven o'clock,
except Sundays, when we were lazy and left at nine. Once
Miss Condon came, on a sweltering August night, to say
she felt faint: I threw her a sovereign and told her to
get back to her machine, " slick." England had a summer
that year, and all through it we worked, canvassing for
orders, interviewing hundreds of people, marketing risks
(for we cut a little into marine assurance), struggling for
obnoxious trade such as guano and explosives. And when
other men had closed their offices, when some of them
were in bed, there we sat, the four of us, Stanley and I
fed by the fury of our young ambition, Baring and Miss
Condon by gibes and doles; there we were, circularising,
applying insolently for contracts that would have filled
the P. & O. fleet, shouting (in English English) that we
were right there with the goods, planning, scheming.

It was wonderful, it was romantic, this fierce creation.
Our business was no wretched child which we would allow
to grow; no, we were going to bring it up in the forcing-
house, feed it on some Wellsian " Food of the Gods,"
made out of our brains and bodies. Stanley saw the
romance of it.

" Here we are," he said, " with our fingers at the throat
of the world, shaking it to make it pay up. All the
world . . ." He indicated the big Mercator map on the
wall. " Shanghai, we're sending creosoted sleepers there

on that old tub the *Urmiah* . . . and Cardiff; coal—coal
for the Port. It's we who're handling it, thousands of
tons of it—we'll handle millions of tons—cranes, baskets
—hear it, Cadoresse? Hear it rattle down the chutes,
millions of tons, to cook the Lord Mayor's dinner and
warm the slippers of Mr. Thirty-Bob-A-Week at Clapham.
And New York City—Bombay—the whole blasted antheap—Good Lord!" He breathed heavily, as if awed by
the globe enormously spinning within our walls.

But I did not see it like that. Enough romance, I
was too old for that silly game. I was out for money,
revenge. The English wouldn't have me? That was O.K.,
I'd not have a nationality at all, I'd be a cosmopolitan,
I'd drip with gold in every European Hotel Métropole,
I'd have three cars at my door, and cars for my servants
that the English peerage couldn't afford; and I would
travel—to the fiords on my yacht, to the East with my
caravan, my armed escort, my camels and my dancing girls;
and if I liked I'd be an Englishman as a pastime, buy
myself ten thousand English votes, the right to make
laws for Englishmen, a seat in the Cabinet if I had to
double the party funds. I'd be rich enough to buy John
Bull's shirt and turn him, naked, out of his island . . .
And here I was, in the principality which was going to be
an empire, well-clad and gloating over our trial balance-
sheet. The first six months showed a profit, capital ex-
penditure entirely written off. It was not every young
firm brought that off; but that was nothing: let England
wait.

III

And so we rushed onwards, urging our little business
to beat every week the record it had established seven
days before and succeeding, pound by pound, so determined
were we to win, so ready to ship anything between a
historic mansion for re-erection in New York State and

a halfpenny packet of pins. Between us Stanley and I
evoked a code of daring, a sort of samurai gospel which
bade us shrink from nothing. One morning we were rung
up by the Lea Ironworks; they were put through to
Stanley and said:

"Can you——"

"Yes," said Stanley, interrupting.

The audacious interruption went the round of the docks:
Stanley, Cadoresse & Co. did not need to know what it
was people wanted them to do, asked no questions as to
place or date, did not care whether there was yellow fever
in every port and a dock strike in the bargain. No, they
just said "Yes." And the joke served us well. I went
one morning into the office of Alston Brothers to charter
a starred A for a new client.

"I don't know you," said the manager. "And I don't
know your principal. Don't care for that sort of business."

Thomas Alston came into the office, a paper in his hand,
and at once the manager grew more truculent, so as to
show his chief what a sound man he was.

"Don't care for it," he growled. "People come along
every day with twopence and think they can do what
they like with our boats—mess up the hold with leaky
barrels of tar—get us into trouble with half-a-dozen
harbour-masters before they've done."

"Stanley, Cadoresse & Co. play the game," I said, quite
as truculently.

"Oh, is that who you are?" said Thomas Alston. He
looked at me rather kindly, winked a cunning grey eye.
"You're the people who always say 'Yes,' aren't you?
Give the babies a chance, Mr. Marston."

We chartered the ship and she made an excellent
voyage. Two months later Thomas Alston rang up "the
babies" to know whether they would like to look out for
freight for his new Tunisian line, in which case he might
break a rule and give them a monopoly.

"The babies" boastfully replied that they would charter

the ships themselves, and they filled them every one, for they went the round of the exporters' representatives protesting they already had the monopoly: as a result they got it. Once only did we come down on a rash speculation, for one of our hired vessels was held up somewhere in the West Indies, by an accident to the only crane that could lift our goods, for four days beyond the lay days. I remember Stanley's anxious face when he came in with the cable that told us we were already liable for two days' demurrage at sixpence a register ton. A hundred pounds!

"Gosh!" said Stanley. "Ten days'll all but break us." Then he impartially damned the authorities, the makers of the crane and the wretched niggers who had put it out of gear.

On the third day I sent an expensive cable telling the dock company we would sue them for damages, which was idiotic, as the company had an Act of God and accident clause that covered it; but the cable relieved me so much that, on the fourth day, I was almost cheerful when Stanley and I talked over our pipes of filing our petition and camping in Carey Street.

The crane was restored on the fourth day and we scraped through with a fine of two hundred pounds; the money was not wasted, for it taught us that a young firm must not speculate. I do not think we chartered a ship again for two years, except once or twice when we knew that somebody was in the market, slipped in and re-sold him the charter-party with a profit of a few pence per ton.

We recovered some of our self-esteem over the great rat case. We had shipped eight cases of Cheddar cheese, destined for India, where Englishmen insist on English fare when the temperature is 108. Two of the cases were so badly stowed that the lids worked loose; as a result rats entered the cases and, when the goods were landed at Bombay, it was found that every one of the hundred cheeses had been nibbled. I can see our client now, cable

in hand; he was a very fat, very red little German, whose
legs were so short and whose voice was so high that I had
to hold down my laughter by force; he was so exactly like
"the dying pig" in indiarubber that the hawkers were
selling outside for sixpence.

"Shpoiled!" he squeaked; "every plessed cheese
shpoiled. I make you reshponshible. I make de captain
reshponshible. I go to law. I prosecute."

We pointed out that the stevedore——

"Damn de shtevedore," he screamed, waving the cable.
"Dis is cheek you talk. You shpoil my cheese. You—
you take de biscuit."

The little German burst out of our office some seconds
later, jamming his silk hat on his square head, vowing
he would "prosecute." But we could not stop laughing;
the association of cheese and biscuits was too much for
us. Besides, we were not liable, being merely agents;
all we risked was the loss of a small client. Still, we had
for our credit's sake to see what could be done; the case
seemed unpleasant, as inquiry showed that the ship had
carried six cats. I had given up hope when Stanley came
into my room nearly five weeks later with an expression
on his ascetic face that made him look like a monk who
has caught a carp on Thursday evening.

"Talking about cats," he said, and stopped to grin.

"Cats?"

"Yes. And cheese. You remember?"

"Oh, yes, that rat business."

"Well," said Stanley, negligently, "I just thought about
it a bit. Slack lot of cats on that boat, don't you think?
Six cats ought to have watched those two cases."

"Oh, do say what you mean. This isn't a missing word
competition."

"I thought," repeated Stanley. "Then I cabled to our
people: 'Any cats on board.' The reply was, 'No.'"

"No," I cried, "but they shipped——"

"They did. Therefore the cats had vanished. I waited,

met her at Tilbury, went on board, got hold of the cook——"

" Why the cook? "

" He was likely to be interested in cheese. I told him a story of a musical cat I used to have—and a story about how my brother-in-law's dog ran away, suggested canaries, kept the conversation zoological. By the time I'd done he was sick of hearing me talk and was just bursting with animal anecdotes. He told me four, including one about a pet chimpanzee, and then——" The thin, dark face became as sly as that of a fox. " Then—well—the ship did take six cats at Tilbury, but they all ate some stuff that disagreed with them or something felinicide happened. Anyhow, they slung the last of them overboard off Dover, absolutely dead."

I took it in. The owners were caught and must pay compensation; of course, they had no chance against a firm conducted like Scotland Yard.

Great days! Now we have our own fleet and our own flag, quite a jolly flag, a white S and a red C on a blue ground, with a yellow edge. But we're so great that, somehow, the days are not so great.

IV

I do not suppose any better cure could have been found for my bruised soul than this successful creation of the firm. When the first of July and the first anniversary came round, I discovered that a little of my harshness had gone. I was not rich yet, could not hope for much more than two hundred pounds or two hundred and fifty that year, but I was my own master and, every month, we were doing that little better which meant we were going to do very well. The hard work had saved me, prevented me from brooding, saved me from dreams and almost from regrets, for a man does not every night of three months collapse as he gets into bed and yet find

time to think of the girl who passed. After three months
habit does the rest. Edith! I did not think of her every
day then, for my business was my love. When I did think
of her I ached, but the pain was bearable, and soon some
commercial anxiety ousted it; Edith had become ghostly,
was no longer the girl I loved but a faint memory, like
the pretty chime of a church bell that one remembers,
or a scent of lavender. I had not seen her once since that
night of encounters; I had seen none of her friends and
was just beginning to have time for new ones. Once or
twice I had met Mr. Lawton, who nodded distantly; I
had spoken to Hugh in the street and received with cold
thanks his good wishes for our success. Edith had not
been mentioned, and often I liked to tell myself that I
had forgotten her, that I loved her no more.

A little for that reason, I think, and a little because I
gained some freedom when we increased our staff by
Mortimer, who superseded Baring, and by an office-boy,
I found that my old taste for adventure returned to me.
Oh, no idealistic interest! Edith, Maud, the others, had
smashed that; I was hard, and my gaiety, my pleasures
were hard. But—I despised myself a little—success was
softening me; I was not quite as hard as I had been, I
began to see once more the dangerous, delicious grace of
English girls. I smiled back at those who served my
meals, sold me stationery, took my name. Once I talked
Shelley with Miss Condon.

I pulled myself up, told myself this would never do.
But I was melting, melting like an iceberg that drifts south.

Folkestone helped me, and its summer girls, but it did
not save me; I shivered when I thought that my old self
was rising again. At Folkestone I met the summer girls
for the first time, as I had never before taken an August
holiday in England; this one I took at Folkestone because
I think I had come to hate the French more than the
English and did not want to join my mother at Pontaillac,
there to see the Southern peacocks strut. Folkestone Leas,

vastness of short, charred grass and asphalt; hotels of
Babelian ambition and boarding-houses with august names;
little, steep streets aiming for the sea, and, far below,
white dots which are bathing machines; enormous pleasure
ground, temporary antheap hoisted into smartness by the
staid grace of some women and the bulky wealth of motor-
cars. And girls! Girls who came from London and are
there unseen, in chrysalides no doubt and butterflies only
in August, who perpetually walk up and down the Leas
in white, or pink, or light blue frocks, in violent-coloured
sweaters and the smallest white shoes; girls whose hair
blows unruly about their fair, arch faces, who are always
laughing, sometimes giggling with elaborate, cheap beaus,
straight from the City but wearing round their hats the
colours of the Grenadier Guards or the Oxford half-blue.
They were adorable, light as the woolly petals of the
dandelions the wind blows from the fields, and so obviously
happy in their brief radiance. They did everything con-
spicuously; they walked arm-in-arm with the beaus, and
their attitude proclaimed that they knew they were walking
thus; they stopped to laugh at anything, a peculiar dog,
a rival sweater, a frock-coated German clerk. They made
love too, with the complete innocence and abandon of their
kind. In the evening, not far from the electric standards,
I could hear giggles, requests for information as to what
they were taken for, and smothered "Don't be sillys,"
followed by the thrilling little noise of baffled kisses. I
was no longer morose; with good-natured cynicism I took
my share of these Saturnalia of the Innocents, the very
small share involved in the exchange of shy looks at the
bottom of the Leas elevator, the shy looks that meant:
"Oh, pay my penny and be my pal." Other trifles, too,
modest mixed bathing and most limited privileges of admiration from a distance, little journeys to Hythe and the
Smuggler's Retreat on the coastline omnibus, more audacious trips to Boulogne, solemn tea at the most imperial
Imperial Hotel, and half-hours next the band, but not so

near that I might not hold firm, sunburnt hands and give,
by very light kisses, cause to be told I must not be so
desperate a kid.

It was nothing, it did not mean anything; it was not
love, but a pretty mummery, a contract of companionship
in which each party found profits of pride because seen in
conversation with one of the other sex.   I remember the
word " Dora," and somebody's tight black curls that fell
over Irish blue eyes.   That is all; for that is all there
was: eighteenth-century badinage brought up to date by
a municipal band and a Virginia cigarette.   My intensities
did not rebel against the code; indeed, I liked it, liked to
feel that I was not to be involved in terrible adventures,
that I might make love—without prejudice.   Lifted then
from the ferocities of my dead attitudes, I could enter
into the spirit of the artificial town, play tennis without
touching hands, cycle into the country and rest in woods,
there to make love so lightly that tea mattered more than
kisses, dance even without emotion; for blue eyes, grey
eyes, brown eyes, aglow and merry, all told the same
tale: let us be gay and risk no suffering; we are the
butterflies, and when the winter comes we must hibernate
until the summer calls its girls again; so do not handle us
roughly, summer beau, do not ask us to thrill and love
and ache, lest we may have to pay the price.   No, summer
beau, be with us another butterfly and flit with us in the
clearings while the sun shines.

I had been lonely, lonely without women: how long is
a day without caresses!

V

Stanley too, and Mrs. Stanley, were in the conspiracy.
Now I often went to the little house at Esher to dine and
talk.   Mrs. Stanley had been given a full account of my
adventures, knew that my engagement had been broken
off and that I had subsequently lost my character; at

first she was a little inclined to treat me like a convalescent, to receive my remarks on the weather and the London and South-Western railway with a sympathetic air, to suggest that I had suffered but should through her be healed.   Soon, however, as she mistook my cynicism for gaiety, she resumed her inconsequent, clumsy and subtly delightful airs; she never, and it must have cost her an effort, alluded to my romantic past, but she took great pains to show me that she thought none the less well of me on account of the scandalousness of that past.   She even discussed free-love in an obtrusive way which amused me very much.

" I don't think it would work," she said, confidentially. " You see, it's all very well when women are young and pretty, but when you get tired of us what's to become of us?   I suppose you'd send us to the workhouse."

" You're too subjective in your theory," I said.

" I don't know what that means, but you must look upon it from the woman's point of view.   Mind you, I don't see that it matters a bit if it's going to last; the registrar and the vicar—after all, they're only details."

Stanley and I both laughed, for Mrs. Stanley was quietly pious and a little ashamed of her fondness for a neighbouring chapel-of-ease: but then a sweet woman will generally be quite immoral if she is required to cheer a man up.   Her simplicity, her transparence, the bird-like agility with which she leapt from politics to domesticity and then, via the baby's teeth, to eugenic segregation, the broad jollity of her, all contributed to crack wherever it touched the hard coating of my cynicism.   When we arrived together from the City she would rush into the hall, and while Stanley was being kissed I could hear her soliloquise to him:

" Baby's been very naughty.   What d'you think he did? He stole all the tape out of my work-basket, tied it to Pat's neck and hauled him about the floor, shouting: Puffer! And Pat was taking it like an angel, but he's been sick.

That was just before Mrs. Hoskin came in. Do you know her brother's going to put up for the District Council? I'm sure I don't know why unless it's because he's a builder. Which reminds me: Did you tell Benetfink that——"

" I told Benetfink," said Stanley, laughing as he freed himself, " and the other topics are adjourned. Now curtsey to Mr. Cadoresse, if a dumpling can curtsey."

She curtseyed, shook hands as she apologised for not having seen me, her eyes round and gay, her mouth pouting because she was mildly snubbed.

"We have such a lot to talk about, old three-yards and I," she said.

They did have a great deal to talk about, this incongruous couple, and they sandwiched it with rather startling suddenness between leading questions, tactfully designed to draw me out on my own topics. Indeed, the conversation at dinner resembled nothing so much as a shower of shooting stars, so rapidly did subject after subject fall into our midst; it was Mrs. Stanley started them one after the other, bewildered us by frequent rushes into side-issues and by literal rushes when the crash of crockery or a wail from the first floor showed that something was happening in the kitchen or the nursery. Stanley gazed at her with silent but undisguised delight: when he had stared long enough she would make a face at him, usually by inflating her cheeks, compressing her mouth and shutting her eyes. Then, suddenly:

"Well, is that a good melon for you, you old scarlet runner? "

They were ridiculous, adorable. Mrs. Stanley's prettiness, her white skin, blue eyes, fair hair, the completeness with which her body concealed her bones, made to me such an appeal that my harshness had always gone before the evening's end. I never thought of making love to her, which I could have done in her husband's presence, for he would not have understood; but I don't think she would have understood either. Besides, her mixture of simplicity and originality baffled me; sweet, languid women, and fierce, wild women—I knew how to manage those, but intellect informed by innocence was beyond me. Besides, I was a sort of Englishman now, and the code of respect weighed heavy upon me.

I think, though, I was happier when alone with Stanley after dinner. Then, slowly sucking at our pipes, we could discuss interminably the chances we had of capturing an order from some exporter, consider whether certain expenses could be cut down or some others profitably incurred. Or, deciding we must not talk shop, we would debate some political question. I was still a Radical, with a touch of the Anarchist, for I detested the organised utopia of the Socialists, but Stanley called himself a Tory Democrat; that is to say, held a license to consider himself more progressive than my own party while defending the Crown, the Church, the landlord and the publican. Also he was a vigorous tariff reformer and converted me regularly once a month, for I fortunately recovered from his attacks as I read my morning paper. He was very exasperating and quite as dishonest as I was; considerable light was shed upon the value of our arguments when we found that, in one of those interminable debates on Protection, we had both quoted from the same table of world wages—only I had selected the countries and trades that proved Free Trade England most bountiful, Stanley those that demonstrated the wretched condition of the British working man. I did not care for those dry economics; but Stanley had his flights.

"You know," he said once, pointing at me a knubbly brown finger, "all this sort of thing, politics, it's a rotten game. Sort of street row. You shout black, and I shout white, and it's grey all the time. What we want is something to chuck all the ideas into until they get mixed; a sort of intellectual melting-pot." The piercing eyes became dreamy as they gazed at the red wall. "All that talk of sending the L.C.C. kids to Paris for a week, and having four hundred German boys here . . . showing 'em St. Paul's and the chute at Earl's Court . . . rot, all that. They haven't got any ideas. They only do what Cambridge and Harvard tell them. We've got to mix up the people who've got a chance to get ideas, not only those who haven't. The Carlton Club ought to swap a hundred members every year with the Reform—or why shouldn't the Reichstag let English M.P.'s make a law or two for the Germans? Mix it all up, that's the idea. Scotch manses for bishops . . . male charwomen . . . Swiss toreadors . . . give the navy vodka instead of rum."

New friends, too, came into my life; Hoskin, the builder, who filled his fancy waistcoats to bursting, and Mr. Shepherd, who thought, probably because I was not an Englishman but merely a benighted foreigner, that he ought to win me over from Rome. Their wives, their daughters, direct people of the tweed and stiff collar type, people who had never heard of the Stage Society, but were willing to play tennis with me or to risk a wetting when I punted. I had found a new England where nobody pretended, where everybody was busy doing simple, muscular things; the women were neither urban nor suburban; they were frank, fresh, and when an occasional flirtation involved me, I found a new pleasure in rapid, innocent kisses after which there lingered in my nostrils neither powder nor scent.

Once more I was becoming human.

CHAPTER II

RECONSTRUCTION

I

EARLY in that year I had rejoined the Liberal Club, less because politics called me than because I found myself lonely; I rejoined in a cynical mood, telling myself that I didn't care what became of the rotten country, but that I might have some fun in the rough and tumble. In my earlier enthusiasm I had been righteously angry when the Lords rejected the Education Bill, the Plural Voting Bill and the Licensing Bill, though I had little liking for religious education in any form and was individualist enough to think a man had a right to be drunk if he chose; after my emotional disaster I do not think that for a year I read a single political speech; the Small Holdings Act, which should have fired my imagination, went unperceived by me through the Upper House, and it was only later, when human desires and human interests began once more to grow round me, that I realised politics as likely to amuse me.

I think it was the new spirit of Liberalism attracted me. Within seven or eight months of the general election I had sneered at the Liberals because they showed no inclination to tackle the Lords; I had even, in the face of a shocked club, likened Sir Henry Campbell-Bannerman to the celebrated commander who marched his soldiers up the hill and marched them down again. But, in the early days of 1908, I discovered in the Liberal papers distinct signs of anger, realised that, faced with so " game " an assembly as the Lords, the Liberals would eventually have to do something, if only because a noisy minority

of the rank-and-file wanted something done. I harboured
no illusions as to the voice of the people; I had heard
it at Hambury shouting more or less beerily, more or less
aitchlessly, and generally talking the most obvious nonsense; I knew too that the mandate the people gave its
elect was on the whole to make the other fellows sorry
they spoke, and that the mandate would duly be reversed
when the people thought they would like new bread and
especially new circuses; I knew that elections were decided
less by alternative convictions than by alternative regrets:
if I had not held the business of politics cheap I should
not again have taken it up, for I wanted an amusement,
not a religion. As I saw looming in the near future a
great row with the Bishops and the Lords I decided to
be in it: for a Frenchman loves a row as much as an
Irishman, particularly when the opponents are prelates
and aristocrats.

It was in this contemptuous, defiant and pugnacious
spirit I appeared before Cloggie. The old man held out
both hands to me, and I guessed that he would have
kissed me if he had been a Frenchman. He looked no
older, for years are nothing after the seventieth; his white
hair was as thick; his blue eyes were as benevolent and
bright under their shaggy white eyebrows. " Good boy,
good boy," he remarked a large number of times as he
held my hand. " Thought you'd never come back again.
What you been up to? Sowing wild oats? Well, well,
I been through it too. *I* know." Cloggie winked at me
as one gay dog meeting another. " Do you know," he
said, confidentially, " they used to call me the Girls' Own,
at Dudley, back in the 'sixties. That was before I met
Him," he added, hurriedly. " He made a new man of
me, did William Ewart. Did I ever tell you about that
night in '74 when He spoke at Bradford and I held His
coat? "

I let Cloggie describe the scene again, displaced this
time some dozen years and located in a new town. As

he spoke, telling, I suspect, the plot of a dream, I liked him more than I cared to think. Old Cloggie stood with one arm outstretched, imitating the great man, with a glow in his eyes and something of the tempest of Gladstone's phrases in his voice. I understood that his leader was Cloggie's god, that his speeches were his creed; sustained by a sentimental passion the old Whig soared, was splendid, was a tribune when he roared in William Ewart's rolling tones the message to all the Smiths in Wolverhampton. And, as suddenly, he was human again:

"Do you know?" said Cloggie, "I remembered you, wondered what'd become of you. Once I thought . . . no . . . I never did, Mr. Clogg; you're quite wrong, Sir—I said that these times were funny times, Mr. Clogg; not a word more."

He communed with the shade of Mr. Clogg and I sighed, thinking of Hambury and Edith. Then I shook him by the arm, for the altercation with the ghost was becoming violent. "I never said he'd gone over to the Tories. No, Mr. Clogg, you've got no right——" I was just in time to save him from blasphemy, from telling the ghost of the pious founder of our library that he lied. Cloggie looked at me with mournful eyes. "I never said you'd gone over to the Tories," he protested.

"No, no, of course not," I said, soothing the old man. "I was busy, making my own business. Down with the Lords!"

"Ah," sighed Cloggie, rapturously. Then he glared at me in a purposeful way, censorious, and a faint North Country accent crept into his voice. "That's all very well shouting 'Down with the Lords,' lad, but tha must gird up thy loins if tha want'st to fight the good fight . . . Beg pardon, Sir? . . . Yes, Mr. Clogg, certainly——"

He conferred with the shade, then solemnly: "What do you say to *Progress and Poverty* for a beginning?"

I pressed one hand upon my heart: the first book

in my political education—Hambury—Edith. . . . Curse
you, weak heart! what's this to start you a-beating?

"Yes," I said weakly, "I'll have that."

I took the dirty old book away. And I was very near
tears when I found a note on page 8: "Ward Four
c:r. 6.30." Little dream girl, whom I had loved and won
amid the dust of that election, you suddenly became the
one reality in a dirty room papered with posters, littered
with leaflets, crowded with canvassers, list-checkers,
envelope addressers. . . . But I fought the dream and
destroyed it: away with sentiment, and up with the struggle
for life, the splendid anodyne.

II

Happy in his enterprise is the man free from love.
Unburdened of the delicious load, his mind occupied by
naught save his ambition, he can march undeflected towards his goal. Because he does not love he spares no
man, and if he no longer hopes to love he stops at nothing;
his brain is clear, he sees without feeling, and because he
feels nothing he understands everything. Sympathy is
a generous draught, but you cannot hold the cup to the
lips of others unless you too have drunk; and the potent
pity that heals another pervades you, softens you;
ordained in the priesthood of sorrow your brain struggles
against your heart; you are drugged, you are beaten.

I was not going to be beaten, for I was not going to
thrill. I would make a great business, love no woman,
but enjoy many, and I would make a toy of Parliaments.
Calmly, then, I chose the Liberals because the chances
of the rich City man were greater with them than with
the Conservatives; that was just a question of numbers.
Also I decided to be extreme, a little because I liked
violent language, a great deal because I saw that the richer
I became the more noble I would seem if I fought against
wealth. I reappeared in the Club debates as an amazing

and suspected figure, as elaborately dressed as possible, never more informally than in a frock-coat; I wore fancy waistcoats, scented my handkerchief; sometimes I came in evening clothes. The little group of tradesmen and workmen hated me, I think, and my airs, but they could not withstand the acrid violence of my speeches. I was happy in their midst because I was playing a part, strutting as a fop and mouthing words that would have satisfied the Labour interest.

Soon I had my party, about ten members out of sixty. We always occupied the same chairs and ostentatiously conferred with one another when the chairman stood up to put a resolution. My party comprised Cloggie, two railwaymen on the edge of Socialism, a gas-fitter, one of the most intemperate temperance men I have ever met; also a secularist elementary school teacher, three shop-keepers called Lewis, Evans and Lloyd, and an extraordinary person, Mr. Misling, who had rebelled against mere Liberalism because the Admiralty refused to try vege-tarianism in the Navy. We were the cranks, the danger-ous people; we followed our parliamentary favourites closely, noted their speeches and their votes. I had a fancy for Palissy, the Radical potter; the school teacher quoted Mr. Beans' questions with relish. There was Pon-sonby too, we liked him, and the member for Tottenham, while Mr. Misling periodically suggested that Mr. Bernard Shaw should be asked to contest our division, presumably in the lentil interest. We were absurd, but I knew what I was doing. I was making the heterogeneous homogeneous by harbouring myself all the oddities and all the discontents; I was extreme so as to collect the extremists, but I was going to use them, not to serve them. In March I was elected to the Executive and signalised my entry into the governing body by calling the Prime Minister weak-kneed and a traitor to his pledges.

I think this was a happy period of my life; I led, I was followed by the few and viewed with undisguised bewilderment by the many. I enjoyed the posturing, the game, the unreality of the business; like Stanley I played psychological chess. I had the keenest sensations of pleasure when I led my little group to the attack of an amiable speaker who had come to us from the Temple Club. He was a young barrister with ambitions, who intended to do everything a gentleman could do to get into the London County Council; he was very round, so shaved and so brushed, so black and so white, so smiling, so bland, so archly daring, that our Radical group had begun to growl and shift its feet long before he was half through his speech. The young barrister had come to explain the Small Holdings Act, a subject calculated to rouse an urban Liberal Club, for it afforded the townsmen a chance of believing that they could interfere with the agriculturalists.

"You see," said the young barrister, "almost insuperable difficulties stood in our path. Faced on the one side by the crying needs of the people who were deprived of access to the land, on the other by the legitimate claims of the landowners——"

A few hisses. Shocked protest of the Chairman.

"We were compelled to progress with moderation and due consideration for the interests involved." The young barrister smiled sweetly at my flushed face and at his elegant phrase. Endlessly he unrolled his periods, excusing the latitude given to Tory County Councils, suavely explaining why limitations had been imposed on compulsory powers. . . . Real anger filled me for a moment as I realised that urbane youth as the conventional Liberal, determined to do as little as might accord with pledges, to shelter behind a convenient syllogism, a dilemma, an anecdote or a joke. "Little fat boy, brief-fed, I loathe you," I thought. Quite honestly I wanted a leader with blood in his body as I leapt to my feet with the group when questions were called for. It was a queer little scene. The Chairman sat framed between his funereal whiskers, horribly shocked, by the side of the bland Temple Clubber,

who still smiled. The portraits of Cobden, Sir William
Harcourt and the prospective Liberal candidate for our
division stared from the walls at the little Radical group
which had stood up *en bloc*.

All together we shouted and shook our fists at the mild
Daniel.

"Why don't you nationalise the land?" roared the first
railwayman.

"Why don't you nationalise the land?" repeated the
second railwayman.

"Will you provide houses?" asked Lloyd, who owned
a country cottage.

"Gentlemen! gentlemen!" protested the Chairman.

Evans demanded a national loan guaranteed on ducal
estates. The temperance gas-fitter behaved so violently
that some one shouted he was drunk.

Amiable and urbane, the young barrister took us up
each in turn, explaining the Act with affected simplicity,
as if addressing a Socialist Sunday School; he assured
the railwaymen that one day, by and by, eventually (and
so forth) "the taxation of land-values would operate in
the direction indicated by their remarks"; he assured
Lloyd that rural housing preyed on the governmental mind;
he took quite seriously the vegetarian grievance of Mr.
Misling and assured him that in the Navy a potato allowance was traditional.

And then I was on my feet, speaking, so hot with rage
that I do not remember exactly what I said. Phrases
remain: "Playing and tinkering with abuses—juggling
with words—foregoing omelets to save the eggs——"
I think that I clamoured for revenge, for the break-up
of the ducal estates, for minimum wages and State agri-
cultural banks—I spoke to the music of hisses and cheers,
and as I spoke I had a vision of a new, a wonderful land,
a hotch-potch of Garden City and Merrie England—bath-
rooms all round and maypoles on the village greens.
Sturdy yeomen, farmers' daughters—farmers riding to

hounds (subject to the right to shoot foxes). And big towns with laboratories, institutes. free libraries (that banned no novels)—athletics for clerks—morris dances in the slums, no, ex-slums, for I dropped rent into the bottomless pit.

I found myself shouting for a new Enclosures Act.

" A new Enclosures Act! No more filching of the people's land by the rich, but an enclosure of ducal land with the dukes outside—and then you'll have an island where it'll be good to live under the Union Jack."

The young barrister glibly congratulated me on my admirable speech and assured me that however distant my millennial ideas might be the Liberals would embody them in Acts of Parliament. I hardly listened to him: I was looking into my soul. What was this treachery to myself? Why had I so genuinely glowed when I pictured the great England that would arise, thrilled at the words " Union Jack? " Was I going to be false to my hatred? to my revenge? No, no. But, very faintly, something whispered:

" It is March, Lucien Cadoresse. Do you know that the violets are shyly clustering on the steep, moist banks in rutted English lanes? Do you not remember the women with skins of milk? and the young Apollos, their brothers, with the delicate mouths and proud, short heads? This is England, calm, gentle-eyed as a heifer, and as strong; alien, do you not love her? "

III

Such was the disaster that befell my hatred, came piling on my success in the City, on Stanley's friendship, on those balms for my wounds. At first I refused to acknowledge the mysterious process, told myself that I hated England, that I would make sport of her customs, butts of her men and toys of her women. I fought for my foreign air, availed myself of the summer to accentuate the colours of my socks, waistcoats and ties; I affected affectations until affectation seemed to be nature; I tried to be a Frenchman because I could not bear to be an Englishman, to feel the suck of the English morass. I did not want to be cold, reserved and dogged, I wanted to be ebullient, cynical, gay, outrageous; I wanted to tell stories that were subtly improper rather than coarse; I wanted to love and ride away.

But England turned towards me her courteous face, took no notice of my clothes and my airs; she asked me to dinner and smiled at my stories; her women returned for the aggressive insistence of my glances the beautiful, tender gaze of the English maiden. It was the general had captured me and made me accept the particular.

Politics, I think, played the chief part in this new birth, and I associate the political emotions of that year with the Old Age Pensions Act. Bathos? No, that is not bathos, for idealism is a god of itself and can live in any shrine. I had laughed at the Bill when it was introduced, made jokes of the " five bob a week when you're dead " kind; I had spoken in its defence at a couple of open-air meetings, rejoicing rather in my contempt for the brief I held and in the dexterity with which I parried questions than in the merits of my case; I liked to feel master of my crowd, to cheat it. When a man called out " Rot! " I didn't want to make him see it wasn't rot; I preferred to say: " The gentleman is a judge of rot," or " That man knows all about rot, he talks it," or give him some such successful, drivelling answer from the electioneering store. I wanted to dominate.

But the summer came and I was stung into fury by the attempt of the Lords to kill the Bill; I went to Folkestone, returned charmed, my memory haunted by the gracious shapes of English girls, by the innocent gaiety of England at play. The Bill became an Act, and I joined in the delight of my party, perhaps because I wanted something to delight me, for I was alone. Stanley had gone abroad with his wife, my few friends were scattered, I had a little time to think. And I found that I was thinking of this Act! Absurd, but a sentimental flood carried me away. I had visions of millions of old men and women freed at last from fear and want; in vain I told myself that the age limit was too high, the allowance too low, that the reduction of the pension for married couples was mean and its maintenance at the full scale for irregular alliances funny. I tried to think in detail, and scoff, but I failed: I began to think in principle.

In principle! Something had happened to my view of English politics. Notwithstanding my experiences at Hambury, and though I knew that our election was more like a game of poker than a St. Georgian contest, I realised that English politics had a material basis, were more than a mean little private wrangle; I saw that the Liberals, unwillingly perhaps, were doing something because England was determined they should do something. Land, religious education, control of the liquor trade, democratic government, all these were being handled with an air of definiteness if not of resolution; the Liberals did intend to open up the fallow acres, to make a better country, and it did not matter much that they were wrong-headed, limited, intolerably prejudiced, for theirs was more than a quality of movement: it was action. And those others, the Tories whom I abused so gaily, they too had something to do. That tariff of theirs, a ridiculous scheme to me who was born in a protected country and knew that a tariff mattered about as much in daily life as a speed limit for motor cars, it was action too. I liked the intensity of conviction that fired Mr. Chamberlain when I heard him at the Albert Hall, the stress he laid on the fact that two and two are four; and the others, the young bloods, Brown of Wolverhampton, Lord Algernon Cust, fated to die in the last ditch, I enjoyed their enjoyment and upon their resolution sharpened my own energy.

An obstructive veil was drawn away by an unseen hand.

Politics remained a game, yet a game played, not for love as in my own country, but for high stakes. The French had not, in my time, done aught save persecute their Church, had not tried to do anything else, had endlessly called one another names, made and unmade cabinets so quickly that not one had been able to realise a plan. Oh, talk, talk, perpetual French talk! talk of income-tax, talk of civil service reform, talk of industrial assurance, and nothing done, nothing save stupid reiteration that the country stood by the immortal principles of 1789.

Revolutionaries! that's all the French were. They could break anything and could make nothing; they were noisy drones, and here in England were the sturdy bees hiving the honey. Behind the futile marionettes of the Palais-Bourbon and of Westminster stood two very different peoples: the French occupied with love-making, egotist art and private economy; the English, determined that the peasant should have land, the workman wages and security, the child training. They were building, and at the steady glow of their will I lighted the ever-ready beacon in my own soul. Almost at once I saw the English as I had seen them, saw them better, perhaps, for I was rid of stupid, old John Bull and his riding-breeches; I saw the English I had dreamed ten years before, the English determined to achieve, to make their dreams materialise, to establish in every corner of the globe the Pax Britannica, to cut roads, build bridges; I saw England sending out messenger swarms to conquer the black and the yellow, to guide and illuminate with splendid common-sense the less steadfast white.

I was intoxicated. Once more I faced London, and the city showed me its soul under its throbbing body, the great business of itself. As I walked its interminable streets, leagues from east to west, and from north to south leagues too, and as I watched from the bridges the flow of its liquid history towards the Pool, out towards the sea and the world, I knew that I was at the hub of the universe, for here was something more than culture, than delicacy, than art: it was purpose, it was life. I was drunk with life, born again. And as if England had planned to reconquer me her skies poured down upon me in those August days the droughty heat in which I live best. Swollen were the flowers in the parks and luxuriant the leaves; the women of the orgiastic town that burst into maturity hung their heavy heads upon their slender bodies like peonies over-rich in sap. I flung myself upon London as if I wanted to embrace it.

Of my adventures, common again now, I remember one best. Her name was Laura Filton, a tall girl whose slim form, when leaning against the warm wind, seemed to bend as a blade of grass. Her close, pleated blue dress and her peekaboo white blouse hid little of the graciousness of her; her languid, rose-white neck was wearied by the weight of a head laden with light-brown hair, dressed high and in a score of curls, of her enormous, flat, black hat trimmed with red roses. I had made friends with her wire-haired terrier near the Round Pond, and then with her; it is six years ago, and her air is archaic, her hat and pleats are of the dead, but Laura Filton, idle tradesman's daughter, stands before me now, calm, sedate and alluring, with all the grace of England in her long hands.

She was irremediably stupid, and I remember little of her conversation. We had exhausted the habits of her dog; she looked at me with calm, blue eyes.

" Have you seen the Salome dance? " she asked.

I had, and suggested its costume must be delightful in August.

She laughed, stated she didn't fancy it for herself.

" I do," I said boldly. " Come, dance it now—or be a dryad. Here are the trees of the Gardens to shelter you."

She looked at me as if wondering whether I was serious, and the memory has an air of unreality, for about us little children play the ancient game of diabolo, and I hear a

nursemaid humming the forgotten ditty, " I wouldn't leave
my little wooden hut for you."

" You are silly," she summed up at last.

Laura Filton had nothing to say, gave me no mental
satisfactions, nothing save an ineffectual acceptance of
caresses she did not desire, and yet I have put her among
the great in one of the niches of my heart; she had no
quality, but I gave her the quality of England. The first
to attract me since my re-enchantment, she figures as the
dove of peace flying towards me, ambassadress of the women
of the isles. I think I tried to express to her something
of the delight that was in me, to tell her that when I
loved her I loved her people, her splendid, conquering
people, loved her as the daughter of the pioneers. She
listened while I ranted of London town and, at last,
said:

" Yes, it's a fine place, isn't it? And those new motors,
the taxis, they're the latest. Have you been in one of
them yet? "

I laughed, pressed her slender arm, told her that she
had missed her mark, that these new-fangled carriages
were French. But I loved her guilelessness, would have
had her more innocent still, so that she might be yet more
serene, serene as England the Conquering.

IV

To Stanley also I showed my new madness, and he
smiled.

" At it again! I thought you'd find out we weren't so
bad, after all. To tell you the truth I saw it coming
in March when you took up politics again; when you began
abusing my side I knew that in a few months you'd be
falling in love with your own."

" I've fallen in love with both of them."

" Evidently. You never do things by halves. Tell you

what, Cadoresse, you'll have no peace until you make an
end of your ambitions and take out your naturalisation
papers."

I stepped back, stared at this tall, untidy person, who
seemed to think me funny because I had lost my heart
to a nation.   In that moment Stanley was more representative of his people than ever before; that he was
articulate while they were dumb did not affect my sense
of his Englishness, for here he was, saying tremendous
things and treating them as trifles.   Careless of the
honours piled so heavy upon him by his birth on English
soil, he stood, leaning against the mantelpiece, shifting
from one foot to the other.   His eyes gleamed wickedly,
as if he were analysing me, observing the emotions that
must have been passing over my all-too-expressive countenance.   This business of being an Englishman, nobody
knows anything about it except the foreigner.

I did it.   I plunged that very day and, in the evening,
read my instructions so many times that I ended in knowing some paragraphs by heart; though they thrilled, they
terrified me a little, for England did not throw herself
at my head; she wanted to know all about me, all about
my family, my work and my behaviour; trusting me very
little, she wanted four Englishmen to affirm in a statutory
declaration that I was respectable and loyal; and having
captured me, England hinted that she would never let me
go but wished me to reside in the United Kingdom.

For a whole fortnight I struggled with intolerable com-
plexities.   It seemed as difficult to be born again as it is
to be born actually.   I spoiled my memorial on a Saturday
afternoon and languished, in a state of suspended nationality, until the Monday.   Then I had to find a referee
who had known me for five years and had to submit with
as good a grace as I could to a cross-examination by
Barker, whom I asked out to lunch for the purpose.   He
consented, but put an unfortunate idea into my head:

"What d'you want to naturalise for, you silly old

josser? You're chucking your five pounds away, anyhow. They won't have you: not respectable enough."

He laughed, and his agreeable face seemed malevolent. "What about that affair of yours? That was a bit of all right, but if it comes out—what oh!'"

The idea preyed upon me; long before my papers went to the Home Office I realised what a man feels like who is "loitering with intent to steal." I passed policemen very fast and stiffly, expecting one of them to come up to me and say: "Hi, you, the Frenchman. What d'you think you're up to trying to become a bloomin' Briton? What about Maud Hooper? And what's that you said last year about the old Queen? And what about——?" In those moods I mentally ran away without listening to those other and formidable "what abouts?" for I knew there were a great many more, that I had accumulated a good deal of disloyalty in the year of disillusion. But I set my teeth and decided to go on.

The chief statutory declaration was made by Barker, and others followed from Stanley, Purkis, Cloggie (I mean Smith) and Mr. Hoskin. These men shocked me, for they did not seem to realise the importance of the affair, except Cloggie perhaps, for he delivered a lengthy speech on human brotherhood, ending on an inference that England was the eldest of the family. But Barker refused to sign until he had drunk a "small port," the only intoxicant he allowed himself as a teetotaler; and old Purkis sent me a jocular message to say that he had a new rose which he would name the "Cadoresse Britonii," while Stanley persecuted me with theories as to the intuitive qualities of the police.

A fortnight elapsed. These were anxious moments, for a plain-clothes called at my address and told the landlady casually that it was "all right at Cambridge Street": that meant the creature was taking his business seriously, that he had called at St. Mary's Terrace too. What had Mrs. Hooper said? Perhaps she had laid upon my not altogether guiltless shoulders her daughter's ruin? But I was fervent, I told myself to try to be brave. I was idiotic, and yet the whole affair was about as fine as being converted. Then, one morning, I found on my breakfast tray a notice informing me that my desire was granted me and requiring me to take the oath of allegiance.

The commissioner for oaths behaved very badly. He was a very dirty little old man whose office smelled like a dust heap; while I read out, Holy Book in hand, my solemn pledge of loyalty to the King, he persistently scratched the place where his skull-cap chafed him. While I kissed the greasy book he remarked: " Half a crown."

It ought to have happened in Westminster Abbey. I had a fancy for red velvet, no, for " imperial " purple or " royal " blue—and there ought somewhere to have been a lion and a unicorn, and a band to play " Rule Britannia." . . . It was as flat as a marriage before the Registrar, worse, for the commissioner did not even wish me every happiness.

But while I stood for a moment on the landing, my eyes mechanically recording the words on the dirty ochre paint, quite unforgettable words: " Reformed Sewage Disposal Co. Ltd.," my heart was beating fast and I was swollen with pride. An Englishman at last—born again. . . .

I can now guess what a man feels when he has just been knighted.

V

" You are becoming intolerable," said Stanley, good-humouredly, a fortnight later. " Since you wasted five pounds you go about as if the place belonged to you——"

" I belong to the place," I said, in a fervid voice. " Do you know, Stanley, it's true; I can't keep it to myself and it's funny how little it seems to matter to other people."

" One's affairs never really matter to other people."

"No—but such affairs! I told Gladys, you know, the red-headed girl at the 'Yemen.' I told her I was a naturalised Englishman, and all she said was: 'Who'd have thought it?'"

"I'm not surprised," said Stanley, "if you will roll several capital R's in the middle of 'naturalise.'"

For several sorrowful moments I reflected that it was rather a pity no Pentecostal, naturalising fire could descend upon my head. But soon I thought: "Anyhow, I'm in." And then: "After all, you need a jolly good R to say 'Britannia.'"

CHAPTER III

THE LAST LAP

I

I walked quickly along Piccadilly, hugging my heavy coat against my body, for a fierce wind blew in my back from the east and, at every corner, split itself into eddies in which danced dust and pieces of paper. I liked the harsh January day, was conscious of my wind-stung face, and of the warmth of wool upon my chest. I was alive, more alive than a man, alive as a young horse. In the sharp air all things seemed unusually definite, made up of angles and lines; and every noise was multiplied; clear came the ringing of the bells of the modish electrics, the trample and bit-champings of the horses, the crashes and backfirings of those new-fangled motor-buses. And above all I heard the tap-tap of the feet, could distinguish the clatter of a pair of little high-heeled boots from the duller, regular sound the big soldier in the fur coat was sowing. Men and women, all in a hurry, borne by the wind, thousands of them, millions all round them. And the imperious demand for alms of a blind man's stick.

I glanced at the shops, the pageantry of ties, the high piles of cigarettes framing like minarets the brown girl who rolled them, the clustering chocolates, the loud overcoats on their dummies, the leather, the gold and silver, the perfumes in their bottles, so abundant that I fancied I could smell them.

Then Devonshire House behind its prison gates, and the plunge into dandydom, frock-overcoats and grey-topped boots. I stopped to look at the Ritz, which seemed very

397

staring and new, and for a while watched the midday
tides of traffic surge past it, blotting out the Green Park,
all save the empty heaven above, which suggested vastness,
for the gaunt skyscrapers of Westminster were very far
away. I saw the scene as part of my life, felt strong,
successful, free; I was making money, making power,
and this scene would soon be my setting. A rough balance-
sheet told me that I could depend now, not on two hundred
and fifty but on five hundred pounds in the coming year.
Success! And freedom: here was I, at two o'clock in the
afternoon, able to walk Piccadilly because such was my
mood. I had been to see the manager of one of the big
Atlantic companies in Cockspur Street, the Rudyard or
the Red Sun, I forget which, and could afford a walk to
Hyde Park Corner: you do not know how wonderful is
Piccadilly at two o'clock unless you work in the City from
ten to six.

But the icy wind drove me on, past Bath House and up
the hill, towards the clubs and the growing solitudes.
I liked to look at the women, little furry animals with
half-muffled faces, at the men, the ruddy and stout in
check trousers, the indolent clean-shaven, and those others
in rather old clothes whose faces showed the sunburn of
India. All the world was a toy for me, all its people, and
that short, plump young man who stood lighting a cigarette, on the steps of a club.

As I drew near I glanced at him, and at once knew
him. It was Edward Kent, but I did not want to speak
to him, I had done with his part of my life; to see him
made me remember. But Kent did not share this feeling
of mine. He, too, had recognised me, and now came
frisking down the steps. As we shook hands I was filled
with a sense of his absurdity. I could judge him better
now, understand his irrelevancy in an ordered scheme. His
jauntiness, his flow of polite platitudes and mild epigrams
exasperated me.

" It's ages since I saw you," he said, blandly. " Where

have you been all this time? Making pots of money, I suppose, from what I hear."

" What have you heard? " I asked.

But Kent did not answer me, having forgotten his own remark.

" I've just been in here for a chop—though sometimes I chop and change. I've been having lunch with Tortini, the musician; I'm thinking of joining his quartette. Of course it'll be rather hard on my golf, not that that's up to much. The other day I went round in——"

I listened, seemed to listen for many minutes, for Kent had a loose abundance of conversation, a taste for elegant unreality that maddened his audience. Not only did he produce a flood, but he perpetually turned on and then off taps marked anything between " Latest Political Scandal " and " Socks." At last I interrupted him, said I must hurry on.

" Where are you off to? I'm going to Burlington House to meet my sister, Mrs. Hugh Lawton, you remember. Louisa's infected me with a taste for sociology."

" Yes," I said, holding out my hand.

Kent did not take it, went on speaking.

" She and Muriel are great pals. Muriel's engaged, by the way."

" Indeed? " I said, my hand still outstretched.

" Yes—she's got hold of quite a decent chap, a sapper. Quite mad, of course, and when he marries Muriel he'll go over to the Liberals and be almost complete." Kent laughed at his little witticism, was so pleased with himself that I think he hardly realised he spoke his next sentence aloud: " I never thought she'd get married, but I suppose it's catching now that Edith's as good as accepted that fellow Shepstone who's been dangling round her for a year."

I knew that I did not blink, that not a muscle of my face moved, but I heard my teeth crunch together. I remained impassive, almost at attention, while Kent told me the chestnut of the barrister and the pickpocket who 'ad a bit o' luck in the Strand.

Well done, Lucien Cadoresse, England had at last given you something of the bulldog.

II

When the ship has gone down she does not suck under all the little matters she carried; hen-coops, life-belts, spars, a litter of domestic furniture float most obviously upon the waves. As I sat at home, an hour later, an impersonal self wondered why my eyes were so interested in trifles, in the row of books and pamphlets upon my writing-table, notably the flaring red " Liberal Year Book," in the polished brass inkstand, the woodcuts of old London upon the green distempered wall, and the muddy golf-sticks in the corner. But these little things are not little except against the broad background of life; when the loves, lusts, hatreds, the ambitions, the fears and delights have suddenly been shrouded, then the little things become important: for they survive disaster, they never die, and sometimes by their permanence they link.

I accomplished a number of mechanical acts in the hours that followed; I trimmed my moustache, made many idle drawings on my blotter; I sorted my books, all the red ones together, all the green ones, and so forth; and I sharpened with great steadfastness a whole packet of pencils.

I do not think my mind worked true during those first hours; its concentration upon the futile tasks was purely automatic, self-protective perhaps, and the hollowness of my purpose showed through my business, for I found I had at once to find something else to do as soon as I had finished with one trifle. While I was idle my brain seemed in a state of continuous, nervous whirl, in a condition akin to fitful half-sleep, through which there perpetually intrudes an undefinable but oppressive preoccupation. I remember wondering whether I were going mad.

I expect I was very near it.

Dusk. I had been sitting for a long time in the arm-chair, rather stupefied now, and therefore more content. I heard the housemaid come in, put a match to the fire, switch on the lights. She asked me whether I wanted tea. I said, " No," without turning round. Then I listened to the fire crackling, got up to tend it, for habit, that petrified fruit of instinct, reminded me that the grate was ill-built. But as I knelt in front of the flame, coaxing it to grow by shuttering it with a newspaper, I found that the sound of a human voice and the performance of a duty which was not futile had worked some change in me, cleared my brain of fumes. The realisation came slowly, so slowly that it must have been some time before it occupied the whole of me, for I managed to build up a good fire without killing it. When I at last walked to the window, I knew that I was no longer feeling as an animal, but thinking as a man. For a minute or so I repeated, " Edith engaged . . . Edith engaged . . ." I paused, then said it again with an air of finality. I did not stop to analyse the relation Kent had implied, to wonder whether she was actually engaged. I accepted the fact. Then I asked myself what it meant to me. At first it meant nothing at all, nothing more than Muriel's engagement or any one of the eight hundred and seventy-four engagements which came about in the United Kingdom every day.

I smiled at my own statistics and, for a while, found satisfaction in my consciousness. But I was not yet all conscious, for instinct took me to the writing-table, made me unlock the drawer in which I kept Edith's letters; there were about thirty there, the first of all written just before the Hambury election, the last, an appointment on a half sheet; there were two picture postcards from Fowey; I found also a programme headed " Empress Rooms," on

which my initials figured seven times, the menu of Ma-
homed's Hindu restaurant with an intricate pattern of
E.L.'s on the back. No photograph, not a lock of hair, or
a fan, or a ribbon. Nothing but these letters, and yet—
I had kept the meanest of them, the most formal, the
unsigned commands to be at a given time at some Underground station. I had kept everything.

I flung myself back in my chair, my hands on the papers,
and knew that I was sane after all, for here was aching
regret shot with flashes of agony. I bent forward, ordered
the letters as well as I could, began to read them. The
first one, its childish round writing and underlined words,
yes, here was Edith, slim, outlined against the sea, her
fair hair streaming on the wind. Some appointments to
meet at Hambury—in ward four—and I thought of the
young Liberals, of Chike, the progressive grocer, of Edith
when the hood fell from her head. . . .

A pain I had never known before went right through
me as I remembered the falling of the hood, the fair head
pillowed on my shoulder. . . .

I read all the other letters, some more appointments, a
picture postcard saying that the weather was lovely at
Fowey, and that they were going by boat to Land's End;
a long letter, too, very tender and very shy:

> " . . . But how can I write what you ask? I am
> not like you, I am afraid to say what I think, it all
> seems so strange and so wonderful that you should
> care for me at all. That is why I can't tell you
> how much I love you; I seem cold, I know, but
> I'm not, I'm not. Oh, my darling. . . ."

I closed my eyes, gripping the letter. " Go on," said
instinct.

> " . . . you must know that I love you, that I've
> never loved any one else. I couldn't, and I'll

always love you, always, always, whatever you do,
I'll always love you. . . ."

I read to the end, mastering the grief that rose in me,
thinking to dominate it, to succeed in being a man. But
I was not prepared for the last line; she had signed
" Edith," and, as a postscript, written: " Is this a good
letter? "

The manliness went out of me. Edith, tender, devoted,
but shy, had broken down her reserve, had forced herself
to write a love-letter because I demanded one, and when
it was written had suddenly asked for appreciation, for
praise, as a child begs for full marks. She had given me
all she could give, then raised towards me the blushing
flower of her face that she might read thankfulness in
mine.

A bitter shame was in me while I wept, uncontrollably,
endlessly wept; hands clasped over my eyes I felt myself
shaking all over; for a long time mine were terrible, dry
sobs, sobs that tore at my throat, pulled and jerked my
shoulders . . . it was later only the tears came, and then
they were wrenched from my eyes . . . and later again
they flowed silently, painlessly, until I sank face down
against the table and found that everything about me was
growing dim, receding. With every minute exhaustion
gained upon me. I was vaguely conscious of the growing
cold as night came and the fire went down, of a torpor
seizing me, pressing down upon me. I slept.

I woke up to hear the clock strike four. I rose to my
feet and found that I staggered as I walked about the
room, but soon my cramped limbs recovered, though I
shivered with cold. I went to the sideboard, poured out
a third of a tumbler of whisky and swallowed the stuff in
two gulps. Then, as I sat by the side of the cold grate,
I felt better, stronger; and I was peculiarly lucid, as if
the exhaustion of my body had freed my brain. Indeed,

I hardly felt my body, I had the sensation of severed limbs that is gained from several doses of absinthe.

For a long time I thought, and it seemed as if some obscure mental process had taken place within me while I slept, as if I had gone on thinking during those hours of torpor. This I knew because I did not awake to weak misery: I awoke in reaction, physically exhausted, but mentally calm. I recapitulated the points of the case, told myself without any passion that I loved Edith, had always loved her, must have her. I did not doubt that she still loved me, that she was preparing to marry the other man only because I had forsaken her. . . .

Yes, I had forsaken her. I had not understood her, given her time. For some minutes I bitterly reviled my own impatience, my intolerance, my sensitiveness, my precipitancy; I had brutally asked her to choose between her father and myself, and had not given her many minutes to make up her mind; unmoved, I had seen her tears flow; I had tried to bully her, I had sacrificed her on the altar of my self-importance; I had trampled on her sense of duty, sneered at her delicacy, despised her scruples; I had seized a butterfly and broken it upon a wheel. . . .

"Brute . . . brute . . . fool . . ." I whispered.

And I found intense pleasure in this vilification of myself. While I once had seen no side other than my own, I now saw mine no longer; I hated myself and enjoyed the punishment, as if I were split into judge and criminal, so that one part of me could rejoice in the retribution which overtook the other. Testimony of my love, also, I delighted in my abasement, for the true lover has no pride, but cries out to his beloved: "Oh, most beautiful, oh, priceless one, deign only not to avert your eyes. . . . I am worthless, soiled, despicable . . . there is no good in me save that I love you. So put your heel upon my neck, beloved, and tread, tread hard. . . . Ah, that pain is sweet, the pain you give. . . ."

Soon I saw my life as it was, a life of hard, perpetual

contest. I had struggled to become an Englishman, struggled to become a free, rich man, now I must struggle to win my woman. Oh, it was struggling did it after all, ceaseless toil, endless resource, unflagging, dogged energy. To try, to be beaten, to try again, that was life, after all. And a fine thing of its kind, adventurous because you could never tell which way the contest would end, bracing because you had to take the blows and come on for more, and come on again, and again, and still come on, until the enemy got tired of hitting, and then you won. . . .

The whisky in my body and the fierce metaphors in my brain inflamed me, evoked in me a response, made me grit my teeth together and clench my fists. They thought they had beaten me, did they? They thought they could keep me out, keep me down. . . . We should see. Edith loved me still, had always loved me, and I'd have her, have her if I had to kidnap her. In that hour I was strong, much more than inflamed; I swore that nothing should keep me from her, that I would call her back, and if, hardly possible to conceive, she loved me no more, win her a second time.

As I sat alone in the icy room, waiting for the dawn, much that is my soul stood forth: a conviction that life has no virtue save in its battles, that it is a poor thing at best, and that all its colour and its dignity come out of contest.

Life is in us only when we fight; fighting makes life splendid, and if we cease to fight we begin to die.

Life is like a tree: when growth is arrested decay begins.

I stood at the window. In the greyness the houses opposite seemed ghostly and unfamiliar. Then day began to dawn in the east.

There are no good causes and no bad causes. There are only the causes that win. There is no dignity in endeavour, but only in victory.

Defeat is naught save the prelude to victory.

The dawn touched the roofs with rose and, fervently, I repeated:

Defeat is naught save the prelude to victory.

III

With extreme care I made ready for the struggle. My face was livid and there were purplish blotches under my eyes, but my black hair lay very sleek, and my hand, nerved by my purpose, had not shaken while I shaved. Resolutely, too, I ate, though my furred tongue revolted from food and I wished only to empty the teapot: I was going to want my strength.

I stood at the corner of Lancaster Gate, watching from a convenient point, and the old excitement rose in me. I recognised the maid. Fiona, older, slower and fatter, came trundling down the steps to snuff critically in the gutter. The little dog gave me my first powerful emotion; Fiona, waddling cautiously down the steps instead of clearing them at a bound, four paws outstretched, as the hound of Artemis, was a horribly eloquent evidence of passing time. I had left her young, and now, after little more than two years, she was old. For some seconds my throat contracted as I wondered whether Edith, too, had grown old. At half-past nine Mr. Lawton came out, walked away towards the Tube station. Still I waited. She was coming: I knew it.

IV

For some minutes I walked behind her; though my heart beat so fast that I thought I must stifle, I was still sybarite enough to want to look at her before I spoke. I had not seen her very well as she appeared, for she had turned sharply to the left and I had followed; I had had time only to see her hair blaze vivid in the sunshine, and now, as I cautiously suited my pace to hers, I found her unexpectedly the same. She walked as quickly, as springily as ever, and gaily she shook her little bag at Fiona in the hope of making her leap at it. But Fiona was old, and peacefully trotted.

If I saw no more than this it was, no doubt, because of the tumult within me. I was overcome by unexpected realisations, subtle convictions of needs and, oddly grafted thereon, a lust for conquest; I enjoyed this careful following, was more than the wild beast tracking its food, was also the sportsman enjoying the chase. But mixed with this feeling that must arise in any man that pursues any woman, after the manner of the male, was a transcendent, swoon-approaching joy, a sense of fulfilment; she did not see me, but I saw her; I trod in her footprints, and I had a feeling that was literally sensuous when my foot crumpled a scrap of paper which hers had touched.

Cautiously I followed across the Bayswater Road, through the postern and into the Gardens. With her I abandoned the path for the lawns, treading warily lest the frosted grass should criss under my feet. The wind had fallen, and now the pale sun threw upon the ground the fine shadow-tracery of the branches: as she passed under a tree the thin reflections fell across her, patterning her with light grey lines. Suddenly she stopped, seemed to gaze at the Speke obelisk, and I knew that my hour had come, for we were almost alone; far away some nursemaids wheeled perambulators along a path, and a few little dark-clad men hurried towards the railway stations and their business. I heard the faint crackling of the bare twigs, the distant whistle of a park-keeper. And then I shrank, for I was so full of happiness, of rediscovery, that I wondered whether I had not better be content and turn away. I was as the Oriental sage bidden add to a bowl already full of water. . . .

The sage, I knew, added a rose-leaf. But I shrank, I shrank; I was afraid. In spite of my aching desire to see her face, I feared what I might see in it. . . . I half turned. But it was too late: Fiona, slowly trotting in circles, muzzle upon the ground, drew near me in her course, stopped, looked at me. She stared at me, and I wondered whether she hypnotised me, for we did not move, either of us, but gazed into each other's eyes. I saw something struggling in the beautiful brown depths, recognition, doubt; Fiona knew me, was desperately trying to remember where she had seen me, wanted to remember. I saw the effort of her little brain.

Then a change came over her. She cocked her ears, opened her mouth a little, so as to show her pink tongue moving in slight excitement over her white teeth. And very, very slowly, she came towards me, gazing at me still, her tail agitated by a nervous quiver. She came quite close, looked up at me, and suddenly lay upon her side, a front paw raised, her tail now beating sharply upon the ground. . . .

I heard Edith cry out: "Fiona! Fiona!" saw her flit towards me.

Then, quite unaccountably, I was looking at her and she, one hand upon her breast, was meeting my eyes with hers.

I do not know how long it lasted.

In those moments I saw her collectively, as an object devoid of details. Through the immediate sense of my delight ran a streak of terror, and even in that clasp of gazes I felt the impulse to fly. But the film dissolved and, suddenly, I saw Edith.

At first I thought her unchanged. Then I observed subtle differences, hair dressed lower than before, a roundness of figure new to me, a suggestion of woman. But the blue eyes that held mine were the same, filled with wonder, some fear, some delight perhaps, as I had so often seen them, and, dark in the pallor of her face, they suddenly reassured me, told me that here was the everlasting woman before me that defied the impermanence of the flesh. I took a quick step forward, holding out both hands.

" Edith," I said, hoarsely.

Swiftly her rigid features relaxed. A heavy blush stained her face to the forehead, and I saw her lips tremble and twitch. Something that was hidden away in me responded to those tremulous lips. I came quite close, gripped both her hands.

" Edith," I said again, so hoarsely that the word came in a whisper.

She did not withdraw her hands, stood facing me, her eyes meeting mine; but the continuous quivering of her hands told me that she too would gladly escape me, that it was in spite of her disquiet her eyes were able to meet mine. Our eyes linked us: we couldn't get away. . . .

With this knowledge came a thrill of delight: Edith joyous, Edith crying out my name might have pleased me, but Edith powerless to free her hands from mine, to lower her lids under a gaze which I knew must be hungry, aroused in me all the savagery of the conqueror and the inexpressible emotions of triumph. . . .

" Mine, mine, mine," I thought, and my love seemed to increase with every repetition. What was this idea of winning her back? I had never lost her. And— " Hers, hers, hers," shouted another voice; I, too, knew that I could not withdraw my hands, avert my eyes. . . . She had never lost me. . . .

I found I was walking with her across the grass, still holding her hands. We sat down on chairs that faced the polished black water of the Serpentine at the bottom of the slope, and as I leant forward I thought I had little to say.

" Edith . . . my darling . . . my beloved . . . I never thought I'd see you again."

She did not reply, but looked towards the ground. Then:

" It had to come . . . in London . . . accidents. . . ."

"This is not an accident," I said. "I followed you."

She threw me a quick glance full of inquiry.

"I followed you," I said, in a low voice. "I had to see you again, to tell you . . . because . . . oh, Edith, what's the good of talking, my dear, my dear? . . . I want you, I want you. . . ."

Her look was startled. Her mouth contracted; furrows appeared between her eyebrows.

"Lucien," she faltered.

"Ah," I cried out, all afire with the tenderness of her voice, "you still love me, you still love me. I've been a brute, a fool, murdered your happiness and mine, and you love me, you love me. . . . Say you love me, say you've forgiven, forgotten . . . say you love me, do you hear?"

Savagely I crushed her hands, leant towards her so close that I could feel her rapid breath upon my face, see all the gradations of colour in her distended pupils. I could feel a ring through my gloves and rejoiced to think that I was grinding it into her fingers.

"Say you love me," I repeated, in a still harsher voice. "I've never forgotten you, I've never loved any other woman, I've never ceased to love you. I went away from you with all my pride torn and with all my heart bloody. I didn't understand, I wouldn't understand . . . but yesterday I heard something that made me understand that I couldn't give you up, that I couldn't let you go, that I'm all—poisoned with you." I stopped, wondering why I had said "poisoned," then hurried on. "I heard there was another man. . . . Is it true?"

She hesitated, then, with a brave lift of her head:

"No."

"There could be no other man after me?"

A long hesitation. A bold meeting of my eyes.

"There could be no other man after you."

"You will . . ."; about to say "marry," my tongue took a quick, wise turn: ". . . let me go to your father?"

" Yes."

" I love you.   Do you love me? "

" I love you."

We did not think of considering whether we were
watched.   Together, I think, we bent forward . . . and
her light hair was in my eyes, my mouth upon her mouth.

V

We did not seem to have to explain.   In very few
sentences I seemed to tell Edith facts that we both of
us knew to be unnecessary.   I told her that after losing
her I had passed through hell, faced loneliness, privation,
endless labour, and the everlasting need of her; I told
her that my business was flourishing, that I could marry
her at once.

" What does it matter? " she asked.   " Isn't it enough
that you have come back, that I said I would take you
if you came?   I knew I would when . . . oh! Lucien, how
often I have cried——"

" My darling, my darling, forgive——"

" Oh, no, no."   She laughed, and there was a shrillness
of excitement in her voice.   " Don't say that.   What is
there to forgive now that you've come back—still love
me——? "

" Shepstone," I whispered.

Her face reddened, and she half turned away.   But
again she faced me bravely.

" I must tell you the truth.   Mr. Shepstone asked me
to be his wife.   He—he says he is in love with me, and I
like him; I said I would answer him later.   Oh, it was
so lonely. . . ."

" My dear, I know, I too."

". . . So lonely.   And I couldn't believe you'd come
back to me.   I knew we should meet again, but I thought
we would be strangers.   Or friends, much later, when we

were old. Mr. Shepstone asked me so often . . . and they said that you . . . that an actress——"

" Ah? you heard that? It's true. I was mad when I lost you. I was ready for anything, anybody. I've lived—abominably. I'm a beast, I'm low——"

" No, no——"

" Yes," I cried, as if anxious to enhance my triumph by self-abasement; " low, despicable—not fit to be touched by you."

" It's all over," Edith murmured. " What do I care what you were? "

I knew that she would not understand, but how splendid was this disdain of the past. As she spoke the future expanded, panoramic.

" You never forgot me," I whispered.

She smiled. " Never. I could not. I wanted to, but . . ."

She freed her hands, suddenly pulled at a little gold chain, drew a locket from her breast, opened it. In it lay half-a-dozen crumpled white petals.

As I bent to smell their faded scent, in which was a hint of suède leather; she whispered:

" The first thing you gave me, Lucien—from the almond tree—you remember? "

VI

Little Dresden Shepherdess, your eyes are pure as the mountain torrent; your hair is golden as honey, you lean light as thistle-down against the wind. Sweet one and brave, who have no reproach for me, naught save gladness, who will raise me, the iniquitous, the soiled from the ground on which I throw myself abased, sweet one and brave, forget my sin against the love you gave me for me to cast away, destroy the foulness of sense and self-seeking that has made me hideous, in the fierce, white flame of your purity; with you, lift me from grossness into that region of innocence where you dwell, and let me dwell there with you. Take my heart between your slim white hands, sweet one and brave, and hold it close to the warmth of yours.

VII

I pause awhile before these terminations, so suddenly do they come, and unlinked with the dragging length of my older life. There is no detail in them, they come too swiftly; as white squalls they overwhelm me. I feel that there should be gradations in their crises, forebodings, then prolonged struggles, hopes deferred, marches and countermarches; one ought not to win or lose a woman so simply; much time should elapse and there should be much skilful play of wits. To stand, as we did, starkly in front of each other, to avoid explanation, shirk apology and absolution, it was—inartistic.

But then I was sincere, and there was no time for the artistic dallyings to which I am given when sincerity is not there and I call upon its wraith. Life is not artistic: its big adventures appear as you reach some appointed spot, and they rush upon you as dragons that have been lying in ambush, compelling you to fight, and at once, lest you be destroyed. There are no slow adventures, slow victories, slow defeats worthy of the name of adventure: the deliberate is the dull, and no forlorn hope ever lagged as it made for its goal.

Thus, and I remembered it as I decided once more to try a throw with fortune, I had lost Edith within four hours. At eight o'clock I had held her in my arms, pressed secure kisses upon her lips. By midnight I had closed in fierce contest with her brother and her father, with her family, with English society and tradition, with the whole phalanx of England, close-packed and ready to receive the intruder upon its pikes. . . . I had lost her in four hours, and now I was going to win her in ten minutes.

I entered the dining-room at half-past nine, as well-groomed as I could be, assured that my shirt-front shone as brilliantly as any English shirt-front, that my hair was ruly and my jewellery almost invisible; also I was ready for Mr. Lawton, a little surprised at having been admitted into the house, and vaguely suspicious that I had been admitted only to be insulted. The maid went up to the drawing-room to hand her master my card, for I had refused to go upstairs, as I wanted a private interview, and did not fancy a sensational irruption among the assembled Lawtons; I rehearsed the scene that was going to take place.

Mr. Lawton would glare at me; he would say: " What do you want? " I would say: " Your daughter." He would tell me to leave the house, and I would reply: " No, not until I have had my say." Then, while he ostentatiously turned aside to examine that most excellent oil-painting on that most sumptuous red wall-paper, I would state the position, in Saxon English flavoured with idioms which would show I was an Englishman, and with 'Varsity slang that would prove me a gentleman. I would make him see that Edith was mine until death us do part (slight Adelphi excursion), that I was doing well, and that I would never, never give in (let loose the English bulldog). At last he would ungraciously give his consent, and in a sporting manner I would hold out my hand. Perhaps my beaten enemy——

" Hullo, Cadoresse! I'm very glad to see you. What have you been doing all this time? "

Ridiculous! Here was Mr. Lawton smiling at me, with a friendly look in his blue eyes, and he was actually holding out his hand. I felt he was not playing the game, playing it as a French father would have, but I took his hand, muttering that the creation of a young business——

" Oh, yes, I understand," said Mr. Lawton. " I hear

you're doing very well, that you're going to be much bigger than poor old Barbezan by-and-by."

I had to smile, to protest we intended no harm to the old firm; his interest in my affairs was frank: he asked no questions, but received with evident satisfaction the confidences I felt compelled to make. I struggled, but I gave way under the pressure of his unobtrusive courtesy. We seemed to talk about business, endlessly. Several times I tried to close with him by alluding to his family, as a beginning, but he interrupted me. That was something, in the land of "Thou shalt not interrupt."

"My wife is very well; you must come upstairs and see her. They'll all be glad to see you."

I ventured to ask whether Muriel . . . It seemed that Muriel, too, would be charmed. . . . I opened my mouth to introduce Edith into the conversation——

"You must have a drink," said Mr. Lawton, amiably.

I did not want a drink, I wanted to get to my work, but I accepted, for Englishmen are always drinking whisky and soda: one has to live up to one's naturalisation papers. Mr. Lawton poured out the whisky, asked to be told "when," and while he manœuvred the syphon, managed to make me tell him that I had taken up politics again, and promise to come and hear him speak on the Budget later in the year. But my opportunity arrived; we both stood glass in hand and, as Mr. Lawton touched the liquid with his lips, I was upon him. As I spoke I was amused, for I could see his nose through the glass that muzzled him.

"Mr. Lawton," I said, quickly, "I've come to ask you for your consent to my marriage with your daughter Edith."

No tell-tale expression crossed his face as he put down the glass. Indeed, his voice was almost cordial as he replied:

"My dear fellow, we discussed that two years ago. You know what I said."

" Yes, but things have changed. I am getting on——"

" It's not that, you know that perfectly well."

" It makes a difference."

" No, Cadoresse, you know that had nothing to do with my refusal."

A stream of rhetoric burst from my lips. I begged him to consider that time was passing, that we loved each other, that his objections had once been well-founded, but that I had become a naturalised Englishman, had acquired the habits, the standards of an Englishman.

" Now don't I behave like an Englishman? " I asked.

" You've become more English, but you're not English."

I went over the whole field, asked him to acknowledge that my hair was short, that my clothes were perfectly unobtrusive; begged to be told whether I was noisy, boastful——"

" You boast about nothing except being an Englishman," said Mr. Lawton, slyly; " and yet you're a Frenchman, a Roman Catholic, to the bone."

I went off on the religious question, and we had quite a spirited little wrangle on the difference between French and English Roman Catholics when they happened also to be agnostics. Then I brought the argument back to its base, and a heavy despair began to stifle me as I realised that this man had made up his mind in the English, bullish way, that nothing would move him: I don't know why an Englishman never moves; perhaps he can't.

At last we faced each other, Lawton calm, and I rather breathless. There was a moment of silence, and I wondered whether Edith would stand by me if I threatened him; she had promised nothing, had merely agreed to my once more going to her father; all I could do was to hope that she would help to carry out my threat.

" So you refuse to let me marry her? " I said, harshly.

Mr. Lawton looked at me with an air of amazement.

" Refuse? You need not ask for my consent."

" But—but——" I protested, and I was angry as well as bewildered by this change of front.

" I have no consent to give." And as I stared he went on:

" Two years ago, or is it two and a half? you came here and asked for my leave to marry Edith. I refused, because it was my duty to refuse. Edith was under age, and I had to protect her. Now she is twenty-two, she will be twenty-three in April; the position has changed. I no longer come in. She must decide for herself."

" Mr. Lawton," I cried, suddenly thrilled, my tongue thick in my mouth with excitement.

He raised his open hand, and it was the first time I had ever seen him do anything so histrionic:

" She is free. I neither consent nor refuse. She has her freedom and she has her responsibility. I will not interfere, for—it is not my business."

Understanding irradiated my mind. Here was the Englishman, the *beau idéal* of his type: his daughter was of age, was free, free to be happy and free to be wretched; the fate of other free individuals was not his business. And I wondered whether I loved this sumptuous English freedom or hated its cold aloofness.

" Thank you," I said, unconsciously imitating his attitude.

He did not reply, but as I turned towards the door, the sportsman said, detachedly:

" Don't go yet. Come upstairs and see them; my wife would be sorry to miss you."

CHAPTER IV

AN ENGLISHMAN'S HOME

I

Life has described a circle, as a preliminary, no doubt, to describing another; I sit at my knee-hole desk, consider my regulation silk hat, then gaze awhile through the window into the misty depths of the trees. Idly I watch the traffic in Kensington Gore, motor-cars speeding towards Richmond, Surrey, perhaps the West Country, ponderous motor-buses advertising English soaps, plays, oats; and horses swiftly drawing the broughams of Englishwomen to Dover or Grafton Street. This is England, wealthy, easy England. And there is the immense policeman at the gate of the Gardens; near him are two blues from Knightsbridge, who flirt with nursemaids in hospital garb. Handsome, well-groomed men, dainty children, women whose clothes are six months behind the Paris fashion, pedigree terriers—England.

And in this room, my study, are Morlands on the brown paper; in the bookcase I read the names of the bigger books: Macaulay's *History of England,* the *Life of Disraeli,* a massive volume on the Pre-Raphaelites; I recognise the novels of Fielding and Thackeray, Boswell's *Life of Johnson;* and a playwright's corner, Beaumont and Fletcher, Sheridan; there are no French yellow-backs. On a bracket my well-beloved collection of Lowestoft china; on the mantelpiece Liverpool transfer. Comfortable chairs are covered with green-leaved black chintz; a pipe-rack hangs over my piled golf-clubs. *The Times* has fallen on the floor, littering the hearthrug, and John, the bulldog, sleeps with his enormous head pillowed on the loose sheets;

418

he snores, and as he sleeps he chokes and gurgles. He is disgusting, he is delightful. This is England.

I have not been to the City to-day, but shall drop in for an hour at four o'clock, when I shall have finished these memoirs. I must finish them, perhaps to begin them over again one day, for I have not had the strength or the wish to extend them over the last five years. Of those years I say nothing now; perhaps I have nothing to say, perhaps I feel obscurely that my alien life ended one morning, when Edith and I faced each other across the little body of Fiona as she squirmed in the rough grass. Yes, everything conspires to give me that message. On the stairs I hear voices raised in shrill protest; I hear Marmaduke clamouring for sweeties and tiny Edna uttering, for reasons unknown to me, scream after scream. Then Edith's voice, very low, very sweet. I wonder why I called those two " Marmaduke " and " Edna." Oh, yes, I remember: there are no corresponding French names.

II

Before me lies a blue paper. Addressed to Lucien Cadoresse, of 200 Kensington Gore, it states that " By virtue of a Precept of the High Sheriff of the County aforesaid," I am summoned to appear before His Majesty's Justice or Justices assigned to hold the Assizes, there to serve as a Special Juror. Can it be that the recreant English-born say " Damn " when they find such a blue paper in the post? It is amazing to me who am thrilled by this little thing I may do for my country. With eleven other Englishmen I am to decide the fate of Englishmen in the stern, but lofty presence of England's law.

Soft-footed, ghost-like, the parlourmaid comes in with the message that Mrs. Cadoresse would like to have the car later on if I don't want it. I nod. No Frenchified familiarities, discussions or pleasantries pass between me and my servant; I don't look at her, I am not sure that I would know her in the street. Yes, I am an Englishman.

III

But what of these English, then? Can they be understood of me at all? or only felt? Ten years have gone, and I seem to see the English only in flashes, as if some psychic stage-manager made them leap across the stage, leap so fast that my mental eye could gather of them nothing but a post-impression.

They leap, the English, all different, all alike; each one has his passion or his equally amazing lack of passion, and yet each one is somehow brother to his fellow. Let me close my eyes, look at you one by one, as if you were bacteria wriggling under a lens.

Here is Hugh Lawton, my brother-in-law. You play a good hand at bridge, but you are not too good to be mistaken for a sharper; your golf handicap is six: you will never be a plus man; you do not belong to the Athenæum, nor to an obscure club in a back yard of St. James's. You are a fair average. You have married a pretty woman, not a beauty, and, of course, you have three children: it would be impossible to imagine you with either none or fourteen. You are a moderate Liberal —did you ever dream of Empire or of Socialism, once upon a time? And now that you have told me so much, tell me what is your passion. What! you don't know. No, I don't suppose you do: Hugh, you are not alive, you are merely there—and yet you have life as has that queeı little animal which lives at the bottom of the sea, alive on its mineral stalk. You are for the Broad Church, the constitutional State, the " good " novels, the vote for women householders; you maintain, and some things you tolerate —you will tolerate the intolerable when it is established. For you are an Englishman: you want to be neither too unhappy, for that is unpleasant, nor too happy, for that

is sinful; you want to earn enough money, play your
games, peacefully love your wife, educate your children
as yourself, work just hard enough to want to play just
hard enough and to sleep well, not too heavily, until you
surrender your soul for the eternal rest.

You are in the middle; you are not among the very
good, not among the very bad; you and your million
brothers, you are always in the middle, and England—
is it because England is always in the middle that England
is the centre of the world?

Yet, all of you, you are not like that. Here is Edward
Kent, an elegant figure, a Regency wit in a morning coat.
Are you England? or only donnish Cambridge? What
are these affectations of yours? What makes you say
"What race?" when, on the greatest occasion of the year,
some girl decked out in light or dark blue ribbons tells
you that it's a fine day for the race? Kent, your revolt
against England is allegiance to England; your French
novels, your unashamed desire to shine in public, your
trim hands, your dislike of sport, all these are revolts you
are trying to engineer against the England that has got
you, that will never loose you, that will force you to do
the decent thing on a battlefield if you are dragged there,
or in the Divorce Court, if you get so far. I do not think
you will ever get into Court, for you will never want any
woman badly enough to suffer because you take her.
Love cannot touch you; like birth and religion it is not
the kind of thing a gentleman should meddle with, for it
involves complications, you know, the problem-play complications, which are so sordid, unnecessary, so unpleasant,
as you say. Luxurious Kent, you would ring for your
pyjamas in Portland gaol, but you wouldn't be luxurious
if you were not trying not to be coarse—English.

Others, Mr. Lawton, Under-Secretary of State, impossible to corrupt (save perhaps with a peerage by-and-by);
Colonel Raleigh, soldier, who believes in efficiency and
making Lord Kitchener Governor of every British Colony.

Gallant Colonel, you made Yorkshire smile last year when you, a Justice of the Peace, were caught in a quiet assembly where cocks were fighting a main. . . . Dicky Bell. . . . I like your round face, your short nose and bright eyes, your devotion to the little slum boys whom you still drill. You have some ideas of education. Games and classics, you say, have gone too far in our country, but you're not going to do away with them. And many more, the acute and the dull, Stanley, Neville, pretty Muriel and her sapper, Farr the abominable, old Purkis, the young Liberals of Hambury, Mrs. Lawton, enjoying a quiet life between an at home, a dinner and the supper that follows on the play, the eighty-seven clerks of Stanley, Cadoresse & Co., and all the others whose nameless faces crowd round me, what are you doing?

Living. That is enough. Asking no more. Just wanting to keep the blinds down so that life may be decently obscured.

England is busily engaged in not pulling the blinds up.

Living cleanly, without worrying about what will happen next. You'd die well, most of you, if it came to that: it's a good deal.

I love you, oh, not blindly as in Edwardian days. I know you're not so nimble as the French, and that you enjoy shooting ideas as much as you enjoy shooting grouse. But I love your calmness in the presence of life; I love your neutrality, your unobtrusive courage, your economy of emotion, and the immense, sane generosity of you. To the stranger within your gates you give bread, and you give him your kindly heart too. Only the stranger makes you shy if he lets you see that he knows that. You are the dignity, the solidity of the world. The French are its passion, you are its reason; you are the bearers of restfulness.

Englishmen, when I want to think of you all together I think of Falstaff. You have lost most of his gaiety, you no longer dance round the maypole of Merrie England;

oppressed by cares and expenditures you stand aloof from democracy and no longer respect aristocracy; your rich men cannot sit in the banqueting-hall where he rioted, for it is tumbling about their ears. But the root of you is Falstaffian: the poetic idealism of the Fat Knight still flowers in your sons, his philosophic acceptance of good and evil radiates out from the midst of you. The broad tolerances of England, her taste for liberty and ease, her occasional bluster and her boundless conceit, they are Falstaff.

Falstaff embodies all that is gross in England and much that is fine; his cowardice, his craft, his habit of flattery are no more English than they are Chinese: they are merely human. But the outer Falstaff is English, the lawless root of him yet more English, for you hate the law, and obey it only because you make it in such wise as not to chafe you. And he is your soul; he is the Englishman who conquered every shore and, a Bible in his hand, planted your flag among the savages; he is the unsteady boy who ran away to sea, the privateersman who fought the French and the Dutch; he is the cheerful, greedy, dull and obstinate Englishman, who is so wonderfully stupid and so wonderfully full of common-sense. Falstaff was never curbed by adversity: no more was the English race; it was, like him, too vain and too optimistic, too materially bounded by its immediate desires. Falstaff, you are the gigantic ancestor of the priests, merchants and soldiers who have conquered and held fields where never floated the lilies of the French or the castles of the Portuguese. Too dull to be beaten and too big to be moved, you were the Englishman.

IV

That is all I have to say, for I am born anew, and all my life lies before me, the past effaced. England has taken me in her strong, warm arms, and I have pressed my face to her broad bosom. Big, strong heart, I hear you beat; there come sorrow, famine, pestilence, and you beat no slower; and now fame and victory, there is no hurry in your throbbing. Fold me close to you, woman with the golden helmet, and hold your trident ready to keep danger at bay: I was not the child of your body, let me be the child of your heart, because I love you, my——

I hear a soft footfall behind me, then a low voice:

"Am I disturbing you?"

I turn, and for a moment consider the young face, unmarked of the fleeting years, the smiling, rosy mouth, the gentle blue eyes. I clasp the slim, white hand, draw towards me the form that so gladly yields. Edith sits across my knees, laughs low as I kiss her neck.

"Have you much more to write?" she asks, at length.

"No," I murmur, "only one word."

"Let me write it," says Edith, and there is in her eyes an appeal with which mingles security.

I whisper into her ear as she takes the pen: ". . . because I love you, my. . . ." Her left hand still in mine, she bends forward, and I can see nothing save the pale gold tendrils on her neck as she writes the last word:

". . . England."

THE END